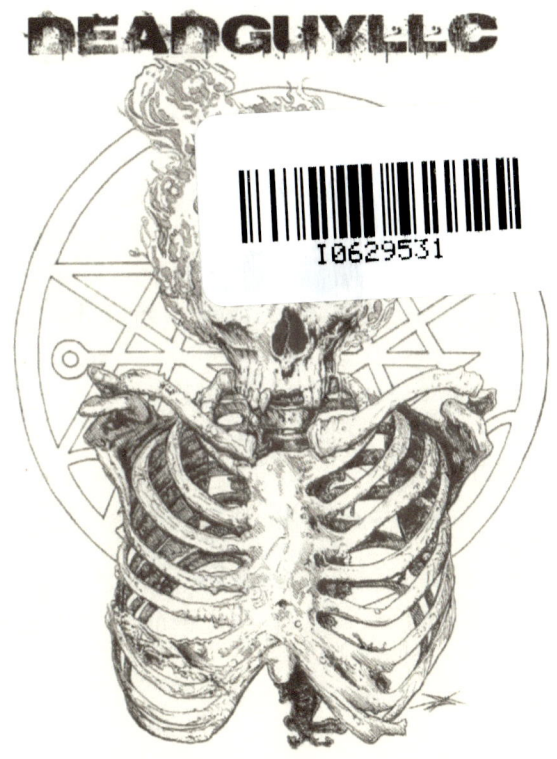

DEADGUYLLC

Published by DeadGuyLLC

Ryan C. Thomas © 2023 Solipsism in the Switch grass
Christine Morgan © 2023 Cosmic Catapult
Jeff Strand © 2023 Avert Thine Eyes

Tales of Terror

The world is indeed comic

But the joke is on mankind

- H.P. Lovecraft

Solipsism in the Switchgrass

Ryan C. Thomas

It was the stupid backpack that did it. Slung over his right side, it was full of books, heavy, and when he'd steered his bike to the edge of the road it had shifted sideways just enough to tip him into shoulder of the road. He wasn't even going fast, but the front wheel got caught up and the bike spilled sideways, and he went over the shoulder and somersaulted down the outside embankment, right into a small boulder. He slammed into it hip-first and felt something go instantly wrong with his legs.

"Fuck," he winced, noticing now that his left leg was toe-up but his right leg was heel-up. As he tried to elbow himself up from his supine position agonizing pain sailed out of some biological nether and raced up his entire body. "FUUUCKK!"

The intensity of it immobilized him. He lay back down and started breathing through gritted teeth.

"No no no," he muttered. "It's broken. Definitely broken. Holy fuck is it broken."

For a few seconds he closed his eyes, willing away the panic. He opened them again and stared up through four-foot-high

5

switchgrass at the baby-blue sky above. It was so bright it hurt his eyes. Where were his sunglasses?

He reached up to his head and screamed again. Every movement was debilitating. His chest constricted and he gulped air to steady his nerves. Steeling himself, he ran his fingers around his ribs. Something was bulging out in ways it hadn't just minutes earlier. A broken rib? Had to be. So not just his leg but his ribs too. Fucking awesome. Fucking wonderful. The boulder was off to his right. Not very large. No bigger than a basketball, but hard enough and angled enough to do damage.

He was only forty years old. This shit didn't happen to forty-year-olds. It happened to octogenarians in convalescent homes.

"Phone," he muttered, realizing he had to call for help. First a friend, then an ambulance. But first a friend. He had plenty of friends, and they had to be close by. The hotel with the writer's convention was only a few miles away, and even though the event had ended at noon, he knew people would still be hanging out in the bar area. Who'd still be there?

Bryan? Izzy? Someone.

At first he couldn't find his back pack, then spotted it several feet away in the switchgrass. When he reached for it, his whole body went rigid with agonizing pain. This was beyond anything he'd ever felt before. He let loose with a scream that momentarily shut up all the buzzing insects around him. When it passed, he looked at the backpack again. So close but a yard too far away. How the hell was he going to reach it?

"Just breathe. Just fucking breathe, dude." His calming mantra did nothing to alleviate the aches that were now swimming up his leg. Even though he knew it was stupid, he wanted to test just how much he could move his leg. Maybe he could get into a less painful position and drag himself to the bag that held his phone.

Again, he looked at his right leg. The heel up, the toes down. He'd either broken the hip or completely dislocated it. He took his watch off and placed the band in his mouth, bit down. Holding his breath, he moved his right foot.

He wailed, saw blackness before his eyes, fought to stay conscious.

Without warning, he began to cry.

"Help!" he yelled, but then stopped because that rib was barking back, and he wasn't strong enough to fight through the agony.

He cried some more.

***

A half hour passed. The bright blue sky was beginning to turn gray. Would it rain? Probably would, knowing his luck.

The insects were chittering so loud it was like lying in the middle of table saws. Bzzzzz. Bzzzzz. Bzzzz. Just shut the fuck up, he thought. Occasionally a bird would squawk overhead, and they'd go silent for a second or two, but then they'd resume buzzing.

Perhaps because he was thinking of this, he glanced down at the ground around him and focused on the dirt. It moved with tiny beetles and ants and other leggy things, but nothing major. No snakes, no rats. Just bugs doing what bugs do. He was aware that the mosquitos would be out at some point, but he figured it was only four or five o'clock at this point.

He also realized the pain hadn't abated at all. If he shifted anything below his waist even a millimeter, the pain nearly knocked him out.

"OK, phone phone phone."

He stretched out an arm toward the bag. It hurt like hell, but he was prepared for it this time. He groaned and cried and pushed the switchgrass aside as if that would bring the bag closer. But it didn't. He stopped, waited for the pain to ebb. How could he get the bag? The grass? Could he make some kind of grappling hook? Was he fucking Batman now?   He grabbed the roots of the switchgrass and yanked, hoping to pull out a large bundle. Instead, he pulled himself half an inch closer to the bag. But there was a cost, and his hip reminded him. He screamed and screamed, and the bugs shut up in awe of the show.

He let go of the grass, weeping.

"Where the fuck is anyone?!"

Where the fuck indeed. Thing is, he didn't even know where he was. The state road leading into town, toward the hotel. Nothing but empty land and some farms from there to the next town. He figured he was halfway between them. Who owned this land? Someone had to. It was a state road, someone had to drive by. Cops had to patrol it eventually, right? He'd hear them coming and scream no matter how much it hurt. Or he'd throw a rock. Could he even do that? Maybe they'd see his bike. It had to still be on the side of the road. Please God or Satan or whatever entity that can hear me, let someone see my bike.

He kept still, starting at his backward leg, listening for cars. Nothing. Just bugs.

***

If he didn't move the pain was tolerable. If he moved, he screamed. But he needed his phone. He grabbed at the roots again and yanked, dragging himself another half-inch closer. The pain was immeasurable, and he wailed for the hundredth time. This time, however, he saw his home screen light up for a second, revealing the picture of his latest book,

Blood Cock Death Orgy Part II: Oozing Fuck Farm of Cum Chunks by Ed Lordge. It was his most disgusting book yet, full of the type of depravity that would cause the Marque De Sade to wince. He'd reveled in reading a passage at the author convention, beamed when people in the audience grimaced and walked out. Knowing he could affect people like that was a powerful feeling. He was too intense for them, too hard. Besides, if they didn't like graphic rape and incest and necrophilia and bestiality that was their problem. He pushed limits because that's what artists did. Those people were all pussies who couldn't handle the darkness. Just like the book bloggers who called out his syntax and grammar. Screw them. You didn't need to know the rules of writing when you had the ability to create images so disturbing, they made people puke.

He watched the screen go dark again, wondering why it had lit up in the first place. Then it hit him. His voice had turned it on. Yes! He forgot the latest update of the phone would respond to his voice commands even if it was locked.

"Siri, call 911!"

The phone screen lit up, showing his book cover again, but it did not dial. A blue wheel spun in a circle. In the upper corner he saw just one bar of service.

"Oh c'mon! You're gotta be fucking kidding me!"

He waited for the phone to reset and tried again. "Siri, call 911." Again, the blue circle spinning. He closed his eyes and waited.

Nothing happened. This was all some kind of cruel joke.

"Um, are you ok?"

He lifted his head, grit his teeth in pain. Who's voice was that? It wasn't on the phone. Who'd said it?

"Hello?" he mumbled.

"Are you ok?"

The voice was weak, frail, tinny.

"Please help me," he begged. "Please, I broke my leg or my hip or something. I'm in so much pain. Please help me."

The switchgrass swayed in front of him and he heard footsteps. With a rush of air the grass parted and a teenage girl emerged. "Oh man, you don't look good," she said.

"Yes! Thank you thank you thank you. Please call 911. I need an ambulance."

She tilted her head and stared at his leg. "Your leg is backwards.

You know that?"

"Hell yes I know. S'why I need an ambulance. Hurry."

"Hurry what?"

"Hurry and call! I'm in so much pain. I need to get out of this field."

"Oh, I can't do that."

Her words stunned him. Had he heard her correctly? "What'd you say?"

"I said 'I can't do that.'"

"What? Why? I need an ambulance."

"I can't have anyone come to this field."

"What're you talking about? Why?"

"Because this is the field where my daddy buries his bodies." Her words froze him. His thoughts swam in circles like fish schooling together to avoid a predator. "The fuck are you talking about?"

"My daddy doesn't even allow me to come without him. It's a bad field."

"Yeah, no shit. And I hope you're just fucking with me. Funny joke. Now can you go call please."

"Like I said, I can't. This is daddy's body field. He said no one's allowed. You fell in the wrong field, mister."

Ed's whole body shivered, and pain throbbed in his hip. He tried a new tactic. "Look, I don't know what you're talking about, and I don't care. I don't even know where the hell I am. I couldn't point this out on a map if you put a gun to my head. Just get me out of here and your daddy's field remains a secret."

"Hmmm. Lemme ask him." She stood up and poked her head above the switchgrass. "Hey, Dad!" Ed's eyes went wide.

From far away came a deep voice: "Yes, Scarlet?" Ed's eyes went wider.

"Daddy, there's a man here says he needs help and if we help him, he won't tell where your special field is.

"Jesus Christ, Scarlet, why is there a man here?"

"I dunno, but I saw a bike out near the road. Might be his."

"Hang on, I'm coming over."

She leaned down into Ed's face again. "My daddy is coming to talk to you. Hang on."

Heavy footfalls grew louder, and the tall grasses all swished in unison. Ed could hear a man's labored breathing approaching and held his breath, wondering if he'd just made a huge mistake.

The footsteps were close. A man was huffing and puffing. Over the top of the grass a shovel appeared, getting closer. Then the grass was folded down and a large overweight man was suddenly there. Slung over his shoulder was another man whose clothes were awash in blood. Ed could immediately tell that person was dead.

The large man dropped the corpse right next to Ed. The head bounced with a loud thunk, then lolled toward Ed, revealing a dark cavity where its nose and mouth should have been. Buck shot had ripped up most of the eyes.

For the first time since the fall, Ed screamed out of fear instead of pain.

"Oh shut up," the man said. "No one's out here but us. What happened? You take a fall?"

Ed nodded but kept on yelling.

The large man raised his foot up over Ed's head. "Shut up or I'm gonna stomp your teeth out. Can you walk?"

Ed managed to stop the screaming. His mouth trembled and he felt a coldness overtake his body. "No," he managed to say.

"What do we do, Daddy?" Scarlet asked.

"Well, we can't just leave him here in this state, I suppose. Get his phone and turn it off."

Scarlet did as instructed, then handed the phone to her father.

Ed began to cry. That phone was his lifeline and now it was gone.

And here he was lying next to a faceless corpse.

"Please, I won't tell anyone."

"None of that now. You certainly won't tell anyone because you are hell and gone from anyone who gives a fuck. And truth be told if you would have just rode by I wouldn't have given a fuck neither. But here you are and I got work to do. So just hang tight."

Daddy took a second to scope out the field around him, then hefted his shovel. "Yeah, this is as good a place as any, I guess."

"I feel like we've been in this spot before," Scarlet said.

"I feel like you think the whole field is the same spot, girl."

"I remember this grass."

"Sure you do."

With that, the large man started shoveling a few feet away from Ed.

With each drive of the shovel into the dirt, Ed whimpered.

Scarlet bent down and touched his face. "You have nice lips."

"Are you going to kill me?"

"Well, I'm not."

For the briefest of seconds Ed had hope he might get out of this alive, but then the sound of the shovel snapped him out of it.

Scarlet moved around him and opened his bag, took out his book.

"Hey Daddy, I found a book. Can I keep it?"

Daddy grunted and kept on shoveling. Dirt flew up over everyone and scattered in the air. Some of it rained down on both Ed and Scarlet but she didn't seem to mind.

Scarlet read the title of the book and wrinkled up her nose. "Ew, that's gross. Who writes this kind of stuff?" She turned the book over and noticed Ed's picture on the back. "Oh my God, it's you! You wrote this? Hey, Daddy, this man wrote this book! How cool is that. A real-life author right in your field."

If the large man was impressed he didn't show it.

"What's it about?" she asked.

Ed muttered through chattering teeth. "It's just a horror story."

"Will you sign it for me? I love books. Sometimes Daddy brings me some but I don't think he's ever brought me a horror one before. Mostly just regular stuff and books about God. Can you make it out to me?"

"Um…"

"I see a pen in your bag." She took it out and handed it to him.

"If I sign it, will you help me?"

"Oh, I can't help you now. But I sure would like a signed copy of your book."

Daddy's voice came booming over the grass: "Sign the book, boy, or I'll make you sign it."

Ed signed it, his hands shaking so badly the signature was nothing but a tiny squiggle.

"Thanks!" Scarlet said, bounding off to show her daddy.

"Fuck fuck fuck fuck," Ed murmured, tears welling up in his eyes again.

***

An hour passed. The sky was striated in deep orange and pink. Bugs had crawled up his pants and found their way to his crotch. He itched them but touching anything near his hips was so painful he found it easier to just let them explore. So far, none of them had bitten him.

Daddy finally returned, his face red and covered in sweat and dirt. Like some poor man's psychologist, Ed figured maybe he could appeal to the man's paternal senses. After all, he seemed to care for Scarlet. He must have a modicum of mercy in him somewhere. Or maybe, thought Ed, I could show him we're simpatico. I mean, he's burying a dead body, and I write really dark stuff. We're practically the same.

"Hey, mister, I don't blame you for what you did to this guy. I mean, did he try to rob you or something? Hey, I'm a supporter of the Second Amendment. I get it. Home invasions are no joke. Looks like he had it coming, right? You call me an ambulance, hell, I'll come back and help you take care of any future trespassers. At the very least I could help you dig some holes. Seriously, so many people deserve a bullet to the head. I get it. You gotta protect your family. So whatdya say? Help me out and I promise I'll come back and help you. Might even be good research for a book. I've never dug a grave before. That's hardcore, man. I like it."

Daddy took a faded red bandana from his back pocket and wiped sweat from the back of his neck. "Oh, I'm not digging the hole to put that body in. No, I'm digging that hole to let something come up from underneath. Bit of a doorway, if you will. Like the holes mice and voles make. The whole tunnel system under the field. But it's down a couple feet. Sometimes it's hard to find the veins. But I found one, so it won't be long now."

"What...what's in the holes?"

"I wish I knew what they were. All I know is many years ago when my own father built our house down the road here, we had a bit of a scuffle with some things that wanted us to leave. They came into our house and attacked my mother and father. They took my sister, though I don't remember that bit because I was only a baby. They took her here and fed on her and we never found the body. They came back a few months later and took the dog. Then later they took some motorist who'd broken down and came to stay with us while the tow truck came out—in those days there was no twenty-four-hour service, so the man had to wait until morning. He slept on our couch, until those things came and got him and dragged him back here. My father figured out two things by then. One: when their bellies were full, they slept for a bit. Same way an animal does, you know. Two: dead people leave behind goods, like wallets and watches and stuff. You can sell that stuff and it sure does beat working at some deadbeat job in the rain and heat all day. Of course, people don't really carry cash that much anymore. But they all carry something. Like your phone, that watch beside you. That looks fashionable. Usually, people have them smart watches nowadays."

Ed had bought the Fender watch at a Hot Topic years ago because he thought it looked cool and he planned to pick up girls by telling them he was a lead guitarist in a punk band. He couldn't play guitar but what did they know. Stupid stupid stupid.

Ed quickly realized his Stockholm Syndrome ruse had failed miserably. He needed a new tactic. "The cops can ping my phone. Trust me, I've researched it. They can get within fifty feet of the last ping." This wasn't entirely true. It was a one-star review of his last book that taught him the police can ping phone signals. It had pretty much nullified the entire plot of that book. But he pressed on. "They'll know I was here.

They'll check this field. They'll check your house."

"Doubtful. There's not much service here. Oh, sure if the wind blows right maybe you'll get a bar, but no more than that. I took a trip to the library way out in town. I learned how to erase a phone. I opened some online seller accounts. Sell those phones for good money. Sell anything I find for money. Those books in your bag. Your bike, even, once I get the serial number off it and stamp a new one in. What else you got? That shirt looks in good shape. Some kind of movie? Someone'll buy that. Yessir, I'd say you brought me a few hundred dollars easily. Enough to keep the lights on, put some gas in the car. Out here things are not so expensive. And all I gotta do is keep the field fed."

"No. No the cops will come. They'll find me somehow. Just let me go and save yourself the hassle."

"Cops ain't coming, boy. I don't know if you've noticed lately but cops ain't working too hard to stop crime these days. They ain't saving anyone from anything."

"Please just let me go."

"Where you gonna go anyway? You can't walk. Probably got lots of internal bleeding going on. Your leg is fuckside up. Looks like some mad scientist attached it wrong. Nah, you're not going anywhere. This field wants you. Probably already smells you."

Ed stammered, fighting back tears. "Are you going to kill me?"

"You want me too? I can go get the gun."

"No. Please."

"Alright then. Figure you ain't moving so I won't waste the ammo."

The man inhaled long and hard, held the air in his lungs for a couple seconds before blowing it out. "You smell that?"

Ed did smell it. The scent of compost. Hot, burning soil rife with decomposition.

"The field knows it's getting fed."

The man patted Ed on the leg, which sent shockwaves of agony through his body. Ed screamed and tried to jerk away but it just made the pain worse. The man stood up and said, "Shit. I gotta go. I think I pulled something in my back a minute ago. I need to go lay down. Not as young as I used to be. Out here digging these holes. Probably need to hand over the job to Scarlet

17

but she's all…" He made bird-flapping motions with his hands to insinuate Scarlet was flighty. He stopped and rubbed his lower back. "Ow, that hurts. Anyway, you just sit tight, it won't be long now." Scarlet poked her head out from the switchgrass. "Should I get his bag?"

"Hell yes, get his bag. And the watch. Get his bike too. He drop anything else?"

"No. I didn't see anything."

"Ok, grab all that and get on back to the house." With that, Daddy turned and walked into the tall grass, which closed behind him like curtains.

Scarlet held up Ed's book. "Thanks again for signing it. I'm gonna read it before Daddy sells it."

Ed reached a hand toward her. "Please don't do this. Just call an ambulance. I won't tell. I promise."

"I can't. It's the field, see? You fell in Daddy's field. You shouldn't have done that. Bye."

She shouldered his bag and disappeared through the same curtain of grass as her father.

Ed was all alone. Swimming in pain and lost in terror. Beside him lay the corpse with its missing face. He could see chunks of bone and gristle and ichor inside the skull. Beetles were scurrying over the wetness of it all. It glistened like prime rib and chicken wings smothered in cherry juice, all mashed up in a bowl. It stank like trash and sweat and piss. Who had this man been? How had he ended up near Scarlet and her dad's place?

The stench of death was once again overtaken by the ripe, pungent aroma of compost.

Ed stared at the darkening sky and frantically thought about how to save himself. He couldn't move, couldn't crawl, his screams reached no one. There had to be a way. Maybe the pain would subside and he'd be able to move. He'd written that once in a story. A character had his arms cut off and waited for the numbness to set in before fighting his way to safety. It could happen, right? He could go numb and then find the upper body strength to move.

He shifted his hip just to check and howled in pain. Tears flowed down his cheeks, realizing he had no chance of moving at all. He was trapped, suffering, scared out of his mind. The corpse next to him moved.

He yelped in fright. "Oh God!"

Was it alive?

The corpse moved again. But this time he knew it wasn't alive. Something underneath it was trying to free itself. It jumped a third time and went still.

"Jesus Christ what is that?"

The switchgrass rustled louder. He could hear things moving near the floor of the field. It sounded like animals. Rats? Squirrels? Opossums?

What was out here?

There was a squeak as a small animal climbed up onto the dead man's back and stood staring at Ed. No, it wasn't an animal. It was something different. Something about a foot tall, hairless, with red and pink skin, the hues of a ripe peach. It was humanoid, if humans could be so little. Two arms, two legs, no tail. Long, black claws arced out of its fingers and toes. Its eyes were off-white with stitches of red veins. Its nose was bulbous, and its face resembled an elder Jimmy Durante (who Ed only knew of from old Loony Tunes cartoons). Between its legs a tiny, wrinkled penis hung down like a dead meal worm. It lifted its head and sniffed the air.

"Ahh! What the fuck are you!" Ed was hyperventilating, a new fear overtaking him.

The small creature opened its mouth, revealing human teeth, with the exception of oversized, sharp canines, like vampires and werewolves had in bad horror films.

"Dear fucking God, go away."

The creature raised its arms and squeaked again, only this time its squeak morphed into the blare of a child's toy trumpet. A second later more of the naked humanoid creatures appeared overtop the corpse's body. Some brushed dirt off their skin, others didn't care. Their body types were slightly different from one another. Some had bloated bellies, some were so thin their ribs protruded, some were taller, some had large penises and longer nails.

The first one that had arrived sat down, felt along the shirt of the corpse, and dug its nails through the fabric into the dead man's hide. It yanked on the skin, pulling and using its claws to cleave the subcutaneous fat. It tore loose a piece of flesh and greedily ate it. The sallow fat globbed through its teeth like gelatin until the creature sucked it back in. It swallowed, squeaked, and trumpeted again. With a sudden frenzy that seemed to come out of nowhere the other creatures began digging into the flesh. They frantically yanked off chunks of skin and scooped out bloody flesh, gnashing it all in their teeth.

Ed screamed. None of this could be real!

The creatures shredded the dead man's clothes in a frenzy and began to carry all the tatters back through the grass toward the smell of compost. Toward whatever hole they'd emerged from. Back and forth they went like worker ants. For a brief second, Ed wondered why they'd bothered taking the swatches of clothes. Did they use it to make nests? Did they eat it?

With the faceless corpse now completely bare the creatures were able to just bite into the flesh and tear out chunks of meat. Their pink and red faces were smeared in blood and gore and Ed now saw that their penises were erect and undulating. Just like living mealworms.

One by one the monsters fell to their bellies and began to spear the corpse's gaping wounds with their dicks, humping up and down.

Jesus Christ, Ed thought, they're fucking it!

The tiny monsters pounded away at the dead man, jabbing their dicks in an out, an orgy of blood and flesh and dirt and grass and tiny little dicks fucking fucking fucking hard and fast. The corpse was completely engulfed in hairless pink and red humanoid monsters thrusting so fast it created the wet popping sounds of suction cups on glass.

One of the tiny monsters let loose with a tinny roar and shot backwards, cumming a stream of dark yellow goo into the corpse's torso.

It wiped its forehead in exhaustion and smiled at Ed.

The other creatures followed suit, each one roaring and then ejaculating thick monster semen. The pressure of each demonic orgasm caused the monsters to recoil up off the body for a moment, landing in exertion.

For a few minutes nothing happened. The little monsters just sat staring at the corpse and at Ed. Occasionally they'd itch their dicks or lick their blood-stained lips. Ed thought maybe they'd fall asleep and he'd have a chance to get rid of them, pick them up and snap their necks.

Then the corpse started to bubble like it was being boiled in a searing stew. The skin started to slough off right in front of Ed's eyes. He heard the bones snapping inside the body, sharp cracks like the nunchucks effects in the Kung Fu movies he liked. The skull caved in on itself, the gaping hole in the face crumbling as if it were made of plaster. Blood oozed out of the body's pores and swam underneath Ed's body. It was cold and thick and flowed incredibly slowly. The monsters now stood up, growling, getting to work, pulling the body apart. The hands came off at the wrists. The feet came off at the ankles. They peeled the skin off in slick ribbons that no longer seemed to adhere to the fat underneath. The fat washed off the muscle and bones like bacon grease.

The creatures started taking all of this away, dragging it through the grass back toward the hole they'd emerged from.

Soon Ed was staring at nothing but striated muscles and pink organs. The pectoral muscles were particularly tough for the creatures to rip apart so again they used their nails to create a gash which they then shoved their tiny dicks in and fucked until they popped into the air with glee.

Ed watched as the gooey semen began to melt the muscle. He got it now; the creature cum was some kind of acid that broke down the body parts. Even the ribs underneath began to crack in half. The creatures then stripped all the muscle and bone and took it away to their hovel.

Over the course of the next hour, as the moon floated above him like a cataract, the creatures finished carrying the pieces of the dead man into the hole in the ground. Ed could only imagine where it went. He imagined a network of tunnels and nests under the earth filled with the bones of every human that went missing and was never found.

Finally, the last creature jumped up on his chest and looked him in the eye.

"Please don't," he begged. "Please don't eat me and fuck my corpse. Please."

The tiny bald thing smiled wide, showing sharp teeth and black gums. Bits of flesh were lodged in its diastemas.

"I don't want to die," Ed murmured.

The creature turned away, leapt to the ground and scurried off into the tall grass.

Ed was alone. The night air had turned cold. He shivered and it made the pain in his hip flare up so he forced himself to stop.

What felt like an eternity went by and he started screaming again.

"Help! Help me!"

He screamed until he was hoarse, and his lower half was nothing but white-hot agony.

He gave up and stared at the night sky. Tiny bugs were crawling all over him now, attracted to the congealed blood on the ground all around him. He swatted at them, but they bit anyway. The mosquitoes were particularly brutal, buzzing in his ears and stabbing at his face.

The night went on forever. At some point he fell asleep.

***

He awoke to the sound of footfalls. I'm saved, he thought. But his heart fell to his stomach when the grass parted, and Daddy and Scarlet reappeared.

"Still alive, huh?" Daddy said. He was rubbing his back and groaning.

Ed tried to plead with them but the bug-bite welts on his face seared and his throat cracked with dryness. All her could get out was,

"Buhh…"

"Why didn't they take him, Dad?" Scarlet asked.

"They got their full of the other guy, I suppose. Even an alligator rests after a big meal."

Scarlet bent down into Ed's face. "I started reading your book last night. It was real gross. Do you really like that stuff? Cutting people up and having gross sex and just all around being nasty?" Ed just stared back at her. It hurt too much to nod.

"Stop reading that trash," Daddy said. "Put that book back in the bag so I can sell it. See what this guy is worth. Go on back to the house."

Scarlet gave a wink to Ed and made her way back into the depths of the field. Daddy scanned the environment around him, all the while caressing his lumbar area.

"Shit. The little guys go back in their hole they cover it all up. Just like gophers. I'd dig you a new one but as you know I wrenched my back yesterday with that shovel. I suppose I could get my gun though. You want me to do that? At least you wouldn't feel no more pain. I'm sure I'll be ok again in a day or two. Dig a new hole then."

Ed had never wanted to wake up from a dream so much in his life. Of course he didn't want to die. Who just gives up that easy? There's always hope, right? He shook his head no

"I figured. Ok, I'm gonna go lay down." Daddy started back through the switchgrass then stopped, faced Ed one last time. "You know, it's too bad you won't die the way you think is cool. All that butchery in your books and Satan stuff. You ask me, this is much worse. Worse than getting hacked up. Worse than getting death-fucked by tiny monsters. Yeah, this is a way worse way to die, just lying here in pain reflecting on it all, knowing it's coming. Coming real slow. Dehydration, starvation, can't move, can't talk, pissing yourself, nothing but pain if you move. Maybe you'll get lucky and a coyote will show up and go for your throat. I doubt it though. Haven't seen them around here in a while. Then again, maybe the little rascals will figure out how to come up on their own. Who knows."

Daddy left the field.

Ed listened to the grass swishing and tried several times to move but just ended up squinting in enormous amounts of pain.

He lost time. At some point his belly ached so bad it overshadowed the pain of his broken hip. Then eventually he choked on the dryness of his own throat and his head hurt and he shook and saw lights behind his eyes.

This is truly worse, he thought.

Cosmic Catapult

Christine Morgan

The blondie, now? She looked like a screamer.

Nineteen, maybe twenty. What Simon's gran would have described as "pleasantly plump," and right proud of it. Dressed to show it off, even, in snug pre-ripped jeans and a low-cut sleeveless top with a push-up bra what did wonders for her cleavage. Real gift of God, there, and if God were feeling particularly generous on this fine summer night, that bounteous bosom might leap spang out of its confinement to give them all a fine show.

She'd love it, too, the blondie would. Oh, she'd fuss, and act all mortified, but underneath, she'd be soaking up the attention. Basking in it, luxuriating, like a cat in the sun.

A screamer, for sure. Loud and theatrical-like.

Good. Always good for business, that.

Her brownette friend? Not so much a screamer. More the fainter type, if Simon Bodean were any judge. Which, after forty-plus years doing this, since he'd been a mere scrap of a lad, he prided himself on being. The brownette had a more bookish, quiet way about her. Pretty, but too serious to make the most of it. Taller and slimmer than the blondie, she wore a pair of them calf-length cottony pants and a not-too-tight tee-shirt with the blue phonebooth/port-a-potty box from that doctor show on it.

A fainter, yeah. Her big eyes would go even bigger, bright with terror, then roll up as her head lolled and her limbs flop-flailed around all boneless. He'd seen it a million times, and it always struck him amazing how none of their necks broke from whiplash.

They waited in line, the blondie clutching the brownette's arm and squealing with excited anticipation as each pair ahead of them took their turn. It wasn't the quickest process on the midway, and other rides ran far more customers through, but the Cosmic Catapult was by far the star of the show, and everyone knew it.

Oh, the Hypercoaster was a popular draw, right enough, and the great pendulum swing of the Ghost Ship. There was always something to be said for the nostalgia factor of the good ol' Ferris Wheel and Tilt-A Whirl. But, for sheer daredevil spectacle, nothing beat the towering twin spires and the two-seater carriage suspended between them on super-long bungees.

That in itself made for an impressive enough sight, but, just lately, Simon had consented to his daughter's urgings to amp it up some. Before, it'd only been the Catapult, plain and simple, nothing fancy, got the job done. Now. After quite a bit of work and even more expense, it was a genuine showpiece. The spires were strung with color-changing bulbs, revolving gadgets sprayed displays of laser beams into the sky, the lights were synchronized to space-age music from a complicated computerized speaker system Simon didn't half understand, and a high mural-painted backdrop curved partway around the whole works.

The mural had been Marco's doing, yet another example of how Simon could hardly deny Ava anything once she had her heart set. He'd had his doubts at first, but even he had to admit, the boy'd done a hell of a job. Swirling galaxies against a star-shot expanse, alien landscapes with planetary rings and strange moons, not quite psychedelic and not quite realistic while having aspects of both. More than eye-catching ... mind catching, somehow. As if there were hidden symbols or messages worked in it that you could sense, if not actually see.

Yes, indeed, the Cosmic Catapult!

Which, technically he supposed, should more properly be called a slingshot, but Cosmic Slingshot -- or (anything) Slingshot -- just didn't have the same ring to it. A slingshot was what a little kid used to ping pebbles at stray dogs or passing cars. A catapult, well, that sounded dang near epic.

Ava, having buckled in and secured the current riders -- a dad-and-son duo -- stepped back and gave him the thumbs-up. The dad was all beer gut and hearty bluster, joshing his boy about how this'd put some hair on his chest. The son, elevenish, who'd just hit the height restriction by a fraction of an inch, appeared equal parts exhilarated and scared shitless.

A pisser? Quite likely. A puker? Simon hoped not. Pukers were the worst, hardest to clean up after, caused the most delay.

The mom, watching from the sidelines, leaned over the waist-high metal fence right quick to snap a picture of the two of them, as Simon gave his customary brief spiel. Everyone in line, as well as passing crowds of fair-goers laden with cotton candy and cheap carnival-game prizes, paused, craning to watch.

He did the three-two-one countdown, yanked the lever, and - KA-SPROOOOIIIIIIIING away they went, hurtling skyward!

The hearty-bluster dad shrieked like a teakettle. The son stayed silent; the Catapult-Cam video screen on Simon's control console showed him clenched tight as a miser's buttcheeks, everything about his grim expression suggesting here he was fully expecting to die before he'd so much as touched a girl's titty.

Unlike the other midway rides, the Cosmic Catapult didn't take tickets from the booklets bought at booths around the fairgrounds. It was cash-in-hand, fifteen bucks a head. For an extra fiver, Lottie would print them out a souvenir pic from the video; for an extra twenty, they could have a copy of the whole thing on one of those minicomputer-widget things. The 'I Survived the Cosmic Catapult!' stickers were free, dispensed by Ava when she unlatched them after. The tee shirts ran eight bucks' kid size and standard, ten for the larger sizes.

Good money. Kept him and Ava right nice, paid Lottie and Jess a decent wage, even let Simon put some away for some theoretical eventual retirement. Yes, the upgrade remodel had been something of a pinch -- even with Marco just about offering to do the mural for free; if Ava so much as batted her eyes, he'd jump through hoops of fire -- but the results were already proving worth it.

The dad-and-son duo pogoed around, up and down, back and forth, in slowing increments against the darkening sky. As was often the case, after that initial teakettle shriek, the dad overcompensated with a lot of whoops, hoots, and hollers; such fun, a real blast, and nope, he hadn't been scared, not a bit! The son remained grimly silent; whether he'd pissed or not remained to be seen, but as far as Simon could tell, he'd at least not done a puker.

His expression, on the Catapult-Cam, had changed, though. Gone slack and distant. He stared blankly off at nothing, with a hollow emptiness downright disconcerting. His face was ashen. Simon couldn't be sure, but he might even have bitten through his lip so's it bled thin trickles across his chin.

The dad finally noticed, once Jess was winching the seat-carriage back to its starting point at the launch pad. He left off the bluff heartiness in favor of concern -- "Buddy? Hey, bud, you okay? It's over. Bud?" -- and the mom rushed forth as soon as Ava moved to unbuckle them, maternal instinct being a powerful force.

"Charlie? Charlie, what's the matter?"

"Come on, bud, don't scare your mother."

"Is he all right? Is he all right? Charlie, look at me, talk to me!"

Ava glanced from the kid to Simon, with a warning-worried wince. He sighed inwardly and cussed under his breath. The parents had signed the release forms, their boy had eked past the height requirement ... legally, all should be in the clear ... but you never knew when someone might cause a stink.

It took the dad and Jess to hoist the kid out of the seat; he was inert as a mannequin but stayed upright when they set him on his feet. His pants were dry, which was a plus. His empty gaze went right through his mother as if she weren't there, which was a minus.

"Charlie!" She grabbed him and shook him.

Everyone waiting in line and watching from the midway blatantly rubbernecked, going up on tiptoes, jockeying for position to get a better view.

Ava winced toward Simon again. He gestured for her to stay cool, just stay cool, play it normal. After a subtle nod of acknowledgment, she put on a cheery smile and pasted a sticker to his chest.

"Awesome job, you did it! Hey, Lottie, I think this guy deserves a free tee-shirt!"

"What's wrong with him?" The mom shook Charlie again, and the dad settled a big hand on his shoulder.

At that, the kid gasped and twitched and did a whole-body shudder, blinking up at them with the shock of someone jolted from a bad dream.

"It almost got me," he said.

The various other adults exchanged puzzled frowns as Charlie's mom swept him into a hug and patted him and fussed over him and told him it was fine, he was safe, nothing was going to get him ... all while glaring this-is-your-fault daggers at the dad.

"Well, now, there we go, let's move it along," Jess said, raising his voice, his tone jovial, as if this was nothing new.

He herded the family in the direction of the exit, and they went along willingly enough, the mom suggesting maybe they'd had enough carnival rides for now and the dad agreeing, saying how he, at least, sure could go for a corn dog or a big ice cream sundae. Charlie brightened, then turned to Ava as she rushed up with the child-sized tee-shirt Lottie had brought over from the booth.

"Something's up there," he told her, soft and solemn. "I saw it. It saw me, too. It almost got me."

Ava's cheery smile wavered. He'd spoken too quietly for most of the onlookers to catch his words, but those closest whispered and muttered amongst themselves. The kid looked at the sticker on his chest and the folded tee-shirt in his hand, tracing his fingertips over the 'I Survived the Cosmic Catapult!' logos. A shaky little laugh, not a happy kid laugh, escaped him.

"It's up there," he said to Ava. "I think it's hungry."

Then he went along with his parents as Jess ushered them to the gate, taking only a single haunted look back at the rising twin spires.

Dubious, Ava raised her eyebrows at Simon. She looked so like her mother when she did that, it about broke his heart all over again. He gave a half-shrug -- what can you do? -- and she grinned, before facing the line of paying customers with a brisk clap and amiable, "Who's next?"   He'd despaired, at first ... him, raising up a girl by himself? But damned if Ava hadn't grown into a fine young lady, hard-working and capable, sweet and kind. If her falling for Marco proved the worst of it, well, could a doting father truly complain? Marco may have been a mite peculiar -- a dreamer, an artist, a head-in-the-clouds type -- yet, what with his parents, he at least came by it honestly. Maggie Zuri, as Madame Magdalena, read palms and cards and crystals out of a burgundy velvet tent with gold fringe, while Tomas Zuri did stage magic under the moniker

Mister Mystic. Fine folks, carnies of long standing. And, whatever else, Marco was clearly smitten with Ava, smitten to the core.

He let go those musings as Ava got the next pair of paying customers secured in. Grown men, the both of them, near Simon's own age. Biker-toughs in heavy denims and black leather vests, one sporting longish hair and a greying ponytail, the other bald as an egg, both liberally tattooed. He kept an eye on them, because sometimes fellas took rude at having a pretty thing like Ava fastening harness buckles between their legs, but these two behaved themselves nice and polite.

The bikers bumped fists as the countdown began, then gripped the padded lap-bar the way they might've gripped motorcycle handlebars.

KA-SPROOOOIIIIIIIING! Up, up, and away, the men voicing

wild shouts more befitting the war-cries of Vikings charging into battle. They had themselves a textbook-perfect ride, returned to earth safe-and-sound, tipped Ava a twenty when she gave them their stickers, and headed off toward Rusty's Beer-BQ tent while loudly declaring the experience

"Fuckin' EPIC!"

Which was all fine-and-dandy far as Simon was concerned. The kid, Charlie, he really shouldn't have gone on it in despite being just barely tall enough. Too much for him. Hopefully, it'd only leave him shook for a while, not traumatized for life or anything.

The blondie and the brownette he'd noticed earlier were up next, the blondie sashaying out to some encouraging wolf-whistles she ate right up. The brownette showed some reluctance, casting her gaze toward the height of the spires ... a height the bungee cords would exceed by almost as much again, at the apogee of the initial launch. She might have backed out, but her friend implored and wheedled and reminded her they'd already paid, the NO REFUNDS sign quite visible on Lottie's booth. With a resigned-seeming grimace, the brownette set her spine straight, squared her shoulders, and let Ava buckle her into the seat-harness.

Whenever young women, especially attractive ones, rode the Catapult, the watching crowd always increased, hosts of teen boys and men of all ages eager to get a glimpse ... and if the blondie's bounteous bosom did bounce free from confinement, so much the better! Simon himself, old as he was, faithful to his wife's memory as he was, still knew he'd be having a gander same as anyone else.

A gander and then some, thanks to the Catapult-Cam, though Lottie would be quick to delete or blur over any inappropriate content. She'd gotten into that habit once she'd realized how many guys thought whipping out their works on video would add to the thrill.

The sky had gone a deep periwinkle, shading indigo to the east and magenta to the west, already shining with the diamond-specks of a few stars. Shadows masked the grubbier daytime aspects of the midway, and the rainbows of lights dazzled magically as a wonderland, transforming everyone and everything into beauty.

Getting the thumbs-up from Ava, as the stoic brownette white knuckled it on the harness and the blondie giggled and squirmed in anticipation, Simon did his spiel, did his countdown, and threw the lever.

KA-SPROOOOIIIIIIIIING, flinging them high! And did the

blondie scream? Did she ever! Full-throated, operatic, an ululation that would've done generations of silver-screen scream-queens proud! It pealed across the fairgrounds, warbling like a melodious police siren – then cut off as abruptly as if throwing a switch.

Screamer and a fainter, then? Simon suppressed a chuckle as he flicked his gaze to the Catapult-Cam and ...

... and what the pan-fried hell?

The seat-carriage was empty. They were gone, the blondie and the brownette, both gone.

Sick horror seized his guts. If the buckles hadn't latched, if the lap bar malfunctioned, if they really had been catapulted or slingshotted off into the open...

He imagined them, blondie and brownette, soaring through the air, arcing like missiles, plummeting toward the unforgiving solid ground ...

No one else knew yet, except maybe Lottie, but a consternation had already begun to set in from the lack-of-screams silence. That consternation would become pandemonium in a flash, as soon as people saw empty seats where, moments before, two pretty girls had been.

Simon whammed the control console with the heel of his hand, as if to knock some sense into the Catapult-Cam and convince it to quit fucking around. The view, though, didn't change. As he gawked, incredulous, he realized the lap bar was in place, the harnesses hanging unoccupied but obviously still fastened. That made no goddamn sense ...

Someone on the ground noticed, shouted, and there came the pandemonium, an uproar of clamoring queries and vying for a line-of-sight.

"Bring it in!" Simon called. "Right now!"

Jess hurried to do so, winching the seat-carriage back to the launch pad and ratcheting it in place. Ava shook her head, aghast, gaping.

"I secured all the latches, I safety-checked! I know I did!"

"She did!" added Jess. Then, to Ava, "You did, I saw you. And ... look .. they still are ..."

Simon joined them. The lap bar was locked into place; he gave it a firm shake to make sure. And even if the lap bar could have unhooked, then slammed back, there was no explaining the harnesses ... which, even if they somehow came unbuckled, certainly could not have re-buckled all by themselves!

But then, how ...? But then, where ...?

Pandemonium, a pandemonium of voices and questions and demands, chaos crashing and swirling around Simon like an insane hurricane. The word spreading wildfire-fast, story no doubt growing and getting distorted in the telling. The crowd doubling, trebling. Fellow carnies, fair-goers, fairground security. Hundreds of people talking at once.

The insistence was that the girls had been launched, terrified and flailing; their broken bodies would be found a quarter-mile away, splatter smashed, burst apart the way pumpkins did during the autumn festival Punkin-Chunk, only red and chunky and strewn with bones and organs instead of orange and stringy with pulp and seeds ... the insistence it was a hoax, a trick, a publicity stunt ... that it had been a terrible accident ... that it had been willful murder ... that the girls had secretly been wearing parachutes and would drift down soft as dandelion puffs to take their bows ...

He heard it all, and heard none of it, and if Lottie hadn't stayed level-headed enough to assert some sort of order, he didn't know what else might have happened. But Lottie, bless her, took charge, drafting a couple carnival roustabouts to help her clear the immediate vicinity, dispensing refund-receipts to everyone who'd already paid and been waiting." What ... what happened to them, Pa?" asked Ava, sounding suddenly five years old again and not understanding why her momma wasn't coming home.

"They were there, weren't they?"

"They were," he said. "And then they weren't."

"Did they get ..." She couldn't even say it, gulping thickly as she scanned the horizon.

"I don't know. Don't think so; everything was secured up good and tight. You saw to that. Ain't no one on the midway more diligent; I'd stake my life on it."

"They couldn't have just ... disappeared, though!" Ava said. "Right out of buckled harnesses, right from under a secured lap bar?"

"I don't know," he repeated. "Sorry, sweet pea, your ol' Pa got no ready answers for this one."

Nor, it turned out as the evening went on, did anyone else. The whole fair came to a near standstill, carnies and townies alike milling about. Members of the small-town media showed up, hoping to score the scoop before the major networks swept in. Local law enforcement, eventually followed by feds, descended en masse to investigate.

The Cosmic Catapult was cordoned off, gone over fine-tooth comb for any sort of clues, with Jess on hand to answer any mechanical questions. The fairgrounds and surrounding parking lots, farmlands, and neighborhoods were searched. Thanks to Lottie's release forms, they had the names of the missing women, but whatever electronic searches the techy types did from their cell phones drew an utter blank. As if the phones, along with their owners, had just up and vanished off the face of the earth.

The Catapult-Cam video, analyzed frame-by-frame, only added to the mystery. Oh, it started off ordinary enough, showing the passengers -- firmly buckled in, with the lap bar secured, thank you very much; there'd be no accusations of carelessness thrown Ava's way -- as the countdown went on and the seat-carriage hurtled from the launch-pad with a sudden burst of dizzying speed, all G-forces and acceleration.

There was the blondie, screaming exuberantly, tossing her head, bounteous bosom bouncing such as to put her bra's integrity to the test. There was the brownette, wide-eyed and apparently holding her breath, posture rigid, holding on white-knuckled.

But then, at the apogee, at the very height of the tensile cables' extension, the video fritzed with a brief jag of static. In the very next instant, the seats were empty. Just ... empty. The women, just ... gone. At that exact moment the blondie's operatic screams had abruptly been cut off. The harnesses still buckled. The lap bar still latched. No violent ejection to send them careening into the wild twilight-blue yonder. As if they'd ... whiffed out, winked out. There, and then gone, in the blink of an eye.

No one, least of all the experts, knew what to make of it. Increasingly crazy theories were bandied about, everything from disintegration to alien abduction to divine intervention, a mini-Rapture, party of two, your table is ready.

Simon's only comfort was to know he and his weren't likely to be blamed, not for the disappearances at least. Nothing could be found mechanically wrong with the Cosmic Catapult itself, nothing about the video supported any fakery, no malice or malfeasance had reason to be suspected.

If he and his were to be blamed by their fellow carnies for the serious blow to everyone's collective income for the night, well, little he could do about that. They'd be lucky if the entire thing didn't get shut down for the duration. It'd be a pinch to all their pocketbooks ...

In the short run, anyway, as was eventually pointed out. Here they were, at the heart of another urban legend in the making! Like the one about the teens who'd ridden standing up on a rollercoaster and been decapitated by a low-arching cross-stretch of track. Or the one about the knife-stabber stalking unsuspecting victims in the hall of mirrors. Notoriety, infamy, and the dirty lure of morbid curiosity would bring in more customers than were kept away.

Simon didn't find that silver lining much comfort either. The mystery of it, the impossibility, the unreality, nagged at him.

Nagged at Ava, too ... as cops and crime-sceners went meticulous about their duties in the harsh sodium-glare of portable lights, flooding the launch-pad in stark white cut with sharp, black-edged shadows, she approached him where he sat on the table-part of a picnic table, watching the proceedings with a lukewarm mug of soup in his hands. Lottie had pressed it on him, insisting he needed to eat or drink something, but he'd managed a couple of sips and then simply held it.

"Pa?" Ava boosted herself up beside him.

"They find anything yet?" he asked, knowing full well they hadn't. Knowing, somewhere deep in his marrow, they wouldn't. There'd be no sensible, logical explanation, no tying up of loose ends into a tidy little knot.

"Nothing yet," Ava said, sounding like she knew it too. "But Pa? I've been thinking ... about that little boy, from before. About what he said."

40

"Charlie," said Simon.

"Maybe ..."

"Maybe what? Maybe it wasn't just a scared kid's imagination?"

"He said something was up there. He said he saw it, and it saw him too. Almost got him. He said he thought it was hungry."

"Yeah." Simon exhaled heavily. "I remember."

"Well, but, what if ..."

"There was? And it ate them two girls? Sucked 'em clean out of their seats and snarfed 'em like popcorn?"

"I know it seems crazy, but so's all this already." She waved at the activity, the crowd, some fella in a mask and gloves and plastic booties tweezing for fibers, some likewise-attired gal shining a blue beam into nooks and crannies. "Also, I had Lottie go back and run me their video, the dad and his boy?"

Simon looked at her, a tingle skittering along his spine. "And?"

"And it's got that same sort of fuzzy glitch. Only a flicker and only for the splittist split-second; wouldn't hardly notice at all on a regular watching. But I swear, Pa, it's true."

"Did you look at other videos --?"

"Sure did, all the ones from tonight, and it's only on those two."

"You mention this to any of them yet?" He dipped his chin toward the bustling investigators.

She shook her head. "They already look at me funny."

"Right. Well then, I'll let 'em look at me funny."

Setting down the soup, he went and found someone in charge, a brusque and efficient woman in a smart pantsuit like she'd choppered in straight from Quantico. He fully expected to get the bum's rush, but she heard him out.

41

Skeptical, she may have been, but with few other leads she must've figured it wouldn't hurt to be open-minded. She compared the videos, called over some other experts, and consulted. They even got the boy's -- Charlie's -- family's information from their release form and dispatched someone presumably to find and interview them.

Simon was glad enough to retreat again to his picnic table as they did their thing. It was near to midnight by then, when the fair would normally be wrapping it up for the night, but he didn't figure any of them would be seeing much sleep.

Ava was over with Marco and his folks now, him putting a comforting arm around her. Tom Zuri, changed out of his top-hat and flashy tuxedo, and stood nearby, watching the technicians. Maggie Zuri, still wearing her headscarf, eyeliner, and bangled jewelry, paced back and forth along the mural her son had painted, frowning pensively.

"Marco, this painting ..." she said at one point. "Have you been reading my books? The ones on the ebony shelf?"

"No, Mama," he replied. "You know I can't read that stuff."

She relaxed. "Ah, good."

"Though I do sometimes look at the pictures," Marco confided to Ava as his mother strolled out of earshot, and the gentle joke made Ava smile.

How exactly it came about, Simon wasn't sure, but the next thing he knew, someone had decided a test was in order. A test of the Catapult Cam, to look for what the Quantico lady referred to as 'the anomaly,' as well as anything else out of the ordinary with the Cosmic Catapult itself.

They were, in other words, gonna slingshot a couple cops up there, for the same reason the bear went over the mountain. It struck Simon with an uneasy feeling in the pit of his stomach, though he couldn't say why. The bikers had gone up and come down okay, after all, and so had plenty of other passengers over the course of the day. Dozens of them, without so much of a hint of an incident.

Bad idea or not, though, what else was there to do? If it was the Cosmic Catapult, he couldn't very well just go on flinging paying customers willy-nilly.

So, he agreed. Best to let them do it, with plenty of witnesses and equipment; if anything did happen, at least they'd have ample evidence.

The officers who volunteered didn't seem to share his misgivings. On the contrary, the younger of the two, a rookie likely fresh from the academy, could hardly volunteer fast enough. He clambered into the seat with an ear-to-ear grin, remarking, "Can't believe we're getting paid for this!"

His companion, a salt-and-pepper brick of a man who would've been right at home busting up drunken brawls, only grunted some sort of affirmation as they strapped him in. The buckles and lap bar were quadruple-checked, the Catapult-Cam and their respective bodycams as well, and a helicopter circled at a prudent distance with a spotlight and telephoto lens.

"Pa, you're not really ...?" began Ava.

"I ain't," he said, shrugging and spreading his hands; the techy types had taken over the control console, readying to do their own countdown once the Quantico lady finished a rather different version of his usual spiel.

Never, in the many years he'd spent on the midway, had Simon heard a crowd go so quiet, seen them watch so intently. The very air about thrummed with a tension that had little to do with the pent-up potential energy of the taut bungees.

Three-two-one and KA-SPROOOOIIIIIIIIING! Off they went,

with a jubilant yip of glee from the rookie. Up and up and up, the cables stretching to the very limit of their extension.

Then came a barrage of frantic curses and panicked shouts from high above, and exclamations of disbelieving shock from the control console and the police van where they were monitoring the body-cam footage, and ...

Long story short, when the seat-carriage was finally winched back to earth, it had one sole occupant and one empty seat.

"He was there, and then he was gone!" the badly shaken older cop, a wet patch on the front of his uniform trousers, reported.
"There was a ... a kind of pop, like when a kid pops his finger in his cheek ... and, poof, he was gone!"

Gone, he was. Harness still buckled, lap bar still in place. The Catapult-Cam showed exactly what it had before, a jagged glitch and then no rookie sitting where a rookie had been a split-second before.

The live video from the rookie's bodycam showed a turbulent first-person view of the launch and ascent, the vast star-studded black sky above, the vast countryside spreading out in all directions below. At the very instant it neared apogee, though, a fizz of static obscured the image, which then went utterly blank, signal lost.

Well, and if it had been pandemonium before ...

Simon felt Ava's hand slip into his, both seeking and offering reassurance. "What now, Pa?"

What now? They were done, done with the Cosmic Catapult at

least. It'd be seized, hauled away ... dismantled and destroyed ... or studied in some secret government lab or military base ... and, but for the huge number of witnesses gathered, he and Ava and Jess and Lottie may have faced a similar fate.

"I'm thinking," he said, "it might be 'bout time to retire."

Avert Thine Eyes

Jeff Strand

"Avert thine eyes, lest ye go mad!" Gerald shouted. "The human mind cannot comprehend the horror that looms above us, and to gaze upon it will surely spell doom for your sanity!"

Edward squeezed his eyes shut. "I shall not look at the accursed evil!"

James put his hands over his face. "Nor shall I! I must protect my brain from this ungodly sight!"

Arthur pulled his wool hat over his eyes. "I'd sooner pluck the orbs from their sockets than allow them to view the cosmic menace!"

"Aw, shit, I looked," said Roy.

"Look away!" Gerald screamed. "Look away immediately!"

"I can't! It's so gross!"

"Avert thine eyes!"

"Seriously, you guys, I'd heard that ancient evils were unpleasant to look at, but this thing is just plain nasty." Roy pointed to the sky. "It's all green and slimy. It's bad enough when I have to look at a normal-sized octopus, but this thing has got to be the size of six or seven Dairy Queens put together! Oh, God, its mouth is disgusting."

"God has no part in this!" said Gerald.

"I take it back—I don't think that was its mouth. I get why they say your mind can't comprehend it, because it's really hard to tell which part is its mouth, which part is its nose, and all of that. Does it have ears? I don't know. Lots of green slimy tentacles, though."

"The tales are true!" Gerald wailed. "It possesses an infinite number of tentacles!"

"Oh, no, I wouldn't say that it's an infinite number. More like twenty."

"Twenty doesn't sound so bad," said Edward.

"It's pretty darn bad," said Roy. "I'm not sure how you'd fit an infinite number of tentacles into the sky, although I guess that could be part of why it makes you go insane. But, yeah, it looks like about twenty tentacles, maybe twenty-two or twenty-three. Twenty-three would be pretty weird, wouldn't it? An odd number of tentacles. When it's tentacles or legs or eyes it's almost always an even number."

"It could have lost a tentacle in a fight," said James.

"Yeah, yeah, that's true. And, like I said, it could also be twenty or twenty-two. It's hard to count them while they're all waving around. You guys should really see this thing. But don't look, obviously. I wish I hadn't."

"Then turn away!" said Gerald.

"I can't! It's like driving past a car crash. I will say that I'm feeling less insane than I would've expected. I'm scared and grossed-out, but I haven't lost my mind. Maybe it takes more than a giant sky-octopus to make me feel like I've lost my grip on reality. I dunno."

"Is it doing anything?" asked Arthur.

"Not really. Hovering, mostly. It's not knocking over buildings or anything like that."

"Perhaps I should take a look," said Edward.

"No!" Gerald shouted. "You must not look!"

"Roy seems to be handling it okay. I was under the impression that if we gazed upon the ancient cosmic evil we'd go completely comatose, or just start shrieking incoherently and rip out all of our hair. I can handle looking at something gross and slimy. I'm a vet."

"I'd advise against looking at it," said Roy. "I may not be tearing out my hair, but I'm definitely a little queasy, and looking up like this is starting to strain my neck."

"What if slime starts dripping off it?" asked Edward. "We wouldn't be able to see it to move out of the way."

"You literally just said that you could handle slimy," said Gerald.

"Looking at it and touching it, yeah. But what if this slime is like acid? Or what if it excretes a blob of slime the size of a house? It seems dangerous to stand underneath the ancient evil without being able to see what kind of goo it might drop on us."

"I think we're okay," said Roy. "Like I said, the tentacles are waving around a lot, and I don't really see anything coming off of them.

I'll let you know if that changes."

"I can't keep doing this," said Edward. "I have to look."

"Don't you dare!" shouted Gerald.

"You're not the boss of me." Edward opened his eyes.

"Ew."

"I know, right?" said Roy.

"It's freaky as hell, no doubt about it," said Edward. "But it's not like I feel my sanity slipping away. I can still speak in complete sentences."

"Right," said Roy. "I was under the impression that it would be a sight that haunted my every waking moment. Don't get me wrong—I'll think about this thing a lot. Probably every day for the rest of my life. But not every hour of every day."

Edward nodded. "My thoughts exactly. I mean, look, it's a gigantic glowing octopus-like monster hovering a mile above our heads in the middle of the city. That's not something I'll forget any time soon. But it's kind of like the movie Requiem for A Dream. It messed me up for a while, but I got over it."

"I haven't seen that one."

"Great acting, but it's a tough watch."

"Did you say it's glowing?" asked Gerald.

"Yeah," said Edward. "It's got this glow surrounding it. Not like it's radioactive, more like it's...uh, what's the word...?"

"Otherworldly," said Roy.

"Yes!" said Edward. "Otherworldly. It has an otherworldly glow, like something that passed through a portal into our dimension. Eerie as hell."

"Oh, yeah, totally eerie," Roy agreed. "But not incomprehensible.

My brain can totally process what's happening."

"Also, I have to admit that it's kind of nice to be able to see what it's up to," said Edward. "When I was averting my eyes, I wasn't sure what it was doing, and that was a lot scarier. It's really just floating around up there. It's not like it's on a murderous rampage."

"I'm starting to think I should look at it," said James.

"You should do no such thing!" shouted Gerald.

"Roy and Edward looked at it, and they sound okay. I like to think that I'm at least as mentally healthy as they are. I feel kind of stupid just standing here with my eyes closed."

"Do not succumb to temptation!" Gerald told him.

"Screw it," said James. He opened his eyes and gazed upward. "What nightmarish presence lurks in the skies above?" he shrieked. "My psyche cannot cope with the unimaginable, indescribable horror!" He let out a maniacal giggle and began to repeatedly slap himself in the face.

"See?" asked Gerald. "You see? He's gone mad!" "It does seem that way," Roy admitted.

"My perception of the world is forever altered! I feel as if cosmic worms are burrowing through my skull, devouring everything I once thought I knew! Why would God allow this being to exist? Or...am I staring into the wide-open jaws of God right now?"

James' pupils faded away, leaving him with pure white eyes.

"I have been stricken blind, and yet I still see!"

James fled. For a newly blind man he did surprisingly well for a few moments, and then he smacked into the side of a Mexican restaurant, knocking himself unconscious.

"See what you did?" asked Gerald. "A kind and decent man is now irreversibly insane."

"I didn't tell him to look!" Roy insisted. "I in no way suggested that my own experience was going to be the same as his. If he went whack-a-doodle, it's not my fault."

"Right," said Edward. "There was no peer pressure. Nobody said that all the cool kids are looking at the giant octopus. He made a choice, and clearly for him it was the wrong one, but I reject the accusation that I behaved irresponsibly."

A giant tentacle reached down, wrapped around Arthur, and yanked him a mile into the air. The creature tossed Arthur into its mouth.

"Oh, wow," said Roy.

"What happened?" asked Gerald.

"It was super-fast. That thing grabbed Arthur and ate him!"

"It almost makes me wonder if Arthur should've had his eyes open," said Edward.

"Nah," said Roy. "You saw how fast it happened. There was no time to run. It could just as easily have been you or me."

"That's true, I guess. Hey, what are those?"

"I'm not sure what you mean."

"Something is falling."

"Oh, yeah, you're right. Jeez, I hope it's not slime."

"It kind of looks like...musical instruments."

"Musical instruments?"

"That's what it looks like to me," said Edward.

"Why would the beast have musical instruments, and why would it drop them?" asked Roy.

Edward shrugged. "We're not supposed to understand it. That's sort of its whole deal."

"Wait, nope, they aren't musical instruments," said Roy, as several bones landed on the sidewalk in front of them. A skull bounced off the cement and struck Gerald in the face.

"Goddamnit!" shouted Gerald.

"Ah, they're Arthur's bones," said Roy. "That makes a lot more sense."

"My nose is bleeding," said Gerald.

"At least you're better off than James," said Edward. "It looks like he got hit by six or seven rib bones."

"So, ultimately, being comatose worked out in his favor," said Roy. "Can you imagine getting impaled by a bunch of broken ribs if you were fully aware of what was happening?" He shuddered.

"I'd say that we should go over there and help him, but three of those ribs went in his neck. I think he's pretty much boned." Edward frowned. "Oh, crap, that pun was totally unintended. I'd never make a joke like that about the death of a human being. Or an animal, for that matter.

As a veterinarian there's a certain amount of gallows humor that goes along with the job, but I know where the line is drawn."

"It was pretty clever, though," said Roy. "Even if it was an accident."

"Still, I feel bad. It was way too soon. That's the kind of tasteless joke that gets you canceled."

"Well, how about this? Arthur is pretty much boned, too! Now we both lack a moral compass."

"That doesn't help."

"I didn't think it would. But it was funny enough to deserve a callback."

"You know," said Roy, "it suddenly occurred to me that if the horror above is snatching people up, eating them, and spitting out their bones, it might not be such a great idea to just stand here. We should take cover."

"I was thinking the same thing," said Edward. "Maybe at that ice cream shop at the end of the block?"

"You don't have to twist my arm. Their peaches and cream flavor is simply divine."

Roy and Edward began to walk off.

"Hey!" Gerald shouted.

"What's wrong?" asked Roy.

"Are you just going to leave me here?"

"Sorry," said Edward. "I assumed that you could open your eyes enough to watch your feet while you walked."

"No! I'm not opening my eyes until the ancient evil has returned to its own plane of existence!"

"All you have to do is look down," said Roy. "No judgment about your safety precautions. You do you. But the ancient evil is a mile straight up in the air. I'm just saying."

"What if it controls my will and makes me look up?"

"If you're suddenly giving it brand new powers, why couldn't it just send magical fairies down here to pry open your eyes and tilt up your head?"

"We should get going," said Edward. "The ice cream shop closes in twenty minutes."

"I hope it's not too crowded," said Roy. "Everybody else around here fled as soon as the ancient evil arrived. Honestly, we look kind of silly still being out here."

Edward and Roy each took one of Gerald's hands and led him down the sidewalk.

"Is it lower than it was before?" asked Edward.

"Is what lower?"

"The ancient evil."

Roy looked up. "Oh, yeah. It was a mile up before, and now it looks like it's about three-quarters of a mile. That's not great."

"Do you think it's going to squish us?"

"Probably not. What would it gain by squishing us?"

"I'll be honest," said Edward. "My sanity was doing just fine when the ancient evil was a mile above our heads. Three-quarters of a mile is a different story. It seems bigger when it's closer."

"Do you feel like you're going mad?"

"Not full-on mad, but I can feel things slipping away. In retrospect,

I wish I hadn't looked."

"I told you!" Gerald shouted. "I told you to avert your eyes! But nobody ever listens to me!"

"Fine! You told me! There's no reason to be a dick about it!"

"How insane are you feeling?" asked Roy. "Do we need to be concerned that you're going to go feral and attack us?"

Edward shook his head. "I'm not feeling violent. It's more of a

'bite off my own tongue' kind of insanity."

"Better than biting off other people's tongues, I guess."

"True."

"Though I think watching you bite off your tongue will probably be more disturbing than gazing up at the ancient evil."

"When I feel uncontrollably compelled to do it, I'll turn around."

"Thanks. Much appreciated."

"How low is the ancient evil now?" asked Gerald.

"Oh, look who suddenly sees the value in using your eyes!" said Edward. "What's the matter? Having trouble gauging the distance of the threat when your eyes are squeezed shut?"

"Drop the attitude," said Roy. "You just accused him of being a dick, but now you're behaving like one. You've become the very thing you just condemned. He asked a simple question."

"That's true," said Edward. "I apologize for being rude." He looked up. "It's definitely lower now. We need to hurry."

The three of them speed-walked down the block to the ice cream shop.

"Son of a bitch," said Roy. "What kind of ice cream shop closes early on Sundays? That's the day people are most in the mood for it!"

"That's really disappointing," said Edward. "Peaches and cream would've been a wonderful last thing to taste before I bit my tongue off.

Speaking of which…" He turned around and bit down, hard.

"Oh, jeez, that sounded horrible!" said Roy. "We've been so focused on our eyes that I didn't even think about covering my ears!"

Edward turned back around and spat out most of his tongue, along with a lot of blood.

"Dude!" said Roy. "If you were going to spit stuff out, you should've stayed turned around! Nobody wants to see that!"

"Thorry," said Edward. He turned around and spat out some more blood. "Thith hurth."

"Of course it hurts. Your tongue has nerves galore. Your insanity was never going to completely shield you from the pain."

A glowing green tentacle reached down and wrapped around Edward's neck. It yanked his head off and rose back into the air.

"Yowza," said Roy.

"What happened?" asked Gerald.

"Edward bit off his tongue, just like he said he would, and then the ancient evil popped his head off like it was pulling the cork out of a bottle of wine. I don't mean like it was using a corkscrew—that would've been horrific. I mean like when you drink part of a bottle of wine, and you put the cork back in, and then you pop it back out when you're ready for more wine. It was like that, but gorier."

"So that warm liquid hitting me is Edward's blood?"

"Yeah. He's got quite a spurt going. His body hasn't fallen over yet. I know you're committed to keeping your eyes closed, but it really is something to see. Oh, wait, too late, he just fell. His leg is still twitching but otherwise the show is over."

"What's the ancient evil doing?" asked Gerald.

Roy looked up. "Not much. Oh, wait, no, it's descending fast. I'm getting a 'devour all of humanity' vibe from it."

"And you're sure the ice cream place is closed? You tried the door?"

"Yep. Okay, the octopus-thing is getting scarier and scarier the closer it gets. They say that the strongest fear is fear of the unknown, but I'm going to call bullshit on that. I can see its mouth now, fangs and all, and that's way scarier than when I wasn't sure what I was looking at."

"Are we all going to die?" asked Gerald.

"That's the direction things seem to be moving, yeah."

"I'm not ready to die. I have so many things left to accomplish. I've never learned to play guitar. I've never eaten white chocolate. I've never made love to a woman, successfully."

"I can feel my sanity going bye-bye," said Roy. "You're welcome to make your own choices, but I will say that I'm feeling less scared as my ability to process information fades. This whole 'turning insane because you're unable to cope with the unimaginable horror' may be the way to go."

He bit off his tongue, spat it out, then sat down on the sidewalk to await his doom in a cheerfully oblivious state.

Gerald opened his eyes.

"Roy, you're sitting in a pool of blood!" he said.

Roy shrugged.

Gerald gazed upward. He looked directly into the infinite eyes of the creature.

"You are eternal," he whispered. "You are what has always existed and will always exist. You are all gods combined. I fear thee, love thee, and worship thee. Take me as your victim. Take me as a sacrifice."

The ancient evil slapped Gerald upside the head with a tentacle.

It spoke in a booming voice that shattered the windows of the ice cream shop: "Offering yourself as a victim is a pussy move. Grow a pair."

"Oh," said Gerald, flustered. "I thought you'd like that."

"No. It's total weak sauce. You are the chosen one, Gerald. You are the one who can defeat me and save humanity. Fight back. Let us do battle."

"Are you serious?"

"Do I look serious?"

Gerald stared at the ancient evil for a few moments. "I honestly can't tell."

"Battle me!"

Gerald punched a tentacle.

"Ow."

Gerald punched it harder.

"Ow. Damn."

Gerald grabbed the tentacle and gave it a vigorous tug.

"Stop it. You're going to yank it off."

"I shall never stop yanking, foul beast!" Gerald shouted. "I shall best ye in combat and save billions of lives!" He tugged on the tentacle as hard as he could.

The ancient evil pulled its tentacle free, then slapped Gerald upside the head again. "A valiant effort, but obviously I was just messing with you."

"Oh."

"Should've kept averting your eyes."

The ancient evil popped Gerald into his mouth and spat out his bones. Then it smiled, though no mortal would recognize it as a smile, and began the process of devouring humanity.

Witchblood

Tim Curran

Last year, when Kirt Vanderheim perished in the fire that consumed his building, there was an awful lot of talk about what had started the blaze. Much of it was gossip, distortion, and sheer nonsense. Sure, it was a strange business, and the fire marshals still haven't figured out what could cause a blaze so hot that no remains of Kirt were ever found. The mainstream press spent a lot of time hinting that the fire started because Kirt was free-basing cocaine, cooking crank, or involved in Satanic rituals gone astray. And the latter, of course, was something the crazies of the religious right went after like sharks smelling blood in the water.

But all the above is bullshit.

You see, I was there the night Kirt died. I saw what happened and what I saw, man, well, let's just say I've been on some serious drugs ever since. I'm afraid to turn out the lights at night because I don't know what might be hiding in the shadows and I'm afraid to sleep because of what might come for me in my dreams. Sounds like some pretty mad shit, but it's true.

And it all started when Kirt called me and said, "Man, you gotta get your ass over here right now, I got something you just gotta hear." Before I go any farther, I suppose I should tell you who Kirt Vanderheim was in case you don't know. Maybe that'll put this whole ugly business in perspective, if that's even possible.

Okay. If you're the type that considers Judas Priest or Iron Maiden relaxing, AC/DC just pleasant toe-tapping old school nostalgia, or Black Sabbath to be the auditory equivalent of comfort food, then the name Kirt Vanderheim is probably well-known to you. Vanderheim was the president and founder of Graveworm Records and its sister label, Morbid Dementia.

And in the arena of independent death-metal, that was saying something.

For it was Kirt Vanderheim that gave birth to such bands as Dismembra, CorpseGrinder, and Decapitated Nun, and turned a love for high-decibel brain damage music into not only a passion and a way of life, but into a lucrative multi-million-dollar industry.

And he did it nearly single-handedly.

Becoming, I might add, not only a record producer, but a marketing genius and a promotional guru along the way. Not so bad for a high school dropout from Milwaukee whose resume consisted mostly of rolling joints, packing bongs, and blowing out his ears listening to everything from Accept to Black Flag. I went to junior college with Kirt, so I know what I speak. G.E.D. in hand, he made a career of cutting classes, hanging out in metal and punk clubs, and selling bumper stickers and t-shirts out of the trunk of his car you know, things with catchy slogans like, FUCK THE RICH and I BRAKE FOR CORPSES, I LUV POODLES—WITH BARBECUE SAUCE and HAVE YOU RAPED YOUR PRIEST TODAY? Cutesy, feel-good Hallmark kind of things like that.

In his sophomore year—don't ask me what his major was—Kirt decided he was going to become the Rick Rubin of thrash metal and you know what? He did just that. What would later become Charnel House Productions was started in a basement apartment with an old two-track analog recording machine begged, borrowed, or stolen, and a handful of extreme metal bands anxious not only to push the envelope of hard rock, but to tear that sonofabitch open and make some ear drums bleed. Kirt dropped out of school, but I finished, even graduated which was really something considering my social schedule.

I had a journalism degree, a record collection you had to move by truck, and an absolute love of what my old man liked to call "sewer music." I worked for a number of underground music magazines that barely paid the bills, made something of a name for myself, graduated to the Ivy-league rags like Cream, Spin, and Rolling Stone. Eventually, pretty much feeling betrayed and disgusted by the corporate maneuverings of these publications, I returned to my roots writing articles for Metal Maniacs, Metal Edge, and Metal Hammer, among about a dozen others. I became known as something of an authority on heavy metal and when high-scale trade rags like Entertainment Weekly or news mags like Time were looking into a series on decibel-driven music, they turned to yours truly. Somewhere along the line, I wrote three books and started my own magazine, Thrash & Grind, which I am happy to say was available in just about every periodical market in the country for some six years.

I did okay, right?

But what about Kirt Vanderheim?

Well, he did more than okay in the twenty years since our college days. Pretty much from scratch, as I mentioned, he built Charnel House Productions into a mega death-metal entity, scoring a tremendous and fanatic cult following and swinging some huge deals with entertainment biggies like Sony and Virgin. He was the mastermind behind Bloody Jesus and Grave Orchids,

Virgin Vivisection, and Pigflesh. His bands headlined the annual Slaughterfest in Copenhagen and the Butcher-Bash in Edinburgh.

Anyway, given the sort of journalist I was, we had a very good working relationship, Kirt and I. I helped him launch the careers of some of his earliest bands like Antichrist and Mother Necrophile and in the process got some of the finest stories any music journalist could hope for. Whenever we'd get together, we'd launch into these incredibly long, intellectual discussions on the state of heavy metal past, present, and future. We'd extol the virtues and criticize the limitations of black metal and thrash metal, doom and grindcore, progressive and power metal, dissecting influences and trends, minutely scrutinizing sub-sub genres like Viking and Goth metal.

But that was our thing.

It was our life and our passion and there was really nothing else for us. No drug in the world could touch what metal gave to us. About a month before the fire, Kirt invited me to Charnel House studios to hear a couple sessions from some new bands he was working with. Like everything else, death-metal was hardly standing still. This new crop of artists had fused black metal and grindcore into a hyperspeed assault of distorted guitars, hammering drums, and guttural demonic vocals—sometimes called Cookie Monster vocals by the uninitiated— trying to prove that they were indeed the scariest, meanest, most psychotic rock 'n' roll bands out there. The band names themselves were almost enough to turn your stomach Rancid Testicle, CorpseFuck, and Disemboweled Fetus, among others. The most promising group was an all-female quintet called Maggot-Cunt, if you can visualize that one. The lead singer's name was Autopsy Angel and she could alternately sound throaty and masculine like Satan possessing Linda Blair and then jump octaves until she was screaming like a soprano being peeled by razors. If that gnarly bitch wasn't possessed, then nobody was. Man, oh man, what a girl.

Kirt let me listen to the first two tracks they had cut, "Fucking the Dead" and "Bride of Chains," and believe me, the lyrics were enough to put you off meat for a month. It was nasty, visceral stuff, and I really shouldn't have been surprised. Death-metal had long been a cult unto itself and these bands were always trying to out-do one another, not only singing about grave robbery and necrophilia, but actually practicing them. At least, that was the buzz they liked to create about themselves.

But there was no getting around one thing and that was that these bands were anti-social deviants on a good day and violent sociopaths on a bad one. I couldn't count on one hand the crimes they committed, the sentences they received, the cemeteries they defiled or the churches they tried to burn down. Some of these guys and gals were simply playing a part but others? Jesus, you didn't want to get on the wrong side of people named Carrion or Vomit Messiah who actually carried dead ravens and wormy rats in leather bags so they could always be near the smell of death.

It just wasn't healthy.

The night Kirt burned-up or vanished, take your pick some people are still saying he went underground, that it was all a carefully planned marketing ploy I went to his penthouse apartment because he had something he wanted me to hear. And it wasn't some new thrash band, but something important, he said, the discovery of a lifetime.

Well, how could I refuse that?

Kirt's penthouse was on the top floor of the office building that housed Charnel House Productions and a dozen other counterculture entities he had created. When I got there, we had the place to ourselves. There were no leather-clad groupies with multiple piercings or Goth chicks with corpse-white faces. That in itself told me this actually was important. Kirt pulled me into his den (about the size of a warehouse) where he kept his CD and vinyl collection, his metal memorabilia, all those incredibly rare bootlegs and master tapes. Kirt was big on vinyl, had something like 100,000 records in there, and if you dug hardcore rock 'n' roll like me, well, it was enough to make your mouth water.

"Well?" I said. "Tell me."

"Pour yourself a drink," he said, "this will be worth the wait." I had a whiskey and Coke, started looting through all that hot wax in the glass shelves: the rarities, the alternate versions, the albums that never made it to press, the songs that were bounced from the final sessions. Here was the ultra-rare Soviet-era bootleg of Bloody Jesus' seminal first record, Shit and Disease. Here were the manic, never released Latin versions of CorpseGrinder's only two records, Fetid Orgy and Children of the Slime. And here also were incredible rare bootlegs of bands like Unholy Incest, Suffocation, and Brainworm. And behind lock and key, I was looking at the master of the only known recording of Decayed Intelligence, a band that committed suicide together after laying it down.

Shit, Kirt had things there worth hundreds of thousands of dollars. He popped in a few minutes later, saying he had to arrange bail for the lead guitarist of Accursed Soul—He-Who-Is-Not-To-Be-Named—who had somehow gotten his hands on somebody's prized doves and bitten their heads off and painted the walls of his hotel room with their blood.

Another day in the life of a death-metal mogul, I guess.

Kirt just stood there, a skinny little guy with long tangled dreadlocks and a beard that reached down to his chest. His eyes blazed like coals yanked from a brazier. And I knew, just looking at him, that he'd found some oddity he wanted me to listen to. Probably some antique metal, what we liked to call proto-metal. One of those bands from the late sixties like the MC5 or Blue Cheer, Lucifer's Friend or Sir Lord Baltimore, who were blowing eardrums and laying down the law long before the term "heavy metal" was even coined.

"Come on, let me have it," I said, getting excited now, too. He grinned and slid a plain white record jacket from inside a locked case. "Okay, my friend," he said. "Tell me what you know about WitchBlood?

I knew all there was to know about that mysterious band. WitchBlood was a German metal group circa 1972, 1973. They were probably the actual originators of death-metal and this easily ten years before Venom and Possessed would pick up the gauntlet. They sounded much like Black Sabbath played at a frenetic pace, but with the obligatory growling demon vocals that would, a decade later, become the mainstay of the death-metal movement. But this was in the early 1970s. At the time, they were radical and demented and anarchistic, considered revolutionaries and terrorists by some, while others thought they were merely a talentless shock band. I recall one reviewer, after seeing their live show, saying they were "sheer and unadulterated vomit, no more, no less." Which led the band to call their first and only album House of Vomit. Maybe an inside joke and maybe their way of yet again raising their middle finger to the establishment.

Okay, those are the basic facts.

They made only the one album, went out on one largely unsuccessful world tour, disappeared into hiding for a year, and then resurfaced meaner, vicious, and more antisocial than before. They had put together some new material and they played it in their hometown of Hanover, Germany in October of '73. And here is where the legend of WitchBlood really gets going. That concert was the only one where they played their unrecorded new material because somewhere during the show, that old concert hall went up in flames and the band with it not to mention some fifty or sixty other people.

A rock and roll tragedy, to be sure.

I briefly went through all that, the entire time my eyes feasting on that cardboard sleeve in Kirt's hands. My pulse was pounding. My palms were sweating. "What…what do you have there? C'mon, man, don't hold it back."

I sounded like a junkie, but that's pretty much how I got concerning rare metal. And particularly when you were talking WitchBlood, who in the folklore of headbangers were akin to the Holy Grail or the fucking Shroud of Turin.

He handed me the sleeve.

My hands were shaking so badly I nearly dropped it.

Just a plain white cardboard sleeve with the words Hexeblut burned into the sleeve. That was it. Nothing else. I reached inside and pulled out a dust wrapper and the album itself. It was made of blood-red vinyl. No name, no pressing info, nothing. A bootleg surely and one that made my stomach flip over. "You listened to it?" I said.

But Kirt shook his head. "No haven't dared. I bought a warehouse full of old records from Stuttgart and this was in one of the boxes. I wanted you to be here when it was played the first time."

"Jesus," I said, "if this has those lost sessions…"

Well, no need to go into it. The rights on something like that would be in the millions. And not because of the musical genius of the band, but because of the historical tragedy itself. But, honestly, the money meant nothing to Kirt and even less to me. From a purely pop culture perspective, something like that would have been absolutely priceless.

"Let's do it," I said, swallowing my drink in one pull.

Kirt took the album and set it on the turntable and, drawing in a slow breath, placed the needle on the wax. There was some static, some scratching, and then a whole lot of noise. But not the kind of noise we liked, just noise. Lots of rumbling like thunder in the distance, some high-pitched pinging sounds, something like voices buried in the mix, booming sounds. All sorts of shit and none of it even remotely like music. We listened halfway through, and I can tell you that I didn't care for what I was hearing. I didn't know why, but something about that distorted, nonsensical noise was making my skin crawl. My hands were bunched into fists and my teeth were chattering. I was sweating rivers. Finally, Kirt pulled the needle off it. "I suppose," he said, "we should play it backwards."

We looked at each other, both knowing that what was on there was meant to be played in reverse, and not caring for the idea much. Why? I don't know. But I think we both had a very bad feeling, only we were too cool and too urbane to admit it.

Kirt set the needle back down and started the turntable in reverse. There was nothing but silence for maybe five minutes and then it began. I heard that thunder more clearly now and the sound of a great bell gonging in the distance. What might have been rain and wind. Weird screeching and scraping noises that made my molars ache. And something like dozens of women whispering and something else like a wet ripping as if someone had been disemboweled with a hook. And through it all, a male voice muttering words that were guttural, garbled, and totally incomprehensible. It was saying something, but I couldn't be sure what. Those words weren't German, at least no German I've ever heard. If anything, they sounded almost like Latin, but debased and rasping and, yes, eerie.

It was all very unsettling, but the worst part was those whispering voices. I'm almost sure they were saying, "hilf mir, hilf mir, hilf mir, hilf mir," again and again which is German for help me.

I wanted to scream, to snatch that record off the turntable as I heard a rising slithery sort of noise that seemed to be beneath our feet but then something happened.

Something awful.

The floor began to vibrate, and the walls began to shake. There was a sound like a heart beating and lungs breathing. All those glass-fronted shelves of rare recordings shattered into a storm of glass. Records and masters and CDs went flying through the air. Tiles fell from the ceiling and then everything was consumed in a mephitic black mist that stank of sulfur and rotting meat. A wave of heat hit me, blasted right into me with what seemed like hurricane force and threw me across the room, singing my eyebrows and mustache.

It also saved my life, you see.

I blacked out, I must have blacked out.

I can't be sure. But when I opened my eyes, I was on the floor twenty feet from where I'd been sitting, dazed and confused, and the room, the very center of the room where we had been sitting had changed. It was like a black hole had opened up, some whirling vortex of matter and energy and force. Except it was living: a funnel of pulsing and glistening tissue that was not flesh exactly, but almost like an organic mist that was expanding with an echoing screeching sort of sound that was so unbelievably loud I involuntarily pressed my hands over my ears.

Kirt was sitting right in the middle of that ever-widening chaos.

I could see him there. He was still in his chair. The turntable was on the stand next to him. Both were caught in that chaos, but as it churned and widened, they were trapped in some kind of stasis, some sort of antigravity sink absolutely motionless. Kirt's mouth was wide open like he was screaming but I couldn't hear a thing above that screeching.

It was at that time probably less than thirty seconds into the whole thing when something came creeping out of the vortex. Maybe creeping isn't the right word because it seemed to spray out of there like vomit: wild, whipping strands of some pustulant white gelatin like fleshy Spanish moss that flowed upward and spread out over the ceiling, consuming and thickening like cream.

I think I screamed.

I think I lost my mind.

But if I had to tell you what that room looked like, I would have to say it was like being inside something alive, a livid, slick biological profusion of tissue and striated muscle and viscera.

Something like coils of squirming entrails came out of the vortex next except they weren't entrails but corkscrewing pink worms that were big around as telephone poles with immense suckering mouths on the ends.

That's what got Kirt: those mouths.

The worms came out in fleshy bunches like the tentacles of sea anemones, juicy and pink and spiraling. They wound Kirt up like pythons and then those sucking oval mouths were on him, draining him dry until he shriveled into a dry husk and broke apart. They must have put out an immense, raging heat because what was left of Kirt was cremated into black ash that blew apart like one of those carbon snakes you burn on the Fourth of July.

The record was a summoning.

That's what had happened in Hanover, and it was happening again. Played backward, that rare WitchBlood record was an invocation, a summoning, and, yes, a sacrifice to something out of time and space, a livid fleshy pestilence from the subcellar of the universe.

The vortex continued to widen and more of that jelly flooded out until it seemed the entire ceiling was fluttering with it. And the worms more of them all the time moving with serpentine convolutions as they sought me out, a vaporous stew of sweet putrescence billowing and steaming around me, fans of creeping web-like nervous tissue oozing from the greasy walls.

I jumped to my feet and ran out the door seconds before there was no door left. The last thing I saw was a rising cyclopean stalk that was slate-gray and scaly. It opened into a mass of corkscrewing appendages like the trunks of elephants.

That's what I saw.

That and the remains of the den glass cases all shattered, records reduced to fragments, streamers of tape tangled throughout. All of it whirling around and around in a tornado. There was no time for speculation, because the room was being engulfed in a gushing sea of tissue and worms and bulbous eyes.

The fire must have started about that time, I'm guessing.

As I stumbled down the corridor, mumbling and sobbing and more mad than sane, I heard smoke detectors whining and then the shrilling of the building's fire alarm. The corridor had become a steaming, pulsating womb expelling the pink of convolutions of wriggling shapes like peeled cobras.

By then, the penthouse was engulfed in flames. I could smell smoke and something sharp like ozone.

I pretty much stumbled down four flights of stairs as the building shook and creaked and groaned like it was trying to pull itself up and walk.

I fell out onto the sidewalk and crawled out into the street.

And that's when I looked up.

Oh, it was a four-alarm blaze, that was for sure. The building was burning, tongues of fire licking out of windows and a rolling pall of black smoke rising from the upper floors. But that wasn't all. I saw what looked like hundreds of those pink twisting worms rise up out of the flames as if they were born from them. They pushed out of the conflagration like a forest of serpents escaping a single egg. They filled the sky and brushed against the stars above which pulsated like beating hearts. And then then the rest of the thing whatever it was rose from the roof in a gigantic, writhing, mountainous mass of flabby lobster-red tissue, swollen and squirming and set with immense liquid sea-green eyes and gelid tendrils and a million roping, slithering feelers.

It's actually impossible for me to describe what I saw.

There are limits to human perception.

But that thing kept rising, swelling, expanding, flooding out in a slushy pink-gray-black-red anatomical profusion that filled the sky, bursting open the building like a flaming shell and stretching chitinous jointed legs that reached from horizon to horizon. I danced around, avoiding bricks and smoldering debris that buried the streets.

And then there was a hollowing rocketing detonation like a sonic boom and the thing was gone.

There was just the collapsed remains of Kirt's burning building across the street, its wreckage scattered for hundreds of feet, the structures next to it going up like napalm

That was it.

It ended right there.

My guess is that the Witchblood record was either destroyed in the chaos or melted down. Either way, its destruction sealed the hole that led into another universe or dimension, call it what you will.

I was on my ass in the rubble, singed, face blackened with soot, and I felt hands on me pulling me to my feet. I smelled body odor and foul breath and was looking into the face of Albert K., one of the crazy homeless people that lived on the street.

"I saw it," he said. "I saw the monster."

I was pretty much hysterical by the time the fire trucks and cops rolled onto the scene. They sedated me and threw me in the back of an ambulance. The next day in my hospital bed I was questioned by the fire marshal. He didn't believe a word I said. He claimed what I saw rising from the ruins of the building was an optical illusion caused by the flickering firelight reflected onto those columns of black smoke. That's all.

Sure, and if my aunt had a dick, she'd be my uncle.

I know what I saw.

Unfortunately, my only corroborating witness was Albert K. who they did not consider exactly dependable. They called him the "Sushi Kid" around the neighborhood because he was always digging in the dumpsters behind the Japanese deli down the way. When he forgot to take his Lexapro (which was often) he went up and down the street peeking in mail slots, claiming he was a government agent whose job it was to interrogate invisible Korean elves that lived in mailboxes.

And that's it.

A four-alarm fire much like that one in Hanover so many years ago.

Can I explain it? Any of it? No, not in the least. WitchBlood, unlike all the others that followed, were the real item. They had summoned something from some anti-world and had the record not been destroyed (I guessed) it would have eaten the world, gutted it and burned it to ash. All I know is that thing was swelling like bread dough, a living flux of matter whose sheer volume was something that our mathematics could not possibly hope to measure. I believe it would have engulfed this world, this solar system, then blotted out the stars in heaven. That's what I think. It was something undimensioned, a cosmic cancer that went on to infinity. Regardless, whether you believe what I've just told you or not, just do me one favor. If you ever come across that rare, blood-red vinyl of WitchBlood shatter it, burn it, but get rid of it.

Because if you don't, you're gonna find out all about rock 'n' roll damnation.

-The End-

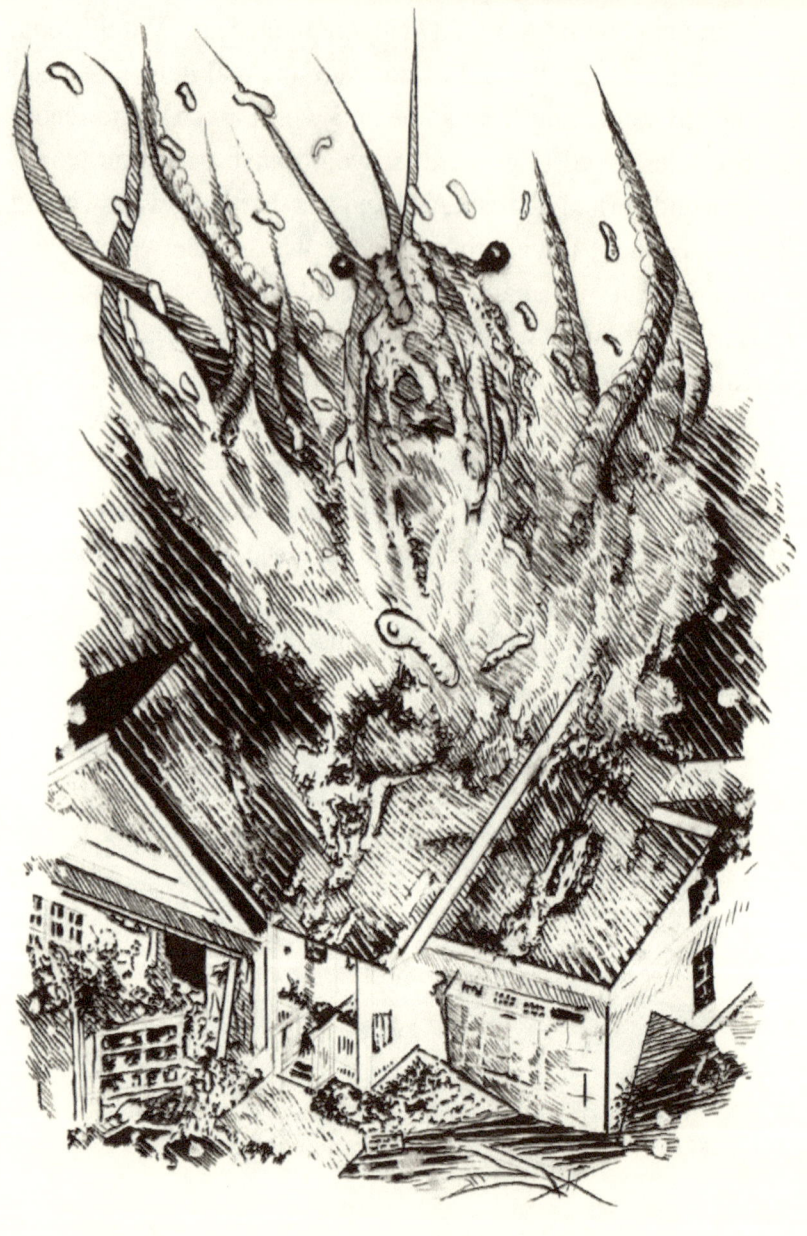

Bad Sounds

Patrick Lacey

Seth finds the tape in a crate filled with donations and spider eggs. One of those eggs' hatches in his palm before he Oh shits it back into the pile. Something dark and small and new tumbles out. He backs away but that cassette he was reaching for, it's still inside, is so inside, that the hatchling has found its way onto the plastic shell. It pauses there, studying him with however many eyes' spiders have. He figures it must be an omen but A.) he doesn't believe in omens (not yet anyway) and B.) that tape's cover has its hook in him.

He swallows a tablespoon of bile, flicks the spider, and hopes mom isn't standing by. Seth lifts the tape and marvels at the lo-fi graphic. It's a skeleton, or at least it's supposed to be, but whoever drew the thing forgot that skeletons don't have noses. On any other day, he'd get a good chuckle, but his run-in with the egg has him on edge. The sort-of skeleton's wearing a robe over what he has to imagine are bone-shaped ears. In the background is a sky that's never known sun, is more like cotton candy if cotton candy were made of storm clouds. And out of those clouds leaks a bolt of lightning the color of mustard. Beneath this glorious mess is the title.

Bad Sounds.

Not exactly original but he's seen worse. Usually they're more tantalizing, like *Blood-Curdling Nightmares or Chilling Sounds of All Hallows Eve* or—you get the idea. Seth is somewhat of an expert with these things, has accumulated quite the collection. These things are tapes manufactured through the eighties and nineties, with a few stragglers post-Y2K. They're sound effects and so-called creepy mood music, meant to add ambience to Halloween parties. Back when Seth was a few inches smaller—vertically and horizontally—his parents would break theirs out each year while his cousins ate too many Twizzlers and their parents got wasted off spiked punch. For them, it was background noise. Every few minutes, they might pay notice to the sounds of cackling witches or clanging chains but then it was back to living in the moment. Seth, though—he's never been great at that part. For him, it wasn't white noise but the essence of the party. Since then, he's become obsessive with collecting sound effects, specifically of the Halloween variety.

The crate is located out back of Jake's Record shop. Given its name, Jake's used to specialize in records, but times change and so do business models. And also, owners, since Jake found himself a condo in the Florida Keys. His son, Jack (how original), took the place over and switched to a more standard thrift store approach. For some reason, he kept the name going, maybe to maintain the customer base. But since the records have been reduced to a single rack out back, Seth figures those customers are long gone.

"Find anything good?" Jack says at the register. He's pretending to price something on the computer, but Seth can see the truth in the reflection of Jack's glasses. What he's really doing is bidding on a half dozen eBay auctions. It's almost common knowledge that Jack has a bit of a gambling problem. He's recovering now, has switched from betting on races, to auctions for retro toys, video games, that sort of thing. But those add up. Everything old will someday be new again and when that day comes, re-sellers will know before you. Up come those prices and people like Jack start increasing their bids, looking to own all the toys they couldn't afford with their childhood allowance.

Not that Seth's judging. Remember: he collects Halloween sound effects cassettes.

"Just this," Seth says, setting down his new copy of *Bad Sounds*. Jack snickers, then clicks. His lenses show a ten becoming one hundred. "You might be the only person in the world who gets excited about these things."

"You'd be surprised," Seth says.

"Yeah? You running a group or something? You guys meet once a week to discuss which screeching cat sounds the best?"

"I just mean there's other fans, that's all. No need to be a dick." "Just busting them," Jack says. "That'll be…" But there's no price sticker yet. The thing's hot off the proverbial press. He opens up a new tab, types *Bad Sounds* cassette into eBay's search bar, and comes up with precisely nothing.

"Maybe it's the only copy," Seth says, mostly joking, but the thought doesn't sit well in his gut.

"Doubt it," Jack says, still scrolling.

"Where'd you get it anyway?"

Jack nods out back, which is code for beats me. He means that someone dropped it off before or after closing time. People want to get rid of their old shit and they don't want to wait around for Jack, since Jack's usually late. Most of his goods are donated this way. Not that Jake's is a charity shop, a la Salvation Army.

All the earnings go straight into Jack's pockets and then into eBay listings for some action figure playset Santa once refused him.

Jack shrugs. "How about twenty?"

Seth snickers. "How about ten?"

"Come on, man. This thing might be rare. Said so yourself."

"And you said I'm the only one who likes these things." He sets down a ten-dollar bill and lets Jack think it over.

The computer chimes and Jack proceeds to whisper *for fuck's sake* under his breath.

"Bad news?" Seth asks.

"Lost again."

#

Northshore Independent Radio is one of the longest running stations of its kind, which is code for *no one ever listens*. It consists of old-timer music, religious talk shows, and historical non-fiction that would lull a coke head to sleep. Not that Seth's one to talk. His show, *The Sounds of Sound Effects*, airs every Friday from midnight until whenever his follow-up stumbles in. Sometimes it's a grumpy pastor from one of those godly programs, real old-testament stuff, and other times it's Hank Lancer, who plays bluegrass better fit for

Kentucky than

Massachusetts. The station's located on a barren stretch of road just before the Middleton border. The lot fits three cars on a good day and the building looks more like a converted auto shop, mostly because it is.

The Friday after Seth finds his new tape, he shows up early for work, though "work" is a misnomer. He doesn't DJ for money. It's a way to unwind after a week of bank-telling, of seeing how bloated most people's accounts are compared to his.

He opens the front door, winces as the creaking metal echoes down the hall. Whoever's his lead-in probably picked up the sound. He waits in the hall until Wendy Grafton steps out.

She favors seventies trucker tunes even though she looks like the nicest and oldest grandma you've ever seen. Her skin is mottled with deep-cut wrinkles, but the flesh smooths out when she smiles, which is often.

"Early tonight, Seth," she says, waving him into the studio like it's a therapy session. Her hair's not silver or grey but pure white, as if something once scared the color out of each follicle.

He raises the tape. "Got something new I want to play for the nice people at home."

"Good luck with that," she says. "Made some cookies for you.

They're by the coffee maker."

"You're too nice to me."

"Someone has to be," she says with a wink and a pat on his shoulder, and that's the most action he's gotten all year. Most people figure Seth's one of those happy-as-a-clam bachelors, but the truth is he finds human connection difficult. That's why he prefers thrift stores. It's easier to buy someone's former belongings, to exist *through* them, than swipe right and hope for the best.

Wendy has cued up two songs to allow Seth to set up. Radio isn't what it used to be. Movies romanticize it with record- and tape-laden archives but really, it's a computer and a handful of left-over CDs. Lucky for Seth, the station held on to their cassette player. He cracks open Bad Sounds and slips it inside.

Wendy's remaining tracks finish up and Seth turns his mic live.

"Hi folks, it's Friday night and I just know your head's spinning from the work week. It's late and you can't sleep, and you've got a drink in hand. Might be coffee but it's probably something stronger. You're looking to unwind but nothing's doing the trick. That's where I come in. Sometimes music doesn't cut it. You've heard it all before or it doesn't fit your mood but the world's full of other sounds. Could be a cricket chirping or waves crashing. Could be *anything*. All you've got to do is open your ears and listen. Tonight, I've got something special for you. I know Halloween's a couple months away, but I saw candy corn in Target this week. If they can start early, so can we. Say hello to *Bad Sounds*, a rare artifact from—"

Seth flips the case over, searches for a date but comes up empty. In fact, he can't find a composer or record company either. There's no information aside from the track listings (*A Horrorble Night, Things That Lurk,* etc).

"Let's not trouble ourselves with the details. After all, that's where the devil lives. So, sit back, sip that drink of yours, and let the spooky sounds do the talking."

He mutes his mic and presses *play*.

The tape begins as all tapes do, with a few seconds of dead air. The speakers hiss. The magnetic strip whirrs. Next comes the fading-in sound of a distant thunderstorm, of pounding rain and crackling thunder. Above that: ghostly moaning and growling wolves, all standard fare.   He leans back in his chair and assesses Wendy's cookies: an oatmeal raisin, a chocolate chip, and something too lumpy to identify. He picks the oatmeal and pours himself some coffee that tastes like it's been on the burner all week.

Bad Sounds transitions from storm to rustling leaves and padding footsteps. Further back in the mix is a synth playing occasional atonal chords. Again: nothing revolutionary.

Not until the woman screams.

It sends Seth rolling back in his chair. He's heard plenty of mock gasps before but none quite like this. There's something desperate in the woman's voice, her pleas more life-like than usual. After that comes distorted whispering, like it's been run through a guitar pedal, like it's not altogether human. Seth can make out a word here and there, like *circle* and *forever* and *suffering*, but it's mostly a syllable stew. Chanting next, a dozen or so voices monotoning their way through what he figures is Latin.

His skin buzzes, like that fictional thunderstorm from earlier isn't so fictional. His head starts to throb.

The chanting grows to a crescendo as the sound of crackling flames enter the mix. Cut back to the woman's screams, which have grown more desperate, more urgent, until they stop altogether.

Side A ends.

Seth wipes sweat from his brow. His pulse pounds, like he just went for a jog. Rule number one of radio is to keep things moving. Silence is the enemy, but speaking is tough business. He turns his mic live, lets out a sigh he didn't know was building. "Well, folks, that was...something. I figured it would be like all the other Halloween tapes I've played over the years. I'm sorry if I put any of you on edge. That's never my intention. Let's transition to something a bit more soothing, shall we?"

He cues up a library of nautical sounds, lulling waves and cawing seagulls, the kind of thing that usually calms him. Emphasis on usually. Because Seth is worked up from those chants. In fact, it's like he can still hear them, like whoever was muttering in some long-dead language is in the control room. He presses eject on the tape player, removes *Bad Sounds*. Side B is ready to go. He could flip the tape for an encore but given his heart's jumping jacks, he slides it back into the case and snaps it shut. He leans back and hopes the waves will soothe him.

They don't.

#

Danvers is a small town, so things like murder tend to make the paper.

That's what Seth sees on the front page the next morning. A man on the border of Beverly, one Frank Hodge, shot himself and his son with a twelve-gauge he kept hidden in the garage for emergencies. His son recently moved back home after a messy divorce. Now he has a messy exit wound. Police are looking into a motive.

Seth sets down the paper on his teller station. The bank opens in five but he's not thinking about deposit slips or his change-your-password notification. He's thinking about Frank Hodge.

The man was in his seventies, was somewhat of a radio enthusiast. Seth knows this because Frank was a bank customer, used to shoot the shit when things were slow, always complaining how radio's a dying art, how broadcasters used to be royalty. What bothers Seth is that Frank was a listener of *his* show. According to the paper, he shot himself and his son around the time Seth went on air last night. Which is also around the time he pressed play on *Bad Sounds*.

"You hungover or something?" Matt, his co-worker says. Twenty years Seth's junior, Matt's probably never had a hangover. He takes frequent bathroom breaks and smoke breaks and any kind of break that will keep him away from his window.

"I don't drink, remember?"

"How's that going for you?"

Seth doesn't answer, is too busy staring toward the headline of today's paper.

Murder-Suicide in Danvers.

On his lunch break, he returns to Jake's Records, though he's not in a shopping mood. Jack is box-cutting a package open, grumbling at the excess bubble wrap.

He pulls out a Transformer, vintage no doubt. He cat calls like some construction worker. "You know, this thing goes for a few hundred, but I talked the guy down. Gonna look great on my shelf."

"We need to talk," Seth says, setting down *Bad Sounds*. He keeps it cover-side down, lest he see the poorly drawn skeleton and its bony nose. But the back's not much better. Now he can see the track listing, the sound effects he didn't get around to sampling last night.

Dark is Night.

Something's in the House.

Hello, Seth.

He gags on his tongue, takes a step or three back, and slips on stray bubble wrap. Ass meets floor. When he gets back up, the last track is *Howl-o-ween Eve*. He must have misread it.

"The hell's with you?" Jack says.

"That thing," Seth says, meaning *Bad Sounds*, though speaking it aloud feels a little too *Candyman*. "Where'd you say you got it?"

"I didn't. Someone dropped it off, remember?"

"Out back?"

"No, on the roof," Jack says, tossing the shrapnel of his special delivery into the waste basket. "Yeah, out back. You sure you're okay?"

"You got a camera out there?"

Jack shrugs. "Never review the footage. Thrift stores aren't exactly burglary hot spots."

Seth's a mild man. He doesn't raise his voice or curse. When he spills something, he shrugs and gets to work. When someone cuts him off on the highway, he figures they must have an emergency. When his last relationship ended, when she shouted *You're a total fucking push-over*, Seth said *When you're right, you're right*. Which is why Seth shocks himself as he grabs the collar of Jack's shirt. "There's something wrong with that tape. And I need to know who dropped it off."

Jack raises both hands, like *Don't shoot*. "Okay, okay. Let's check it out." He unlocks his computer, minimizes a half-dozen eBay tabs, and opens his security footage. "It's set to motion detection. Saves me from having to store every second on the cloud. That shit costs money. And business isn't exactly booming."

He gestures to the otherwise empty store, then skims through the videos from this past week. Most of the footage is rats and raccoons setting off the sensor. Jack skips ahead. A couple kids pass through the alley, taking turns swigging from a bottle, probably lifted from one of their moms. Seth's beginning to think the dropper-offer of the tape remained still enough to avoid tripping the camera. Then the next video starts. At first, it's just a breeze dislodging junk from the dumpster's cracked-open lid. A figure trudges into view. They're wearing black sweatshirts, the hood pulled very much over their face. It's like they came here to steal then thought better of it. The figure looks both ways before reaching into a pocket and pulling out a small rectangular object. Bingo. They set *Bad Sounds* down on the back stoop and sprint in the opposite direction, like they just pulled the pin on a grenade.

"That's the only camera?" Seth says after the video's run time is up.

"I keep the second one turned off."

"Seems like a waste."

"Like I said, I sell old shit for a living. What's this about anyway?"

Seth spots a copy of today's paper on the counter, slides it over and thumbs the headline, like that explains everything.

"I don't get it," Jack says.

Seth heads for the exit but Jack calls after him.

"Forgetting something?"

Seth knows he's holding the tape, but he doesn't turn around. "You keep it."

"You know we don't do returns."

"Consider it a donation," Seth says, letting the door slam behind him.

#

A week passes. A week free of *Bad Sounds*. Seth drives to and from the bank listening to his standard sound effects. Hooting owls and clanging wind chimes. No screams or pleas. Most people would balk at his choice of soundtrack, but most people don't think twice about what they put into their ears. They tune into whichever top forty single's peaking that week or the hourly traffic report that never changes. Seth prefers sounds to music because sounds indicate life, and life is always happening—at least for others. He saw a shrink a few years back who harped on that little detail, said something about Seth being unable or unwilling to admit he wasn't living life. He was a passenger, not a driver.

Said shrink was probably right but Seth stopped going after that.

He avoids Jake's Records. Jack has no doubt placed *Bad Sounds* on the rack. If Seth were a betting man, say, like Jack used to be, he'd put money on a price tag of forty bucks and a rare sticker for good measure.   When Friday rolls around, he shows up at the station just in time for Wendy's trucker songs to wrap up.

"You feeling okay?" she says, setting out another tray of cookies.

Unfortunately, they're all the unidentifiable mushy variety.

"Never better," he says, pouring himself a cup of burnt coffee as his first tracks of the night play. Usually, he opens with a welcome message, but his microscopic audience won't mind if he pushes it back.

"Why do you ask?"

"Because I worry about you. Someone has to, right? Look, I don't want to pry, and I mean this is the nicest possible way, but you seem a bit lonely."

"What gave it away?" he says, sipping and wincing at the acid that doesn't stay down for long.

"I mean it. I'm no stranger to loneliness. My husband kicked the bucket a decade ago. Sure, he was a royal pain in the ass, but we fell into a rhythm that wasn't exactly horrible. I miss that bastard like you wouldn't believe. I miss the way he grumbled when he took out the trash and I miss the way he'd fall asleep five minutes into anything he watched on TV. I used to find his snoring unbearable. Sounded like a jackhammer going off at midnight. Now I'd cash in my social security to hear it again."

Seth sets down his mug too hard on the console. A few specks of radioactive coffee splash over the rim. "I appreciate it.

Honestly. And yeah, I'm a little lonely. But only a little. Relationships have never been easy for me. Neither is interacting with most people. Too much effort and there's always the risk of rejection. Don't take this the wrong way, but I'd like to avoid getting attached to someone because what you just described doesn't sound like a blast."

"Better to have loved," Wendy says, lets the rest hang. "All I'm saying is you should get yourself out there, rejection notwithstanding.

Doesn't have to be serious. Hell, come to bingo night if you want. Because this, sitting around and listening to sound effects, there's more to life, you know."

He smiles, nods, says he'll think about it. Wendy means well. And bingo doesn't sound half bad.

He does his intro, cues up a collection of wildlife ambience, and heads for the bathroom. In the mirror, he sees what Wendy was talking about. He looks…if not sick, then unwell. *Bad Sounds* really did a number on him. His skin's got a grayish hue and the bags beneath his eyes are darker than usual. But the good news is he's recovering, has put a week of distance between him and the tape. And besides, maybe he blew the whole thing out of proportion. Frank Hodge seemed normal, sure, but plenty of murderers seem normal. Everyone's got a dark side. Maybe whatever was brewing in him had been there for some time. And Seth might've been coming down with something when he first spotted *Bad Sounds*. The mystery virus has been slow to leave, that's all. Life's full of coincidences and also sound effects. And speaking of the latter, he's got to get back to the control room.

He heads down the hall, past posters of long-gone DJs, broadcasters no one will remember. Before stepping through the soundproofing door, he does a triple-take. Through the glass he sees a figure hovering over the console.

It's wearing an over-sized black hoodie and it spots Seth watching. What was that about coincidences? How many black-hooded figures does he know, save for the one on the cover of *Bad Sounds*? His heart forgets to beat. His lungs forget to breathe.

He backs away but the studio door's opening and the figure's heading his way and—

And the figure is Jack.

"Hi?" Seth says, trying to cut the tension. The problem is, his blade's too dull. He needs something sharper.

"Tried to plan it just right," Jack says, like he's mid-way into a conversation. "Figured I'd wait until you headed to the pisser."

"I did head to the pisser."

Jack steps closer, which is when Seth detects his foul breath.

Smells like sewage and rot, like he hasn't brushed since they last spoke. "I know what you're thinking. You're thinking 'Hey, that hoodie looks familiar. Didn't I see it on the camera?'"

"Crossed my mind."

"The answer's yes you did, to which I'd add I'm sorry about all this."

Seth holds up his hands in hostage-negotiator fashion. There's just one problem. He doesn't know what Jack's demanding. Also, that makes Seth the hostage. "Let's sit down and talk about it, okay? You tired? You look tired. Got some coffee in the control room."

"Yeah, I'm tired. That's how it starts. You ought to know."

"You mean *Bad Sounds*?"

Jack shooshes him. "Keep it down, will you? They'll hear."

"Jack, you're starting to freak me out. And after the week I've had, that's saying something."

"You're not paying attention," Jack says, raising his voice a few decibels. He speaks through his teeth. Spittle flings every which way.

"Floor's yours," Seth says, reaching into his pocket for a cell phone that's not there. Must have left it on the console.

"What you saw on that security camera, it was me but not *entirely* me. That tape, it seeps into you, you know? Makes you do things you normally wouldn't. I tried to get rid of it after I listened."

"I thought you hated sounds effects."

"I did. I hate them even more now. A few tracks in and I got all itchy. Felt like I was coming down with something. Then I blacked out. Woke up covered with dirt. That's when I realized the tape isn't just a tape. I drove across town and dropped it into one of those little neighborhood libraries, stuffed it behind a couple of romance novels. But here's the thing. The tape didn't want to stay there. So, I wake up in the alley behind the shop, hand-delivering it back to myself. After that, I figure I'll leave it in the back room, in a box of junk. No one's going to sift through that stuff anyway."

"No one except me."

"Like I said, I really am sorry."

"Shit," Seth says. Through the studio doors, he can hear his block of nature tracks coming to an end. He didn't have a chance to cue anything else up. There goes rule number one of radio. "So, what're you saying?

The tape is cursed?

Jack says nothing, which is really just saying *Give the man a prize.* "The way it works, far as I can tell, is you've got to have someone else listen to it. It's like passing on a cold. When you brought it home, I figured 'great.' End of story. I also figured you're a smart guy. You'd realize what needs to be done. When you played it over the air, you passed it on to anyone else listening."

Seth's pictures Frank putting on a pot of coffee, sitting in his den, and tuning into Seth's show. What he hears makes him lose time just like Jack. And in that trance, he unearths his secret twelve-gauge, shoots first his recently divorced son, then himself.

"Then why are you here? I listened after you. That means you're cured."

"Not quite. When you brought the tape in, I blacked out again. Maybe it hadn't gotten all the way out of my system. Maybe it's a proximity thing. Fuck if I know. What I do know is it made me listen again and now it's in here." He taps a finger against his temple.

The dead air from earlier turns to a familiar hissing. In comes a thunderstorm.

"You bastard."

A crane of his head and Seth can see Bad Sounds on the console, right next to his phone. The case is open and the tape deck's doing its thing. He moves forward but Jack blocks the way.

"We need to ditch this place, get far enough so we can't hear it.

That's the only way."

"What about whoever hears it on *air*? They don't have the luxury of tape trading."

"We can't worry about them. Now turn around and let's go."

"Jack, move."

Jack doesn't move. Not aside at least. But he does wrap both hands around Seth's throat. "They're still listening. They're still *with me*. You don't want to wind up like that old bitch."

"What?"

But Seth pieces together the puzzle when Jack shoves him back, when his shoulder bursts the front doors open, and most of all when he trips over Wendy's limp body. One eye's still open. Her mouth is frozen in a forever gasp. Her cookies may have sucked but she was the closest thing to family that Seth had.

"Bastard," Seth says just before he loses his lunch and breakfast onto the cement.

"Keep moving," Jack says and maybe he was on to something with *Bad Sounds* still circulating inside him. Because his eyes are too wide and unfocused, like some junkie chasing the dragon, only the dragon's more like a poorly drawn skeleton.

"You got it," Seth says, but he moves in the opposite direction, as in past Jack. Toward the studio. He fumbles with the handle before he pulls open the door and is met with the chanting at full volume. He feels *Bad Sounds* crawling into his ear canal and taking the elevator down. His skin tingles, Pavlov style. He reaches for the eject button and—

#

And wakes up next to a dumpster. He's battling the headache of the century. His mouth tastes like a landfill, and you'd be forgiven for thinking he's mid-bender. He tries to get up but his equilibrium has other plans, sends him back to the hard surface. It's a give and take until he manages to pull himself into a crouch. His breath's not the only thing that stinks around here. The dumpster smells like it hasn't been emptied in some time, like it belongs to a restaurant or commercial business, not a radio station most folks don't even know exists.

That's where he is, standing behind Northshore Independent Radio, one hand on his aching skull and the other waving away a murder of flies. They're coming from inside the dumpster. Seth doesn't crane his head over the lip, doesn't confirm what—or who—is causing such a stir. But if he did, he knows he'd see Jack in there. What's left of him anyway. It's like Jack said: the tape makes you do things you normally wouldn't.

Seth stumbles around the building to find the front steps empty. *Bad Sounds* must've made him toss Wendy too. The lights are still on inside the studio. He can see the half-assed coffee maker and his phone and also the cassette deck that's still very much on. If he tries a second time for the eject button, he'll wind up out cold again. He takes Jack's advice, heads away instead of toward *Bad Sounds*.

Like his phone, his car keys are still inside but he doesn't mind. At this time of night, crickets are chirping, and twigs are snapping. In the distance: the cry of a coyote, the skitter of a bat. Life is happening all around him, just like that shrink spouted. But she was wrong about the other part. Tonight, he's no longer riding shotgun, no longer a passenger.

He listens to the night and the night provides.

The Beach

Dan Henk

The Vacation

Tim's family was pretty working class, but his RPG buddy Drew had wealthier parents. They both attended the same Christian private school in North Carolina, and quite often hung out on weekends. Most of the time at Drew's much larger, two-story Tudor house. It was an elegant white stucco and dark wood framework dwelling, all hidden within a few acres of wooded property.

Drew's parents owned a vacation bungalow on Brunswick Island, and they would often take Tim out there for weekends, grabbing a burger at a famous local restaurant along the way. This time however, Tim's parents rented a room at some cheap hotel near Carolina Beach. They invited Tim to bring along Drew. Being church buddies, Drew's parents were all too agreeable.

As was typical, once they arrived at the motel Tim's parents disappeared. Leaving Drew and Tim to their own resources. In a ramshackle motel that had seen better days. It was, however, within a stone's throw of the beach.

The two trekked out to the beach, built sandcastles, dug foxholes, and tried paddling out until they almost drowned.

Drew was a bit chunkier, so he did a little less of the deep-water activities. But come sunset, they both scoured the shore for sand hoppers. Curious little crustaceans that could be found by the air bubbles they left in the wake of the receding waves. They'd scored a yellow plastic pail and spent the last hour before sundown filling the bucket.

Sand Hoppers

Back at the motel, Tim flipped through the TV looking for anything decent. All he could find was a low budget, alien conspiracy movie. Flying saucers hidden in industrial garages, guarded by hardnosed, uniformed men. That eighties version of military personnel, all running around and hassling intruders. Dark shades, nondescript uniforms, all the stereotypes present and accounted for.

The plot wasn't the greatest, and the film was a bit needlessly dark, so Tim diverted himself by sifting through the bucket.

The sand hoppers squirmed around like they were annoyed at being displaced. The mere sight of them slightly repulsed Tim. He wasn't sure what they were exactly, or if they could actually bite. He poked at them with a plastic straw, and a few latched on. Tim frantically whirled around the straw until the creatures dropped back into the morass.

Restless and bored, he shook the bucket, and something caught his eye. It was a little rounder and had more of a metallic sheen than the creatures. After a few pokes with the straw, he managed to isolate the object. Pushing it to one side, he extracted it from the bucket.

It looked like an old, corroded coin. The hue more of an aqua-green than anything. Sort of like those pennies that stayed in the fountain at the mall too long. The markings were so worn they were unreadable, but they were definitely nothing he'd seen before. This could be valuable! He'd read plenty of those made for kid's stories where they find valuable letters from ex-presidents in the back of some old drawer.

Tomorrow he'd hit up the locals and see if they had any clue what this was.

The Locals

His mom cooked eggs, bacon, toast, and topped it all off with a glass of OJ. Drew and Tim were still mulling over the food as mom stuffed a satchel full of clothes and announced-

"Me and your dad are going to the beach. You and Drew have fun dear. Let's meet up at 6 for dinner!"

With that, dad tossed his silverware on an empty plate and brought it to the sink.

"Thanks honey, Delicious meal."

A brief flash of light from the door, and Drew and Tim were left to their own devices. In a musky motel room that stunk of mildew and brine. Everything looked so old and worn, Tim wondered how long this place had been standing.

He dug into his pocket and pulled out the coin.

"Look what I found Drew!"

Drew seemed less than impressed. He glanced at it briefly, pushed back his mop of brown hair, and inquired-

"What is it?"

"I don't know. Some old coin I found in that bucket with all those sand hoppers."

"Let me see that."

Tim dropped it in his palm and Drew flipped it over. In the light of day, it looked even older and more worn. Roughly oval, the edge was chipped and the whole thing looked sort of hand made. The patterns on had oxidized to green, the depressions a scummy a dark brown. Drew flipped it over and nonchalantly asked-

"What do you think it is?"

"No idea. Let's check it out. It might be worth something."

Tim was a bit more hyped up. But then again, he always was.

"Sure. Where you thinking?"

Tim had no idea, but there were some local fishing shacks around here. If he could muster up the courage, he'd ask them. Talking to grownups you don't know was a bit intimidating, but he didn't want to leave and miss out on what could be buried treasure!

"Let's just hit a couple of the local fishing shacks and then we can go to the beach."

Drew looked skeptical, but he was usually pretty agreeable. Tim pulled his flip flops on, stuffed a towel, flippers, and goggles in his backpack, and tucked the coin in his pocket.

"Hold on a minute"

Drew complained, scampering to get his gear.

Outside, the sunlight was blinding. The gusty winds kicked sand into their eyes and blasted their bare legs. Squinting, Drew peered around the motel parking lot and inquired-

"Where did you want to start?"

Tim had no clue, but this was his idea, and he didn't want to act like he didn't have a plan.

"I think I saw a fishing shack just down the road."

Drew shrugged, his shirt whipping in the wind as it highlighted his belly and chubby arms. Tim doubted anyone would give them the time of day. Two kids in swim shorts and flip flops bothering grownups who had real jobs. He debated just heading to the beach, but it was a matter of pride. Now that he'd brought up the idea, he might as well get it out of the way.

Cars roared by, pelting the kids with rocks as they navigated the thorny bushes of the roadside. They passed a few more commercial looking fisheries, a cheap motel and a no name gas station. The heat was muggy and suffocating, warming up even the soles of his flip flops. Tim was sweating and feeling the start of a sunburn. But he was too stubborn to give up yet. Pebbles kept slipping into his flip-flops and poking the bottoms of his feet. Drew was obviously struggling as well. The armpits of his t-shirt sported huge circles and he was puffing heavily. His demeanor looking less cheerful by the moment. Tim stopped and surveyed the landscape. Just beyond a slope ahead, was a promising looking shack. Just run down and isolated enough it didn't appear too intimidating. It was now or never, and Tim had to pick something before Drew gave up.

"C'mon! I think I see one!"

Drew wiped sweat off his forehead and tried to spy what Tim was pointing at.

"That place?"

"Yeah!"

Tim took off, galloping along the roadside. He hurdled a dried rain gully and raced up the asphalt driveway.

"Wait up"

Drew yelled, huffing and puffing as he tried to catch up. Tim halted at the wooden door and let his nerve build up. Once Drew had made it, all out of breath and gasping for air, he turned to fully face the entrance. The hovel looked almost ready to fall over. It was all whitewashed clapboard and the door didn't even have a real handle. Just a rusty iron loop. Tim grabbed the rung and pulled it open. Inside wasn't much better. The walls, roof, and even floor consisted of rough slats, a few stacked up into a homemade looking counter. No one was present and Tim was a little creeped out, this resembled the scene from a million different horror movies. After a few tense moments, anxiety overtook his curiosity, and he was ready to make a quick exit.

"Hello?"

A gravelly voice emanated from some back room. It started Tim and gave him pause. Drew burst through the door. Grasping his knees, he tried to say something, but was too out of breath. A middle-aged man sauntered in from the back. He was sporting a mesh trucker hat and clothes that had all seen better days. Wiping his hands on his T-shirt he planted them on the counter.

"You kids need something?"

Tim paused, unable to think of the right words.

The man's piercing blue eyes stared at him mercilessly, which only made Tim more uncomfortable.

Finally, he muttered.

"I found something on the beach. I thought maybe you might know what it was..."

He was already thinking this was a bad idea.

"What have you got? Let me see it."

Now Tim felt even more ridiculous. It was just some old coin. This was definitely a bad idea.

Digging the coin out of his pocket, he reached up to drop it on the counter. A counter that was almost level with his head. Boy did he feel small and irrelevant.

The man picked it up, and holding it aloft, rotated it between his fingers.

"The beach you say? Maybe the sea caves? Did you wander in there?"

Tim wasn't quite sure how to answer. In the glare of scrutiny, it all seemed a bit ridiculous.

"Uh, yeah, the beach. I didn't know about any sea caves. It just looked really strange. Like maybe old or something."

"It's nothing special. Maybe some foreign tourist dropped it. Go back to your vacation kid. Some of us have work to do."

The man sounded contemptuous and a bit irate, but Tim couldn't help noticing that he looked a little startled. Tim reached up, snatched the coin out of the man's palm, and muttered-

"Thanks mister, sorry to bother you."

As he bee lined for the door. It slammed behind him, and he was almost to the street before Drew caught up.

"Tim....what's...what was all that about..."

Tim leaned over and whispered-

"I don't trust that man. We might have a real find here."

Incognito

Wary about that guy, Tim pulled Drew sideways. Through a rash of overgrown weeds and towards docks that sprawled across the beach. It was only a few feet from the fishing shack, and still a way from the motel, but Tim figured they were still safer here than following an open road. Tim ducked between a few small beach houses, pushed through a rickety old fence, and erupted onto the shore.

The wood of the old dock rose up on his left and Tim ducked underneath. Slipping behind it stilts, he waited for Drew to catch up. The whole thing was a bit silly now. He was hiding behind rotted old wood, his feet half buried in sandy piles of tourist crap. Cups and fast-food wrapping. Drew joined him, panting and out of breath.

"What's going on Tim?"

"Let's hang out here for a minute."

Drew shrugged his shoulders.

An hour passed and Tim was running low on excuses. He had spent an hour poking through plastic garbage and half dead vegetation. He was about to suggest heading back to the motel, when he heard a noise. It was the hum of a four-wheeler, and instinctively he ducked behind one of the interior posts. Drew looked confused and snuck over.

"What is it, Tim?"

An ATV bounded up the beach and stopped at a cluster of tourists. A man in a tan police uniform dismounted and started with some very aggressive gestures. Tim was half hiding behind a strut, all his attention focused on the distant commotion, when a sound behind almost made him jump.

"What are you guys doing here?"

Tim tensed to run, but that cop made him think twice. Quickly turning his head, Tim realized it was just a kid. Maybe he was being too hasty. This guy looked more like some scruffy, latch-key local than anything dangerous.

Tall and thin, he was outfitted in filthy jeans and a worn t-shirt. Not anything that struck Tim as a cop. The kid's long blond hair blanketed his face in softly shifting strands of silver, and he had the smell of engine oil, cigarettes, and dirt. He was also wearing a white Metallica t-shirt, with a bloody skull behind the logo. That definitely gave him more cred.

"Just hanging out."

"You the guys the cops are looking for?"

Tim grew nervous again and tensed to run, but figured he better ply the waters first.

"What are the cops looking for? Hey, it's cool. Fuck 'em."

He slightly muffled the word "fuck", as if it struck him as a bit audacious. Tim looked at the ground and shuffled the sand. He wasn't sure what to say, but he figured the safest bet would be to feel the guy out. He really didn't seem to be a cop.

"I'm Tim. This is my buddy Drew."

"You found something, didn't you?

That is not what Tim was expecting.

"No, seriously. Fuck them. When we find stuff, we just bury it. Anyone who gets too involved tends to disappear."

"I found a coin. A weird looking coin."

He pulled it from his pocket and held it up. The kid took it, raised it to a light beam from the rafters, and twisted it around slowly.

"Bury it. I hope you didn't show it to anyone."

"Uh oh."

"Oh shit, what'd you do?"

"Just showed it to the guy at the nearby fishing shack. He acted a little weird so I took off."

Pulling out a pack of camel's, the kid lit one and took a puff.

"Did you tell him who you were?"

"Nah, we high tailed it pretty quick."

"Just avoid that cop out there, bury the coin, and I'd leave as soon as you can. Things have gotten really weird around here.

New people that seem slightly off, and way more cops than usual. Ones that don't look like cops."

Drew looked quizzical. He'd stayed back the whole time, observing something he clearly didn't understand. Tim, on the other hand, was going down a mental rabbit hole. He'd read plenty sci-fi and horror books. This sounded like some serious grown-up shit, and we all knew you could never trust the government. Thanking the kid, he turned down an offer of a smoke, and went back to poking around in the sand with his toes. He was done talking to anyone he didn't know, and figured that if he didn't engage, the kid would just leave.

"I'm not kidding. There've been legends of weird events around here for years. Sea monsters and all that. A few months ago, some government guys showed up, and people started disappearing. That fishing guy came around the same time they did. No one knowshim and he's definitely not local."

The kid finished his cigarette, stomped it out, and sauntered off.

"I'm scared Tim. This sounds like something big."

Drew was scared of everything. Tim figured if he just downplayed it, they'd have a better chance come sunset.

The Motel

It was dark by the time they left. Tim and Drew wandered down the shore towards the motel. There were just a few stragglers left on the beach. They were all reduced to the black silhouettes in the distance, piling up their towels and folding their chairs like some old stop motion film.

The trip back was much longer than Tim remembered. He kept glancing up at the wood shacks bordering the shoreline for reference. He was about to double back when they finally made it to the outskirts of the motel. The small parking lot held only a few cars, the open door of their room spilling a thin shaft of light across the gravel. Mom and dad were almost done with dinner when they entered.

"You missed supper! There should be some leftovers in the fridge, I hope you boys had a good time. We need to checkout by eleven tomorrow. Have fun and don't stay up to late, me and your dad are going to bed."

Dad glanced at Tim but didn't say anything. He piled his knife and fork on the plate, topped it off with his napkin, and headed for the sink.

"Thanks, honey, for the dinner. I'll wake you up at 9 tomorrow, Tim."

"Awe dad, can we do 10?"

"You've proven you're not good with time Tim. 9, bright and early."

Drew darted for the fridge and started pawing through the plastic wrapped plates. Two were piled high with fried chicken and rice. He grabbed one and headed for the silverware drawer. Tim's head drooped as he wandered over to the fridge.

He took the other plate and headed for the couch.

"Hey Drew, can you grab me silverware and a napkin?"

He pulled out the TV table and dropped his plate on top. Walking over to the tube, he flipped the dial until it landed on some sci-fi show about radioactive roaches. A minute later, Drew joined him. Moving Tim's plate over, he set down his food and started stuffing his quickly smeared face.

"What are we watching?"

"Some sci-fi movie about ravenous radioactive cockroaches."

"OK. You want me to grab you a drink?"

"Sure. Just water"

It All Goes to Shit

Tim woke up in handcuffs. Wrists bound tight behind his back, the first thing he noticed was how uncomfortable he was. Propped in a corner, the contours of a wooden chair bit into his butt, the sharp edges of the metal cuffs scraping his wrists.

"What's going on?"

The room was full of cops. Spread out on a plastic sheet in the middle of the floor were the remains of Drew. Blood splatter was everywhere and all that remained of the face was a soupy mess of mangled flesh and shattered bone. One eyeball trailed out of a broken socket, hanging down the left cheek at the tail of a crimson string. The eye cavities were mashed into an oblong grove, the slightly more sunken remains of the other eye hole a gory fissure. Most of the nose was a tangled mess of cartilage slivers and gelatinous blood. The body looked fairly intact, if a little pale and swollen. Mom was curled in a corner, sobbing into cupped hands. Dad sat opposite on a folded chair; face buried in an upraised palm. He shook his head back and forth slowly, disbelief clearly evident.

One of the officers approached holding aloft a short brass pipe.

"Drug paraphernalia. Did you know your kid was smoking marijuana?"

Dad shook his head slowly and mumbled

"No idea officer."

"Where did he get this? By the looks of it, I'll bet it was laced with something. Angle dust most likely. We've had a bit of an epidemic recently"

Dad looked disgusted, and still refused to make eye contact.

A cop pawing around the floor near Drew pulled up a lead pipe crisscrossed in splatters of blood.

"Looks like we have the weapon here!"

Tim glanced around in desperation and pleaded.

"Dad, you know I didn't do this! Dad! Look at me!"

For a moment Tim's dad stilled his head and opened his eyes fully. Tim could almost hear the gears turning. The moment passed, his eyelids dropped again, and he resumed shaking his head.

"They'll find you the help you need son."

"But dad! You know me! Really! It's me! Your son! You know I didn't do this!"

Dad turned to face Tim; his tear swollen eyes now visible. A questioning demeanor passed over his face. As if he wanted to believe. But it was brief. He lowered his face in his hand again and resumed the melancholy shudder.

"Look officer. Just tell me what to do..."

The closest cop, Tim guessed he was the chief investigator, walked over to Tim's dad and rested a hand on his shoulder.

"We have to take him downtown. You can follow us if you want.

Something this serious tho, he'll be in for quite a while. You might want to get a hotel close by."

It Only Gets Worse

Over an hour passed. Medical examiners came and left. Yellow tape was draw across the crime scene. Tim sat aghast, trying to remember anything from last night. His parents slowly became more solemn and just sat stoically in their chairs. Their tears had long dried, their eyes staring out into oblivion.

Eventually only two officers remained. Gesturing for Tim to rise, they escorted him out and into a police cruiser. A few minutes later his parents followed. They grimly climbed into their mustard yellow fiat, started the engine, and waited. Two cops clambered into the front of the wagon.

Refraining from making eye contact, they peeled out onto the main road.

Tim's mind raced. What could he possibly do? Recalling the coin in his pocket, he twisted his handcuffed hands. They wouldn't reach far enough, so he awkwardly twisted his hips in an attempt to reach the front pocket. The cuffs bit into his wrists, his shoulder felt about to dislocate, but he finally clawed to the bottom. The pocket was empty.

Revolution

Bobby Lisse

Todd stood at his dying son's bedside. His hair was greased with a week's worth of sweat and a head full of dread. A bouquet of wilted flowers sat in a vase next to the bed. A single, green cymbidium orchid stood bright and lively. The tubes and leads that snaked their way to his boy's body looked like vines growing on a neglected giant. A cruel memento mori.

Todd had not uttered his son's name since they were admitted. Every time he felt Dylan dance on his tongue a shriek would threaten to escape from his gut. He would struggle to catch his breath for what seemed like hours. "My son" brought on no tracheal fit, so he had resorted to the possessive moniker.

A missing patch of skin on his son's hand held Todd's tragic gaze. The wound looked like a burn which had become infected, and Todd shamefully kept his own hand away as if it were the result of a contagious, zombie apocalypse inducing, flesh-eating disease. It wasn't. He wanted to hold his son's hand, but he was afraid of the lifelessness he would feel.

Todd thought back to the first time he saw a dead body. His grandmother lay peacefully in the casket. Her eyes closed, her cheeks sunken, her hands grasped and resting on her pelvis. He knew who she was supposed to be, but he stared at an imposter. His young brain imagined her a villain. An evil, undead, doppelganger of his grandmother. Her skin always seemed to have texture when she was alive. Porous and moist, her cheeks hung low on her jaw signaling the late life of a woman who was much heavier in her youth. In that time of mourning Todd looked at her cheeks and saw a thick layer of wax. It reminded him of Madame Tussauds, the wax museum his mother had brought him to in the city the winter before.

When Todd's mother led him to the side of the casket to pay his last respects and pray with her, she did her best to prepare her son for the grief that was sure to follow.

She told him "God takes his favorite children." as if that would make sense to an eight-year-old.

Todd responded, "Like Jesus?" with naivete.

"Exactly like Jesus, honey." She put her hand on Todd's back and steered him to the corpse.

"You don't have to look, if you don't want to." Todd's mother helped him kneel.

The smell of the flowers which surrounded the coffin would never leave Todd's nose. He would smell it again in other places of less mourning, but it would bring him right back there, beside the remains of his loved one where a fit of anger came over him that can only be described as wrath. Wrath against God for taking a piece of his heart. The boy's outburst startled everyone into gasps and clenched fists. His mother rushed him away as he kicked and screamed.

"You're not dead! You're not dead!".

His trust never healed after that.

Todd stared down his forearm at his fading tattoo. The irony sneered at him and the words "In God We Trust..." made little sense to him now. An outburst from an eight-year-old child rose in Todd's paunch. Again, he was angry at God, but God wasn't there to feel his ire, so his son's stiffening body was on the receiving end.

"It's not like if you die the world will stop spinning!".

A pathetic spittle flew from Todd's mouth. His eyes poured tears that he despised but he was in too much pain to worry about seeming weak. He hated the world for how he felt at that moment. The heart monitor signaled the end. In that exact second the world stopped spinning and the worst day of Todd's life would last for the next six months.

Distance and Time

It had been almost six months since the Earth stopped rotating.

It was a static, floating marble for so long that people had already gotten over the "still-sickness". It was a panic that was spurned by an imperceptible unmoving; a cocaine rage or caffeine fit from hell that usually ended in tears or death. A schizophrenic meltdown that can be blamed on the augmented polarity of the planet if only someone knew scientifically just what was going on.

Half the world was chafing and freezing and the other was peeling and burning. Geography had made solar messiahs. The new gold rush had become battery banks. Those who resided in the day and had retained some semblance of pragmatism knew the night would come, eventually. They did their best to store as much energy as they could, but it wasn't without tragedy. Equipment was wearing out ten times as quick without the reprieve of darkness.

Theft became a matter of "national security" and bulked up the private security industry, or as Jerrod liked to call himself 'The Panel Police'. One thousand miles or so from the tragic death of a boy, mankind's final conflict was primed to explode.

Back to the Grind

It was Jerrod's first day back on rotation.

Not all the Solar Bank sites, storage facilities that cultivated the steady power of the sun, had been built around buildings as secure as a Prison, like Jerrod's had, but they were all fortified locations. What was left of the government had identified a few preferred existing sites to stage their greedy, natural energy hoard. Installations were limited by the wildfires which left a hazy overcast hundreds of miles around. Schools with safe rooms and multi-level entrances that were designed to keep the weekly school shooters out. A profession that had thankfully dried up once the world stopped turning.

SB-7, as the old prison was dubbed, stood with its back to mountains, which made it vulnerable to only one side. Shield Pledge Security had begun fourteen-day shifts about a month after everything changed. So far it has been working out. Temporary sleeping quarters and "swivel watch" had kept the on-site guards fresh and alert.

The union had suggested what management called 'extreme caution' safety measures which included uniforms staying on site for fear of off-duty attacks or hijacking. The proposed security detail for off the clock personnel was rebuffed. Management's argument was that if an armed security guard with as much training as their company claimed to have on staff was unable to protect and defend themselves, they shouldn't be defending matters of national security, and tried to use it as a maneuver to force employees to live on-site. They even started building barracks, but the labor washed up as the sun persisted. The wood ended up sitting, rotting, and becoming home to creatures seeking shelter rather than guards.

Jerrod was no "Prepper" but he had resorted to living as independent from the grid as he could. He had cured and cold smoked everything. Curing the meat would make it last and smoking it was just for flavor. He knew the power would eventually shut down for 'preservation,' but what he was most worried about was the supply chain.

He was one of the lucky ones that only had himself to care for. He had seen shootings over food at the grocery stores, which became the wild west of this still Earth, and always assumed it was some poor father of four who was doing what he needed to feed his brood. He had empathy for family men in this new, post-turn world but it wouldn't stop him from shooting one of them if they stepped onto his field. The kill order was cut and dry: Shoot to kill; no warning.

Jerrod fancied himself a poetic man. He didn't care to read poetry, nor did he care to follow any established rules of poetry, but he assured himself he had both rhythm and "...a way with words". There were no more public readings, not that Jerrod would have participated if there were. His verse lived solely in a moleskine notebook - the tool of any writer who was flatulent enough to believe their words were too valuable for fleeting digital technology like a notes app and would much rather kill some trees to doodle on. Today's entry:

"The morning air used to feel crisp and foreign, but its edge has dulled and become familiar like adjusting to the horrid stench of a room that your nose no longer registers. Last night's chill has faded from existence."

He was right, there had been no break from the energy of the sun. The morning dew may now live only in prose. Jerrod always kept the book on him in case the right words were to tickle his brain and today was no different as it was snuggly contoured to his thigh. The ballpoint was its bedmate.

Jerrod removed his .38 special from his nightstand and snapped it safely into his ankle holster.

The Commute

Public transportation had become as close to an exclusive means of travel, besides walking, that has existed during the century of individual vehicles. Gas prices and scarcity made driving a combustion engine car the ultimate superfluous gesture of wealth and indifference. The train brought Jerrod within three miles of work which took a fit fella like him around forty-five minutes.

There was a park about halfway through the walk that Jerrod would sometimes stop at to recapture some semblance of the "old normal". He'd write in his moleskine, eat a sandwich, or just stare at nature. He figured that the lack of foot traffic probably wasn't new and that it was probably what saved the park from looking like every other allotted zone for recreation and reflection.

The tents that used to occupy the stone below the bridges had hiked up their skirts and sunk their stakes on more scenic real estate. No one could blame them. The Rangers had all but been wiped out. As well as all ex-military had been sucked up and transferred to active-duty policing or taking jobs with the private security firms. The same kind that signed Jerrod's own paycheck.

That day he sat there, an apple making the rounds in his palm as he chewed sweet chunks of red delicious. No one else had come down the overgrown path. Jerrod checked his watch, noticing it was about time for him to complete his journey. He tossed the apple core into the overgrowth and walked through the covered trail. The trail opened to a large field where one day long ago kids frolicked and flew kites and families sat on blankets that promised the security of a false reality.

Normally, in the post-turn world, this field was a flat plane of sun scorched grass. Today it had transmogrified. What Jerrod didn't realize is that the park, to him, was the last bastion of hope to hold on to his former self. On that day his past was buried. Finally, he had lost his paradise to the destitute.

A throng of cloaked, unkempt, humans stood in a half-moon. A single man stood at the centroid. His robe hung low enough to conceal the apple box he stood atop, as if he were preaching. Jerrod was careful in his approach. His father had ingrained an important lesson in how to carry yourself when he was a young boy.

"Never walk with your eyes on your toes. Keep your head high and proud and no one will ever think you're weak.".

At this point in his life, he no longer heard the echo of his father's mantra, but his neck muscles had been trained to keep his gaze straight forward. His security training taught him to keep his hands out of his pockets as they could act like loose handcuffs that can turn into an obstructive restraint quicker than you could pull them out. His quick pace was a result of a dedication to cardio. Despite the size of the field there were enough mendicants gathered to force Jerrod into a close flyby.

As Jerrod got close, he could get a better look at what he suspected to be the evangelizer. He played the part well. The long, greased hair. His thick beard stricken with gray streaks looked more like a fungus growing upon a tree rather than a growth of human hair. His robe, unlike the others who wore soiled earth tone garb, was stark white. Not laundry white, but the type of white that could be accomplished washing clothes in a cool stream. The Man's face was hard to make out even though Jerrod could hear his sermonizing. It drew Jerrod closer than he wanted to be. The dusk of man is upon us. Do not let their fear mongering steer you towards compliance. Do not fear the night. Welcome its cool embrace. For when the sun finally sets, when the day is finally over, the son of God will have returned. This is the Revolution Summer!"

The crowd roared in a wave of approval. The undulating harmony sounded more like a congruent military force than a bunch of vagabonds. Jerrod knew this song. It was a symphony of destruction. His training urged him to learn more, but his watch beckoned him to punch the clock or risk losing the stability and boku pay.

The crowd broke their crescent formation and filed away neatly. They truly behaved like a military encampment when their tents were erected with incredible haste. Jerrod hung back enough to remain a face in the crowd but close enough to get a good look at the Preacher. When the cleric finally turned and gave Jerrod a clear view. It was not what he had expected. There had been plenty of reports to the of folk who had poisoned minds from prolonged exposure to the merciless sun, and skin disease had increased at an unimaginable rate, but Jerrod had never seen anything like this.

The man's face was cracked and peeled in sickening dermal waves. The splayed ends were blackened like the wick of a candle. The stretches of skin that weren't lifting away from his face seemed to be slicked with an oily substance. Not sweat, nor sunscreen, but more of a whale oil sheen. It appears the Preacher had not stepped away from the glare of the sun since it had decided to keep its gaze on this side of the globe.

The Preacher did not move from his pedestal. His gestures were minimal and deliberate. The extent was a raised hand as if he were blessing his parishioners as they assembled their temporary quarters.

Jerrod had seen groups like this before, led by false prophets promising salvation and screaming about the night side of the earth. This was the biggest one by far and looked like a traveling city. There were rumors of militia cannibals coming from the dark to steal the benefits of the sun, but that had to be hyperbole or misplaced foreboding as the grass on this side of the Earth was no longer green, but burnt and brown. Those who lived closest to ports lobbied for walls to be built along the coast, but resources were focused elsewhere. Jerrod originally wondered why the government didn't send forces in to distinguish any type of uprising that may cause chaos, but you don't separate dogs as soon as they growl at each other. You give them a chance to adapt.

Jerrod thought about his contract which obligated him to report if he suspected an attack on the station was imminent. These people may have behaved soldierly, but they looked like "tree huggers". Still, he would have to file a report when he checked in. He approached the Preacher as genially as he could.

He put on an inquisitive face and led with what he thought would steer the conversation as far away from violence as possible.

"Excuse me, do you mind if I ask you a question?"

The Preacher turned towards the outsider's voice and now Jerrod could get a clear look at the masterful orator. His eyes were sunken so deep you could hardly see how cloudy they were. It was as if a layer of diffusion had been laid into his orbital cavities. It looked more like a corpse than a living man.

"How can I help you, stranger?"

Jerrod tried not to cringe at the gruesome sight of charred skin, even if he did not think the Preacher could even see his expressions.

"What book do you read from?" Jerrod thought the question was benign enough.

"There is only one book." The Preacher's answer didn't reveal much but Jerrod figured he meant the Bible, so he fashioned his follow up towards a God he was familiar with in a former life.

"OK, I think we're praying to the same God. I don't mean to be offensive, it's just some people nowadays are looking to start new religions and…"

"I'm not interested in creating a new religion." The Preacher's words had no reassurance attached to them. "I want a new era of mankind."

Jerrod wore his fret clearly on his face. He could only hope those glassy eyes did not register his worry. The more he stared at the Preacher the less human he looked.

"Now I ask you, curious traveler, would you evolve with us?"

Jerrod felt the words he would choose next were important to his immediate survival.

"I once shook hands with the Devil, but we could not agree on what kind of bread to break."

The Preacher nodded his head slightly, understanding Jerrod's careful refusal. "I believe you will find sweet bread elsewhere and I bid you good fortune." He stepped down from his apple box revealing a solid, two-foot-high rectangular platform. He was eye level with Jerrod as he walked past him, two of his followers close behind, one of them grabbing the box as they scurried. Jerrod waited a moment before making his way past the camp.

He felt compelled to gaze back over his shoulder to see what type of massive tent the Preacher must have helped himself to, but he fought that urge successfully. If he had looked back, he would have seen the Preacher on the edge of the field. He never broke his stare from Jerrod's departure, menace somehow breaking through his mangled face.

Punching the Clock

Jerrod approached the first guard tower with guns trained on him, but he had no worry of being shot. Around his neck was a high-tech perimeter sensor. Enter the kill zone without it and you were treated like any other trespasser; you were shot in the head. Not as forgiving as forgetting an I.D. badge at a corporate office.

Inside the first fence was the incomplete employee barracks. In big blue graffiti on the side of one of the roofless buildings was written:

"The Panel Police - Every Day is Sun Day".

The next gate opened into a large steel fence corridor. At the end of that were reportedly impenetrable doors into the facility. There had never been an attack that reached this far so no one could prove them vulnerable, but Jerrod had little faith in any hinged barricade when it came up against the will of Man. As he swiped his badge, he engaged the deadbolt and pulled on the hefty door noticing its every weakness. Rust, a single locking mechanism, and a double walled corrugated structure that made it look vulnerable regardless of how heavy the metal was. The weakest point he could see was that it required power to open and close.

The second he swiped his badge he was officially "on the clock". He wasted no time in reporting his encounter. Men are creatures of habit and in the post-turn world the hierarchy in military-like installations was no different than before. The titles might have meant nothing

besides a shared obedience and myth of power, but regardless Jerrod reported to his Lieutenant that he had seen a group of at least three hundred who seemed to him to be operative, as they called it.

"Armed?"

"With the "good book", but besides that I'm unsure."

"Hostile?"

"Self-Righteous."

"Hmm." The Lieutenant pondered for a moment before scribbling a minor note in his logbook. "You've done your diligence." He didn't care to look back up at Jerrod which meant he sensed no threat.

"Have you done yours?" Jerrod knew once the words escaped that he was about to get a strike on his jacket. The Lieutenant kept his eyes from meeting Jerrod's.

"I apologize Sir, I don't mean disrespect. With the other facilities losing coms and all, I'm on high alert. It's just the whole reason we're mandated to report is…"

"I know what the requirements are and why. I'm not going to send out the ranks for some bible thumping hippie. Not with so many no shows today. The coms situation has got everyone on edge, but per corporate they're working on it so don't worry, ya pansy."

Jerrod didn't like the sound of missing personnel. It all added up to too many red flags for him. Ever the company man, he submitted to the bureaucracy.

Shift

Jerrod was covered in grease and grime. Regardless of how much he looked like a car mechanic, he couldn't change an oil filter before he started working at the solar bank. The ad read "Will Train" and they did, but Jerrod was a mercenary as most of the other employees were and he wasn't mechanically inclined and wouldn't be able to translate any of his newfound skill to anything besides panels and leads and energy piles. With a flashlight in his mouth, he greased the four-inch-thick cables to prevent friction and wrapped the insulation back around.

Jerrod radioed for the lines to be reconnected. They had to sever power from the panels while the feed was serviced, and the entire compound was fed by those panels. They were completely off the grid. If the panels went down, they were "dead in the water".

Jerrod had asked his supervisor early on why they couldn't run off the battery power. His answer was a herald of a dying capitalist society.

"A farmer grows crops for the consumer."

That answer made little sense to Jerrod, the pragmatic man that he was. "If a farmer were starving, he would eat his own crop." he thought to himself.

"Turn on Main, over." The walkie talkie bleeped, ending Jerrod's relay. A loud thump and metallic click brought on a crescendo of energy. A whir with lights coming on and systems energizing. The compound was alive again.

Another day, another shift, another duty. Jerrod stood guard in one of the many towers around the compound. All the towers had a three-hundred-and-sixty-degree view but this post in particular saw the most action. They called it "the kill perch" because this is where the shot was taken to stifle every attack that had ever surfaced. It was an easy job if your conscience didn't get in the way of the trigger. There was no debate, no negotiating, and no hesitation. If someone approached unannounced, you shoot them. Jerrod had eight circular notches on the stock of his rifle. All head shots, hence, the circles. He had been a sniper in a former life, in a war that meant no more than the one he was in now - protecting the assets of the wealthy. The dead space that day had him writing in his moleskin.

"They called me God because I could choose who lived and who died. I was that accurate. I hated that nickname and maybe that's why I couldn't stand any Jesus Merchant I came across. It's kinda like once you work at a pizza joint it just becomes dough, sauce and mozzarella to you. Knowing the ingredients robs the magic. I'm a far cry from that action and it's been a while since anyone stumbled into my kill zone, so I've resorted to training my eye tracking insects. Lately it has been mosquitoes, mostly, thanks to the heat and humidity from this bastard Sun. It sticks around like a jock itch. My favorite thing to watch were the bees. The way they danced from flower, to bush, to hive removed any fear I used to have of their stinger. Especially the carpenter bees. I watched them come out of the old split rail fence, flying around like little minivans driven by overworked Moms trying to quiet the horror of screaming kids and playing bumper cars around town. Now, I'm left with these flying vampires who have nothing

to feast on except a dwindling population of cattle who look malnourished grazing on sun dried grass."

Shoot first

There was a fly in the tower. It was the most fun Jerrod had on watch since the last shot he took. He built a five-sided box with manilla folders and attempted to direct the fly in. He would get it close but over ten times it had deked at the last possible moment. It sat on the opposite window, pivoting around as if it were wary of its approach. Jerrod smacked his hand on the window to the right of the fly and it took off towards its target. It was in line to enter the pseudo trap, but Jerrod had seen this flight path before. He ran along behind it waving both his hands up and down thinking he could create a vortex that would force the insect into the Smead enclosure. It worked!

Jerrod jumped, both fists in the air. "Yes!".

Just as quickly as the fly went in, he flew back out, but Jerrod was already satisfied. The alarm sounded like a hell trumpet. A badgeless man had made it halfway through the kill zone, sprinting as if his life depended on it because it most certainly did. Jerrod's gun was resting against the far wall. He lunged for it as quickly as he could, released the safety, and pulled back the bolt. He pushed the awning window up with one hand, planning out his shot as he moved. The fly escaped through the opening, but Jerrod ignored it. He propped, steadied, closed one eye, and shot.

Another circle to add to his gun.

Don't Move

Jerrod stood over the body. It was against protocol for the tower guard to leave his post during duty but being so understaffed, no one else was going to retrieve the kill. It was a perfect shot through the center of his forehead and looked like a third eye was emerging from the wound.

The blood had formed a vermillion nimbus around the bald head. Jerrod poked the body with the muzzle of his rifle. He looked the man up and down, assessing the threat. Was he from a larger group? Was he armed? Was he just lost and wandering, hoping for some salvation in this wretched post-turn world? His garb looked like the group Jerrod saw in the park but was far cruder. It was brittle burlap, and it must have been torture on his skin.

There were no pockets to check through. A three-strand rope acted as a belt around his midriff. It was taped in the center with two loops of black electrical tape anchoring an aged paper cylinder. Jerrod tugged at it, ripping the paper at one edge before finally prying it from the adhesive. He unfolded and read it. But did not understand its message was for him.

Obey and you live.

Jerrod stared at the warning as if it were a foreign codex. The sound of a single footstep brought his confused eyes right into the butt of an elephant gun.

Your Clothes, Give Them to Me Now

Jerrod awoke drenched in sweat. His bare chest was glistening. Tacky blood split past his nose like a river around a massive boulder. A three-inch gash in his forehead mimicked the headshot he had put upon the intruder. The striated muscles in his shoulders looked to be stretched to their absolute limit.

His hands were fastened to a large tree and tied behind his back. He leaned forward on his knees. He had been unconscious long enough to ache and his legs were too stricken with pins and needles to tell if his .38 was still on his ankle. Although he highly doubted it was. He couldn't wipe the salty water or gore from his eyes, so he blinked trying to clear his vision.

He could make out a large shape not far from him. Ten feet, maybe. It was low to the ground but had a wide base to it and came up to a rounded point. He kept blinking to no avail. The shape grew skyward. The distance between it and Jerrod shortened and he braced for what was to come.

It was soft, silky, fabric wiped across his face. It wasn't moist but it was cool and a nice respite from the sweltering sun on his skin. He blinked a few more times as the cloth was removed from his face and now, he could see what the shape was.

It was the Preacher.

He returned to his apple box and sat down returning his handkerchief beneath his robe. His hand came back with a book. It could have been a bible, but it was very old looking. Its cover seemed to be made of some type of animal flesh, dried of course. Not leather, at least not made by any professional tanner. It was crude and somewhat gruesome.

Jerrod didn't keep his stare on the book long as he dismissed it as just another faith dealer's tool of manipulation.

"I warned them about you." Jerrod's breath was short.

"I expected you to."

The Preacher talked like a man who could see nothing new.

"They didn't listen."

"I expected them not to. Not many are afraid of a blind preacher." Those were the first words Jerrod heard from the Preacher that didn't ring true.

"I didn't mention that." Jerrod conceded. The Preacher thought for a moment, his sunken orbs and swollen face revealing no mannerisms. He leaned back, lifting one foot and adjusting himself.

"Did you not think that was an important part of the story?"

"If you were blind, I would have told them you were blind, and the result would have been the same."

The Preacher gave too much credit to Jerrod, who was sitting there tied, tired, and in pain.

"So, what now? Are you going to storm the castle?" Jerrod said that with hope in his voice. He knew the chances of success were almost nil, even with his pass. He hoped the Preacher did not.

"Is that your strategic advice?" The Preacher allowed some air to settle between them. "No, you know better than that. You don't think I'm cavalier enough to attack barbed wire fences and walls and steel reinforced doors, no matter how many men I have in my legions."

"I can't help but feel like you're going to tell me the plan." Jerrod had acceptance in his throat.

"I have no qualms sharing "the plan" as you call it, with you." The Preacher stated.

"Because you're going to kill me?"

The Preacher had reclaimed some of the credit Jerrod had earned. He removed Jerrod's pass from his shirt. Jerrod chuckled. "I see now. You lured me out to get the badge. You're going to walk in there and kill off forty trained killers, open the doors and let your people in. What you don't know is that the whole facility compartmentalizes like a submarine."

"Some of my men have the training to do such things. Though, unless you're counting the entirety of the people who have been employed both present and past by your firm, I don't think forty is quite an accurate headcount. As you've been told, some didn't show up for their shift and the ones who did have grown weary of constantly opening every interior door. Which would leave only a single obstacle in the shape of a rusty door. There are twelve men on duty, "trained killers" as you call them. The commanding officers are hardly capable of protecting much beyond their own impotence."

Jerrod instantly knew how serious this threat was. This wasn't a fly by night operation. They had been scouting the compound, the personnel, the protocols, and who knows what else. They probably knew where Jerrod lived. All at once he realized they were not in that park by happenstance.

"Why didn't you take me when you saw me in the park? Why wait and let me kill one of your men?"

"As I said, some of my men are highly trained. Some serve other purposes."

With those words a group of men started gathering around the preacher. Not as many as Jerrod had seen in the park, but enough to do damage. They were all dressed in company clothing. They all had badges. The Preacher handed Jerrod's badge to the one man who did not. "You've heard the rumors of the other facilities falling?"

"I hear a lot of rumors but they're all bullshit." Jerrod spit back.

"Ah, but this one is not. I admit, some of them have become quite imaginative. Dubbing us a horde of cannibals, with thick, bushy beards. Attacking out of the dark lands is fear and fantasy. What is not an invention is how calculated we have been in dismantling every power grid we've come across.

Jerrod laughed, half in fear and half in hopes that none of it was true. "So, you're the zombie army that all the nutcases are yapping about?"

"Come, watch a plan of certainty." The Preacher stood and pointed to Jerrod. He was cut free from the tree and lifted by two followers in cloaks. "Everyone serves a purpose in our parish."

They walked to the edge of the brush which was about four hundred yards from gate one; clear of the kill zone. The Preacher gave calm instructions to a select few men. "This is our warrior sect. Our finest. Our bravest. The community you bore witness to, they remain behind, comfortable but able and ready to step in if one of their brethren shall fall."

"You said you wanted to create a new mankind." The Preacher held his hand up to his militia as if he was telling them "Hold". He walked through a crowd that parted like curtains riding a strong gust.

"And so, I do."

"Well, if you go in there and kill everyone, you're just committing genocide."

"I believe the term you're looking for is speciocide. I'm at peace with eliminating those too nearsighted to see what the future for man holds. Those stuck in the light like a moth."

"What makes you so worthy? What makes you the one to start a new mankind?"

The Preacher postured his body in a way that displayed offense.

"Were you a devout man in your past life?"

Jerrod shook his head no, vehemently. "What kind of man were you?" The Preacher inquired.

"A killer." Jerrod's teeth flashed like a dog warning "not a step closer". His eyes dipped inward and there was an audible snarl from his maw. His glare would have struck fear on the face of almost any mortal man, but the Preacher had a shield for a face. An imperceptible reaction thanks to too many moments in the unabating sun. He stepped close to Jerrod. Close enough for their breath to meet. Through the edema in the Preacher's face Jerrod could see a hint of white. Nothing he would call eyes, but objects, nonetheless.

The Preacher kept his voice soft. "When you steadied your hand, held your breath, closed your eye, and pulled the trigger, which God did you pray to for a hit?"

"The only one." Jerrod spit with vitriol.

"And did I ever fail to answer your prayer?" Jerrod looked at the Preacher with wide eyes. He had thought the man may be a bit crazy, but now the fear of God was in his bones. He knew the Preacher was God.

Not the one he had known as a boy. The New God.

We Move When the Good Book Says So

They stood four men wide and five men deep. The Preacher remained directly behind them. He held the skin covered book close to his chest. No one made a noise. There was wind but not enough to relieve the heat. Jerrod wondered what they were waiting for. A sign from above? He felt resistance was futile, but he tried to sew doubt in the followers.

"There's no way they don't take twenty men approaching at once as a red flag. Even if they have badges."

The Preacher gripped his book tighter. "In the best of conditions, you are the only guard who can make twenty lethal shots in time. In the best of conditions."

Jerrod pondered what the Preacher meant by that. The sun may have been a hindrance, but it was a clear day. It had been for the past three months. The wind wasn't enough to throw a shot off target. He knew the Preacher was right about everyone else being a terrible shot.

"They might not be expert marksmen, but there is enough ammo in there that they don't need to be. After the first shot is fired, they'll never open the gates. All the interior doors will get locked" Jerrod told no lies.

The Preacher turned to Jerrod, "We have the good book." He patted the skin. Jerrod rolled his eyes. He had long ago found holy rollers to have the realistic intelligence of a child. "Your God bleeds just like your men will."

"Then let the water from the heavens wash away our gore." The

Preacher tossed the book down. It was slick with an oily substance. Jerrod heard him strike a match and drop it on the book. He was puzzled as to why The Preacher would destroy something he so coveted just moments earlier. The book burned slowly. Its dermis dust jacket wasn't quite flammable, but it did melt like a thick layer of wax. Jerrod watched its steady destruction and then saw the book's true cover as its wrapping disappeared. "Farmer's Almanac". Thunder struck like a war siren. The skies darkened in the time it took Jerrod to crane his neck. Visibility had become compromised and then in an instant it had become impenetrable as the rain fell.

Jerrod was stunned. The Preacher was a practical man after all, not some crazy Jesus freak preying on the manipulative minds of those who needed someone to follow; someone to call a leader.

The formation of men fell into a single line spaced apart in what Jerrod could only assume was calculated since they measured by using their arms to touch the soldier in front of them. They moved quietly forward, towards the compound. Two cloaked men stayed behind holding Jerrod in place. The Preacher, taking up the rear, stopped a moment and looked back at Jerrod. When he turned his face seemed to be repelling the water, but it was falling so hard it was impossible to tell what you were looking at.

"Time has not mattered. Not for quite a while. Now this day has finally ended. You can come live with us in the darkness, or you can wait, hopelessly, for a new dawn."

The Preacher brought his hands to his eyes and stuck them within his orbital cavities. He pulled at the skin tearing it apart. Jerrod's mind could not comprehend the self-destruction. The skin of his cheeks broke away like a thin candy shell revealing heavily wrinkled skin below and bright eyes. He kept pulling at this outer layer revealing that more of the protected skin beneath It was shriveled like he had spent an eternity submersed in water.

Jerrod knew then. A wax-like covering had protected The Preacher's skin from the sun and radiation that everyone else was subjected to. The wax body suit now lay in the muddy puddle at The Preacher's feet.

"Move quickly. The power will not last long." The Preacher's followers moved with pace and all Jerrod could do was watch.

Your Face will Stay that Way if You Keep it Up

There was no alarm. No warning of the impending doom. The first barrier was too easy. The second wouldn't be hard either. Once the metal door was open The Preacher knew all hope for his enemies was lost. The lights had finally gone out once they were inside. The sound of the power shutting down was frightening. It sounded like the end of the world.

His army of twenty strong moved with calculation and large curved knives came out from their waistbands. They slaughtered everyone they encountered. They cut them like a butcher bleeding a pig: belly, throat, wrists, and femoral artery were all sliced as deep as the blades allowed.

The blood coated the concrete hallways.

The Preacher followed behind as clean up, a shotgun hidden in his robe. He didn't need to take a shot until every employee was dead. Then, he unloaded.

Outside

Jerrod heard a few muffled shots but not enough to sound like any type of resistance. His colleagues were impotent soldiers. They might have killed intruders, but they were no more "killers' than a drone pilot sitting thousands of miles away from its target or a video game cowboy.

The rain relented. Jerrod had become so accustomed to the hum of the harnessed energy that once it stopped a void itched in his brain. He looked at the robed followers and saw blank stares. They were automatons, waiting for a cue.

"What did he promise you, a wealth of virgins?" Jerrod ribbed hoping to break their facade.

"He didn't have to promise us anything." One follower remarked with no fracture in his armor.

"You don't think he's going to exploit his power at some point? It's what Men do. We are patently corruptible." The other follower was less amused. When you see something, who is the authority on the truth of that vision, your eyes or your brain?". Jerrod didn't quite understand where the follower was leading him, but he knew better than to leave the air floating and empty. "They work in tandem."

"Exactly! He would not spite his nose to save his face." Jerrod got it, but he felt like a disillusioned belle at the conspiracy ball.

"It's time." The cue came without Jerrod noticing it. They moved towards the dark facility.

Welcome to Tomorrow

The followers' flashlights seemed to be lit for diligence only. They walked the halls with a familiarity of the layout that Jerrod could only credit to some pre-scouting they had done. The pools of blood were beginning to congeal, and it made Jerrod queasy. He wasn't a man unaccustomed to grim .deaths. His former life as an exported wall street bodyguard was filled with death.

The bodies were breadcrumbs. As they advanced, they were no longer just the guards but the followers of the Preacher that had fallen dead as well and their corpses were leading to the old chapel. It was used as the temporary sleeping quarters slash break room. Pull out posters of scantily clad and nude women were taped to the walls of God's house. Where criminals once paid penance, you could now see large bare areolas which were the mortal enemy of the pious man. It seemed a natural palace to find the Preacher sitting alone, drenched in blood. There was no longer a large cross on the wall but rather an outline where it had once been nailed. The stained-glass windows had nothing but walls behind them making the beams of the flashlight bend and reflect in odd ways.

If this were a movie and there was a score being applied to the moment an appropriate soundtrack may very well be the opening organ of Mercyful Fate's "The Oath". Only this isn't a movie, this was the end of the world.

Jerrod stood a few feet inside the chapel, his eyes adjusting slowly as the silhouette of the back of the Preacher's head became clear to him.

"I'm guessing you want me to get it back up and running?" The Preacher didn't answer right away.

"No."

His voice was one of defeat, or more severely one of submission.

"You have someone that can…"

"I have no one. I don't want it back!" The Preacher responded with anger. Then, his voice changed to sorrow. "We'll never look at the same sky again. My boy."

Jerrod could hear the globus sensation in the Preacher's throat as he spoke. Two shots rang out and the Followers dropped to the ground. The flashlights had fallen in such a way that the Preacher was illuminated. He held a bright blue, solitary flower to his nose. A gun protruded from under his arm. Smoke billowed from the barrel. Jerrod was in shock.

"I used to recite this epigram before I shot my enemy. It started with 'In God we trust…'. Which sounds innocent enough but the intention behind the words was that God guided my bullet. I'm not sure I ever believed that. I just thought it was some cool shit to say. I started doing it after I saw Pulp Fiction. I don't have the capacity to memorize an entire scripture, so I took this line from a book I read as a kid. 'In God we trust, all others pay cash.' Then, Boom! I'd shoot that fucker dead. I never thought about the other side of that bullet. I'm not talking about the devastation it had caused inside his body. Tearing through flesh and organs, or if I was lucky, which I often was, it would make his brain explode inside his skull and maybe spray some out on the dirt for a little fireworks finale. I'm talking about the family that was on the other end of that body. The hurt, the true pain that bullet could cause. I never felt pain like that. Not until I did. You know what happened when I finally felt the suffering that I had caused to so many children, parents, siblings, wives?"

Despite the rhetorical nature of the question Jerrod tried to read between the lines. There was something deeper he could sense. Something that seemed more malevolent than some "asshole on his high horse".

The Preacher's voice fell to a dulcet whisper. "The world stopped.".

Todd rose from the last remaining pew. He dropped the pistol and turned towards Jerrod. "I was a Marine, once upon a time. I thought it defined me. Made me who I am."

"I was in the Army, Green Beret. You led those men to slaughter." "They served their duty. I served mine. I promised them transcendence. What difference does it make whose rapture they incurred, mine or some fictitious God in the sky?"

"You don't get to choose who lives and who dies. No one does."

"I've lived the worst day of my life for far too long. Now that day is over, and the darkness has begun. This world no longer deserves to exist in the light. Not since my boy died."

The Dark Army Engulfs the Last Light

Todd was a smaller man, but he fought with temerity. Jerrod struggled to keep balance with his hands tied behind him. Jerrod's forehead burst open again, bleeding plentifully. As the two men struggled the sound of the impact echoed with discordance. Like the Venice library scene in The Last Crusade, while Indy breaks through the ancient floor. Todd slammed Jerrod to the ground breaking his wrist which allowed him to wiggle his restraint loose. All he needed was one hand. The rhythmic thunder did not cease. It came from a foreign source. A horn wailed like a Celtic carnyx, instilling fear in the hearts of enemies and mettle in the Celt Warriors.

Jerrod took advantage of the diversion. He reached into his boot and removed the .38. He aimed it at Todd's head, but his wrist could not hold the weight of the pistol and the bone broke further, diverting the muzzle toward Todd's belly, instead. The shot rang out as the approaching doom became imminent. Todd stumbled backward holding his gut. His mouth was agape, but before he could blurt out some pithy final words a wave of bearded, wind burned creatures tore him apart like soft bread. His entrails spilled out and were gobbled up before they could stain the floor.

Jerrod played dead with his eyes wide open. The wound in his head tricked the cannibal horde into passing on dead meat. He had slowed his breath enough to avoid detection, but his eyes began burning and his pulse raced at the fear of blinking before they could finish their snack.

Luckily there were enough mouths in the trough to make short work of the once prophet turned protein.

There was no shred of Todd left. His being had been devoured. He would compost in the tenebrous belly of the creatures of night. Once the dark army had moved on, Jerrod pulled himself from his faux grave with his face covered in sticky, coagulated blood.

The solar banks were destroyed. The prison had taken back its walls. It was a single purpose facility again, to jail hope. Jerrod scanned the field which once showcased children flying kites. It was a gruesome landscape of robed death. Steam rose from the blood and bone left behind.

The chill of night settled. This was the end of mankind.

Dreamers

Bracken MacLeod

For David Cronenberg

He worked at the cuff securing his wrist. Without one free hand he couldn't release the other restraints. What was it Carl Sagan had said? *If you want to make a pie from scratch, you must first invent the universe.* This wasn't as difficult as that. Before he could get out of this room, he had to get out of this bed, and in order to do that, all he had to accomplish was undoing a single buckle. Before it came back.

Might as well invent the universe.

The cuff holding his right arm in place was fastened with a simple strap and buckle. No lock or complicated mechanism to outsmart. Just the kind of something he'd manipulated a million times in his life, getting dressed or using the bathroom. A single buckle was all that stood between him and… not freedom exactly.

His neck hurt from craning it around and seeing wasn't helping anyway. The problem wasn't sight; it was reach. No amount of observation could make his wrist bend more or his fingers lengthen. These restraints had been designed for this very purpose—holding him in place—and there was nothing he could do to undermine their function. Not from his side of the transaction. He took a breath and decided to try something different.   Tucking his thumb as close to his palm as he could, he tried to slide his hand through the cuff. Without that digit, he imagined he could slip free with little effort, even though the strap across his chest and upper arms limited his movement, he only needed a few inches of motion. Once out of that, everything else would fall into place in easy sequence. Undo the chest restraint, move to his left arm, then his legs and ankles. And then, the floor and the door. But for a thumb, he would be free.

The door at the far end of the room opened. No sound of the slide of a key or clack of a deadbolt. He was immobilized; no need to bother with securing the room. He closed his eyes, tears fighting their way through the tight slit between his lids and escaping down the sides of his face. They caught in his hair, and he sympathized at them having been ensnared. Heavy footsteps approached. He dared not open his eyes, knowing what he would see. The smile. Those eyes. The knife.

The odor of decay settled on his face in a gentle, warm exhalation. His stomach cramped like it wanted to turn inside out. Another breath descended on his bare skin. This time, on his chest, as it turned its head to appraise the meat on the metal table. "Mr. Koenig. Shall we?" it said, low and gentle as if to assure him everything would be just fine.

He closed his eyes tighter as he felt the sharp edge of the knife tip lightly touch his belly just below his belly button. A hand followed it, holding his panicked belly steady as it drove the tip in and pulled up. With a sharp, hot stinging, he felt his skin and flesh separate. Warm blood flooded down his sides, running off his back onto the table. He tried to buck, throw off the hand and the blade, but his ruined stomach muscles wouldn't comply. The knife edge continued apace on its journey up his body, opening him like a garment bag. Breathless, he tried to scream, instead letting out a whimper.

"Now, Mr. Koenig. What will that accomplish? Shhhhh." Like a parent calming a child having a nightmare, it patted his chest, before making the final cut and reaching deep inside of him. Fondling, feeling, caressing.

A nightmare.

He focused on his own hand. Slowly raising it, without resistance and drawing a palm down his face as if pulling away a shroud laid over him.

He sat up. Straps all gone. He got to his feet and felt the slide of his insides threatening to spill out onto his feet. He wiped again with a hand down his chest and belly and the line of severance ripped into him vanished.

It stood, staring at him, jagged mouth turned down in a scowl, its conjunctival gaze weeping redness. "Mr. Koenig?" The stink of its breath drifted to him. He turned and walked toward the door. "See you again soon," it said. He glanced over his shoulder at it. Long arms hanging at its sides, red knife tip dripping on the floor. It cocked its head and smiled like a gash. He drew another hand down his face, and when he opened his eyes again, it was gone.

Maxim Koenig walked through the door.

The woman leaning over him winked as she detached the wires from the sensors stuck to his forehead. Her breath smelled like tea and honey. A man behind her was typing into a keyboard on a standing table beside the bed. He glanced over at Max and said, "Welcome back. Your readouts were all over the place. That one was pretty intense, yeah?"

Max nodded. His mouth and throat were dry. "A drink, please," he rasped. The woman disentangling him from the sensors leaned past him and retrieved a salmon-colored plastic cup from the steel rolling table opposite her. She aimed the straw toward his lips.

"The compound does make your mouth dry, doesn't it?" she said.

"Sorry."

He sipped at the water like someone trying to burn the length of a cigarette in a single drag. She pulled the cup away and told him to take a breath, promising another drink once she removed the last of the leads.

Her partner typed more, his fingers quietly clacking the keys. The door at the far end of the observation room opened and in walked a silver-haired man in a white lab coat. Two younger people followed him in, each holding clipboards. He checked his hair as they passed the two-way mirror. He smiled and slid up beside the bed. "Hello Max. Given what we could see, that looked like a considerably intense one."

"Yeah. It was a doozy."

"Was it the same dream?"

Maxim nodded. "The Corpse Surgeon." It felt like a small charge of electricity passed in a wave over his skin as he thought about what he'd just woken up from. The thing had been haunting him for nearly two decades. A spindly, cadaverous man with a scalpel and desire to plunge his spiderlike fingers into Maxim's insides.

One of the interns beside the man said, "You mean a coroner?"

"No. Mr. Koenig's recurring nightmare is of a living corpse who performs surgeries on him. Isn't that right?"

"Yes, Dr. Zeifman" Max said.

"And how did it go?"

"At first, it was the same. I was tied down and couldn't move. But then... I just... did things. I thought about my hand being free, and it was."

"Excellent. And this is your..." He checked one of the intern's clipboards. "Third dose of the Lucidity Compound. Excellent."

"I just wiped it all away. Except…"

The doctor and his wingmen stepped closer. "Yes?" he said.

"It… the Corpse Surgeon—it seemed to realize what I was doing.

It was there until the very end, watching."

"I see. Your dream experience differed as your took control?"

Max shook his head. The nurse removed the last of the wires connected to him and helped him sit up in bed, tucking a pillow behind his shoulders. He gestured for the water again, and she gave him another sip. "I guess. It was like it was *observing* me. Like you are now. Taking mental notes."

"Curious. Possible, I suppose, that's the influence of the clinical setting. Your subconscious recollected you were under observation and added that detail to your dream. It's an unsurprising development. Your nightmares are..." he looked around the room, "already rooted in a clinical setting. That your sleeping mind would adapt is to be expected."

"It sure didn't feel like my subconscious. More like, it was figuring out how to... adapt."

Zeifman turned to his intern and tapped the tablet, silently commanding her to record that feeling. "Well, Max, we anticipated that the process of moving you from passive to lucid dreamer would involve... odd developments. Side-effects, perhaps, of the unconscious mind resisting having to cede control to an active dreamer. It seemed like your monster was plotting, when in reality it was emblematic of your dream state accepting the shift of power. You had control. In there," he said, tapping Maxim's temple, "that's threatening to the dreamed entity." He let out a quick sigh, straightened his back and added, "I think it all sounds very positive. You were able to purposefully engage with your recurring dream and change the narrative." He nodded at the woman at his bedside and added, "Once Mr. Koenig is certain to be clear of any sedative effects, please make sure to let me know.

"In the meantime, Max, I am heartened by your success here. I look forward to hearing a play-by-play about what you experienced, once you've fully awakened." The doctor turned and exited the room, his two followers on his heels.

Max looked at the woman still holding the water carafe and asked,

"Do you think that's what it was? A shift of power?"

She smiled. "I don't know. But I agree it sounds like a good thing."

"Yeah," the researcher at the keyboard said. "It didn't try to come at you, right? Just stood there and watched you go?"

Max nodded.

The man grinned. "You were in control. You beat it."

"The Lucidity Compound beat it."

The woman put a light hand on his chest and his stomach clenched for a second. "The drug gave you the tools to stand up for yourself. You're the one in control, Max."

Maxim sat in his room trying to focus on the book he'd downloaded. He read the same paragraph a third time, feeling as if he'd not forgotten the language as much as become interiorly deaf to it. He could see the words on the screen, but they weren't getting through. He closed the cover and set the device on the desk next to his chair. There was no bed in the room. He was only permitted to sleep in the observation room, like all the other volunteers, though, the drug—the Lucidity Compound—made him feel drowsy most of the next day after he received a dose. He would've liked to have a nap. At the same time, a nap brought with it the possibility of being sliced open by it again.

Over the years, he'd tried a half a dozen things to avoid dreaming. Prescription sleeping pills, Benadryl, alcohol, pot, and meditation. They all worked differently on his sleep, but not one touched his dreams. Most nights, he didn't remember his nocturnal adventures, but three or four times a month, it came to visit him. The Corpse Surgeon. Unlike any other nightmare he'd ever experienced, those dreams felt extra real. Almost as if he weren't dreaming at all, but existing in some other space parallel to this one. Though he always woke up without injury—*physical* injury—in his own bed.

When he'd seen the subway ad for the sleep study—RECURRING NIGHTMARES? YOU MIGHT BE ELIGIBLE TO PARTICIPATE IN

OUR PAID STUDY—he figured it was worth a try. At the very least, he'd make some money. If he was going to have nightmares anyway, why not scan the code and apply? Lately, he'd been regretting that decision. The drug they gave him every few days made him feel nauseous. And his visits from the Corpse Surgeon were more frequent since getting it. Except today, he'd been able to take control and wipe it all away. Next time, maybe he could do it faster. Before it cut him open.

He wiped his moist palms on his pajama pants and stood to look out the window. Though the view was nice enough, there wasn't much going on. A parking lot and a fence separating it from an expansive wetland. A crane lived out there, but he only saw it occasionally. Otherwise, it was still. And dull. Like everyone else, he'd agreed to live in the research facility for the six-week duration of the experimental trial. The team insisted it was for his safety. Their drug, while shown to be safe in lab animals, had yet to be tested on humans and they wanted to have all their participants onsite, in case. Of what, he didn't know. Between what they were paying for the study and the potential of stopping his chronic nightmares, he was happy to be... not a prisoner... *sequestered.*

Signing up for the study, he'd agreed to have no outside contact. He hadn't counted on that meaning not having access to his phone, laptop, or even a tablet. His cellphone was secured in another room, where a volunteer accessed it twice a day to check messages and texts for emergencies. They said it was to ensure no leaks of their proprietary research. He imagined everyone, like him, had signed an NDA, but then, again, they were paying him enough to cover six months of rent on the outside. Fine. Only the preloaded e-reader they provided was allowed with him in the room. No horror or crime. Nothing that might influence his dreams. He read some literary nonsense about a brother and sister in love with each other out on the prairie and jerked off when he could get the image of them out of his head.

A loud sound in the hallway outside startled him out of his reverie. Excited voices. Not everyone was adjusting to the isolation well. A lot of the participants played board games and hung out in a common room watching television. It felt a little too much like a different kind of institutional setting he'd had experience with before. *I'm not crazy, I just have a problem with my drea—*

Another shout, followed by heavy footsteps hurriedly thudding past his door. Gotta be Monty again. *Guy's got a bug up his ass, I swear.* He crossed the small room, pulled open the door, and stuck his head out.

A pair of men in blue scrubs, hands extended out in front of them, stood between Maxim and whoever it was they wanted to calm down. He rose up on his tiptoes to see.

"Just put it down, Misty. We're all friends here," one called out. *Misty Hill*! He'd laughed when she introduced herself in their introductions circle, thinking it was a joke—or a porn name. She deadpan stared at him and he felt like an asshole. She was nice and was one of the few people who liked to talk to him about things other than the study and their nightmares. He hoped to see her again on the outside.

The men ordered her to "put it down" again. Maxim couldn't see whatever it was she needed to let go of, but reckoned it wasn't a feather duster. He stepped out into the hall, joining a small group of other test subjects who'd gathered to watch the spectacle.

"What's going on?" he asked.

Gunnar Nilsson jutted his chin at the woman and said, "Fucking

Misty's gone off her nut."

Maxim leaned to the side to get a look around the hulking Niveau Institute security officers to see. Misty stood with her left arm extended, palm out. In her right hand, something narrow and familiar glinted under the fluorescent lights.

"Don't come any closer! I mean it! I just need to get this off of

me."

Maxim wondered what she meant. She was wearing the same PJs they all were and while—

She raised her arm and drew the scalpel across her forehead at the hairline. Blood spilled down her face. She pulled the knife from left to right along the length of her brow with a shriek that echoed through the facility like a siren. Maxim's mouth hung open silently and he blinked, trying to banish the image from his eyes, while Gunnar and Paula beside him shouted. The security men closed on her, one lunging for Misty's scalpel hand while the other tried to pin her other arm to her body. She disappeared for a moment in the mass of bodies, until one of them screamed and staggered back holding a hand to the bloody flap dangling off his face. She slashed at the other and slid the sharp edge along his forearm, opening him up. He joined the chorus of wails filling the hall, redness wetly gushing from him, splashing with hers and his partner's on the floor in a growing pool. He let go and staggered back, gripping his arm. He slipped and his head hit the floor, sounding like someone dropped a wooden ball. He stopped screaming.

"Get it off me!" She reached up again and with a hand gripping at her hair, cut along the length of her forehead again. She pulled and lifted a portion of her scalp away from her skull. A fast curtain of red descended down her face and she blinked and sputtered and staggered against a wall, continuing to saw at her skin. She tore and pulled and slid down the wall sitting in a pool of her blood, crying and choking and ripping at her slippery skin. A trio of unbloodied men appeared behind Maxim, shoving him into Paula and Gunnar as they passed.

She tried to slash them, but was growing weak as her blood cascaded down her face, staining her purple pajamas glistening black. They tried to haul her up, but she was wet and slipped out of their grasp, flopping on the floor, banging her head against the slick tiles. Another slipped and fell after her. She lashed out at him and Maxim lost the sense of whose body and limbs belonged to whom.

All their blood was communal.

An alarm in the building sounded, making his ears ring. Shouts of "Get them to their rooms," and "The fuck out of here," floated under the repeating buzzer and more orderlies and security arrived. A tight grip settled on Maxim's arms, and he was whipped away, thrown back toward his room. He fell through the doorway as it slammed behind him. A deadbolt clacking shut.

Sequestered

"Mr. Koenig, would you like to talk about what you witnessed yesterday?" The study counselor regarded him with a neutral look. Surely, she'd been having sessions with Misty as well. Knew her. They were all supposed to talk about their dreams, for the record and their well-being. At least that's what they told him at the start. So how could she be so… unaffected.

"What I witnessed?"

"Yes."

He shifted, flannel pants catching at the seat fabric. "What I *saw* was someone I knew fucking skinning themselves. What am I supposed to say about that? How it made me *feel*?"

She blinked. "That's a good place to start."

"It made me feel like I want to get the fuck out of here." He looked at the door behind him, knowing on the other side waited the man who'd brought him from his room to the counselor's office. Standing sentry with a can of pepper spray on his belt until it was time to escort him back.   "I understand the impulse, Max. You agreed to the residential provision of the study, and—"

"I didn't agree to *this*." He gestured toward the closed door. "To watching someone rip her fuckin' scalp off!" Without realizing, he started to rise out of his seat. The counselor gently gestured for him to relax, waving at him to sit. It made him feel ever more agitated. He stood. "*You know* she had nightmares about ripping her hair out. So, why the fuck would she do *that* to herself?" he shouted. "What are you people doing to us?"

"Mr. Koenig, please sit down so we can talk—"

"I am fucking done talking. Fuck your 'study' and fuck the 'residential provision. I didn't agree to be a prisoner. I'm leaving." He turned and took a step toward the door. The counselor pressed a button on her desk. The door ahead of him clacked.

"Mr. Koenig, I am doing this for your own good. You need to sit down and calm yourself before things get out of hand." She gestured again toward the chair he'd vacated. "Please."

"Are you fucking kidding me?" He turned.

"Unlock it. UNLOCK IT!"

The cellphone on her desk buzzed once. She pressed the button on her desk again and the door behind him unlocked. Maxim yanked it open before she could change her mind and lock him in again. He felt the heavy thud in the center of his chest before his eyes registered what might've delivered it. He struggled to catch his breath as he staggered backwards, deeper into the counselor's office. Faintly, behind him, he heard her say, "Take him to the dream center." Hands fell on him, gripping his arms and legs. He felt his body lifted off the floor and whisked away as he struggled to breathe. He tried to writhe out of their grip, tried to protest. The fluorescent lights in the hallway ceiling passed above him like glowing white lines on a bright highway. His head swam and his head fell back.

Following, upside down, Dr. Zeifman strode behind.

The men carrying him, deposited Maxim roughly on the bed in which he'd slept for the last week and a half. He weakly tried to roll over and out, but they pulled him back into place. His mind suddenly cleared as he felt the first cuff close around his wrist. Then his ankles and other wrists. "No," he shouted, thrashing at the restraints. "Don't! I won't go, I promise. I'll do anything you say! Please don't do this! Don't tie me down."

Dr. Zeifman appeared beside him. "Mr. Koenig. Please try to calm yourself. You are not in a nightmare, but this is for your own good."

"Fuck you!"

Zeifman turned to the woman who always hooked him up to the machine leads and said, "Give him fifteen milligrams of midazolam and then start him on a ketafol chaser. Hook him up. I'll be back in…" he checked his watch. "An hour to establish his fourth dose of the Compound."

Maxim thrashed. "No! No! I want out of here. Let me go!"

"Will that take him off the schedule?" the technician asked.

"No. He's due to get it tomorrow anyway. A 24-hour bump won't have an effect on the results." The doctor glanced at Maxim. "If you calm down everything will be much easier, Mr. Koenig."

"I revoke consent. Yeah! I revoke my consent to participate in this study. You have to let me go. If you give me anything, it'll be assault and you'll all go to jail." Maxim frantically searched the faces of the people in the room, looking for a single expression of appropriate concern or even simple agreement. The people surrounding him went on with their tasks as if he hadn't said a word. "Do you hear me? You can't perform medical experiments without consent. I want out of here, now. You'll be hearing from my—OW!"

The needle slid into his right thigh as he looked left at Dr. Zeifman. A wave of dizziness and disconnection washed over him. The room blurred and he felt as though he was going, after all. "Zei… ffff.

Do… not… cons…

He stared at the swinging doors, knowing he should turn and walk away, seek instead whatever world existed outside, if any. Something moved him forward. He felt compelled to push through.

I'm in control. I am.

The affirmation didn't lower his arm or still his step as he entered the operating theater. Bare and stark as always; it was not yet reddened with his spilled life. The steel autopsy table stood next to a metal rolling tray of gleaming instruments and… the Corpse Surgeon beside it all. "Closer," it said, curing a long finger, beckoning him. Its voice was broken glass grinding with a resonant deep bass below, almost as if there were two voices speaking in concert, one comforting, the other the sound of suffering. Its breath drifted across the room to him.

"I'm fine right here." Maxim glanced back to assure himself the doors behind hadn't vanished in silent dream logic, replaced with a blank wall. They remained.

"Please." It took a step toward him.

Maxim stood his ground. *I can wipe it all away, like clearing a whiteboard.* "I don't want to."

It tilted its head, looking at Maxim with an expression approaching sympathy. Its reddened, bulbous eyes considering him with almost sad pity. It said, "Max, I invite you to talk." A viscous line of saliva slid out of its mouth as it uttered his name.

Maxim almost laughed. That it wanted to talk was absurd. His belly twitched at the memory of its knife. Its hands. He watched its sinewy body for a sign it might lunge. It seemed at rest and stood out of reach of its tools, though not by much. "What do we have to talk about?"

"Our relationship."

"We don't have 'a relationship.'"

Its thin slash of a mouth curled up all the way to an ear, lips cracking and weeping red as they stretched. It bent an arm and stared at its own hand. "What a thing to say after how often I've been inside you.

Touching your heart."

"That's not intimacy! It's a violation."

It nodded. "Complicated, isn't it."

"Not from where I stand."

The Corpse Surgeon lowered its hand and looked at him again. The smile faded, and a hint of its cruelty played in its eyes. It said, "You rarely stand when we're together."

Maxim took a step back.

It reached out. "Please listen. I'm... I'm afraid."

"What are *you* fucking afraid of?"

"What's happening to you. Out there." It pointed to the doors behind him. I can't protect you from... that."

"Protect me? You cut me open."

"To hold your heart. Max."

"Stop saying my name. Stop it!"

It cast its gaze at the floor. "I am the barrier holding back the flood.

I am—"

"The monster that's been torturing me my whole life!"

"The coherence of incomprehensible pain. I am what stands between you and the thing that would destroy you. Without me, you are naked in the thresher of memory."

The muscles at the back of Maxim's neck tightened. He didn't want to think about it. Wounds from his past crept at the margins of his thoughts waiting to be opened like...

"So, you're my protector now? And what am I to you?"

"You are everything. Without you, *I* do not exist."

"I don't want you to exist. I want you gone!"

It held out its rawboned hands, fingers splayed out. "You'll get your wish soon enough. When they kill you, we'll all be gone forever.

Your memories along with us both."

"They're trying to help me. Help me escape you."

Its laugh was a box of broken glass tumbling along a drumhead. It thudded in his chest and made his stomach sour. The Corpse Surgeon's gaping mouth drooled freely, splattering the floor with grey wetness. It drew the back of a hand across its chin and flung the dull slaver away. "You are a lab rat with an open skull waiting to be harvested. They'll dissect your brain to see where and how the Lucidity Compound found a home and write up the results before throwing your cadaver in an incinerator to be forgotten ash."

The mention of the Compound was an intersection of nightmare and reality that frightened him worse than the autopsy table and scalpels.

It cocked its head quizzically at him again. "You wonder how I know.

Of course, I know. The Compound was made to bring me to the surface. Make *me* live behind your eyes instead of deep in the palace of your repressed thoughts. It is the mechanism by which I will become the driver, leaving you a passenger deep in my mind. Observing all, helpless to stop what I do."

"Bullshit!"

"What do you think happened to Misty Hill? She of the lovely locks who feared most of all losing... her... top. Her exchange was inchoate, and she awoke to a nightmare."

"You don't *want* to be in control?"

"Don't you listen, dear boy. I am what you created to protect you from the darkness deep inside. The focus of fear not midnight fumblings and liquor-scented threats of retribution if you make a sound. I hold your heart so nothing else can touch it. What am I if you are lost? A demon without a purpose. The idle damned in a stale Hell."

"I don't... what do we do?"

It held out a hand. Maxim stepped closer. He hesitated. The Corpse Surgeon didn't snatch at him, but waited. He reached out. The Surgeon's hand closed around his, cold and dead—a loose suit of skin that might pull right off with a strong tug. "Good boy." It guided him toward the table and the tray of instruments, picked a scalpel off the table, and pressed the tool into his palm. "*We* can't do anything. It's all up to you."

"What can I do?"   "You must wake up."

"Wake up. Wake up," the voice hissed at him as he slid from the grey twilight into bright white. The light stung his eyes and his head pounded and in front of him a shadow whispered, "Wake up."

He shook his head trying to clear away the fog. Nausea swelled and subsided. A pair of cool hands slipped behind his back and pulled him upright. "We have to go. Do you hear me? We have to get out of here, right now. My partner will be back any minute with the doctor."

"What... I..." He blinked and the face of a woman who'd been his sleep companion for the last few weeks came into focus, framed in tight black hair. She looked at him with kind, but urgent, dark eyes.

"I was supposed to give you another round of sedatives before they come back with the net dose of the Compound, but I brought you out instead. And if you're serious about wanting out of here, we have to get moving. Now." She helped him swing his legs off the bed, holding him behind the knees. For a moment he felt off balance, ready to fall, then he found himself. He steadied a hand against the mattress before pushing off onto uncertain feet. He stood, wobbly but upright. The cold of the floor infiltrated through his no-slip socks. She guided him toward the door.

Everything was dizzy, like waking up still drunk.

"Why... are you..."

"I took this job to help people. Not watch them cut their own faces off and bite people's throats out."

"Wait. What? When did—"

"No time," she said softly. She shoved a bundle of clothes at him. Not his. Scrubs. "Get dressed. My car's right outside, but we won't make it anywhere if you don't look like you're one of us."

He stripped out of the pajamas, embarrassed by his feeble nudity, and stepped into the blue hospital clothes. She slid a pair of rubber sandals on his feet and opened the door. "Don't say anything. Just stay close behind me." She stepped out into the hallway and marched toward the secure door separating the patient's wing from the rest of the Niveau Institute for Dream Studies. She swiped her badge and the light on the lock turned red. A low buzzer sounded audible failure. She glanced at him, wide eyed, a bead of sweat forming on her upper lip. She swiped again. The light turned green, and a click echoed in the hall. She pulled the door open and held it as Maxim shambled through.

She led him into a side stairwell. The world swooned as he stood

on the high landing looking down. She said, "It's okay. I've got you." She held his elbow and they descended together. At the bottom, she pushed the bar to open the door and peered out. "We're good. Come on." She hurried out onto the ground floor.

In the plant lined hall, they passed offices, wall paintings, and the waiting room where he'd first registered for the study. Several people waited inside, and he wanted to run into the center of them and scream for them to get away before they were— sequestered—taken prisoner. She pulled at him when his step faltered. "You have to go to the media. Tell them what's being done here."

"Why not you?" he managed as she pulled him out the automatic sliding doors into the parking lot.

She stopped and looked him in the eye. "People will listen to you. If I try to come out as a whistleblower, they'll ruin me. No one will believe me. But you. You can bring it all down. Tell everyone what they did to you."

"Come with me. Verify."

She shook her head. "I can't. They know where I live. Where my kids go to school. Where my parents are. They know everything and can get to everyone I love." She clicked her key fob and a car a dozen yards away gently beeped.

"And I've got nobody."

"You have to do it fast. The rest of the subjects, the people in that waiting room. They're all depending on you." She opened the passenger door and gently guided him with a hand as he slid in.

"I've got nobody."

She ran around the car and climbed in behind the wheel. The engine purred to life and she pulled out of the parking space she'd backed into without looking. A long angry horn sounded. She raised her hand in quick, dismissive apology and tore off. He looked behind them waiting to see security guards come racing out of the building, jump into cars, and speed after them. She slowed for the stop sign at the exit but rolled through. He saw someone help a child out of a car in the lot before disappearing.

He turned and leaned back against the seat. Head swimming, still full of fog. He closed his eyes.

Just a minute's rest. So tired.

He looked down at the mess. Red and glistening wetly in the light of the bedside lamp. He watched his hand reach forward and shove aside intestine and organs while his other sliced a long tear in the woman's diaphragm.

No!

He watched as his hand set the paring knife beside her body and then returned to pull the rent in her body wider. Her wide, dark eyes stared at him. He saw a silhouette of himself reflected in them. His hands plunged into to her and disappeared. He felt nothing.

Please stop!

His voice rattled in his throat like gravel. "I wish you could feel this."

And he didn't know whether the speaker meant him or her.

It's a dream. *A nightmare. I'm asleep and must wake up and this is all a dream, it can't be real. It can't!*

"Hush, Max." his voice replied. "Be still and see with me."

The Void

Nathan Robinson

In a way, she was thankful that she had run out of food because the decision had been made for her. Laird didn't want to starve to death for Christ's sake, and the alternatives made her want to vomit. She had belts and knives but had already ruled that method out, as she physically couldn't bring herself to do it. She had aspirin and flu medicine. Her mother had stockpiled plenty simply because she was so absent minded, so the option was there. She had been taking an aspirin every day simply for the nutritional value, health benefits, and for a sense of routine to maintain what little sanity she had left. Any sane person would go crazy given what had happened. But she was still here, she was alive, and pretty sure that she wasn't insane, despite the circumstances.

The apartment stunk. She should have moved, but that would mean leaving everything that still made sense to her, even though she was living in abject squalor. All of her things were here. Well, most of them. Apart from what she had left at Mark's, though she didn't hold much hope for getting that back.

Laird looked around in the dim glow the tealight offered, taking stock of what her existence had become.

The black refuse sacks were filled with tin cans and food packets. Her water bottle collection on the kitchenette table, once filled with energy drinks and fruit juice, were now filled with water that she had harvested from the toilet, pipework, and water heater. She wasn't on the top floor, so she had reserves above her that had trickled down for a while. She had limited herself to a liter and half a day, keeping her exertion to a minimum. She had considered venturing and raiding what supplies she could find, but something in the darkness waited. Early on she had opened the stairwell to the fire escape, shining her meagre torchlight into the beckoning darkness that seemed to eat the light, diffusing its power. The light reached the far wall of the stairwell, then began to fade as the darkness enveloped. As if sensing the light, something moved downstairs on the floor below, pushing an object aside so it clattered to the concrete floor, sending a bone-shaking echo throughout the entire building. Laird retreated and closed the door, never opening it again. Finding a tow rope in one of the apartments, she tied off the fire escape door to the handle of the closest apartment. She had hammers and nails and screws, but she dare not make too much sound for she feared piquing the interest of whatever had taken up residence downstairs. The elevator hadn't been a problem as there was no power, so the door remained closed. Though sometimes she was sure she could hear something scratching steel on the other side.

It's just the cables.

Outside, there was no wind.

There was no nothing. It was dark, but a strange darkness. It seemed pitch out there, but deep in the dark, there seemed to be a haze. Orange for some of the time, purple for others. But it resided behind the darkness, contained within it. It didn't get any brighter or darker, it lay suffocating in the distance. Laird had partly convinced herself that it was pitch out there and that the light was a wishful trick. Photons hitting the back of her eyeball maybe. There was no color out there, it was just her mind playing games. It wasn't black. It was an absence of everything. Anything she saw must be her imagination. The light came from the horizon, not the sky, so it was too low to be the sun or moon. It was either something else or just her mind entertaining her with a vague hope that something other than the top floors of her apartment block existed. The sounds of society had ceased. She no longer heard the hustle and bustle of the city below. The shouts, the horns, the occasional siren rushing to save someone's life.

No birds. No dog barks. No squeal of children.

There had been a day with noise. A day with all the noises at once. It had been morning. Then it had been night, rising from below. It wasn't a mist or a fog seeping from the soil and cracks in the concrete like sulphureous gas. It was a shadow, deep and endless. Every shadow cast across the city streets grew Vantablack. Whatever was there ceased to be, and it became a *nothing*. A void. Hearing the shrieks and screams, Laird had looked out of the window and onto the streets below to see what was happening. Just in time to see a city bus drive into the sudden shadow of an adjacent building, Plummeting into nothingness, engine revving.

There had been nothing seismic. It wasn't a sinkhole as surely, there'd be some noise as soil, concrete and cars fell into the void. No screams came from the void.

Laird watched as awareness grew and people braked to avoid driving into the suddenly malevolent shadows. Yet disgruntled drivers behind failed to notice those that had stopped and ploughed into the back of them, sending vehicles over the edges of the holes. Those inside screaming until the shadows sponged the noise from their lungs.

The shadows stretched across the city creating abominable prison bars, trapping those below in the intersections between buildings. Some headed southeast, in the gaps of light towards the sun. Others made their way into buildings, or smashed shop fronts to escape the madness that had eaten the roads and pavement.

Laird went to get her phone to find that the network had gone down. Then the power went out. Her lights were already off, but the radio crackled once then died and the washing machine stopped mid-cycle with an abrupt gurgle.

From the bedroom, her mother hollered in distaste at her loss of television. Then called for Laird.

Laird ignored her and continued to look east out of the window as the chaos unfolded below.

She watched for an hour, and all the while her mother screamed for her.

As the sun moved, it spread the shadow, remaining where it had already touched.

The hours passed and Laird watched as people trapped in between the shadow cages backed themselves into a sunny corner. She fetched her father's old racing binoculars and watched as three streets away a group of about twenty found themselves trapped at the back of a car park. All the vehicles in the car park succumbed to the shadows, tipping into the void with nothing more than a scrape of metal on the tarmac. The group in the corner attempted what looked like a human pyramid. It was more like a mad scramble for the top, as body climbed upon body, man pushing woman down, woman scratching man as the only thing that mattered was putting as much distance between themselves and the thing that wasn't.

Laird watched on entranced, grimly betting on who would be next to give themself to the void.

The Darwinian pyramid folded in on itself repeatedly, each time with fewer members. It ended with two figures clinging onto one another until their sunlit upland became a square foot of sanctuary. One fell. The other held on, only to be pulled into the void. Then there were none. Hidden screams continued across the city as the shadow spread. Now it was moving faster than the shade cast by the sun. Like spilt ink, it soaked the ground, before spreading out, soaking upwards into buildings and trees. The darkness behind the great oak in the nearby playground leached into the trunk, and the tree became a shadow of itself. A bird landed on one of the thicker lower branches and fell into the great oak. The darkness spread around the tree and soon it vanished altogether as shadows blended.

Her mother started hollering again. Laird reassured her and brought her a glass of water. She asked for tea and Laird explained that the power was out, so the kettle would not work. She asked for the radio and Laird gave the same answer. Laird had the feeling that silence was imperative.

By 4 pm it was like night as the shadows poured upwards into buildings. The building that Laird occupied was one of the tallest, so she had more time. She watched as one by one, shadowy fingers reached up past concrete and brick, seeping into windows. Some of the buildings had lights on, and people had lit torches and candles. For some reason, the shadows crept here first. A fresh wave of panic flushed through Laird.

Being high up wasn't enough. It's going for the lights. Anywhere light is, it will go. It spreads from shadows and eats light and anything that it touches.

Laird rushed to the coat cupboard and threw out boots and boxes until she found a tin of paint. It was peacock blue. It was left over from when she had painted her bedroom when she had first moved in. Grabbing a crusty brush, Laird took the paint can to the window and gripped then pulled at the lid. She should have used a knife or metal edge to open it, but panic blinded her foresight. She broke a nail, but the lid came loose.

With frenzied slaps, Laird pasted the paint onto the glass, starting from the top and working down, the light reducing inch by inch with each stroke, until the entire window was peacocked, though, in the inside gloom, it could have been any color.

She dropped the brush into the tin and waited.

Light still permeated through the odd semi-transparent streak, but not enough to light the room. Laird stood in the gloom. Patient and panicking.

She slowed her breath. Listening.

A scream came from downstairs. Then another. She was sure her neighbors were all at work, apart from Mrs. Deary down the hall as she worked nights. She wasn't sure about those above her.

A scream came from down the hall , then fell away as if dropped down a well.

Laird waited. Then it came. A shadow stretched up from one corner like a puddle of oil, moving up and across the glass, thick and malevolent.

Laird shuddered as the phantasmagoric sight ate away at the available light, narrowing into a corner. She thought of the poor souls in the car park as they watched their chances and numbers dwindle.

The light got all eaten up and Laird experienced a darkness she never thought possible.

She stood for what seemed like hours. At some point, she collapsed from sheer exhaustion, having burnt out all of her adrenaline. Laird had dropped to the floor but did not remember any of it. There had been darkness, a blur, then more darkness, but this time with carpet stuck to her face.

The darkness seemed to take a breath. Then it started to scream.

Having rested, her adrenaline levels had replenished somewhat, helping to fuel the panic that now swept through her.

There was darkness and there was screaming. That made up the universe.

I exist. Laird thought. I can hear the screaming and I know that it is dark. That's one other thing that exists.

Her throat was dry, so water (or the lack of it) existed.

She was hungry.

She gripped the carpet, grounding herself. She breathed and breathed air. Not nothing. Laird realized that she was still in her apartment and not adrift in nothingness.

The scream came again. It wasn't the dark itself, but the apartment.

It was a familiar scream. But still, it frightened her.

Her memories came back in fragments as she tried to piece her existence back together.

She was alive, but it was dark.

She remembered yesterday. This morning? What time was it? What day was it?

She felt in her pocket and found her phone. It lit up at her touch, the light exploding and blinding her. Laird blinked. Squinted. Then the phone came into focus. It was five minutes to eight AM. It should be light. She looked at the phone again. No service. She turned down the brightness.

Details of the room came into focus.

The scream came again. With the light, she determined that it came from her mother's bedroom. Laird scrambled through the gloom, rising to her feet, and burst into her mother's bedroom. Her mother was flailing about on the bed, thrashing her arms and trying to get up.

Laird pounced on her mother to offer comfort.

Shhhh. Please just shhhh!' Laird pleaded.

Her mother gripped onto her, digging her nails into Laird's back. She screamed louder and her hands tightened, hammering her nails in deeper. Laird tried to pull away, but her mother's frightened anguish held fast. She dropped her phone. It landed beside the wall, lighting up the skirt and not much else.

'Please...be quiet.... let...go...'

Her mother was thankful she was back, she was scared. She'd had hours in the dark whilst Laird had watched society crumble and disappear outside the window. She didn't understand. She was old. She got confused sometimes. She had good days, but she had a lot of bad days. Today would be the worst. She couldn't be reasoned with. She was being loud, and nothing that Laird said seemed to get through to her.

Laird braced her hands and pushed back to get up from the bed.

Her mother clung on.

'Laird! Don't go. Don't leeeeeave!'

'Please, just let go. I'm trying to help. You're hurting me.'

'No, no, no, no, no, no, no.' Her mother repeated, her voice getting higher.'

'You have to be quiet. There's something outside. Please! Please!'

It's not that her mother didn't care what happened, it was more likely she didn't understand. She hadn't been with it for a while, being mildly confused at the best of times. The sudden, unending darkness would have made her mental state much worse.

'Laird!'

Laird felt pain then wetness as her mother's frightened fingers clawed deeper into her back. Embedding hieroglyphs of agony into her skin. Laird screamed then pushed back against her mother's hands. It hurt more, but it gave her some space. She pushed up and rolled to the side slightly, grabbing a pillow, and moving it between her chest and her mother's.

'Please, just let go.'

Larid couldn't see what she was doing. She was holding her mother back, pushing the pillow down to create a barrier to stop her mother from hurting her. Her mother screamed and Laird began to worry about whatever was outside finding a way in.

Could it hear? Did it follow noise as well as light?

She was about to find out.

Laird pressed down with her arms, locking them, then lifting herself to utilize her legs to help wrangle her mother. Her mother's hands released from her back and now clawed at Laird's face, scratching for purchase.

Her mother's screams were now muffled beneath the pillow.

'Please...stop.' Laird cried as her mother scratched her eyes and mouth.

'Please. Please. Please. I'm your daughter. Please stop. I don't want it to come in here.'

Her mother must have listened as her hands went limp and fell away. She stopped screaming.

Laird got up from the bed and reached down for her phone that came to rest by the wall.

'Something has happened. I don't know what, but it's happened every....;

The phone torch lit her mother's grim face, posed in agony. Her eyes were open, but with the angle of the torch, they were dark.

Laird shook her mother, but her head lolled to one side, eyes fixed.

A guilty conflict bloomed within her. Her mother had been suffering with her health for some time. She had never mentioned it explicitly, but Laird had guessed that her mother was tired of life as the quality dwindled. She hadn't left the apartment in months since Laird had taken over her care full-time.

Now it was over. Her suffering was over.

No more medicine. No more screams of pain and fear in the middle of the night. Bedpans, bed sores, bed soiled. No more.

It had been an accident. She just wanted to keep her quiet. To save them both. To stop that *thing* from getting in. She had ended her mother's life. She had ended her suffering. The apocalypse had arrived, and the first thing Laird had done was remove her mother from the equation, simply because they had both survived whilst others had not.

An instinct had kicked in as she looked towards the future. Darkness had soiled the land and city. Civilization was over and out. Was it a panicked self-preservation that had kicked in? Had Laird not wanted to care because she would struggle to care for herself. With her mother gone, Laird would probably survive longer on the food they had. She wouldn't have to share. She wouldn't have to care. Her mother was gone.

Laird held her mother's hand, telling herself that she had done the right thing. She had ended her life before she would have suffered more. The darkness was most probably permanent. A cosmic event that scientists had not expected. This was it for humanity. Laird and possibly a few others had survived. She had certainly seen others perish. As soon as the rampant darkness touched them, they vanished into it. Laird didn't know where to. She didn't want to think about it. Maybe it would end as inexplicably as it had started.

Laird looked at her mother. At peace. Pain gone. Everything gone apart from her husk of a body. She would grieve, and then she would think about what to do with her mother's body.

She started to scream when her mother tried to get back up.

NOW

Laird was amazed that she had lasted this long. She had tried to outlast it.

But now it was over. All of the food was gone. Every morsel had been scraped from the cupboards. She had eaten paper from books to stave off the pangs, and at one point considered eating a leather jacket to enable her to stretch her rations. It had been three days since she had eaten anything, and she had downed the last of the water just so she felt full.

Everything edible, apart from herself, was gone.

There was her mother. But she dreaded seeing her.

It had been weeks since she had seen her last, but she heard her every day, shuffling around her bedroom, banging into walls and furniture, whilst Laird kept mouse quiet. Her mother had died weeks ago, maybe months now, yet she still stumbled about, every clatter possibly alerting the dark authority that had taken over outside.

But the dark did not care for noise. Only light. Laird could have been as loud as she wanted, and she wouldn't have piqued its interest.

Neither could the waking dead.

She could smell the decay. She had bundled towels up at the bottom of the door and duct-taped the edges, but still, the smell of death permeated everything.

She dared not explore the dark halls beyond her apartment. Fear kept her caged. In turn, that had kept her alive. She supposed that others were out there. But then she supposed she could just as easily be the last one left.

But her mother was left. Shuffling and possibly rotting. She had died but she was still here. Why did she still move? Laird had pondered on this for hours. Days even.

Why?

She had a theory, but it made no sense as she wasn't religious.

There was nowhere for souls to go. The darkness had taken heaven and possibly hell. This was purgatory. This is what it was like. There was nothing.

But there was something. Her apartment existed. She existed. She had defied purgatory. But now she needed to know the truth. Time was up.

Laird had survived. She had been smart. Too smart. She had lasted as long as her sanity would allow. She didn't want to be driven mad with hunger or dehydration over the next few days. She had to make a choice.

She had lit her world with her phone until the battery died. She had tealights and a few dim torches that had lit the apartment when she needed to. But for most of the time, Laird had sat in darkness.

Waiting.

Waiting for whatever she thought was coming. A monster.

Her worst nightmare. Spending hours filling herself with dread, then overspilling with it, quaking and sobbing with anxiety as she realized that the only monster left was time. Nothing was coming. Because nothing was all there was. She was alone.

Laird lit the last tea light with a match. She then ignited a balled-up piece of newspaper and tossed it into the corner of the room. It ignited pages torn from her favorite books. They licked at the furniture she had smashed up and piled against her mother's bedroom door.

She had been a coward, so she wanted a one-way ticket. She didn't want to back out. She needed flames to push her forward.

She opened the window fully, and the flames devoured the oxygen.

It felt like the most light she had ever seen. Laird stood on the sill and straddled the frame, her right leg hanging over nothing. She swung her left leg out so she was dancing on darkness, fully expecting to be grabbed or pulled down by some great invisible maw. She held the candle out into the darkness.

The flame did not move. It kept straight and unbothered by the great nothing. She dropped it and watched it fall. After a few seconds the minute flame disappeared. She had warmth on her back now. Her mother's doorway was fully alight. She sensed the light and now hammered from the other side. The heat was nice. She had gotten used to the lack of it. She felt like she had become cold-blooded.

She had one question. The only thing that had bothered her since this began.

What was next? What was waiting for her in the great beyond? The question had eaten away at her as she pondered it again and again.

The flames grew and the door gave way.

A black, stinking shape shuffled through the flaming door and shambled through the fiery rubbish dump and toward her. Her mother's husk moaned and screamed at the same time reaching out with flaming claws.

Laird pushed away from the window and felt the most freedom she had ever felt.

By the time she turned and looked back, the blazing apartment was gone. Ten seconds passed and she waited for the inevitable thump into the concrete slabs below, but it never came. She fell and screamed until she tasted blood.

She fell and wet herself.

She fell until she was dry again.

She fell and slept and woke up from a dream that she was falling to find she was falling again and again. Dreams and reality blurred until she couldn't tell if she was asleep or not because they were both the same.

Hunger came and went. She thirsted, and that also passed. Sleep became a dream. Dreaming became reality.

But she got her answer as her mind somehow carried on after she was sure that she had died.

Nothing.

She fell into nothing because nothing was all there was.

Nothing ever ended. And she didn't really die. She couldn't die, because there was nowhere else to go.

Everything was nothing. Nothing was everything. This was it forever.

Nothing.

Forever.

The Ties That Bind

Bridgett Nelson

Prologue
1991

The baby slid from between Meredith's thighs, pink, healthy, and crying lustily. Her husband cut and clamped the cord, gently wrapped their daughter in a white blanket, and handed her to his wife. They gazed down at their miracle in awe. "She's perfect," Meredith whispered.

"Yes, she is." Lou kissed his wife's nose. "You did beautifully, honey." They watched their daughter suck her tiny thumb.

"She's hungry. I need to feed her." Meredith expertly latched her daughter onto her breast.

"Look at you, you're a pro!"

"Pure luck." Meredith gave him a half-hearted smile. When she spoke again, her voice was raspy...her manner anxious. "Honey, do you think she's like us? That she has the mutation?"

"Given that both her parents do, I'm going to say it's a safe bet our baby-girl does as well." He paused, thoughtful and silent. "But does it matter? We're going to love the hell out of her, regardless."

Meredith flinched. "No. I don't suppose it does. I just...I want her to have an easy, normal life."

"As do I. But normal is a relative term. And besides, we'll know soon enough." He looked at the calendar. "In a little less than two weeks, in fact."

Meredith rubbed her fingers over the reddish peach fuzz covering her baby's head and said, "What should we name her?"

"You carried her for nine months and just suffered through hours of debilitating labor pains. I think you've earned the honor of naming our tiny princess." This time, Lou kissed Meredith's lips. "I love you, Mer.

And I'm proud of you."

Even after all these years, her husband could still make her blush like a teenager. "I've always been fond of Louve. I love it's meaning, obviously, but it's also an homage to her father…to you, my love. Lou and his Louve."

Lou's eyes watered. "Wow…yeah." He cleared his throat. "Louve is a beautiful name." Crawling onto the bed, Lou snuggled against Meredith, wrapping his arm around her shoulders. He placed his finger on Louve's palm, and her tiny hand instinctively wrapped around it. "Yes," he murmured. "Our little Louve is destined to make this world a better place."

2023

"You're going to be just fine, Mr. Hearst. We caught the infarction early, put a stent in the affected valve, and you're as good as new." I smiled at the elderly patient and his wife. She had tears running down her wrinkled cheeks and was vigorously squeezing her husband's hand inside her own. He grimaced following a particularly hard squeeze, but the smile was back on his face a second later.

"I can't thank you enough, Doc. I'm just…" He grabbed a tissue with his free hand and wiped his eyes. "I'm overwhelmed. Speechless." After a round of grateful hugs, I escaped to the break room, where I fell onto the couch, placed a yellow throw pillow beneath my head, and closed my eyes. I was three-quarters through a twenty-four-hour on-call day, and I was beat. Residency was no joke. I was in the final months of my general surgery residency, after which I'd begin a three year cardiothoracic surgery residency. There were days I wondered if I'd made one whopper of a mistake; thankfully, those days were few and far between.

Five minutes, I told myself. Just five measly minutes and then I'll finish up rounds. Five…measly…min…

…the night was clear and cool. A million stars twinkled in the deep celestial blue sky. Crickets merrily chirped amongst the pastel-colored blooms. Strains of a pop music cover band's song—"Landslide" if I wasn't mistaken—could be heard from the park's pavilion, along with the gentle gurgling of the river we strolled beside. My skin flushed as he took my hand in his.

"I've had a great time tonight, Louve."

"Me too." I looked at him, smiled, and…

"Hey, Dr. Chastain…time to wake up! We need you in room 317!" Michelle, my favorite nurse, let the break room door slam shut. I heard her sneakers running down the hallway and fading as she rounded a corner. As tired as I was, I was glad for the interruption. That night had no place in my memories. He had no place in my memories.

***

Walking through the front door of my apartment, I kicked off my sneakers and took a deep, cleansing breath. I desperately needed sleep, but first…a shower. And maybe some ice cream. Twenty minutes later I was in the same holey, heather gray Imagine Dragons t-shirt I'd been wearing since high school, four plump pillows strategically placed behind my back, covered in cozy blankets, with a bowl of pistachio ice cream sitting on my belly. Even though I'd seen it a million times, Ginger Snaps was playing on the television.

I watched as Ginger got attacked on the screen and felt my eyes getting droopy...

"Do you have any idea how beautiful you are?"

I shook my head and stared at the ground. We'd stopped walking in the middle of an arched, wooden bridge that spanned the river in a secluded area of the park. Hunter pulled me closer toward him until we were standing face to face. He wrapped his hands gently around my upper arms. My heart pounded in my chest, the anticipation of this deeply romantic moment flooding me with excitement.

"Then I'll tell you, Louve. Your beauty, your intelligence, your charm," he paused, and his thumb grazed the side of my breast, "it makes it hard for a guy like me to control myself."

I was flattered that Hunter Quintrell, a co-worker I'd had a crush on for ages, was interested in me...an average-looking, lowly surgical resident. I began to thank him for the kind words, but before I could, he turned me around, wrapped his arms around my chest, and began grinding himself against my buttocks. "See, babe? No control. You make me crazy." His breath was hot and heavy on my neck.

It happened so quickly, and with such intensity, my head was spinning, and I didn't know what to say. What came out was an uninspired,

"Come on, Hunter, cut it out! This isn't funny."

"It wasn't meant to be." His arm encircled my neck. "Now shut the fuck up, Doc."

As his arm tightened on my throat, his other hand slipped beneath my skirt and pushed down my best lacy panties. It suddenly occurred to me this wasn't foreplay. It wasn't a joke.

There was nothing romantic about his intentions. He was going to fuck me, with or without my consent.

I looked at the sky, at the waning crescent moon that hung there. If only...

I heard Hunter's fly unzip.

"Bend over, bitch."

I wanted to wail, to scream, to fight...but the muscular arm squeezing my neck made that impossible. He grabbed the hair on the back of my head and rammed my face into the bridge's rail. Blood poured out of my nose and down my throat. I couldn't breathe, and I panicked, sucking more blood down my windpipe. My coughs weakened as I felt him pushing inside me and...

I sat up in my bed, the sound of my shrill scream still echoing throughout the room, my body covered in acrid sweat. I stumbled to the bathroom and splashed cool water on my overheated face. The bloodshot eyes staring back at me from the mirror were haunted, vacant. Opening the medicine cabinet, I grabbed the bottle of sleeping tablets my physician had prescribed, and washed one down with water cupped in my hand from the bathroom sink.

The conclusion of Ginger Snaps was playing out on the screen as I walked back into my bedroom. I shut off the television, crawled into bed, pulled the covers over my head, and fell asleep, my body curled tightly in the fetal position.

***

"Are you okay?" Steve asked, concern in his voice.

I gave him a halfhearted smile. "Yeah, I'm fine. Just tuckered."

"Of course you are. We're all run-down and ready to collapse." He took a bite of his goulash and grimaced. "Remind me again why I thought the hospital cafeteria's daily special was a good idea?"

"On-call brain," I said. "When your body is willing to accept anything but pinecones and rocks as food."

"Right." I didn't even get a laugh from my usual jovial friend.

Instead, Steve pushed the elbow macaroni noodles around on his plate. After a very long minute or two, he said, "If I'm being honest, you've seemed on edge for months now. Not yourself."

Steve was perceptive, I'd give him that. There was a reason he was my very best friend. My date with Hunter had been nearly three months ago. I hadn't told a soul—for two reasons. First, I didn't want to deal with the fallout it would bring to the hospital and residency program. Second, and most importantly, when I finally killed the motherfucker, I didn't want any bread-crumb trails leading back to me.

"Yeah, I guess you're probably right," I replied. "I'm nervous as fuck about my cardiothoracic residency, and dad's chemo isn't working this time. Just dealing with a lot, Steve-O, but it's nothing for you to worry about, I promise."

"Damn, Lou, I'm sorry to hear about your dad. How bad is it?"

Hearing him call me by my dad's name caused the tears to flow. "It's not good. Reading between the lines, I think his oncology team has run out of treatment options."

"Jesus, that's heavy. Especially when you have a high-pressure residency starting soon." He placed his hand on top of mine. "What can I do to help?"

I started to answer but noticed Hunter entering the cafeteria. He strolled confidently to the counter, placed his order, then surveyed the room while he was waiting. When he saw me, he winked. Noticing my distraction, Steve turned and looked in the direction I was staring. "Oh.

Quintrell. God, that guy's such a dick." He shook his head and turned to face me. "Man, oh man, the things I've heard about him!"

"Like what?" I was intrigued. Prior to our date, I'd known nothing about Hunter—only that he was fantastically good-looking and, from what I'd seen in the OR, a very competent scrub nurse.

"He sexually assaults women."

"Wait…*what*?"

"Several have come forward, but nothing ever sticks. The women have rescinded their accusations every single time." Steve's voice faded out…

"Hey, Louve, can I talk to you for a minute?" Hunter was standing in the hallway outside the surgical recovery room and caught me on my way out. Only two days had passed since he'd left me bloodied and broken on the bridge.

I bristled and walked past him. "No, I don't want to talk to you,

Hunter. Leave me the hell alone."

He grabbed me from behind, his hand gripping my arm hard. Enough to leave bruises. "I was trying to be nice about this, but I see that's not the way it's going to be. So listen here, Louve, because I'm only going to say this once. Nothing happened on our date. We had a nice time, but there wasn't any chemistry. Are you feeling me?" His hand gripped tighter. I grimaced as my breaths came faster and faster. "Everything will continue to be nice and normal at work—I'll act the same, you'll act the same—and nobody will suspect a thing. Otherwise, I will make your life the worst kind of living hell. Nod if you understand."

I nodded.

"Okay, then." He let go of my arm and gave me a big grin. "I'll see you around, Louve. And, hey. You have a great day now!" He whistled as he walked away.

"Louve? Louve? Earth to Louve!" Steve waved his hands in front of my face.

"Oh…gosh. I apologize, Steve. Totally zoned out there for a moment." I took a drink of my very bitter coffee. "I guess I don't understand. Aren't people suspicious of him? How is he keeping his job?"

And how the hell did I not know this guy was a serial rapist before going out with him? Christ. I really needed to pay more attention to the people around me.

"The hospital can't fire him for what are, essentially, rumors." Steve shoved his still-full plate aside. "If they did, I guarantee he'd have a defamation lawsuit filed the very next day."

I watched as Hunter carried his tray to a table where a petite blonde was sitting alone. She looked stunned by his attention. I heard her laugh.

"So he's a sexual predator," I said to myself.

"Yep. As far as I can tell, he has never had more than a single date with any one girl," Steve responded to my whispered statement. I hadn't realized I'd said it loud enough for him to hear.

I couldn't stand the thought of him making that vulnerable young girl his next victim. The full moon was a week away, and if I could figure out a way to get him alone, he would never violate another woman. Not ever again.

***

I made sure Hunter was assigned to my operating room that afternoon. I had several cholecystectomies and a couple hernioplasties scheduled. I'd performed so many of each of those surgeries, I could practically do them in my sleep.

The last thing I wanted was to be confined inside a small room with the man who'd assaulted me, but I needed intel. I'd let this go too long. During the full moon immediately after my assault, I simply wasn't mentally or emotionally ready to deal with him. The month after that, Hunter had been across the country visiting his family. I could feel it, though—the third time would be the charm.

Fortuitously enough, Hunter was at the sink outside the operating room scrubbing his hands. I joined him for the five-minute preoperative hand prep. "Hey, hey, hey, Dr. Chastain!" Because we were both masked, I couldn't see his face, but I could tell by his squinted eyes he was smiling.

The guy could act. I'd give him that.

"Hey, yourself!" I said and returned his smile. "Shouldn't you already be inside and prepped?"

"My last surgery went long, so Martha volunteered to do the setup."

"Okay. That's fine."

An awkward silence descended.

"You're not upset that I never called you again after our date, are you?"

I inhaled so hard that I choked on my spit.

183

Jesus Christ, was he was delusional? Playing dumb? In his fuckedup mind, had the sex become consensual?

When I finally stopped coughing, I croaked out, "No, not at all. I was pretty nervous that night and likely didn't make the best impression." Then I took a deep breath and went all in. I only hoped he bought it. "In fact, I've been thinking about a do-over. If you're not busy on Friday, I thought maybe I could plan a little something. Maybe give us another shot?" I tried to look and sound vulnerable, but I'm not sure it worked, given our current location.

"Uh, so…hmm." I'd rendered him speechless. Good. "What are you playing at, Louve?" he whispered.

Ignoring his question and trying my best to sweeten the pot, I said, "Aw, come on, Hunter. I bought a brand-new dress last week, and I've been dying to wear it." I lowered my voice to a seductive whisper. "And I may have gotten waxed in a very naughty spot since we were last together."

Hunter perked up. "Yeah?" I gave him a coy nod. I could tell he was struggling to process the sudden turn of events. "Fine, yeah, we can do that. Friday should work, unless it's a problem for you that I'm taking Destiny out on Saturday." That was the blonde from the cafeteria, if I recalled correctly. At least I'd be getting to him before he had the chance to get to her.

"Sure. But I'd like to think that after Friday, you won't have eyes for Destiny any longer."

Hunter laughed—a sanctimonious, pompous snicker that had my nerves in a tizzy. "Yeah, sure," he finally said.

"Eight?" I asked, struggling to keep my composure.

"Works for me." He gave me another smug wink as he pushed through the OR door, his hands elevated and dripping.

I sighed. It was going to be a long afternoon with that egomaniac in my OR.

***

"Hey, dumplin'! How's my baby-girl?"

"I'm fine, Daddy." I kissed his bald head and took a good long look at this man who no longer resembled my father. He was so frail and gaunt.

The tears came as I asked, "How are you?"

"No, no. There will be none of that, Louvey." He'd started calling me that when I was in kindergarten, and it had stuck. I'd always be his Louvey. "I'm good," he continued. "There's no pain at all, and I'm sleeping like a champ."

"Snoring like one too," my mother said as she came into the room holding a tray filled with three glasses of lemonade and a plate of homemade cookies.

I laughed and wiped my eyes. My parents still had an incredible relationship. "I love you guys, but I need to know, so please be honest. Are we out of options?"

A long look passed between them. Letting out a defeated sigh, my dad finally responded. "Yes, Louvey. We've gone through the entire regimen. I'm officially a member of the esteemed Hospice group."

"And in wolf form...?"

"In wolf form, I'm healthy. Still have a full body of hair, even. But I don't want to live the rest of my life as a wild beast, Louvey. Surely you understand that. And besides, not every day is a full moon."

I did understand. In werewolf form, I was free, strong, wild, uncaring. Human attachments meant nothing. It was all about the hunt— the bloodlust. I gave a curt nod. "I get it, Daddy. I do. I'm just…" A small sob erupted. "I'm so sorry."

"Aw, Louvey-girl, don't cry." He motioned for me to come to him.

I did. He pulled me in for a weak hug. His body felt brittle in my arms. If I squeezed too hard, I thought it might shatter. "Life has been sweet to me. I have zero regrets. You and your mother have been my entire world; I wouldn't change a thing."

"I love you, Daddy."

"I love you too. And Louve? If I can offer just one piece of sage advice—never feel guilty for your actions as a werewolf. Hell, I'm about ready to fall off the precipice, but I'm not scared. If there is an after-life, I'm confident I'll be happy there." He rubbed the back of my hand. "Being dual-natured isn't easy, but it's a weight we must bear. Who you are as a wolf is not who you are as a human being. Do you understand?"

He stared into my eyes, and I saw something in his— empathy, compassion, concern—almost as if he knew.

"I understand, Daddy." I kissed his feverish cheek.

A couple hours later, as I walked out the front door…I knew we'd said our final goodbye.

***

"Wow. Lookin' good, Louve!" Hunter held up his hand so I could give him a high five, which I did, fighting the urge to roll my eyes. He sauntered into my apartment without invitation and looked curiously around. "Huh. I would have thought a surgeon would have a nicer place." "I'm a resident, Hunter, with massive student loan debt. I can't afford more than this."

"And here I was hoping for a sugar momma." He bellowed out a laugh, then noticed the picnic basket sitting on the table, along with a large lavender blanket. "Wait, we're going on a *picnic*?" The disdain in his voice was obvious.

"Yes!" My enthusiasm wasn't feigned. "I whipped up a few dishes for us to enjoy, and I know a gorgeous spot beside the lake."

"Good thing you look hot in that green dress," he said, his voice pouty.

The truth was, I felt pretty. Auburn curls hung down my back— a far cry from the braids I usually wore in the operating room— and carefully applied makeup made me look less like a corpse than usual. I felt…ready. Strong. Invincible.

"Oh, come on, Hunter. It'll be fun!" I slipped on a pair of flats, picked up the blanket, and said, "Can you grab the basket, please?"

"Yeah, sure," he huffed.

On the drive to the lake, he blared country music, so talking was impossible. What a *charmer*. I was still trying to figure out what the hell I'd ever seen in his dumb ass. At the very least, I could console myself that I was saving the world from his unfortunate progeny. When he finally parked the car and shut it off, my ears were still ringing with the strains of

"Achy Breaky Heart."

Who listens to that twangy shit? Hunter, apparently.

Stifling a giggle, I climbed out of the car. "The location I have in mind is a bit of a hike." Without giving him a chance to respond—to complain— I turned and began following a westward path around the lake.   "Here we are," I said, twenty minutes later. We were on a tiny beach, completely cut off from everything due to a thicket of pine trees and a few large boulders. "Nice and private, right?" I spread the blanket out on the sand.

Hunter turned completely around, checking out our date-night destination. He smirked. I knew exactly what he was thinking. "Yeah, this works. Privacy is always good."

I kicked off my shoes and took a seat on the blanket. Opening the wicker basket, I pulled out a battery-powered lantern, which I turned on. It was nearly sunset, and the trees blocked what little light there was. Next, I removed my portable Bluetooth speaker. Turning on some easy-listening mood music—not country! —I stood and walked barefoot to the lake. Hunter followed. I ventured into the cold water, causing the hem of my dress to get wet. Movement behind me suggested my date was removing his shoes and rolling up his jeans. A moment later, his arm was resting on my shoulders. He gave me a soft smile, and I was briefly reminded why I'd initially been attracted to him. He was undeniably handsome. He leaned toward me. "So, you got waxed?"

I couldn't help it. I sighed. Loudly.

"You hungry?" I asked, ignoring his question.

"I could eat, yeah."

I walked back to the blanket, opened the basket, and took out caprese sandwiches on homemade baked focaccia bread, fresh spring rolls, cherry tomato couscous salad, deviled eggs, mason jars full of sangria and fresh fruit, a bottle of white wine, and strawberry-rhubarb bars for dessert.

Hey, even assholes deserved a proper last meal.

"Damn, woman! You went all out. Somebody knows the way to a man's heart."

I played along, giggling. "I enjoy cooking. With the insane hours I work, I don't get to do it enough. This was fun for me." Handing him a plate laden with portions of everything, I said, "Bon Appetit!"

Hunter worked through the food on his plate and helped himself to seconds. "This is delicious, Louve. I think you missed your calling."

"Thank you. I consider it more of a fun hobby. I've wanted to be a surgeon since I was a little girl." Vivid images of ripping bodies apart beneath the ethereal glow of the moon and feasting on them with my parents swept through my mind. "I've always wanted to help people.

Make up for some of the wrongs in the world."

"Very noble. I just wanted a good-paying job that didn't require twenty years of schooling!" He swallowed a large gulp of sangria and scooted closer to me. I could sense we were just minutes away from June's strawberry moon making her appearance. My heart pounded in anticipation. It was time. I rested my hand on his knee and leaned in for a kiss. He obliged. Soon enough, my dress was in a pile on the blanket beside us. I hadn't been wearing a bra or panties, much to Hunter's delight, and he was currently lapping at my waxed pussy with reckless abandon.

The moon crept over the trees, lighting my nudity in a luminous blue glow. I could feel my muscles beginning to stretch. My teeth lengthening. My hair thickening. This couldn't wait any longer. I bucked against his face, wetting it with my cum.

"Fuck me, Hunter. Please. Just...fuck me."

He wasted no time pulling off his shirt and kicking off his jeans and boxer briefs. My eyes were changing, allowing me to see everything around me in exquisite detail. Reddish-brown hair was beginning to sprout in various places over my body. Thankfully, Hunter was too preoccupied with one specific body part to notice. He knelt between my legs and slid himself inside.

"Fuck, you feel good." He moaned and thrusted harder. "So damn tight."

My fingers and toes began elongating, claws protruding. Hunter leaned down to kiss my lips but kissed my snout instead. He reared back, staring at my evolving canine face. His expression was full of disgust and confusion. "What the hell, Louve?"

I laughed, though it now sounded more like a menacing growl. My abdomen hardened, breasts flattening as hair covered my once smooth skin.

He tried to pull his dick out but couldn't. He pulled harder.

I laughed again and said in a deep, raspy growl, "I'm a werewolf, Hunter. Like all female wolves, my vulva contracts and swells when I'm penetrated. My partner can't get away, so I get all his semen to aid with breeding. Waste not, want not— Mother Nature at her best—it's called a tie."

He stared at my still-contorting face and shrieked, as his fists pounded against my chest in pure panic. "Let me go, Louve," he wailed,

"Or I'll fucking kill you, I swear!"

I motioned to my wolfish body, which was now significantly larger and more muscular than Hunter's. "Do I look worried?" I wiggled around, feeling his pathetic member inside me, and making sure our tie was firm. "In fact, dear boy, I think it's time the *Hunter* became the hunted."

Wrapping my legs around his waist, I began gyrating against him, faking sexual pleasure. "Oh, that's so good, you bad, bad boy. Do me, do me!" My claws tore down his back leaving deep gouges. He screamed, still trying to disengage our bodies. "Oops, my bad," I growled. "Got a little too excited there. Let's try this again. Maybe with me on top?" I effortlessly flipped our bodies around until I was straddling him. I rode his cock enthusiastically, my arms swinging around, the razor-like claws taking large chunks out of his flesh. The scent of his blood titillated me, and my tongue lapped at his wounds, just like he'd done to my pussy mere minutes before.

"Please stop! I can't take it, Louve! I'm fucking begging you!" I put my pointer finger to my chin. "Hm. Let me think for a second. Did you stop when I asked you to on the bridge?" I tapped my chin as I contemplated. "No, no. I don't think you did. In fact, I think you said I'd made you lose control and that you couldn't help yourself. Funny, right? Especially since I'm a wild animal. A monster. I have zero control,

Hunter, and even fewer fucks to give, you sick son of a bitch!"

I stuck my claw into his eye socket and plucked out an eyeball. His screams didn't sound particularly manly. When I knew he was watching, I popped it in my mouth. "Ah, delicious. Though, based on the shape, I'm guessing you had a little astigmatism, no? Maybe we should sample the other one?"

"God, no. NO, NO, NO!"

I plucked the remaining eye out. It hung on my claw like a gelatinous shish kabob. "Such blue irises, Hunter. No wonder the ladies love you." I popped the eye into my mouth. It popped like a grape. He sobbed, his tears streaked red.

"Now, now, Hunter. Did I not tell you that you wouldn't have eyes for Destiny after our date?" I clicked my tongue in pretend disappointment. "You really should start paying better attention to the women you go out with. That's what the best boyfriends do."

"Just get off me, you hairy fucking bitch! Now!"

"Was that 'bitch' comment supposed to be a joke, Hunter?" I snarled. "Not terribly clever, but given your current level of physical and mental distress, I'll let it slide."

I sensed our tie loosening, so I did what any intelligent she wolf would do. I tightened my vaginal muscles. The bulging pressure building in the tip of Hunter's cock pressed against my sensitive folds as I pancaked that bitch. Seconds later, I felt more than heard the pop and grimaced as his juices trickled down my thighs, matting the hair there.

Hunter didn't scream. His mouth opened in a rictus-grin, as the veins on his forehead protruded and pulsated with blood. A tiny shriek escaped, but nothing else.

I pulled myself off his flappy, exploded appendage and stood over his inert form. Unable to see, but realizing I was no longer on top of him, Hunter slowly stood. He was hopelessly clumsy as he acclimated to his sudden blindness. Holding his arms out in front of him, he began moving away from the lake. Viscous blood dripped down his naked legs from his ruined manhood. "You stay away from me, Louve, you hear? Let me leave, and I promise I won't turn you in. I just want to get to a hospital." His voice was gravelly with tears.

He tripped over a rock. The sound of a bone snapping was followed by screamed curses. The rapist laid there, chunks of flesh torn from his body, eyeless, creamy-white bone shards protruding from his arm, flaps of decimated skin hanging from his pelvis. He was truly pathetic—something all the women he'd so carelessly assaulted already knew. The time had come to end his misery. Palming both sides of his head with my enormous paws, I twisted and pulled at the same time. Not only did his head separate from his neck, but his skull was cleaved in two.

Brain food really was the best. I thought as I swallowed the gray mush.

I gazed at the moon…and howled.

Epilogue

I stayed out all night, galloping through the trees and enjoying the sights, sounds, and smells of the forest. Every so often, I'd throw back my head and bay at the brilliant Goddess moon. It was an uncontrollable urge and one I savored. At dawn, as I reached the edge of town, I unwrapped the dress from around my neck, and slid it over my now human curves. Walking barefoot down a silent street, I felt a vibration in the pocket of my skirt. Pulling out my cell, I peered at the screen. It was my mom. "Hello?" I said hesitantly, knowing a call this early in the morning wasn't going to be a happy one.

"Louve, baby…is that you?" My mom's voice was hoarse... choked.

I cleared my throat, bracing myself. "Yes, it's me. What's going on? Is Daddy okay?"

A long pause, followed by a few soft sniffles. Finally, "He's gone, baby-girl. He passed away about thirty minutes ago."

I sat down on the edge of the sidewalk and stared unseeingly at a line of ants working on a piece of potato chip.

The tears didn't come.

"I'm so sorry I wasn't there. Was it…painful?"

"No. He seemed very at peace. Just tired, Louve. I think your father was ready."

"Okay." I took a deep, shuddering breath. "That's good." "There is something I need to tell you though." I could hear her crying again. "His final words were a message to you."

I rubbed my dry eyes and swallowed hard. "Tell me," I said. "He talked in a whisper, so it was hard to hear everything, but I think he said, 'Tell Louve she did good. I always knew that girl would make the world a better place.'"

The tears came.

Howl of the Leather Dog

Patrick C. Harrison III

She had a pussy like a worn-out catcher's mitt—if the catcher's mitt had caught a stick of dynamite.

When she spread her legs and you got a good look at it, you could imagine Mike Tyson giving that sucker twelve rounds of pounding and then some.

If pussies were people, this particular pussy would be the angry alcoholic who'd lived about seventy years longer than he should have, wearing a wife-beater shirt and drinking one Schlitz after another, a Pall Mall jutting from his gaping, toothless, stinking maw, every inch of his flesh a sagging mass of wrinkles, complete with worrisome moles and oddly long stray hairs.

Perhaps that comparison was a bit cruel.

Despite its flaws, it was a wet hole, and that's all Brad cared about.

Unfortunately, he'd promised to stay the night. That's what a ballbag full of jizz will make a guy do—promise to do shit he doesn't fancy doing.

Then once the load is blown, regret for pledges made sets in.

Brad groaned as he sat up, swinging his legs off the side of the bed. Looking over his shoulder, he spied Kathleen on the other side, her body only half covered by the comforter, the curves of her nudeness on display, her back to him, her dyed-red curls splashed across the pillow as if designed that way for a photograph. She wasn't bad looking for her age, which Brad guessed was somewhere in the late fifties, and he hardened as his eyes crept across her, noting the plumpness of her bottom even while hidden beneath the cover.

Though her cock-gobbling lady meat stretched like raw bacon pulled from the package, that rump of hers owned no droop at all. Either she did squats like a dedicated powerlifter or she'd had ass implants at some point. It didn't much matter to Brad. Though, if she wasn't opposed to cosmetic ass lifts, she might oughta consider cosmetic snip-snip to her meaty honey pot. But, again, Brad didn't much care either way.

He was twenty-nine and good-looking, and not too shabby below the waist either. And Brad, being the confident braggadocios guy he was, had a bit of personal challenge—to try and fuck someone, *anyone*, every single day. Kathleen, being a sex-obsessed single older woman, was perfect for this. Any time Brad couldn't find an easy lay via Tinder or some other app, he could always give Kathleen a ring.

One thing about having to stay, he thought, I can hit it again before leaving. He intended to do just that after taking a piss and finding a little snack in Kathleen's fridge. No sense letting a good boner go to waste, but something to cease the grumbling in his stomach first. Kathleen had money (God knows where it came from) and her giant stainless fridge was always stuffed with food and beer and wine coolers.

Grabbing his crumpled boxer briefs off the floor, Brad pulled them on, stood, and adjusted his manhood. Looking back at Kathleen again, he almost asked her if she needed anything while he was up. Lord, what if she said yes?

What if she wanted me to make her a sandwich or some shit? he thought. *No thanks.* Kathleen was fun, sure, but Brad wasn't about to start waiting on her like a goddamn butler or a pussy-whipped husband. He was here because she was a good lay, a real freak in the sack, and easy. But that didn't change the fact that she was old and her cock cavern looked like it had sustained a nuclear blast of dicks during its life.

Making his way into the master bath, he closed the door gently and flipped on the light, eyeing himself in the mirror as he walked to the toilet, flexing his muscles. After a few moments of straining to piss because of his recent orgasm, the urine flowed and Brad sighed satisfaction, leaning his head back and looking at the ceiling. When he finished, he tucked his manhood back in his drawers and stepped in front of the mirror, looking himself over, flexing his pecks, an approving grin emerging on his face.

Brad wished he'd grabbed his phone from his jeans pocket before heading to the restroom. He wanted to check the hookup aps and see what kind of prospects he'd have tomorrow night. Kathleen was a blast, but busting his cum cannon in her every couple of weeks was enough. It wasn't just that her penis pocket looked like it should be thrown on a griddle with onions and peppers, but that damn dog of hers was just a pain in the ass to be around. No wonder she wasn't married yet.

Sighing and tugging at his dick, Brad left the bathroom, flipping off the light before opening the door, afraid of waking Kathleen. She didn't need to be awake until he was pulling the covers off her and plunging into her moist sinkhole. Hell, she didn't *really* need to be awake for that. But Brad liked how lively Kathleen was when they fucked. A real freak, that woman, a lot of fun; except when she tried to involve her dog in their sexual escapades.

Creeping out of the large master bedroom, Brad gently closed the door behind him, his pedicured feet tapping quietly on the porcelain tiles as he made his way down the hallway, its walls decorated with original oil paintings of men and women in leather and latex, performing all manner erotic acts, from the sensual to the depraved and everything in between— paintings of whippings and peggings and gangbangs and orgies, each with various instruments of torture, like whips and floggers and paddles.

A real freak, that Kathleen. The paintings were not only art, but memories.

That's why her cunt looked like it had been used for target practice by a whole brigade of marines.

Brad emerged from the hallway, passing through the smallest of the house's three living rooms, and into the kitchen, which was lit dully by lights on the underside of the cabinets. He whistled a song he couldn't remember the title to as he made his way to the fridge, his hand groping himself again, as if his cock may wander off if he didn't grab hold of it every few minutes.

Opening the fridge, he immediately snagged a Bud Light and twisted the cap off, tossing it in the general direction of the wastebasket, where it clanked on the tiles. He took a long swig, gulping the cool suds down his gullet. Sighing with satisfaction, he brought the bottle back down, half its contents now in his stomach. Fruits, Vegetables, lunchmeat, and condiments galore were before him, along with beer and a couple bottles of high-end champagne. After staring for a few moments, Brad decided on an apple, which he snatched off the middle shelf, then grabbed the neck of another Bud with his thumb and forefinger of the same hand.

Kneeing the fridge closed, Brad guzzled the last half of the first beer and set it down hard on the counter, doing the same with the apple. He twisted the cap off the other beer and took a small sip this time, enjoying the mildness. Nothing was better than a couple of beers after sex. Remembering the liquor cabinet above the counter beside the fridge, he opened it, spying the numerous bottles of amber and clear liquids. Brad wasn't typically a fan of the hard stuff—he'd probably spewed up almost as much as he'd swallowed—but tonight he thought he may try some, perhaps dropping a shot into his beer. What was that called, a boilermaker?

He didn't know much about liquor but he thought Glenlivet was an expensive brand, so Brad grabbed it from the top shelf. Inspecting the label, he noted it was a fifteen-year-old Scotch. *Scotch is the best*, he thought, because he'd heard as much in the movies. He adjusted his balls then twisted the cap off the Scotch and breathed in its scent. His stomach almost turned at the whiff of the hard stuff. But that's okay, he planned to dilute the bitterness in beer and drink it down. Then he'd be ready to get back into Kathleen's seasoned meat muffin. Maybe he would even take her ass this time.

Setting the bottle of Glenlivet next to the bottle of Bud, Brad turned to make his way over to the cabinet where he would retrieve a mug for his drink. He gasped, halting his stride before completing his first step, his heart suddenly leaping uncomfortably.

There in the wide entryway of the kitchen sat Kathleen's dog, Herman.

He wasn't your conventional house dog. Not a poodle or a golden retriever or a beagle. Not one of those tiny dogs that chicks like to get groomed every other day and carry around in their purse. No, this was one of those new types of dogs that were all the fad among the rich, especially the rich and kinky like Kathleen. He was a human dog. Flesh and blood human, but by God he was a dog.

"Jesus, Herman," Brad said, shaking his head as he resumed his walk over to the cabinet with beer mugs, "you scared the shit out of me."

Herman followed Brad with his eyes but didn't budge from his spot in the entryway. Nor did he say anything. Human dogs, like real dogs, did not speak. If one were to judge Herman by his looks alone, he was a naked man, hairy and slightly overweight, crouched on his hands and knees, wearing a black dog mask, fashioned from the finest leather Kathleen could find. The mask aside, Herman's anatomy wasn't entirely humanlike. He bore a surgically attached tale, its flesh as pale as the rest of him, with curly black hairs sprouting here and there.

Brad wasn't sure where the meat for the tail was transplanted from, but most human dogs had it taken from their lower abdomen or inner thighs. The tail was splayed out behind Herman like a dead snake. It was without muscle; thus it would not wag like a traditional dog's tail, rather only hang there limp between his sagging ass cheeks, a useless extra extremity.

"Go on back to your cage," Brad said, waving his hand at what Kathleen called her leather dog as he opened the cabinet. "It's night-nighttime. You shouldn't be up." Grabbing a beer mug, Brad spun back toward the other counter, then cut his eyes at the dog, scowling.

Herman had not moved an inch. He sat there, his hands and knees on the tiles, his ass lowered to his heels, his tail like a fleshy, hairy earthworm.

"You can understand what I'm saying, goddammit. Shoo! Get the fuck back to your cage."

Brad was not a fan of human dogs, Herman in particular. In his opinion, most human dogs were just people that didn't want responsibilities of their own. They wanted to be coddled and cared for, fed and bathed and walked on a leash. They wanted to laze around the house all day without a care in the world. They were freaks, crawling around naked, pissing and shitting outside like they didn't know how to use a goddamn shitter.

But Kathleen called it a lifestyle choice. A fucking lifestyle choice to act like a helpless dog all day and night. *Do you let real dogs fuck you, Kathleen? Do you let real dogs shove their dicks down your throat while your boy toy fucks you from behind?* Of course she didn't. Herman was no more a dog than Brad was. He just had a fucked-up dog kink, and Kathleen had a fetish for his fucked-up dog kink.

"Herman, take your ugly ass back to your cage," Brad said, his back to the dog now as he poured the Bud Light into the mug. He lifted the Scotch and added a healthy dose to the beer, then set it back down without bothering to screw the lid back on. He turned around and leaned on the counter, sipping at the concoction and wincing at its bitterness.

The leather dog was still there. With Brad's eyes on him again, Herman's head tilted to one side the way a curious dog does. If its tail could wag, it would probably be wagging right now. His eyes were wide beneath his leather mask. Brad had never seen what Herman looked like behind the mask. No doubt, he was a pathetically ugly man. Why else wear a fucking mask? Not all human dogs wore masks; some just played the part.

Herman, though, he clearly wanted the mask to cover up his insecurities.

Leaning forward, speaking slowly and sternly, Brad said, "Get the fuck out of here you stupid fucking dog. I'm not dealing with you tonight." Herman tilted his head the other way.

"Goddammit," Brad said, slamming the boilermaker on the counter and snatching up the apple, "I said go!"

He hurled the apple at the dog and it hit the top of his right shoulder and tumbled into the living room beyond. Brad was trying to hit Herman square in the leather snout, but it had been a few years since he'd been a college ballplayer, so his aim was off. Nevertheless, the grazing shot to the shoulder was enough to send Herman crawling quickly away from the kitchen, whining the way an injured dog whines, his limp tail trailing behind him.

"Stop that fucking crying," Brad said between gritted teeth. He took a deep breath, watching the entryway for Herman to return, but he didn't. After several moments of nothing, he drank the remainder of the boilermaker, forcing himself not to gag.

Stupid dog, he thought as he slammed the empty mug on the counter. *This is the last fucking time I'll come over here. If Kathleen wants that fucking freak crawling around, she can find some other dick to pleasure her flesh flaps.*

Leaving the mug and bottles where they sat, Brad stormed out of the kitchen and through the living room, looking around for Herman but not seeing him, then down the hallway with its walls of smut. *One last fuck and I'm out of here*, he thought, flinging open the door to Kathleen's bedroom, sending it bouncing off the wall.

Kathleen rustled under the covers at the sound of Brad entering, but she didn't waken. She'd pulled the covers up over her shoulders in his absence, only the crown of her fake red hair peeking out. Brad stood at the foot of the bed, adjusting himself and looking at the lump of covers. She hadn't left the bed after taking her earlier fucking, so she no doubt had cum leakage seeping from her cunt, like a pita pocket dripping queso blanco.

Brad stroked himself slowly over his underwear, imagining the moistness of Kathleen's cum-filled cooter. He quickly grew hard, ready to go. Dropping his drawers, a sly grin emerged on Brad's face as he climbed onto the bed. Since he was certain this would be the last time he fucked Kathleen, he intended to make sure it was a pounding she'd never forget. *She likes that rough BDSM shit, huh?* he thought. *Well, let's see just how rough she likes it.*

The image of that fucking dog kept creeping into his mind, threatening to soften his erection. The night Kathleen brought Herman to bed with them had been a nightmare. It wasn't Brad's first threesome by any means, but it was his first with someone who thought he was a fucking dog. And it had been clear that night who was capable of delivering the most pleasure to Kathleen: Herman.

Not only was his cock absurdly large, but he possessed stamina that knew no bounds. Long after Brad had spent his load, the dog kept thrusting into her, howling at the ceiling through his leather mask, bringing her to orgasm repeatedly. And when he'd finally splooged his spunk, Herman curled up next to Kathleen like a good dog does, keeping her warm, his eyes, though, staring at Brad on the other side of the bed, as if wishing he'd make a move.

Brad wanted to fuck Kathleen up ever since that night. *Really* fuck her up. How dare she bring her dog into the bed with them. Sure, she'd asked if it was okay first, but Brad wasn't expecting it to turn out the way it did. He didn't know he'd be out-fucked by a goddamn fake K-9, leaving him feeling insecure and unworthy. In truth, that's what led him to challenge himself to fuck *every-single-day*. And in his romps with Kathleen since that night, he'd become more and more aggressive and rough. Only, she liked it that way. Nothing he did scared her or *really* hurt her, not even the cane he'd broken across her ass last time.

Well, all that was about to change. Brad had had enough. Seeing that stupid fucking dog tonight, remembering how it fucked, it burned into Brad's pride. The boilermaker coursing through his system didn't help to cool his temper. And while thoughts of Herman wavered his hard-on, thoughts of *really* hurting Kathleen made him harder than perhaps he'd ever been.

Brad jerked the covers back, flinging them not just off Kathleen but off the bed entirely. Lying on her side, Kathleen shivered and scrunched up, pulling her creaky knees up to her abdomen, exposing the sagging lips of her fathomless flower between her upper thighs. Her eyes did not open, however. Brad inched up behind her on his knees, his cock standing at attention, a snarling smile on his face as his eyes slithered over her plump behind. *Yeah, that has to be a fake ass, he thought. That's why she can take a beating without crying like a bitch.*

He decided to test this theory, rearing back with his right hand high above and behind his head. He swung done with all his strength, smashing his open palm against her left ass cheek, causing a loud smacking sound, like a balloon being popped.

"Ouch!" Kathleen yelped, suddenly awake, her eyes popping open and her head turning to look at Brad with wild confusion. "The fuck are you doing?"

"Spread those ass cheeks, baby," Brad said. "It's high time I tried your other hole."

Kathleen raised an eyebrow at him then let out a little giggle—she actually giggled—as she laid her head back down and rolled her body away from him. "Lay down, Bradley," she said, closing her eyes and tucking her hands beneath her pillow. "You've had enough play time tonight."

Was she really blowing him off like that? No one said no to Brad.

Certainly not some borderline geriatric slut.

"I said spread those ass cheeks, bitch," Brad said, raising his voice, trying to sound authoritative.

"Fat chance," Kathleen said, matter-of-factly, as if his request was of little concern to her. "Go to sleep."

"If you don't do it," he said, angrily now, "then I'm just going to take it!"

Kathleen sighed—actually sighed—not opening her eyes or turning his direction. Then she spoke, almost in a sad voice: "Brad, honey, you're fun and all, but you're not man enough to take *anything from me.* Now go to sleep. I'll make you some scrambled eggs in the morning."

Brad, on his knees behind her, softened a bit, his mind picking apart the things Kathleen said. Not man enough? Go to sleep? She'll make him fucking eggs in the morning? What, did she think him a child? A fucking pussy who wouldn't stand up to a misbehaving woman?

Fuck that!

Quickly, Brad leaned over Kathleen, slamming his palm into the back of her head with one hand and twisting her to her belly with the other. He swiftly hardened with this act of dominance, straddling her thighs as he rolled her, his erect cock aiming straight at her puckered asshole.

"You're gonna learn, bitch, when I say to spread your fucking ass cheeks, you spread your goddamn ass cheeks!"

"Goddammit, get off me!" Kathleen yelled into the pillow, Brad's hand still hard against her head.

Using his free hand, he spread her ass cheeks apart, inching forward, aiming his cock for the poot shoot.

"Get off me, Bradley! If that little prick of yours comes within an inch of my ass, you'll fucking regret it!"

"Oh yeah?" Brad said, pushing her head harder into the pillow. "I guess we'll see about that!"

Hawking a slimy, thick loogie into his mouth, Brad expelled it like a rocket, splatting it perfectly against Kathleen's asshole. He plunged forward, penetrating her before she had the opportunity to protest further. Her asshole clinched tight, trying to push him out but only succeeding in making the penetration more pleasurable.

"Get off me!" Kathleen screamed, turning her head from the pillow.

"I'll get off when I damn well please," Brad said, pulling back and slamming back into her.

"Herman!" she screamed suddenly. "Herman, I need you, boy!"

Brad almost laughed. He was half shaft into her coco hole and she was hollering for a fake dog to come to her rescue. What, did she think someone so lazy and worthless that they would pretend to be an animal would suddenly hop up and prevent her from receiving the best fucking of her life? Because that's what she was about to get, in Brad's opinion, the best goddamn pounding she'd ever been pounded. A fucking she would be reminiscing about on her death bed. An orgasmic encore for the ages.

Only, Herman had different ideas.

Brad heard him bounding down the hallway, sounding like a drunken mule at half-gallop, knees knocking on the floor at a painful pace. He laughed as he pushed hard against Kathleen's ass, making her cry out once again. That dumb human pooch had answered her call by the sound of it, but he was still crawling along on the floor like the animal he pretended to be. And dogs couldn't open doors. Herman would reach the bedroom and be unable to do shit unless he intended to give up the act long enough to turn the door handle. At which point, Brad would momentarily halt relishing Kathleen's rectum so he could knock Herman around.

Then Brad remembered . . . he had not closed the door upon re-entering Kathleen's bedroom.

His head whipped around as the pounding hustle of the dog grew ever closer. Then he was there, screeching to a stop just inside the bedroom, crouched there on hands and knees, his eyes angry beneath that ridiculous leather mask, a low rumbling growl seeming to leak out every pore.

Brad stopped his thrusting, his grip on Kathleen loosening but not letting go entirely. He realized, suddenly, he was sweating. Not from exertion— he'd only just started his work on Kathleen—but from a nervousness that had come on as quick as a spring thunderstorm. Could that fucking dog actually hurt him if it so desired? Anger flashed, attempting to overtake the anxiety.

"Get the fuck out of here, dog," Brad snapped. "You can have a piece of her when I'm done."

It occurred to Brad that Kathleen was no longer fighting him. She wasn't laying there like a dead fish either, the way some women did when he'd taken them without exactly getting consent, like they'd given up, figuring that simply letting him get the splooge out of his sack was probably the safest option. Instead, Kathleen had propped her head up on her hand, her elbow digging into the mattress as she crooned around him to see Herman in the doorway.

"I suggest you pull your withering dick out of me, Bradley," she said, almost amused, "unless you fancy Herman biting it off."

She was right about one thing: his cock was withering, embarrassingly fast. There was no need to pull out of Kathleen; he was shrinking out of her. One last clinch of the ol' asshole from Kathleen sent his manhood dropping out like a room-temp shrimp. With her rape seemingly brought to its conclusion, Kathleen didn't move from the bed or even scoot away from Brad. She simply laid there, a sly smile on her face.

"I said get the fuck out of here," Brad said, though there was no confidence in his voice.

Herman growled—still quietly, but with more intensity. He inched toward the bed slowly, dragging his tail, as if waiting for an order. *Of course that's what he's doing*, Brad thought, *waiting for goddamn Kathleen to holler 'sic 'em' or whatever the fuck.*

"You may want to go ahead and leave, Bradley," Kathleen said, almost sighing the words out, as if she was tired of this spectacle and just wanted to go back to sleep. "Once Herman gets riled up, he can be hard to control."

How had this happened? Moments ago—seconds ago! — Brad was balls deep in her crapper. Now she was *suggesting* he leave. *Or what?* Or this fake dog—this leather dog—was going to pounce on him like some oversized infant wanting to wrestle. With that naked, useless glob of flesh crouched in the floor like a devout parishioner at a church of disgust, Kathleen thought Brad should be intimidated? She thought he should bend the knee and bid farewell?

Fuck that!

"Tell your stupid dog to get out of here," Brad said sternly, his cock getting a sudden rush of enthusiasm as a result of his dominant tone. "We can finish what we started, then I'll be on my way."

"What we started, huh?" Kathleen said, raising an eyebrow and laughing under her breath. "Bradley, dear, get the fuck out of here while you still can."

"Excuse me?" he said, the dog in the doorway momentarily forgotten.

"Nobody fuckin talks to me like that."

"Get the fuck out," she said mildly, without concern. "Last chance." Brad boiled over.

Before he had time to consider his move—to think better of it and perhaps accept Kathleen's offer to let him leave—his right hand crossed over his chest, then swung downward, backhanding Kathleen right in the nose, kicking her head back and causing blood to spray from one nostril as she hit against the pillow, her eyes wide with shock.

"Fuck!" she hollered, her hands going up to her face. "Herman!"

Brad turned, having forgotten the man mutt was still in the room.

Herman was bounding toward the bed on all fours, snarling and barking as his body moved, his muscles contracting, each stride knocking hard against the floor. He leapt, the tail floating up behind him, as Brad, his hands balled into fists, turned to face the dog head on. But as he leapt for the bed—for Brad—one of the dog's hands reached for a clasp on the side of the leather mask, undoing it, pulling the mask free from his head just as he landed on the mattress, revealing himself in full to dear Bradley.

The leather mask had been in the shape of a dog's face, with the long snout and jaws, but beneath it . . . beneath it too were a long snout and jaws. Whether by surgical design or a mutation of

Mother Nature, Brad did not know. Herman's pale flesh extended out to a dog snout below the eyes, with a pugly flesh-toned nose at its end. Below the nose was a wide mouth, with loose skin drooped around, black stubble sprouting here and there. And, as he growled that hideous growl, Brad could see long, sharp teeth within that mouth. Not human teeth, but those of, perhaps, a German shepherd or Doberman.

"Jesus Christ," Brad managed to say in the brief moment before Herman attacked. He didn't move to flee or fight, only uttered that one plea to his creator or simply the empty air between them.

Then Herman was upon him.

Amidst his disbelief, Brad lowered his arms, and with his opponent's limbs no longer a threat, Herman struck the way any dog would, lunging at the neck of his victim—whether tearing open the throat or jugular, it made no difference; either would disable, if not kill. As it turned out, Herman's wide jaws got both.

With Brad falling backward toward the mattress in a pathetic attempt to avoid the dog, Herman's massive jaws wrapped around his neck, the long teeth sinking in only for a moment, before his head jerked to the right violently, the teeth not releasing, but taking as much flesh with it as possible. Blood poured from Brad's jugular and sprayed from his carotid artery, arching over his shoulder and decorating Kathleen's cream-colored sheets like an abstract painting.

Losing his balance, his hand going uselessly to his neck, Brad toppled from the bed, his head colliding with the corner of the nightstand, opening another wound for blood to flow. His eyes and mouth were wide in an equal measure of fear and disbelief.

But the dog wasn't done.

Kathleen had warned of what would happen if Brad didn't leave.

Most dogs only understand a handful of phrases. They understand their name. They may understand 'sit' or 'stay' or 'go potty.' But Herman understood everything. He was a very smart dog.

Brad was screaming from his back—a horrible, gurgling scream—as Herman jumped from the bed, his jaws once more open to the max. The dog's human-like paws slammed into Brad's knees, spreading the man's legs as he fell upon him, dislocating the left femur from the pelvis as he went. In a snarling fit of rage, Herman's open maw descended upon Brad's shriveled genitals. A pit bull, were it capable of jealously, would've indeed been jealous of the power of Herman's bite. In one single, perfectly aimed snap, the dog severed Brad's twig and berries like he was plucking a couple of grapes from its stem, leaving nothing but a bloody orifice between the man's legs. After only two quick chews, the cock and balls were swallowed and resting pleasantly in Herman's belly. And as Brad gasped his last wet breaths, Herman relaxed, panting, squatting beside the man, his tongue hanging lazily out the side of his long, fleshy jowls. "Good boy, Herman" Kathleen said, sitting up in bed, admiring the corpse and her loyal doggo with a satisfied smile. "That's my good leather dog. I hope you don't think your night is done though. You know how horny Mama gets when you protect her."

Herman looked at her, returning his tongue to his mouth, and howled softly—sweetly—toward the ceiling, then jumped into bed.

The Onion Club

Jack Bantry

John was at his allotment digging over the soil in what would be this year's onion bed. He dug in the garden compost with some well-rotted horse manure. Now his back was aching. He straightened, arched his back, trying to rid himself of the pain. It was no use. He was sure he would have a bad back for the rest of his life.

He'd been growing vegetables on his allotment since he took it over at the beginning of lockdown.

The ground was muddy after all the recent rain, but he had to get it done in time to plant his onion seedlings. They had been taking up precious room on the conservatory windowsill and he needed space to plant on the runner beans and butternut squash.

He resumed digging, turning the soil with his fork. He was now in his third year at the allotment. Sometimes things went as planned, he didn't have any trouble growing beetroot and parsnips, or courgettes. Another couple of months and he'd have courgettes coming out of his ears. He couldn't give them away.

Other times things failed for no apparent reason.

The good old English weather was the common excuse. You never really knew what it was going to do tomorrow, never mind next week.

Last year the majority of his leeks went to seed, and the slugs ate his radish. The trick was not to become disheartened and to learn from your mistakes - water regularly and make some beer traps for the bloody slugs. It's not always straightforward. There hasn't been a spring this year - heavy frost until the recent rain. Now the ground was soft enough to dig. In fact, it was too soft. He put some cardboard down to stand on, otherwise he was going to sink into the earth. If things failed, you knuckled down and tried again.

John stuck the gardening fork in the ground, walked over to the shed and poured himself some tea from his flask. He spotted the *Fish Blood & Bone*, and he used that to feed the onion seedlings some nutrients. His back was still aching, but he needed to get the onion seedlings in. He picked up his rake and returned to the muddy cardboard, back to the onion bed.

John had lived in the village most of his life. He ran a successful restaurant in nearby York. Prior to lockdown he was negotiating with two long-time employees and trying to sell them the business. The hours were long, and he was getting too old. He wanted to spend the evenings at home with his wife. They had no children, hence no one to leave the business to, and the sudden pandemic forced him to literally give away the restaurant. He was glad to be rid of it and the pressures the pandemic brought to the hospitality trade. It was simple, he'd made enough money and didn't need the hassle.

When he took early retirement, he had no plans to spend his afternoons growing vegetables. The restaurant business was all consuming, so he hadn't had time for hobbies, until he'd seen the allotments while out on his daily walk. John soon came to love the vegetable garden. It was a way for him to escape the isolation. To save himself from certain madness. John had never grown vegetables before. Shown no passion towards it. He hadn't even taken a previous liking to flowers. He doesn't grow flowers now either, except for a few daffodils, but he does grow all kinds of vegetables. Onions are his real passion, though, thanks to the Onion Club.

At the end of the first season John noticed some of the folks taking more care with their onions than other vegetables. He couldn't understand why. It wasn't as if they were the most interesting vegetables on the plot. When he got chatting, he discovered they were members of the Onion Club.

A club for onion growers.

There was an allotment related club in the village. His interest immediately peaked.

It took place in August at the local pub, The Sowerby Arms, so you could have a couple of pints too. Main prize (club members only) was for the heaviest onion. John applied to join the club. You can only join if the other members voted you in - and they all did, there were no objections, which was good.

He came last at his first attempt last year. Became a bit of a laughingstock. John was always competitive in the restaurant business, you had to be, last place in the Onion Club was a failure. It didn't matter that it was his first year. He was conditioned to be successful. He didn't expect to win on his first attempt, but he expected to do better. Now, John was addicted to growing onions and strived to grow the largest in the village, where they take it very seriously. This year he hoped for a good placing. He'd put too much effort in, and invested enough time, to finish last. John was surprised at how serious he was taking the competition and aimed to have the last laugh.

The bed was raked over, nice and flat, with large stones removed. He loved prepping in March and April, getting the allotment ready for the new season. The daffodils were flowering. It meant spring was near and lighter nights were coming.

He loved spending time on his plot. You had to get the soil ready, put the seedlings in, water them, do the weeding. You spend a lot of time observing and talking to them.

He heard the main gates creak open as he reminisced.

More gardeners.

John walked over to the shed again and brought back a tray of onion seedlings.

He was lost in his own world and didn't notice whoever had arrived until he heard a large cracking sound, like wood splintering. He was kneeling at the time - not good for his bad back - and when he stood, he saw a young man, sixteen or seventeen years old, dressed in black tracksuit bottoms - the ones with the three strips down the side - and a black sweatshirt. It was Steph's shed and her children were much smaller.

John had seen a few of the teenage kids roaming around recently in groups, ignoring the lockdown rules, which instructed people to stay home.

He imagined the young man was stealing to buy drugs. He's heard York, like most towns and cities, had a problem.

"Oi," shouted John. "What do you think you are doing?"

The kid looked back over his shoulder, a startled expression on his face. Probably hadn't seen John knelt and thought he was on his own.

"Can I help you son?" asked John.

"Me mum sent me down for some gardening tools," said the kid.

"She's gardening at home."

"What's her name?"

"Eh?"

"What do they call her?"

The kid stumbled with his word.

He had to get past John to get to the gate. Instead, he took off towards the six-foot fence bordering the allotments. On the other side was a local park. Some kids, possibly this one included, broke in last summer. They damaged the padlock in the process - and trashed some of the allotments. They broke into a few sheds and stomped some pumpkins. It took all season to grow the different crops, most were grown from seed packets in February and March. It was bad enough loosing things to the weather, seeing the smashed pumpkins was heart-breaking.

John pulled his fork out of the earth and chased after the kid. He was going to make a citizen's arrest.

"Get here," shouted John.

"Fuck off, old man."

The kid clutched hold of the awkward wire-like fencing and attempted to haul himself up. John planned to pull him back down and phone the police from his mobile phone.

John grabbed hold of the kid's sweatshirt. Before he could get a good grip, the kid kicked down, connecting with John's nose. John landed hard on his backside.

The kid was climbing higher, almost high enough to swing a leg

John clambered to his feet. Without thinking his swung the fork, which he's somehow kept hold of, and stabbed the kid in the back. The tines sunk into the soft flesh of the kid's lower back, like sticking a knife through butter, all four inches of dirty metal.

The kid let out a bellowing scream of agony, his grip fumbled on the top of the fence. The fork was stuck right into the kids back. He imagined the times sticking out the front of the kid's torso, somewhere around the belly button. All four tines sticking through the kid's stomach. John hadn't meant to hurt the kid. The shock of what he's done was like being zapped with electricity. He pulled back on the fork and it slid out.

The kid let out another scream as he fell back, landing hard on a John's head, knocking the gardener back down.

Panicking, John struggled to throw the kid off him. He managed to pull his head free and push the kid's body away.

His first reaction was: had someone heard the scream?

John looked down.

The kid was laid on his back. He looked terrified, spat blood out of his mouth as he blubbered. His hands were covered in blood as he fumbled with the soaked front of his black sweatshirt.

John looked the kid in the eyes. They were wide open, pleading eyes, they said: *help me, please don't hurt me anymore.* The kid had quickly gone from a cocky teenager to a wounded animal.

The kid coughed again. Blood gurgled out from between his lips.

John pulled out his mobile phone and contemplated calling for an ambulance. He'd also need to phone the police.

He couldn't go to prison. He could hide the body. His car was in the car park. John could take the body to the car using his wheelbarrow, but it would be easy for someone to spot him if they looked his way. He couldn't do prison. John didn't know what to do. He was panicking. No way could John do prison.

If you can't do the time, don't do the crime.

What had he done?

The kid lay still, motionless, the coughing had stopped and his eyes seemed to have glazed over.

What had he done? John wasn't a killer. He was the kind of person who would put a spider outside instead of killing it.

John's mouth went dry as the shock of what he'd done kicked in.

He started to shake.

Oh fuck. No. Fuck. Fuck! Shit no.

John could hear people in the park.

Luckily their view would be obscured by bushes at the other side of the fence. If they'd heard the screams and came closer to investigate, they would surely see through the early springtime branches.

John, in a state of panic, looked around, searching for people, trying to see if he'd been spotted. What was he going to do? He killed a kid for breaking into a shed. Not exactly a crime deserving of the death penalty. He was fucked. *There goes your peaceful retirement.*

John dropped the fork and grabbed hold of the kid's ankles. He pulled the kid back over to John's allotment. He could shove him in the shed, but that would make it hard to clean up any spilled blood. *Arrrgh!* John wanted to pull his hair out. What had he gone and done? Jesus, there was no going back from this.

He looked around himself. At this time of year, the allotment didn't have much growth. It was too early in the season. The only plants with any height were the overwintering brassica - his few remaining Brussel sprouts and the purple sprouting broccoli. That would have to do. He dragged the body between the rows of large overgrown plants.

The body was out of sight, but it was obvious it couldn't stay there.

The only soft earth was where he had dug over his onions.

Fuck!

He needed to get the body to the car, parked in the small car park outside the allotment. The path down was too narrow to drive and he'd already ruled out the wheelbarrow. What was he going to do?

Could John risk leaving the body until it got dark, before hauling it down to the car park? That was an option. There was a good chance he could get it to the car once the sun went down.

He could then drive it out into the surrounding woodlands, but rigor mortis would have set in by then. The blood would be starting to congeal.

John went back into the shed and picked out his spade. He was going to have to bury it here. John got straight down to it. Digging easily in the soft earth. The problem now was the big hole and pile of soil couldn't be anything other than a grave.

He was sweating and his back hurt like hell.

John made sure no one was looking before dragging the body out from under the broccoli leaves and dropping it into the hole.

Come on, nearly done.

He picked up the spade, noticed sore spots on his hands, which were starting to blister. Ignoring the pain, he tossed in the earth, quickly covering the body. He discarded the spade and frantically searched for the rake.

John smeared mud across his forehead as he wiped away rivulets of sweat. God only knows what he looked like.

The ground was flat enough.

John noticed the tray of onion seedling near where he had been kneeling when the kid broke into the shed.

I should plant them, he thought. *They'd naturally avert any suspicion.*

***

John walked through the village on his way to the Sowerby Arms village pub. It was a typical midsummers day with a cloudless blue sky overhead. The village was very picturesque, with quaint limestone cottages lining the narrow winding road. Each cottage sat beyond a typical lawned front garden, surrounded by colour. A cabbage white butterfly flapped lazily above John's head. The common insect was a pest, as the eggs it laid turned into caterpillars that devoured the brassicas.

John was heading to the pub to take part in the annual Onion Club awards.

He was extremely nervous and was hoping for an improvement on last year.

John's onions were definitely bigger than his previous attempt. The initial lockdown had come to an end and people were out and about, many refusing to wear masks and ignoring social distancing.

He walked through the pub car park, which was full, and into the rear beer garden. The club had erected a marquee on the lush green lawn, probably in case of rain, as you can't trust the British weather. People bustled in and around the tent, most with a drink in their hand. John wandered into the marquee, he nodded his greeting or shook hands with a few of the other growers. He had another twenty minutes before the advertised start time, long enough to get himself a pint.

John drank from his pint glass as the Onion Club toasted his unexpected victory. Winner at only the second attempt. He savoured the victory as the other growers looked on enviously. George, the pub landlord was asked to judge. It was a simple enough task, as the heaviest onion was the winner, and the club had some state-of-the-art electric scales. John had his photo taken stood in front of his giant award-winning onion. In one hand he held his certificate, while he shook hands with George with the other.

"What's the secret to your success?" asked Liz Arnold, reporter for the local weekly newspaper.

That interested a couple of club members who wanted to know John's secret.

"Well, I water the plants regularly and get plenty of nutrients into the soil," replied John.

"What do you use exactly?" asked Graham Hogg. Graham, a retired doctor, had won heaviest onion three years ago, and was considered one of the favourites, but had only come in fourth place.

"I'm afraid that's a secret," said John, with a wry smile. It was a secret he wasn't willing to share. John, lost in thought, drank more of his ale. Unfortunately, due to

crop rotation, he wouldn't be able to replicate this year's success. The soil this year had been exceptionally fertile and had produced great results. When growing vegetables, the grower had to rotate the crops to avoid exhausting the soil and help stop diseases which can occur if a crop is repeatedly farmed in the same ground.

John had his own questions, like would the fertile benefits of the decomposing body last for future years, next year he planned to grow pumpkins and courgettes where this year's onions were grown; how was he going to replicate this year's success with his onion's? He'd surely be one of the favourites next year. Maybe he would have to make do with regular growing techniques, that is, unless he could procure another

body…

THE END

Skinheads Ruin Everything

Dan Henk

THE FIND

I'd never really felt 100%. Like my life was my own and everything made sense.

Society had always been a strait jacket. I wasn't even sure who or what I was meant to be. Or if that was even a thing. My parents were deeply conservative, which only became more of a burden as I grew older. I tried running away. Twice actually. As I evolved into a young adult they felt less like my parents, and more like the people I was stuck with. Not that any of it mattered now. They'd found the body. And I'd done such a good job of cleaning up. Hours upon hours of scrubbing and digging.

A LITTLE BACKSTORY

I was living in Virginia at the time. At my parents' house in Burke. Dad was barely around. Mom was present but she was usually pretty oblivious to anything outside of her small, milquetoast suburban world.

Some bug had crawled up their ass and they had decided to vacation.

Puerto Rico was the original destination, but the storm prevented all that.

So, they settled on Florida.

They did offer me the token invitation. Family gathering, fun in the sun, all the usual amenities.

But the last thing I wanted was to waste four days of my life sharing a house with my lame ass parents.

Mom still gave running commentary on the immorality of every TV show, and somehow managed to overcook all the food. Her very presence was annoying.

Not to mention that everything about me seemed to embarrass them. My Mohawk. My attire. My late rising and even later evening hours. Dad always said I looked like a girl, as if that was some sort of insult. He'd chased me around the house with scissors trying to cut my hair and rip my earring off.

So, I stayed home. In my boring suburban house. Nestled ever so wholesomely among trimmed maple trees and boxwood shrubs. Like every other crappy domicile on this block. The conformity of it was almost smothering.

Of course, I was going to throw a party the minute they were gone. I told a few people at school, but it grew out of hand in no time. People I barely even knew were talking about it. A few friends were bringing kegs, Milwaukee's Best, (or Beast as they all called it), but beggars couldn't be choosers! I had a few hits stashed in the freezer too. Just in case.

Come Friday night, the place was swarming.

There was the aggravation of having to corral people smoking in the house. All in an attempt to avoid the parental "smells like smoke" feedback. And the aggravation of getting all the dipshits to not leave plastic cups everywhere. Other than that, it all seemed to be going pretty well. My buddy Dave showed up with his hot sister. I always found it difficult to have normal, relaxed conversations with people I felt I had to impress, but just maybe I could pull something out of my ass this time. I really should say something. Angela was always friendly, although maybe that was just because of Dave. The last thing I wanted was to make our friendship awkward by making moves on his sister.

Things were going swimmingly. We were all outback surrounding the pool. The lamps blanketed everything in a blue glow, which somehow made the environs seem slightly surreal. After a few drinks, not too many I hoped, I figured I could make small talk with Angela. Hopefully feel out what she was thinking. It might even give me the confidence to talk past my flaws. The imperfect skin. The weak jaw. The higher pitched voice. If I could just act the part of someone interesting, maybe I'd have a chance I couldn't bring myself to dive right in, so I made a little small talk with Dave and shuffled around nervously. As time slipped by, I tried to come up with things to say. My leather pants kept snagging in the plastic webbing of the chair, accentuating my awkwardness. Every time I told myself *"It's now or never"* something seemed to interrupt, and I paused for too long. Maybe she really didn't look at me like a potential love interest? What was the perfect thing to say without sounding stupid? I kept running through lines, but they all seemed flat.

Just as I worked up the confidence to try, a voice broke through the din.

"What the fuck do we have here Nelson? It looks like these little pansies are having a party."

SOME PEOPLE MAKE EVERYTHING WORSE

Who invited those morons? Skins felt entitled to pop up anywhere. My mom was Syrian, so my skin wasn't exactly white, but they usually left me alone. My friend Dave, however, and his sister, were black. And these guys were definitely of the racist variety.

"What's this?"

Even with the overwhelming aromas of chlorine and cut grass, I could smell the body odor and cheap cologne. The scrawnier guy was almost a stereotype come to life. He was wearing a crimson flight jacket, straight cut blue jeans, and Doc Martins laced up in red.

"You think you're a girl?"

I was confused for a moment, then realized I was sporting black eyeliner and nail polish. I often described it as my "death rocker" look. This was my house. I'd dress however the fuck I wanted. Besides, I didn't want to look like a pushover. Especially in the presence of Angela.

"No. Do you think you are?"

That was a little ballsy, but too many people were here, what was he going to do? All three of the skinheads, the scrawny guy, his muscle-bound friend, and some older looking jerk-off circled around. The scrawny guy drew closest, his hard, angry face staring at me. A few moments passed in utter silence, the whole crowd looking on, but the skins were silent. They turned and walked away.

The party continued like before, as more drunkenness ensued. At one point I could hear shouting, and the sounds of a distant scuffle. But nothing followed, so I shrugged it off. Besides, I was too drunk to do anything.

More people arrived, a few left, and yet again I missed my opportunity to talk to Angela. The skinheads had rattled me and now all I could bring myself to do was calm my nerves with more alcohol. I made excuses that I would have botched it regardless. But I knew they were just that. Excuses. I was twenty-one and felt like life was slipping me by. Next year I will leave for art school. Maybe I could re-invent myself there. I had started a band, and in the fresh environs of a new state I could possibly parlay that into something that made me cooler.

Come four in the morning, only a few stragglers remained. No one I particularly recognized, but no one I hated either. Drunkenly, I tried to survey the damage they'd done. It didn't look that bad. Then again, I could barely even see, and everything looked better in the late hours.

My bones cracked, and I groaned as I drew up my feet. I wandered over to the pool and gazed at the watery reflections. Soft ripples of aqua-green broke up the dark edges of my shadow. For a moment I was distracted, in some drunken trance. Then the strong stench of chlorine wafted over, and my stomach turned. I rocked back and forth on the ledge, daydreaming about how lame it would be to fall in. Something slammed into my back. Arms waving in desperation, I belly-flopped into the pool. A rush of cold water engulfed me and stinging chlorinated liquid invaded my nostrils. Thrashing about, I tried to break for the surface, but a hand grabbed my Mohawk and held me down.

Pounding the water like a madman, I attempted to break free. But there was nothing to grab onto, and I kept plummeting lower. The follicles on my scalp stung under the tension, as a palm crushed into the back of my head.

My eyes burned and I started to lose all focus. Then vision escaped me, little dots of color flashing into an overwhelming field of blackness. A strange sensation burned through me. My body grew warmer as my blood started to boil. A veil of crimson seeped in at the corners and consciousness escaped me.

THAT NEVER DEAD

I had this crazy dream. More of a nightmare really, but I can't say it was all bad. That skinhead was scared. He was running and then howling in pain as something tore into his spine. Blood was everywhere, bathing me in the sickly-sweet aroma of raw iron.

Then I awoke.

I was sitting on the pavement in front of my sidewalk, under the shade of a giant oak tree. All around me spread a dark splotch. The mangled form of a man, bulbous entrails jutting out of a heap of mashed flesh and distended bone shards, lay just to my left. A patchwork of dark puddles trailed towards the pool that surrounded me. I blinked and tried to clear my vision. Was that mess one of the skinheads? Some of the splotches amid the torn flesh resembled denim. I glanced sideways and noticed that the remnants of suspenders peaked out of the gory pile. Their tips waving gently in the breeze.

All was deathly silent. What could have done this? How did I get here? I glanced about. The stench was overwhelming. Excrement and the sickeningly metallic smell of blood. I looked down at my hands. They were coated in a thick, syrupy sheen. My arm felt damp, and I stretched it to see that the gore extended up towards my armpit.

Flashes started to flit through my head. Snippets of screaming and blood, like the scenes from a movie.

I started to panic. I had to do something. This couldn't be me, but the evidence was damning. How could I explain any of this? A rogue murderer? Someone framing me? In northern Virginia, looking the way I looked, no one would believe me. My own parents would rat me out.

I'd have to clean up this mess and hide the body. That was the only option. That was probably the wrong move, but I didn't want to spend my life in jail.

Rising to my feet and walking over, I looked at the viscera. Jutting out of the gristle was the rounded edge of a skull. Definitely the remains of a person.

What could I do to deal with this? Maybe a bag? I looked around. Aside from a few parked cars in the distance, there was nothing. No sign of life. Some large bags were in the shed. I just had to make it there and back before anyone saw any of this. A few neighboring houses loomed nearby.

No lights were visible. Maybe I could pull this off.

Scooping the slimy bits into one central pile, all while fighting back the urge to retch, I dug out what was left of the shirt and jeans. I brushed off as much of the gore as I could. I took off my shirt and twisted it into a makeshift satchel. Scooping in the remains, vomit rising in my throat every time my hands bumped into the stubby edge of a bone, I managed to pull the majority of

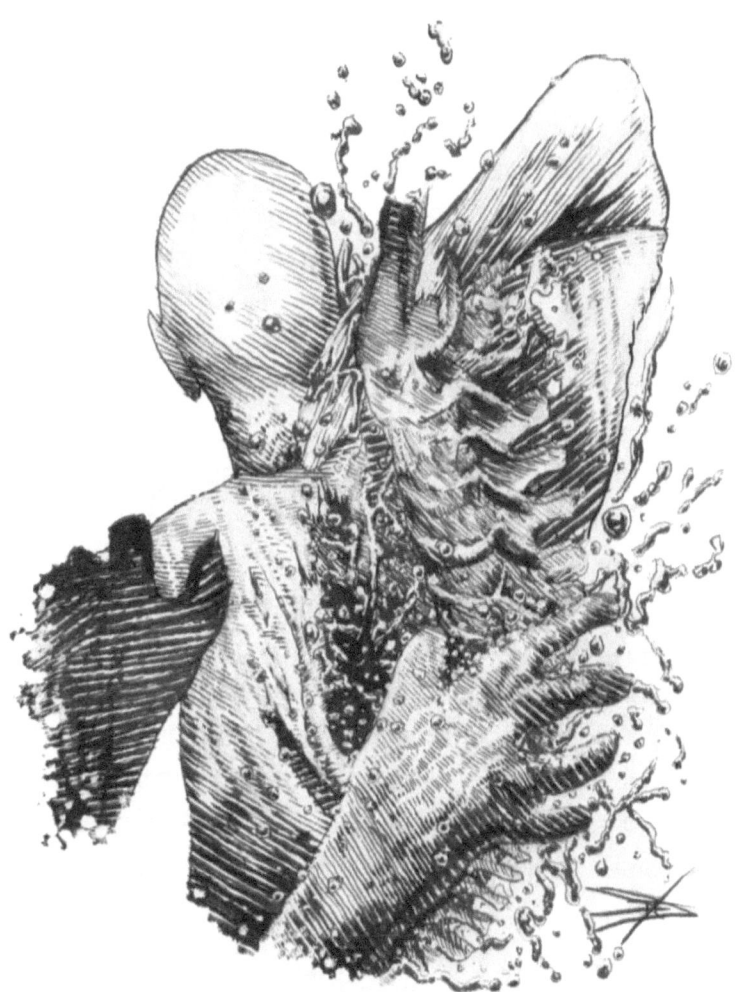

the slop into a makeshift satchel. I tied up the edges, and hoisted it all aloft, almost falling over under the weight as I swung it onto my back. I stabilized myself and headed for the house. Traipsing along the edge of the front yard, the fence of bushes a partial wall, I crept through the yard. The smell was horrendous, hitting me with a putrid gust every time a breeze passed. Clumps of gristle and rivulets of blood steadily dripped onto my neck, gluing the strands of my mohawk to my skin.

As I reached the rear porch, I stopped in the shade and scanned the backyard. Nothing. All was deadly silent. Where did everyone go?

The pool was rimmed with bottles and cups but devoid of life. Squinting, I could make out where that skinhead had tried to drown me. Just shimmering ripples now. There was a little puddle of water on the edge of the pool, but that was it.

Stumbling up the bevel and onto the patio, I hauled the corpse in through the rear glass door. In the darkness I could just make out the water closet entrance.

Shifting the mass on my shoulders and pausing for any last remnants of blood to drip down on the patio (as opposed to the carpet), I crossed the living room and pried the closet door open. The space was small. Smaller than I remembered. Only a tiny expanse of concrete, the hot water heater hogging up most of the space. I dropped the satchel and squinted into the darkness. No tools. Just a little hand broom and dustpan. But I remembered that the tool shed in the back yard harbored a pickax and shovel. And a bin of liquid concrete. There were dish rags and bleach under the kitchen sink. Desperate times called for desperate measures. I could do this.

THE KNOCK ON THE DOOR

The sound repeated itself. A harsh, booming crack.

My head still ached from the show last night, and to top it all off, that rash on my arm had gotten worse. I cupped the aching sides of my skull, the skin on my arm pulling tight and aggravating my rash. I stumbled out of bed only wearing my boxer shorts. My skinny chest was a constant source of embarrassment but fuck it. My head hurt too much to try and find a t-shirt.

As I cracked open the door, the light blinded me. A gust of Old Spice hit before I even recognized the uniform.

"What's...what can I help you with officer?"

My stomach knotted as I tried to run through what I could possibly have done. I mean, aside from the worst-case scenario. And I think they'd bring a lot more force for that. It could be my recent petty crimes, like shoplifting at 7-11. That was months ago, and an employee stopped me before I made it to the door. I'd been caught shoplifting at Kmart, and they had already banned me for a year. It could be last week's vandalism. None of that was anything serious. Just a few tags on wet concrete and a smashed bus sign. I'd done a little breaking and entering months ago when I was drunk, but only at the abandoned project buildings nearby. It was late at night, and nothing really happened. This was a college town. There were way worse things going on. Like that recent stabbing at the train station. Maybe they were just picking on the town misfits.

"Put on a shirt and pants. You're coming downtown."

"What's going on officer?"

"You're Ryan Argarwal right? 21 years old. Originally from Burke, Virginia?"

My heart sank. It wasn't a local drama. Burke was years ago but I figured it must be serious to tie me there. I'd moved all over the country, but there was only one thing in Burke that would draw them this far out.

The blazing morning heat was overwhelming. I tried to clear my vision as

I fumbled for smokes. Pulling a mostly empty pack from the bedside table, I withdrew one and mumbled

"You mind if I smoke this first?"

Convinced the cop would say no, I was a bit surprised when the officer turned and shot me a friendly smile. I tried to stretch my neck for a better view but the shine on the cop's head was almost blinding. A glimmer of mirror shades, an overweight officer, and a way too wide row of teeth were all I could make out.

"Sure."

Inhaling a few puffs, I kicked some of the gravel off the sidewalk and glanced about. The sky was that washed-out blue of early morning. The air always smelt a little different in these hours. Like the day held promise, even when I knew it didn't.

Peeling painted wood houses lined the cross street but no one seemed home. This might be my last smoke as a free man. I thought about running, but realized there was no way that could end well. I wasn't much of an athlete, and I was in no shape to outrun an officer. Even if the cop looked a little chunky.

I mulled over the incident from long ago. I could have sworn I'd cleaned up well. I was soaked in sweat and the sun was coming up as I gave the gravel it's once over last pass. Not that any of that mattered with modern forensics. Once they got down with all their modern blood splatter analysis equipment, the whole incident would be clear as day.

DOWNTOWN

The ride was uneventful. I had been in the back of cop cars before. The police never talked, usually they were dour and serious. These were more genial, and although I rode along in handcuffs, it wasn't that bad. The sharp edges bit into my wrists, but the cops cracked the windows, and I could smell the fresh air. In line with my usual bad luck, my arm really itched. With the handcuffs restraining me, I couldn't even scratch.

As the car rolled to a stop, the police up front stepped out. The fat one bent over and opened the rear door, motioning for me to follow. I passed through a grime smeared glass door and into central booking. Inside, a strong, chemical scent made me queasy. Antiseptic tinged with the aroma of last night's regrets. The seriousness of the situation was finally settling in.

As I strolled up to the central counter, I couldn't help but notice how all police counters seemed to look the same. I'd never been here before, but this looked just like the one back in Fairfax, VA. All cheap particle board painted in some passive tone, like gray. Just as I scrolled up my vision to the officer at the counter, a heavy hand clamped down on my shoulder and guided me to the right. I traipsed down a neighboring corridor and into an intimidating looking room.

White and bare, a gray table in the middle was the only occupant. It looked metal, but there were so many layers of paint on it, the true composition was long gone. I'd never been in an interrogation room, but judging by all the police shows I'd seen, this looked like one. Maybe a little more terrifying in real life.

The cop took a seat to the left of the table and gestured for me to grab the opposite chair.

Claustrophobia was starting to kick in. My head was damp with sweat and the mugginess was stifling. The door cracked open and a tall, slender man stepped in.

He had the look of some military official, not a regular cop. His shirt was gray and sported a few unreadable logo patches. It reminded me a bit of service employees at the bases my dad had been stationed at. The man held aloft stuffed manila folders and a slight scent of mold seemed to follow him.

"This is chief inspector Walter Gilman."

The pudgy cop drawled.

Walter spoke.

"Ryan, The man of the hour."

That did not sound good. The man sat down next to the cop and dropped the folders on the table.

"Quite the adventurer huh?"

Something about this guy was slightly repulsive. I couldn't nail it down, not that the alcohol from last night helped. But there was that smell and his skin looked waxy, like it was buried under a thick layer of makeup.

Maybe the hangover was fucking with my vision.

The man opened the top folder and spread out a slew of pictures. They were all gruesome scenes. A ruptured concrete floor split open to reveal the decayed remnants of something once human. A few of the photos beside it looked like they were taken the night of the incident. All fresh gore and carnage. Only that was impossible.

"I don't understand? Are you accusing me of this?"

"Oh, we know you did it."

Oh shit. But if that was true, why had they waited this long? My mind raced, and my headache was getting worse. I had to think of some alibi.

But all I could draw was a blank. The man leaned back and smiled.

"You know how long you were under the water? Thirty minutes. We counted."

I tried to scroll through my memory of the incident. That was impossible. I should have drowned if that was the case. But then again, maybe this was a good turn. If it all was retaliation in self-defense, and they knew it, then maybe there was a chance.

"You died. Well, that's not quite correct. It was the event that pushed you to the next stage. A half hour later, you emerged from the pool and massacred that man. But you don't remember any of this, do you?"

How did this guy know more than I did? I slumped back in my chair, the metal contours biting through my t-shirt. The blinding overhead light drowned out everything. Maybe that was on purpose. Part of their interrogation technique? I rubbed my eyes, but that only made things worse. My temples pounded, and I felt lightheaded. It all seemed a bit surreal. I couldn't shake this cotton in my head, or the chill that kept pulsating through me body. The man opposite me had a trace of an accent. German or eastern European I guessed. It made the whole scenario more surreal. Was this a dream?

"I don't...I don't understand..."

"Of course you don't."

"But am I in trouble..."

The man smirked. A bit of his makeup rubbed off onto his lip. It was barely noticeable, and I wondered if my eye were fooling me. Then I noticed his eyes. Maybe he was just wearing contacts, but they didn't seem to move quite right.

"Maybe this time."

The man grinned, emitting a weird, slurry cackle.

What had I taken last night? None of this seemed real.

"I hope you understand, we need to hold you a bit longer. It's really for your own safety as much as anything."

With that, the man scooped up the folders, rose from his seat, and strode out.

ALL IS NOT AS IT SEEMS

The inspector turned towards the adjacent room. Catching the closing door, the cop followed.

The inspector turned and muttered.

"You can go now."

"Excuse me?"

He turned and shot the cop an irritable look.

"You're not needed."

The cop sputtered.

"Look, I don't know who you think you are..."

Before he could muster more of a response, a man rose from the central desk and pulled the cop aside. Attired in the same odd uniform the inspector was wearing, he whispered in the cop's ear. The policeman turned bright red and wandered away.

Gesturing for the inspector to enter the neighboring room, the man muttered something as they entered. The rest of the conversation was an unintelligible series of mumbled words as they disappeared. Who were these guys? Hold me a bit longer? I'm not in trouble? My own good?

What was going on?

RYAN

I rested my arms on the table. I still felt sick, and my arm was getting worse. Peeling back the sleeve of my hoodie, the cloth tore off clumps of yellow crust. Dried striations of it riddled the sleeve, The skin beneath was inflamed and spotted with pus filled bubbles. It looked like a severe case of poison ivy to me. The rash itched like hell, but I fought the urge to scratch.

The door creaked open and to my surprise, it was the chubby cop.

"Are you OK little man?"

The cop seemed to be harmless. Not that I'd had good experiences with the police, but this one seemed nicer than most. He did let me get one last smoke in before he took me away. Then again, this whole thing might just be a calculated trick. That whole good cop/bad cop thing. There was definitely something very strange going on here.

"Yeah. I guess. My arm hurts though. Do you have anything like Calamine lotion? I think I have poison ivy."

The cop looked genuinely disturbed.

"Aw man, that does look pretty bad."

Pulling a pair of nylon gloves out of his back pocket, he snapped them on and drew in closer.

"Here, let me take a look at that."

Cupping the bottom of my forearm, he pulled the skin tight and gently poked at the rash.

"Yeah, it looks pretty bad. Let me see what we have in the medicine closet."

Hand still holding my arm, the skin abruptly split open. I grimaced in pain as crusty pink flesh sundered apart to divulge a silvery under layer.

"What the fuck.."

A LITTLE ACCIDENT

It was like a repeat of that long ago incident with the skinhead. As reality started to fade, I could feel the heat rising. In a nightmarish flash of images, scenes of tearing skin, flying entrails, and spinning coils of brain matter flitted through my consciousness. Then, all faded into blackness.

When I regained consciousness, I was splayed atop a table. Leather belts gripped my wrists and ankles, their sharp edges biting in. I was naked, freezing cold, and couldn't clear the fog in my head. I tried to move but was pinned. Something dug into the back of my skull and every time I tried to move pain shot through. Intense overhead light bleached out everything. Two blobs edged into view. As I blinked and tried to clear my vision, I could make out oddly shaped black facades that resembled overcomplicated gas masks. As they drew closer, I could see eyes underneath that had slits for pupils.

"Subject is ready."

The chimeras pulled away and a needle descended into view, its point growing more in focus as it descended. Panic washed over. I tried to scream but only hoarse gargles erupted. The syringe steadily closed in, its tip aimed at my forehead.

"Stop! I'm conscious!"

The needle rotated slightly and centered itself. Resuming its drop, it gently tapped my forehead, stopping just as it punctured my skin. The sharp tip scraped my skull. Something dropped down the length of the needle. As it impacted my forehead, I felt a multitude of sharp metal barbs dig in. Blood trickled into my eyes. I thrashed about, spurts of pain pulsing through my joints. The needle punctured my forehead and my body locked up. This was the worst pain I had ever experienced and I was frozen as it dug into me.

"Oh god, what is this? No Stop! Please...."

With a soft shucking noise, the needle burrowed in ever deeper.

"Oh my god! I can't take this! Please-it's too much!" I mouthed he words, but nothing came out. One of those things leaned over and slapped something gelatinous into my mouth.

I was choking and could barely breath. My eyes bulged out of their sockets as blood pooled in.

The syringe started to vibrate. I felt like my brain was being sucked out.

Froth built up at the corners of my mouth.

Consciousness eluded me.

ALL IS BACK TO NORMAL

I felt good. I wasn't sure what it was, but that show must have gone well last night. Not that I could remember much. Maybe it was all the alcohol I'd consumed. Maybe it was the coke. You'd be surprised what these Ivy League types got up! Well, it was back to the grind. Growing up in Jersey, I always knew my parents expected me to work for the government.

They were pretty tolerant, and I didn't break too many rules. Just a little youthful steam letting before adulthood kicked in. They knew I wanted to be an artist but had talked me into getting an architecture degree as a backup.

Man had that worked out. Tomorrow, I had an interview with some guy from North

Hatch

Bobby Lisse

THE THING I LOVE ABOUT DINERS IS YOU CAN GET BREAKFAST OR A ROAST

"It's not an abortion."

Greg uses a single tine of his fork to tear at the thin membrane. The viscous deutoplasm surges across the plate. A sliver of bread drenches itself in the embryonic protein and ends up gnashed between Greg's coffee-stained teeth.

"They were never going to be little baby chicks. They breed them that way, ya know?"

Shelly grips her fork tightly with its stabbing end pointed to the sky. She's hesitant to poke the cobb salad in front of her. It looks delicious, with perfect grill marks on the chunks of chicken, flawlessly crisped bacon, and the freshest looking tomatoes, cucumbers, and lettuce.

"Why did you have to bring up baby chicks?"

"I said they WEREN'T going to be baby chicks."

"Please don't say baby chicks again."

"You don't want me to say cute…"

Greg stabs his sunny side up egg.

"…fluffy…"

He lifts the egg in the air, readying it for lift off.

"…yellow, little adorable fluff-ball" The fork speeds down the runway.

"…baby chick!"

Greg violently shoves the egg into his mouth which makes the runny yolk splash across both cheeks. He looks like a toddler who has been given free reign of their meal; the soft puree splattered like a Pollock painting across their grill.

Shelly drops her fork.

"You're an asshole."

Greg chews with a devious grin.

"You're right, Shells." Greg concedes as he swallows the last of his food. "Baby chicks   might be the cutest creatures on the planet. I mean, they're the Asian baby of the animal kingdom. There is nothing cuter than an Asian baby, except a baby chick. But you can rest assured…" Greg wipes the massacre from his face. "…these little guys in my stomach were never going to be baby chicks. I wouldn't eat eggs if they were."

Greg grabs Shelly's plate and slides it across the table to himself.

"I'd eat the fuck out of their mother though."

He forks the succulent chicken and shoves it in his maw without dithering.

CAN YOU ACCOUNT FOR THIS GAP IN YOUR WORK HISTORY?

"The way Ignacio explained it to me is it's the same type of machine they use in shit processing plants to make it all flow smoothly. You put something solid in and it comes out all mashed up. It is like an unstoppable blender. So, look at it like that. If we do not send them little yellow balls through the macerator, we'll have a big clog. Production quotas don't allow for any clog, let alone big, yellow, furry, cute ones. You do not have to see them get smashed to bits either. Not today at least."

Enid cringed as Mark did a poor job of sugar coating the fate of the male chicks as their bodies would be turned into literal minced meat. To be used in pet food, mostly. Mark can smell the stomach acid traveling up her esophagus. He can tell a postscript is in order:

"Ok, think of it this way - at least you don't have to make a choice. If it is a male, he leaves the belt. You don't even have to lift their skirts until you've learned how to vent. Two stripes, it's a male. For all you know they're off to live a plush life on an all-male chick farm. Also, you get to go home with a dozen eggs every day if you want! That is a few hours pay right there. Just remember what I said..."

As Mark continued to talk Enid recalled the tour of the factory this morning. As she passed the section that housed the macerator, the sounds it emitted were something she couldn't describe. But it made her stomach instinctively clench. An ear trained for a diverse cacophony may place the sound alongside something like a Mike Smith blast beat or a dissonant tribal drum circle, but that was before the byproduct was making its way through the steel teeth. The chirps showed no awareness of the pending doom. Their sound did not alter; it was chirping and then crunching. A human might scream, even for a split second, as they were crushed mercilessly. The chicks had no such reaction. They entered the machine as innocently as they looked.

Enid's ears had begun ringing as Mark had finished his instruction. The sound of thousands of chicks was no longer just recall. Less than fifty feet away sat an industrial laundry bin filled with tiny live foul. They looked like a ton of loofahs. But loofahs don't chirp. She asked herself how she ended up here.

Enid never expected to be starting a new job this late in her life. In fact, the entire second act of her life had been unexpected. A pre-teen son built like a splintering match that can't be left alone sucked up more than half her weekly paycheck at her last job.

Eleven years she lived paycheck to paycheck with no raise in sight. Her salary sat under living wages with comfortable room for the corporation. She can still taste the day she was fired. All eleven years of regret washed around her mouth like a warm cup of salt water, burning every open sore. She wished she had never taken that gig but It's all she could get after being fired from her previous "career". That was the one job she thought she would have for the rest of her life.

The day she was fired from job one still stings like a divorce. She had considered that family her own after being in their house for so long. She started with the Samuels when she was just eighteen years old and had watched three of their children born wealthier than she could ever imagine. Their bank accounts were larger than her life's earnings before their umbilical cords were even cut. She always wondered whether the boys were birthed by a surrogate. There was a lack of connection that was evident between them and their mother; and she never seemed to show any normal signs of postpartum pain or discomfort. There was some sort of belly, but it never showed before seven or eight months along and it could never be considered much beyond bloat.

Biddy Samuel always took care of Enid during the holidays. A beautiful and luxurious basket of high-end products, everything from snacks to toiletries was a real treat and something Enid could not have bought for herself, but the thousand-dollar bonus felt like she had won the lottery. It never lasted long between rent, taking care of Mama and of course a lavish night out on the town with her cousins. She wouldn't let Tatí or Sandra pay for a single drink and always brought them to the new "hot spot" in the city for dinner. Once a year Enid got to pretend, she was someone else. She lied to herself and with her shoulders forward and chin high had allowed her proximity to wealth and power to infect her brain for those eight hours. That one night a year she would change her last name to Samuel, at least in her own head.

Biddy always brought Enid back to earth quickly by letting her know just how charitable she had been with the bonus:

"It's important to take care of the little people, Ay-nid.", Biddy always pronounced her name with a manufactured accent. Enid could never figure out where the affectation came from as Biddy's normal, round the house, speaking voice lacked any discernible diction. She did of course put on a real "southern miss" dog and pony show whenever company was over. The Samuels were known to host expensive, pretentious parties where local politicians of all imagined hierarchies would rub elbows and make deals as if they ran the world. Nothing exciting ever happened at those parties. Nobody ever got too drunk or caused a scene. Enid would have known because her job was always to chase the boys around and make sure they weren't sneaking a sip of champagne or stabbing each other with the cocktail swords.

The only thing that sticks out from those soirees was the time when the oldest boy, Stewart, broke into Mister Samuel's office. Enid went to reclaim him, and she found the boy frozen as a small cadre of guests feverishly dined on some special dish which the rest of the partygoers hadn't been privy to. Enid apologized for Stewart's interruption, but they never even acknowledged her presence. The light was warm and dim and their heads moved like a pack of lions gorging over a kill.

Then came Enid's turn at legacy building. She tried to hide it at first, unsure how the Samuels would react, but the morning sickness was completely unmanageable, and Enid was cursed with one of those screaming vomit voices. The type that announces spoiled food or inebriation to the entire house. She didn't try to conceal the pregnancy solely out of deception. It was because of an old wives' tale she had heard but she can't remember where. The way she recalls the myth is it was bad luck to talk about the baby before it was born. She didn't think someone of her means could risk letting go of any luck whatsoever. Even Enid's superstitions weren't her own.

Inevitably Enid's hesitance to disclose her "precarious ailment" as Biddy called it was well founded. Mrs. Samuel treated the news as if it were the ultimate betrayal. As if Enid had stepped in and tracked feces across the Persian carpet. There was no recourse for her firing, being an independent contractor; she was simply told that her "...services are no longer required.". Even if Enid knew it was illegal to fire someone for being pregnant, she was too meek to press the issue. "What are we to do, Ay-nid? Shall I have my children unsupervised for the next nine months while you take care of this little gaffe?". Biddy's callousness hurt but Enid could not argue with it. The Samuels were busy people, and she knew better than anyone that the boys were prone to bruises and bedlam.

"I'll make you one last offer." Biddy pointed her chin to the sky as she proffered. "I'm not even sure why I'm being this obliging. I will pay for this mess to go away. You may have three days to recover from this... course of action, but you must promise to never tell mister Samuel. He just wouldn't suffer that his hard-earned money supported the murder of a child. Regardless of how dire its life would turn out to be.".

For a moment Enid appreciated Mrs. Samuel's patience. She thought on it long enough to convoke a heel to stomp and arms to cross.

"Well?"

She couldn't. She wasn't sure why. She wasn't religious. She didn't have some entrenched stance; she just knew this was the one chance for her to do something that could make her life worthwhile. She was tired of being bland and alone.

She didn't even have to refuse. Biddy was a smart woman.

"Undoubtedly the father will take care of you then. Farewell Enid.". She dropped her contrivance as if she couldn't waste an ounce more of effort on her Nanny of ten years. Somehow that frail Woman could make even the most veiled and insincere sentence sound threatening, and those were the last words Biddy ever spoke to Enid.

NEW MOTHER

Mama was around those first six months. She could hardly get out of bed, but Enid appreciated having the moral support. She loved to listen to her mother talk about how difficult a pregnancy it was but how Enid was the most pleasant and easy baby. It made Enid hopeful that her baby was going to be spectacular. "You can't have something great without some hard work, right?". Mama always called her a "gift"", but Enid had trouble feeling like any type of prize, especially once Mama was gone.

Enid's water broke at Mama's wake. Her Mama's cousin - Tatí's mother Nina - was the only other person there, along with Mama's nurse. Tatí had claimed she had a "work thing" and couldn't get out of it but the whole family knew that Tatí's entire existence was upheld by her dope dealing boyfriend and she didn't work but fifteen to twenty hours a week at a car wash; ringing up customers while filing her nails and exchanging thick envelopes with enigmatic names like "Boston Tom" and "Lazy Eye".

The whole scenario made Enid happy that she no longer had the means to bring her cousins out for the yearly bonus party. Though it never stopped Tatí from making Enid feel bad about it.

"E, remember when you used to slave for that rich family? You really fucked that up, eh? What'd you do, suck the Daddy's dick? That old rich bitch catch you shining the golden rod?"

Enid didn't even bother to defend herself. In fact, Enid has never bothered to defend herself.

Mama technically died at the hospital, but she was gone before her body even left the front door. She had collapsed in the bathroom. It wasn't all that embarrassing. Mama's one wish towards the end was that she would go with "clean bottoms on", but that was a futile hope once her bowels let loose. At least she was wearing a muumuu to keep up some semblance of pride without the EMTs seeing her britches. Enid had begged Mama's nurse to drive her to the hospital, but the Nurse was adamant that no one but patients and Holy Cross personnel could ride in their vans. It was "...an insurance thing.". Enid had to take a bus, three buses to be exact. By the time she got there Mama was gone and Enid's belly was ready to burst.

It was the hemorrhage toolkit that had saved Enid's life. The Doctor said she should consider herself lucky and then referenced an outdated tv show that Enid was unfamiliar with, "You're all out of lifelines. Take the sixteen thousand and go home. Enjoy your baby boy.", but Enid wouldn't be able to take Carlo home for another month. She got to know her son through plexiglass and an oxygen hood. He made it. She could take comfort in that and the fact that she had an extra month to get his nursery ready. The apartment still stunk of Mama's death, but she did her best to cover it with frequent sprinkles of baby powder and baking soda.

The survivor's benefits weren't enough. She would have to find work. The best she could do was maintenance at a local venue. Six nights a week twenty-nine hundred people would pack into the theater in the round to see their favorite doo-wop group or a standup comic that had grown too large for clubs. She was never allowed to watch the performances, but from the break room they could hear the rumble of the bass or the echo of laughter.

Most nights it was a small crew. Gilbie and his girls. They would wait for the show to be over and then clean up the twenty-dollar plastic drinks and spilled popcorn. No one ever spoke to the girls. The boss would holler Gilbert's name and they would spring into action like little soldiers stabbing and grabbing the ephemeral junk.

She had heard stories, mostly from the other girls. Some of them didn't speak a word of English but she had learned enough Spanish from Maria the past bunch of years to figure what "violación" meant and "culo" was easy to figure. It wasn't until her last day on the job all the rumors proved to be pregnant with more than hyperbole.

Gilbert had gotten sloppy. He didn't even lock the door to the break room. The edge of the work bench splintered and cut across Enid's throat like a dull razor blade, causing painful abrasions. He grabbed her ponytail and pulled back so hard that her throat flapped open as if it were the skin of an apple being peeled. She tried to scream but it was as if he could feel her breath gathering the energy and every time, she was about to let the cry for help burst he would inflict some other demonic pain that kept her speechless, and her blood and tears flowing. She could feel his stamina waning. It will all be over soon, she thought. The door to the break room swung open. "Gilbert!". It was the boss. All five feet nothing of her. Her call was a lioness' roar. "What the fuck are you doing!?".

Enid sat on the curb. She could feel Gilbert dripping out of her as she rubbed her still bleeding neck. Some twenty yards away at the backstage door she could see the boss yelling at Gilbert but she couldn't hear any of it. She assumed he was being fired just like she had. His skin had become leather from sleeping outdoors with a belly full of cheap vodka but somehow his cheeks were still visibly red when he was scolded. He fiddled with a dirty rag like a child who twists their toes into the ground, refusing to make eye contact as they're admonished for some puerile faux pas. Gilbert wasn't fired that day. He was sent home to the woods out back. Enid wasn't even fired by name. Her pink slip was the soreness that made the curb she was sitting on feel like it was paved with glass.

FIRST DAY ON THE JOB

She gathered at her workstation. It looked like a luggage carousel, only it was stuffed with live baby chickens. She had asked Mark why they didn't just use the males for their meat. His answer was less than satisfying and somewhere along the lines of "...that's not our department.", but one word stuck out to her, "puny ". The males would never get big enough to be worth their weight. It made her think of her son Carlo. No matter how much she put on his plate and how clean he left it he could just never seem to put on pounds.

She stared as a throng of chicks passed by her. She grabbed a single yellow chick.

"Hey, puta."

Enid knew that term of endearment well from her prior life. One she was still healing from. She looked towards the cold voice. A Latina woman in her forties with a hair net and blue apron held two chicks and pointed them at Enid as she spoke with her hands.

"Tonight, you won't sleep. Hell, the rest of the month you won't sleep. But you'll get used to it.". The mercy at the end of Tina's promise was short-lived. She tossed the two males into the hopper with a ruthless thud. Enid's stomach geysered as if the callous attitude of her coworker was like a mentos in soda. She covered a batch of chicks in brown, gravy like stomach bile.

"Oi, what did you eat, shit?". As disgusted as Tina sounded, she didn't even try to waft the stench of regurgitated breakfast away from her face. In fact, the smell hardly registered with her. Tina slammed her hand on a large red plunger attached to the machine and a loud buzz echoed through the factory floor, like grazing the sides of a leg bone in "Operation". The entire conveyor in front of them changed angle and all the chicks, regardless of sex, dumped into the "bad egg" hopper.

Enid wiped her mouth with her sleeve, clearing the remaining mucus from her lips. Unintelligible foreign languages clashed as supervisors yelled at shift leaders. Enid realized she was still holding a chick. The last survivor of her puke party. She checked the chick's down.

Two stripes. It's a male.

Tina was yelling at Ignacio, whose belly hardly fit under his white lab coat. His hard hat sat so far forward on his head that it gave his profile the illusion of a beak. It was bright yellow as well, without a hint of dirt or blood on it. It bounced up and down as he quacked at Tina, animated with a clipboard swinging in his grip. Mark came over to calm them both down but instead drew the ire of both Tina and Ignacio, from which he quickly retreated in cowardice. Enid took advantage of the commotion and pocketed her survivor. She smiled, pleased with herself.

The conveyor belt started back up and Enid noticed the fight was over and Ignacio was inches from her face. "One Strike. Uno.", he said sternly as he held up three fingers. "No more.". He finished his confusing signals off with a throat cutting motion and then slammed his hand down on his clipboard, mimicking a macerator. It made Enid jump and her hand smacked her hip, bringing a chirp from the survivor.

The sound of the machine drowned it out. She nodded her head subserviently, freeing herself from Ignacio's breath.

Tina joined back on the conveyor and shook her head in disapproval as they waited for a new batch of chicks. As soon as the first few came through Tina grabbed them and slung them at Enid. "Maybe you should have a light lunch.". Thud, thud, thud, thud was endless as the crew segregated the males.

Enid walked in the door of her apartment with surprising zeal. The fatigue of the day held long on her face, but her favorite part of the day was upon her. She put the carton of eggs on the small kitchen table with the chipping Formica and waited to hear the clumsy patter heading her way. Like coming home to an

overexcited puppy, Carlo never failed to run at her and wrap his thin arms around her legs as tight as he could muster.

This time, there was no welcoming party. It sent a panic through Enid.

He should have been home from school for three hours at this point. Did Maria forget to pick him up? Did something happen to her, or worse to him? She stifled her overactive imagination to cry out, "Carlo!?". It didn't take long to settle her nerves. Carlo responded the moment his name left her mouth.

"Living room, Ma!". Enid rushed as quickly as she could and found Carlo on the couch, his legs propped up on the small ottoman with pillows between them and covered in white plaster.

"Carlo!". Enid dropped to the side of her son.

"What happened?".

"I fell." Carlo was smiling. A result of the painkillers. Behind Enid the toilet flushed. Maria exited the bathroom and dried her hands on her apron. She's only in her late fifties but had that perpetual matron look to her. The type you would see in Southern Living magazine or on some baking show from the nineteen nineties. "They said he bet another boy that he could fly. He climbed to the top of the monkey bars and jumped off.". Enid looked at Carlo, shocked at her son's behavior. "Carlo Euclid Alsted!". Carlo's smile signaled that his brain wouldn't be open for a debate on his faulty logic or grandstanding until the synthetic narcotic had worn off.

A tiny chirp reminded Enid of the gift she brought home. Her purse dismounted from her shoulder. "I brought you something from work." she said as she unlatched the buckle. Maria leaned in to see what it was. "Ay, Dios Mio!" Maria protested as she turned away in disgust. Enid palmed the survivor. He stood perfectly on her hand.

"Woah!!!" Carlo snatched the chick, rough. "Carlo, careful!". Enid recognized the irony of telling her son to treat the young bird compassionately.

"This is why I don't eat eggs." Maria paced, uncomfortable.

"You eat chicken though." Carlo barked at Maria, calling out her duplicitous consumption. "You eat more chicken than anyone I've ever seen.".

"Carlo!". Enid was surprised by her son's brashness. "I think it's time for you to sleep."

"Can he sleep with me, Ma?"

"Ay, you'll crush the poor thing!" "Maria held her face.

Enid grabbed a shoe box from a side table. She turned it upside down, emptying the contents. The Knick-knacks would stay out in the cold tonight. The Payless box would be reserved for members of the family. "Chum! That's what I'm going to call him. He's, my Chum!"

Enid was pleased that her son's boyish demeanor was returning. She rubbed his head as he held Chum close and whispered secrets into his tiny beak.

HOW MANY EGGS CAN ONE FAMILY EAT?

It's been five months since Enid started her new job. Thankfully she had learned to hold the contents of her stomach down after the first month but the sour taste in her mouth never went away. Tina had lightened up a bit, but they had become anything but friends. Tina had done everything she could to get Enid fired at first, but Ignacio said filling the job would be impossible until college break. Tina let it go but still resented Enid's snail-like pace.

"Enid plucks male chicks from the belt at a rate that is hardly one tenth the speed of her co-workers. She drops them into the hopper as if they're in an eggshell and she's trying not to crack them."

Tina watches this and slams her pull harder and harder against the rim of the hopper. Each rattle of steel made the chicks squeak less and less as the impact steals the glory of the macerator. Enid refused to take notice, but she couldn't hide the wince each time she heard that sick thwomp and crunch.

Every bite Tina would take of her homemade empanada

sounded like the broken back of her little fluffy kills. That day she sat directly across from Enid who was slurping on cold soup. There was no microwave in the break room, just a hot plate and Enid always brought lunch in a plastic container, leaving her little option other than cold or freezing cold.

"Do you want to see it?" Tina goaded Enid, as her tongue slapped in her mouth.

"See what?" Enid knew what.

Tina slammed her hand down on the table, mimicking the macerator, which made Enid spill her soup. Enid looked down into the remaining broth and slurped.

"I don't think I'm ready and Mark said I would have to..."

"I can show it to you. I'm a shift leader." Tina lifted her brow in a display of authority that had never intimated anyone except Enid at that very moment.

Enid declined the invitation as her nose almost touched the frigid liquid.

Back at the belt Tina kept a close eye on Enid, who continued her soft handling of the doomed foul. Tina abandoned her display of dominance over a creature that can't help itself and began softly, but swiftly placing the male chicks in the hopper. Enid sensed the energy change and looked up, locking eyes with Tina. Tina very deliberately placed a single male chick in the hopper as gently as she possibly could.

She did so with a face that seemed to concede some humanity or mercy.

Enid grinned with delight. Maybe she had cracked Tina's hard exterior?

Quitting time had come and Enid watched Tina from a couple of lockers over, removing her apron to reveal a well-worn sweater with a nondescript college screen printed on it. The type you see sticking out of donation bins. It breeds a kinship that Enid misread. She approached Tina with an olive branch.

"What does it do, exactly?"

Tina unfurled her long black hair from the hair net. She made quick work of her bun as she checked the game she had snared in her trap.

"Mark didn't tell you?"

"Not in any way that makes sense."

Tina shut her locker. "Come in fifteen early tomorrow." Tina grabbed her purse and walked away.

"OK." Enid hollered, making sure Tina heard her as she vamoosed.

"And don't eat breakfast." Tina said without a pause in her departure.

On the way out Enid grabbed another carton of eggs.

The Macerator

The sound was completely metal. It didn't have the rhythm of a car engine. It was too violent to sound like a washing machine. It sounded like a train at full steam without that soothing hiss, beating down the track in a motion that couldn't be stopped and would destroy everything but air. When Tina turned it on, she smiled like a man in mid-life crisis showing off his new Harley. Tina didn't bother trying to talk to Enid. They both had aviation earmuffs. Tina pointed to the machine, urging Enid closer. She pointed down with one finger and back at her eyes with two.

Enid stepped close and looked in. The metal prongs took each other's place with exceptional speed and the elegance of a synchronized dance, but there was never space for anything but metal and air. Whatever found its way into those hellish teeth would have no wiggle room. It was a paper shredder that would not jam.

A bout of vertigo rose up the back of Enid's neck and she pulled back from the destructive force. Tina was all smiles. She smacked her hands together hard enough for Enid to feel the plume of air on her face. Tina snapped her thumb and middle finger together to animate the speed at which the whole murder would happen.

The sound of chicks chirping had joined the symphony. Enid's head had begun to spin. She looked down into her hand and saw Chum resting on her palm, chirping playfully. The Macerator called for its meal.

Enid could feel the sweat pour down her face. Her vision had tunneled. As she looked up, she was at the conveyor belt. Tina was talking to her, but she couldn't hear a word she said. Enid fell backwards and before she could hit the ground everything had gone black. Her last conscious thought was "Please don't let me fall into that hell.".

Complications

The next time Enid's eyes were open Biddy Samuel stood over her.

"Now what will you do Ay-nid? You rebuffed my generous offer and now look at you."

Biddy eyed the length of Enid, three quarters of her body covered by blankets, and made her assessment.

"You're nothing now but a cut of meat."

Enid awoke from the dream covered in sweat. She felt relieved that she hadn't fallen into metal death, otherwise she wouldn't have woken up, would she? No one, nothing could survive that. Her back itched from the beginning of bed sores. Carlo's cast legs were propped up alongside her left arm. The boy was jamming his fingers at a handheld video game. Maria was sitting with her purse clenched tightly in her sleeping grip. Her mouth was a bucket collecting rainwater.

The Nurse had come in and spewed out too much information for Enid to ingest so shortly after waking up. Enid did focus in on one word, but she thought she must have misheard the Nurse. Surely, she hadn't heard her say she's pregnant. Was she telling Enid SHE is pregnant? Why would a stranger share that type of information so up front?

"I'll write you a note to take it easy at work, but you're going to have to schedule your first gyno appointment. You're already over sixteen weeks. Lucky you, you must have some good genes cause you're not showing at all."

Her ponytail swung back and forth as she bopped out of the room. Enid's head began to spin again. She looked down at the IV in the top of her hand. A bracelet on her wrist read 'Fall Risk' in large bold font. Enid's eyes closed again.

The bell rang signaling a batch of chicks on their way to be sorted. Enid sighed, trying to close off her lungs to the wretched air of murderous selections she was about to make. Tina stretched like an athlete. She interlocked her fingers and turned them palm forward, bending her knuckles back and cracking them. The pops made Enid cringe thinking of those little fluffy bodies being smashed to death. The conveyor belt seemed to be moving at an increased pace today, but Enid couldn't understand why there was no product to sort. Then she heard the clunking. As if something errant was falling down the belt, out of sight, banging against the steel shute. Finally, the cause of the ruckus had arrived. Carlo landed on his back with his skinny, bowed legs stuck out like puny popsicle sticks from a ridiculous chicken. He had landed right in front of Tina who had no expression of surprise or confusion. She grabbed Carlo by the scruff and tossed him in the hopper. Enid couldn't find breath to scream, and her legs could not compete with a lack of traction. It was as if she was standing on ice. She lurched forward, her hand stretched out as far as possible, but the belt was moving so fast there was no chance for her to save her feeble little chick. She tried to scream for Tina, but the sound of the Macerator had drowned out any possibility of communication. Carlo's chirps crescendoed until they fell in unison with the rolling hammer sound of steel obliteration.

The lunch bell rang. The belt ceased action. Tina removed her hair net and retired without so much as glancing at Enid. She could feel the sadness in every nerve, but she felt no water and heard no sobs. Everything else had stopped except the Macerator. The calamitous pirouette seemed to be getting closer. A monster approaching. The clang entered Enid and grew from her belly up. Her throat shook and her vision blurred. She tried to scream to release the pain of the rattle but her open mouth only made it louder and more agonizing. Her teeth fell away like the edge of an unstable dune as the steel tusks of the death machine embowed her like a human banana peel.

Enid stared at the drop ceiling. Its simplicity brought her solace and allowed her brain to find itself abdicated of her grisly factory shift. She was still in a hospital bed and for that moment that was comforting. Carlo and Maria were gone. The only bedfellow was the beeping and pumping of machines that she was somehow, or another attached to. The euphony of their life sustaining mission was far too evocative of the Macerator's cacophony. Enid felt her heart quicken. She held her chest as if she was consoling a crying child, hoping it would quiet its racket. Between her legs she felt a pop, like a sack bursting and then the gush of warm liquid rushed through her inner thighs. In that instant Enid believed what the nurse had said and panic set in. She knew she would bleed out if she didn't get help. She looked around the foreign room and found the Nurse's call button next to her head. She pressed the button over and over like an impatient pedestrian.

The Nurse walked in casually and Enid did not recognize her. Her hair was down, her skin was darker, her whole build much leaner.

"What is it, sugar?"

"I'm bleeding." Enid squeezed the words through tears. Her throat had locked up. She pointed to her lower half. The Nurse grabbed the covers and pulled them back so quickly that a spray of liquid geysered over her head, narrowly missing her face.

"Oh, your foley line came out. Don't worry doll, it happens. Let me go get some help and we'll get you cleaned up."

The nurse left the covers pulled back keeping Enid's mess on display. Enid mustered the gall to look at it and the color was not what she had expected. Her clinical, white sheets were sopping yellow. The catheter line was actively dripping out at a slow pace. There was no blood.

Bed Rest

Enid rotated her 'spot' weekly. She didn't want to wear out any one seat or get any type of chronic indentation. Plus, the left side of the couch became exciting to her after spending a week in the middle. There was nowhere for her to lean her arms in the middle, so Carlo had built her a throne of pillows, emptying the beds of all their head rests to accommodate his Mother's comfort needs.

While Carlo was at school Maria would stop by occasionally to check on Enid, but her visits had grown fewer and less common. Enid didn't need much. She ate sparingly, showered infrequently, and found herself an expert on a number of daytime television shows.

There was a knock at the door. It was hesitant or dainty, she couldn't tell which, but it was light enough for her to not trust her own perception, so she waited for another round to pull herself from the left side of the couch and answer.

Behind the door was a Woman with long black hair and auburn

highlights. A fresh hair style that could have been a wig. If Enid's attention hadn't gone straight to the large basket in the Woman's hands, she would have recognized her sooner. Enid couldn't believe it. How had Biddy Samuel known? Why, after all this time would she send a basket? All at once a wave of warmth washed over Enid as she felt the faux familial connection, she believed she had established with people that were not her own, grabbing roots again.

"Hey Enid."

"Yes!" Enid could not hide her giddiness.

"You look... good. Healthy. You've put on some weight."

Enid was confused by the courier's comments. She took no offense. How could this woman know one way or another if she had gained...

"Tina!?" It had been almost four months since Enid left the factory. Since even Enid didn't know she was pregnant and never disclosed it to the company they found it to be an acceptable loophole to terminate her. Corporate policy also mandated any worker's comp claim denied and challenged. It would be too long to matter before Enid got any type of financial aid due to her.

"Hey. I, we just wanted to bring you something to help, ya know?

It was messed up that they fought your disability and... anyway. Here." Tina pushed the basket towards Enid who took it like a kid unwrapping clothes on Christmas.

"I thought. Um, I just... Thank you." Enid was stunned. The emotions betrayed her. She was alone in the world again. A single mother with no family. She turned to place the basket on the small kitchen table.

As she did, Tina noticed the reason for Enid's apparent weight gain.

"Oh shit. I'm so sorry. I didn't realize you were knocked up. I guess I should have." Tina's yielding was anything but merciful. She meant it as an empty apology for thinking of Enid as a bad employee.

"It's OK. You couldn't have known. I didn't know."

"Damn, I didn't know you get down like that."

Enid could not hide the embarrassment of Tina thinking she was a "loose woman".

"I don't. I mean, I just thought I was too old. You know?"

"My Auntie got a bun in the oven when she was fifty! Oi, let me tell you, you think it's hard for your body to pull back together in your thirties? When she sits down it's like a pancake. I told my husband if I get pregnant at that age just take me out back and shoot me."

Enid found no succor in Tina's words. Tina noticed.

"But you'll be fine. You're still young." The pause in Tina's cadence gave away her lie. "Well, enjoy the basket. Everyone put something in there, even Ignacio."

Enid looked back at the basket.

"Eggs, of course." Tina concedes. "If you need anything, um, just ya know, reach out."

The pleasantries danced in unison with discomfort. Tina turned away, not knowing what else to say. Halfway down the hall she heard Enid call out her name. Her voice had need and worry attached to it. Tina stopped and walked back to the still open door. Enid stood, legs apart, holding her belly. The floor was covered in amniotic fluid.

"Ay, dios mío." Tina never expected Enid to take her up on the offer.

Begotten

There was too much said and done for Enid to have understood exactly what was happening. "No time…" was what she heard most. Her vision was a constant blurred vignette. Doctors and Nurses in scrubs rushed around her. Once they wheeled her into the operating room her arms had been secured to metal planks. She was the crucified mother. The air that circulated through was cold and biting. The Nurses raised a curtain below Enid's breasts and blocked her view of whatever was going on below. She had a natural birth with Carlo, so all of this was foreign to her.

"You're going to feel some pressure." The voice came from the other side of the curtain and Enid couldn't be sure they were speaking to her. The pressure was intense and drew tears from eyes which she could not wipe because her arms were still restrained. She could smell flesh burning. She looked below the curtain where all she could see was ankles and clogs, the favorite footwear of hospital workers.

While Enid watched the feet shuffle and replace each other's positions a huge puddle of blood splashed on the floor. Not a single voice on the other side of the curtain reacted with any concern, but Enid could not help her panic. She knew it was her blood. She knew it could not be normal. Something was wrong.

"OK, here comes baby."

Enid felt relief physically as the pressure slid out of the incision. She waited for the cry of life but sometimes it takes a few moments for the newborn to wail.

"It's a boy!" The Doctor called out. The next thing Enid heard was urgency.

"She's hemorrhaging."

The beeping of the machines Enid was hooked up to sounded like the chirps of a bin full of chicks ready for the Macerator and it brought mortal dread to Enid as she realized what that meant for her son.

"No! No!" Enid began to scream but the anesthesiologist dosed her with morphine that made her feel like she was falling.

The Lion's Den

The next moments of Enid's consciousness were in transit. She was wheeled out of the operating room and transferred to a different stretcher. Lights and ceiling panels passed at too quick of a pace. The stretcher then barreled through a set of double doors and into a room that was much darker than the hallway. A room Enid found familiar. Gone were the drop ceiling panels and diffused fluorescent lights. The popcorn ceiling had warm lighting that cascaded out across shelves of books. Thestretcher had stopped, and two male Nurses transferred her onto a flat, solid bed. Enid felt nauseous from the drugs and blood loss. She didn't know how many conscious moments she had left.

Enid thought to herself she must be dreaming. Biddy Samuel was standing over Enid, which she knew was impossible. She wished this old haunt would stop. It had been so long since she had seen them, why would the family she never had invade her mind now? There she was, though, standing over Enid with a smile. She tucked a fancy cloth napkin into her collar and bent over Enid as if she was inspecting something of importance.

"Quite the cut, is she not? This one will bear no more."

Enid closed her eyes, wishing to wake from the nightmare, but she could still hear Biddy's voice.

"They say you can taste the anguish of a beast's life in its meat. I always preferred the taste of sorrow."

A collective laughter scared Enid's eyes open. Standing around her were faces she'd seen a lifetime ago. Their teeth were sharpened and needful. Enid knew where she was.

Wires

Marc Schoenbach

In twenty-three years of working homicide, Detective Moretti had never seen somebody in such bad shape that wasn't already dead on the slab.

The girl on the bed stared catatonically at the hospital ceiling, her eyes frozen with a look of unimaginable horror. Her mouth was agape, but no sound emanated from her dry lips.

The detective could tell that the young blonde was once beautiful. But now her frizzy hair did little to cover the countless caterpillar stitches and bruises that marred her swollen face like the stall door of a gas station restroom.

Thick bloodstained gauze bandages wrapped most of her arms, leaving only a slight space in the bend of her elbow. From that crook, a steady flow of maroon coursed through plastic IV tubing which led to a bag of blood hanging from a metal pole.

All but two of her fingers had been wedged into aluminum splints. A hard cast secured her right leg, while a mound of dressing hugged the short nub of what used to be her left leg.

The lingering stench of antiseptic stung Moretti's nostrils as he took a sip of lukewarm coffee from a Styrofoam cup. It was around nine o'clock on Christmas Eve when the detective received the phone call from the hospital.

"Is this Detective Moretti?" the voice on the phone said. Moretti had been working on his second glass of bourbon in his one-bedroom apartment—spending the otherwise meaningless holiday alone—when he coughed into the phone receiver, "Did I win something?" The conversation with Doctor Gladwell was brief and to the point. "The mangled girl you guys found on the road three days ago has just opened her eyes. She isn't talking, but you should be here."

Moretti gulped down the rest of his bourbon before throwing on his olive-green trench coat with the collar drawn up. His bushy auburn mustache barely distracted from his horrible comb-over, but at this point in his life vanity was the last thing on the detective's mind as he floored his 1981 Dodge Diplomat on the snow-slickened road. He arrived at the hospital in just under nine minutes.

The detective had been standing at the catatonic girl's bedside for almost an hour. Nausea and anger splashed around in his belly like a poisonous concoction. No matter how hard he tried, he could not ignore the jarring similarities of his own eight-year-old daughter being hooked up to those same goddamn tubes and wires. It was fifteen years ago when he'd been looking into his little girl's eyes, knowing her battle was coming to an end. He held her hand until her last breath, promising that he would catch the bastard who did this to her.

But vengeance never came and the sick fuck who'd raped and stabbed his little angel in the neck with a broken beer bottle ended up hanging himself in his own closet.

He tried to be strong for Sarah, desperate to convince her that bad things just happened—that life didn't make sense, that it wasn't supposed to, but that everything happened for a reason.

"And just what the hell would be the reason for some random psychopath to have kidnapped and butchered our little baby?" His wife's final words replayed in his brain like a tired song at a dingy dive bar.

Moretti was just a rookie when Sarah packed her suitcase and his naïve idea that justice would always somehow triumph over evil faded quicker than the air from his dying daughter's lungs.

Back at the catatonic girl's bedside, Moretti's throat began to tighten when suddenly a wave of horror flashed across the girl's eyes. Her body jolted upright from the bed. Flailing her arms, she screamed, "I don't know who you are!"

Then, as quickly as it all happened, she fell back against her pillow in silence.

"What just happened there?" Moretti asked. "Who don't you know?" But the girl did not respond.

Moretti inhaled deeply. "My name is Detective Moretti." He gestured behind him with a steel click pen. "And this here is my partner,

Detective Ross."

A second man loomed behind Moretti. He too had a mustache, although it was black and much thinner despite his thick curly hair. He was wearing a dull brown suit and navy-blue tie. He held a grey cassette recorder with a small microphone attached to it.

"We should officially get started," Detective Ross said into the microphone. "It's Sunday, December twenty-fourth, nineteen eighty-nine.

The time is approximately ten-thirty p.m. We're here at Charity Grove

Medical Center—"

"Detectives," a warm nurturing female voice beckoned from the other side of the bed.

Nurse Wendy, a middle-aged African American woman, stood in front of a small Christmas tree on the ledge of a curtained window. Its string of colored lights bathed her white uniform in a warm glow. "Maybe start out slow. I'd hate to see you two frighten her." The nurse adjusted her cap.

"I don't think we're the ones frightening her," Ross said.

Just then Doctor Gladwell rushed in from the hallway. "It's okay, Wendy. They're here to help," he said, tugging on the lapels of his white lab coat.

Moretti shook his head with displeasure. "You were in a coma for the past three days. Are you able to tell me your name?"

A tear ran down the young girl's cheek as her cracked lips parted, leaving a trickle of blood dripping down her chin. Her strained voice sounded like wet rusty nails. "No."

Wendy quickly tended to the girl, rubbing a thin layer of Vaseline on her bloodied lips.

"What's the last thing you remember?" Moretti asked.

The young girl just stared at the detectives.

"Look, honey," Ross chimed in. "There's a madman on the loose—"

"Can you remember anything at all?" Moretti continued.

"What happened to my leg?" the girl groaned.

Moretti turned to Doctor Gladwell. The white-haired doctor leaned forward. "You've had multiple lacerations and fractures. We tried everything we could to save your left leg but the hypothermia was too severe. You've lost a substantial amount of blood, to which we're giving you a transfusion as we speak. But as serious as your condition is I assure you, we're going to do everything we can to make sure you make a full recovery."

The doctor began to walk away but stopped at the room's door.

"Detectives, I'm giving you ten minutes. But I don't think you're going to learn anything new tonight." Then he disappeared into the hallway.   Moretti was more than eager to accept the challenge. He cleared his throat and clicked his pen. "Now I know you can do this. A moment ago, you jumped up from that bed and screamed that you didn't know someone.

Who don't you know?"

The girl shook her head. But Moretti was determined. "Where were you?"

"I don't know," the girl stammered. "I had my arms outstretched over my head. It was dark. And it was cold."

"Three nights ago, a trucker found you lying in the middle of Platte Clove Road," Moretti said.

"Said it looked like you got torn apart by a grizzly bear," Ross added. "But the doctors here say an animal didn't do this to you." Just then Moretti wanted to shout, *"Whoever did this to her most certainly was a goddamned animal!"* Instead he took a sip of coffee, pinched the wetness from his mustache, and said, "By the time they got you outta there, you had lost almost four liters of blood. Any idea who might have done this to you?"

The girl shook her head.

"They found four hooks and eye bolts screwed into both of your shoulders," Moretti was reading from his notepad. "They removed eleven screws from your arms and legs. Looked like maybe piano wire or something was used to bind you."

"Was it more than one person? Did you get a good look at any of their faces?" Ross shook the microphone.

"We were able to follow your track marks in the snow for about a mile. I got my guys combing the area like fleas on a stray mongrel, but we're coming up short." Moretti ran his fingers through his thinning hair.

"Were you sexually assaulted?" Ross asked.

"Look, she can't remember anything." Nurse Wendy adjusted her skirt in frustration.

Moretti waved the nurse away with his pen. "Look, I know it's hard. But I need you to try to remember. Because if you don't, I'm afraid a lot of other girls are going to end up—"

"Okay, that's enough!" Wendy pulled off her nurse's cap and slapped the back of her own hand with it. "You two should be ashamed of yourselves."

"Maybe you better step outside," Ross shook an empty Styrofoam cup at the nurse. "I can use a fresh one."

"I'll take a refill too. Black, four sugars." Moretti rubbed his brow, his head beginning to throb.

Suddenly the girl turned towards the window and stared at the Christmas tree lights.

Wendy scurried to the bed. "Lord have mercy, hasn't this poor girl been through enough?" She reached up and grabbed the green privacy curtain, her knuckles tensing. She began sliding the curtain across the tracks when the girl lifted her head from her pillow.

"I was hiking," she said. "And that's when he grabbed me."

**

Hank Lee Gaskins' heart swelled with the Yuletide spirit as he sat at the head of the long mahogany table. Dressed in his grey wool suit with suede elbow pads, he gazed at his seven family members gathered around the magnificent Christmas Eve feast.

The private dining room epitomized elegance with its gold and red Victorian wallpaper. The floral damask pattern crawled up the walls toward a stunning chandelier—one with crystal teardrop pendants that hung from a ten-foot ceiling.

The Lenox China dinnerware—engraved with illustrations of

hollies and red ribbon—caught the brilliant reflection of the flickering green candlesticks that were at either end of the table. The polished silverware twinkled while the crystal glasses gleamed under the chandelier's warm ambience.

But the meal itself was the real showstopper.

The glazed turkey glistened in succulent juices with sprigs of fragrant evergreens as garnish. Steam rose like playful children from porcelain dishes of candied yams, mashed potatoes, cranberry stuffing, and steamed vegetables shimmering with butter. Mounds of freshly baked loaves of bread were nestled in a wicker basket swathed in white linen. An array of cheese and fig jams sat on an ornate silver tray.

From an adjoining archway that led into a cozy living room glowing by the flickering light of a crackling fireplace, Hank's six-month old daughter was being soothed in her bassinet by Nat King Cole's warm caramel voice oozing from a record player.

Hank turned to his wife Heather to the right of him and was instantly spellbound by her beauty.

Her auburn hair was done up in a round bouffant and her makeup hadn't looked this wonderful since their wedding night.

Her green polka dot cocktail dress hugged her hourglass figure just right.

She took a bite of turkey, trying her best not to smear her red lipstick. Feeling Hank's gaze, she covered her mouth with her palm. "Is something the matter?" she asked.

"Nothing can ever be the matter as long as I have my loving family with me." Hank's chest grew warm. He could feel his throat swell with joy.

"Good," Heather said, wiping the corners of her lips with a green cloth napkin. "But you don't have to gawk at me for so long. I'm not going anywhere."

God, if only that were true, Hank thought. He knew Heather was only being sweet, that it was in her nature to say such things. But to promise that she would always be there felt as fragile as the porcelain dishes at the table.

Hank's heart began to ache. He calmed himself by observing the rest of his family.

To his left was Brandon, his sixteen-year-old son, who, despite his awkward lanky body and shaggy hair, was adored by all the girls at Hudson High. Hank was proud to say that his son's love life never interfered with his grades and when the time came, the boy could go to any Ivy League school he chose.

"I sure am going to miss these home cooked meals when I graduate." Brandon shoved a heap of mashed potatoes into his mouth.

"I would hope you'd come and visit for the holidays," Heather sneered at the boy.

Next to his son, Hank's twin eight-year-old daughters, Brianna and Bellamy—dressed in matching lavender Peter Pan dresses—were running their tiny fingers across the velvet tablecloth, watching the red fabric morph into a lighter shade of pink.

"It's like magic," the girls giggled in unison, flashing their adorable toothless smiles.

Across from the twins were Heather's youngest sister Sheila, and her husband, Roman, who was being a great sport about not smoking his briar pipe at the table. The couple had been drinking enough merlot that Roman's tired jokes and inane puns seemed as fresh as the juicy turkey they'd been devouring.

"I don't suppose you two little cuties heard about the forecast for tomorrow?" Roman tilted a glass of wine to his lips.

The twins shook their heads.

"They're calling for rain, dear!" Roman tried to keep a straight face, but when Sheila gently punched him in the shoulder, he lost it.

Hank's brother-in-law barked like a seal and soon the entire table succumbed to the absurdity. A cacophony of laughter filled the dining room.

Hank wanted to laugh. But a force he did not fully understand began to stir in him, as it often did whenever he felt great moments of joy. The dreadful feeling of guilt coursed through his blood like an infectious disease.

The disease of *Loneliness*.

The word itself felt like a force eternally looming over his shoulder. Like Death itself, its sickle of isolation poised to strike at any moment, screaming, *"Hank, you do not deserve to be happy!"*

Hank stared at the sliced turkey on his plate. But he could not rid his mind of the intrusive thoughts.

The *darkness*. The *isolation*.

His windpipe began to constrict, and his heart rattled behind his ribcage.

He remembered how she made him feel. His own goddamn mother. So unloving, so cruel.

His knuckles went white as he gripped the tablecloth, the memories of his childhood crushing him like a falling boulder.

She locked him in that godforsaken cellar for weeks at a time with not even a stale crumb to nibble on. His stomach howled in agony in the cold, damp darkness as the spiders and cockroaches crawled over his naked body.

And so, he ate the little critters, their wiry legs tickling his dry lips as their thoraxes slid down his throat, suppressing his hunger at last.

But that wasn't the worst part.

The creeping, impending isolation somehow tortured him more than all the beatings, the burnings, the humiliations, the eating of those filthy insects. Because when he was alone in that awful dungeon, he was allowed to think, and his own thoughts could drive him to madness.

But then one night he discovered *Herman*.

The pitiful wooden marionette puppet had been discarded in the corner behind a stack of old detective magazines years ago, its face covered in strands of cobwebs and dust.

Hank held up the puppet, rank with dampness and rot. It didn't take long to untangle the brittle strings and figure out how to work its arms and legs. Soon, Hank was making Herman walk, talk, jump, and dance until he and his new friend fell asleep laughing.

As long as he had Herman, Hank knew that he would never again feel The Reaper's blade of loneliness pressed against his throat. That was until his mother found the thing and threw it into the fireplace. *"No son of mine is going to be playing with dolls,"* she cackled as Herman's body curled up like a matchstick.

The clink of Hank's trembling fork against his plate shook him back to the present. He gasped for air.

"Hank!" Heather grabbed her husband's wrist. "You're turning blue!"

Hank was huffing and puffing like a steam engine, his brow beaded with sweat. "It's fine—I'm fine." Hank wiped his brow, his breathing stabilizing. "It's just that I love you all so much. And when I start to think about it, I get overwhelmed with such joy that it's hard to breathe."

"Well, good. But you've hardly eaten a thing," Heather said. Hank saw his family smiling at him with tender eyes. "I'm just so happy you're all here to celebrate this lovely Christmas Eve with me. I love you all."

"We love you too, Dad," Brendan smirked, a mouthful of buttered bread in his mouth.

Brianna and Bellamy flashed their toothless grins and cheered,

"We love you, Daddy!"

Roman was quick to hoist up his wine glass. "I'll drink to that!" to which Sheila joked, "You'd drink to anything." Then her face straightened, and she nodded at her brother-in-law. "But seriously, we love you, Hank." *"But we're not all here are we, Hank?"* A familiar voice like muddy gravel echoed from the opposite end of the table.

Hank's eyes widened at the sight of his eighty-four-year-old mother seated directly across from him, her ashen grey wasp nest hair glowing underneath the chandelier.

"Mother?" Hank's jaw went slack. Had his mother been there the whole time?

With a gnarled boney finger Mrs. Gaskins pointed to an empty chair next to her. An undisturbed place setting sat in front it.

"Your *other* daughter should be here," the old woman croaked. "Where is she, Hank?"

**

The snow crunching underneath the SWAT team officers' boots echoed in the stillness of night to the tune of stampeding bulls over a pile of crushed bones.

The officers scavenged the woods donned in their tactical gear and helmets. Curved ice axes hung from their belts as their assault weapons mounted with flashlights sliced through the dense forest, casting long ghastly shadows across the frozen ground.

Detective Moretti lumbered twenty feet in tow, a cigarette nub dangling from his cracked lips. He was a city cop, and his awkward, burly body had no business for this kind of terrain.

The cold wind snuck through his trench coat, making his lungs feel like they'd been stabbed by a hot butcher's blade. A mixture of smoke and moist breath poured from his mouth like a boiling teakettle. And though the lactic acid was searing his quadriceps to a mushy pulp, Moretti was determined to catch this sick sonovabitch, even if it killed him.

For the past two hours, the team from Grove County had been trekking through the dangerous icy terrain of *Devil's Kitchen*—a bastardized region of Saugerties, New York—in search of *"rows of gigantic white monster fangs that protruded from a mountain."*

It wasn't much help, Moretti realized, but it was the only landmark the girl from the hospital could remember.

"Remind me again why we couldn't just get the choppers out here." Detective Ross stomped at Moretti's side, a pair of tinted amber snow goggles shielding his eyes from the cold wind.

"It isn't enough I have to hear this shit from Rambo up there, now

I gotta hear it from you too?" Moretti motioned with a gloved hand to Commander Dempsey, the man in charge of the SWAT team. The yellow haired Irish commander had been busting Moretti's balls the minute he'd been told the two detectives would be accompanying the special tactics team on the hunt. *"I don't care how brutal this hike is gonna be,"* Moretti had shouted into the commander's face at headquarters after receiving the expedited search warrant from a weary judge. *"I want to be there to see the look on his goddamn face when we nail him!"*

Moretti hawked a wad of phlegm onto the ground and was surprised to see that bits of his lungs hadn't come up with it. He turned to Ross. "Besides, this guy hears choppers and he's running; it'd take weeks for us to find this creep in these fucking woods."

Under normal circumstances, Saugerties was a beautiful region of the Catskill Mountains, just over a hundred miles north of the city. With sprawling hills of pine and maple, and gullies etched into the earth by running waters, it was the kind of place you took your family in the fall to watch the leaves change color. A perfect vacation spot with your spouse for a relaxing afternoon of wine tasting.

But the upstate woods had trails less travelled. And tonight, under the asylum of a moonless winter sky, Devil's Kitchen was living up to its name. A frozen hellish abyss where black trees guarded the forest like menacing sentinels. Where razor sharp boulders tore flesh from bones. Where one careless step on slippery pine needles could send you over a cliff, plummeting you to your death.

"How many hikers have gone missing here?" Ross asked as he slid on a patch of pine needles.

"A lot," Moretti grumbled. While he wasn't entirely familiar with the area, he'd heard countless stories about hikers who vanished. It had been assumed they had all fallen, their bodies lost and decomposing in the vast woods. But that didn't stop the detective's mind from wondering back to a story his grandfather once told him about *The Kitchen.*

Moretti was just a kid when he heard about the horned creature that slaughtered hunters and lost hikers.

Legend had it that the abysmal creature climbed high in the trees looking for anyone unwise enough to get too close to the cliffs. Without warning, it'd leap off branches, revealing its awful hairy body—all eight feet of it—before hurling its victims over the edge. The foul thing would then scale down the mountain where its disfigured meal awaited. Locals claimed that if the creature pushed you off the cliff, you'd better pray you died on impact, for there was no sound quite as horrifying as the screaming from being eaten alive by the Devil himself.

Even as a frightened child, Moretti swore to his grandfather that when he got older, he'd catch and kill the damned Devil once and for all. But that was a long time ago. And Moretti knew his grandfather's monster was just folklore.

The thing that Moretti and his team were hunting tonight, however, was no fairytale.

He was as real as the trees and frozen snow. A man—if you could call him that—whose soul had been scorched black as coal. And just like the lunatic who had taken his little girl from him all those years ago, there could be no redemption for such a vile being. The only cure was to either lock him up and melt the key or snuff out the bastard entirely with a barrage of hot lead.

"The next thing I knew, he had my arms outstretched over my head..."

Moretti remembered the one-legged girl from the hospital sobbing, *"...and that's when he pulled out the power drill and a spool of wire."*

The thought sent a chill up Moretti's back, and for the first time since the long dreadful hike began, he felt the Devil's presence in The Kitchen. *"I begged him to stop—that I just wanted to go home—but he kept telling me this was my home now."*

The pain in Moretti's legs slithered up his lower spine like a snake made of razor wire. He winced, but he knew he could not stop moving. That poor girl didn't stop even when she was gushing blood from all her limbs. His own daughter's smiling face flashed in his mind once more. "This son of a bitch is going to pay," Moretti rasped, his throat dry as a desert.

"I wasn't the only one... There were others he kidnapped... He

drills holes into them," the girl's voice howled in Moretti's brain like the artic wind. *"Then he takes the wires..."*

"Halt!" Commander Dempsey shouted, his clenched fist punching the air. The SWAT members froze before the foot of an impossibly steep cliff.

Moretti's stomach sank as he watched the team anchor rappel rope onto the rocks. One by one, each team member clipped to the line and repelled down the hill with ease.

When the last SWAT member had successfully made it to the bottom, Dempsey kneeled and took hold of the rope. He looked up at Moretti and flashed an obnoxious red-faced grin.

"Should we send a unit to pick you two up?" Dempsey laughed, repelling down the hill with the skill of a mountain lion.

Now it was Moretti and Ross's turn. "Jesus," McMillian groaned when he'd reached the foot of the cliff and looked down. The SWAT members huddled in formation about seventy feet below.

"What's the matter, you afraid of heights?" Dempsey's shrill voice shouted.

Moretti yanked off one of his gloves. Then he buried his hand inside his trench coat and pulled out a steel flask. With a flick of his wrist, he spun the cap off, sending it sailing over the edge of the cliff in silence before it made a high-pitched clink at the bottom. He took a swig, but the bourbon did little to calm his nerves.

"We can go down together." Ross was kneeling at the foot of the cliff.

"Just get your ass down there and don't worry about me," Moretti snarled.

Moretti watched Ross rappel effortlessly down the mountain with as much skill as the SWAT team.

"Okay, boss, I got you!" Ross shouted from below.

There was no sense in stalling another minute. Time was not on their side and if what the girl from the hospital said was true, then this nut was most likely firing up his power drill to do God knows what to his other victims.

Moretti hiked up his trousers at the crotch and got down on all fours. His knees responded with a loud pop. Using the clip that Dempsey had supplied everyone, Moretti secured himself to the rope. He didn't descend nearly as smoothly as the others, his body swaying like a broken yo-yo, thrashing into the jagged rocks with the force of a wrecking ball. His bones ached but he kept his composure by singing *"We Wish You A Merry Fucking Christmas"* until, finally, he had made it to the bottom.

Unclipping himself from the rappel line, Moretti looked over at Ross who had been standing by Dempsey and the rest of the SWAT team on a series of large rocks. Their flashlights were trained on a huge wall of glistening white stalagmites.

It took a moment for Moretti's eyes to focus but he soon realized that the sharp pointed spikes embedded in the mountain had once been waterfalls that were now completely frozen over. And it was at that moment that a tinge of excitement warmed his belly better than any bourbon could.

"Well," Moretti said, "looks like we found our *gigantic white monster fangs.*"

"Now what?" Dempsey patted the butt of his rifle.

Without responding, Moretti ran to the highest rock formation he could find. He stood a good eight feet above the rest of the officers as he waved his flashlight in every direction.

And that's when he saw it.

Hidden beneath dense brush, ice glistened off the caved-in roof of a small, dilapidated cabin one hundred yards away.

Moretti lit a cigarette and blew out the smoke with weary pleasure. "Let's go wish this son of a bitch a merry Christmas."

**

"Well?" Mrs. Gaskins said, drumming her boney fingers on the table. "Why isn't your other daughter here?"

Hank stared at the empty place setting. He was biting his lip so hard it began to bleed. "Mother, I told you on the phone; she went away to school and because of the inclement weather she could not make it here this evening."

"The rain dear," Roman added dryly, this time without any hint of humor in his voice.

"Is that so, Hank? You want to blame the weather?" Mrs. Gaskins' thin lips curled upwards, revealing a mouthful of rust-colored teeth stained with lipstick.

Hank was digging his fingernails into the tablecloth when a knock at the front door rattled the dishes on the table.

"Maybe that's her now." Mrs. Gaskins pulled her cashmere sweater closed.

Hank's heart pounded like a hammer forging steel.

Heather looked to her husband, her face pale as a ghost. "Could that be her, Hank? Has she come home?"

Hank's mouth was agape. His vision began to blur and he felt lightheaded.

"I don't know," he said. But Hank knew. Deep in his trembling heart, he knew it could not be his daughter—would *never* again be his daughter at the front door.

A second knock shook the house. As it did, the chandelier began to flicker, the crystal teardrop pendants quivering like a child locked in a cellar.

"Looks like a storm is brewing alright." Roman took a puff from his now-lit briar pipe, a plume of cherry tobacco smoke rising in front of his face like a wavering ghost.

"I'm scared," Brianna and Bellamy said, throwing their arms up, hiding their blanched faces behind their palms.

A third blast at the door sounded like the wooden frame had splintered into a million pieces. With it, Nat King Cole's voice from the other room screeched like knives on a tin roof. When the record needle found its groove again, it began to play in slow motion, this time ominously in reverse.

"Well, aren't you going to answer it?" Mrs. Gaskins asked. The candles on the table blew out, sending wisps of smoke towards the ceiling. The room had grown cold and dark, the warmth from the fireplace snuffed out from all the turmoil. Hank sighed, his blue breath now visible in front of him.

"What have you done?" Heather moaned.

Hank's eyes went wide. Heather's swollen tongue lolled out of her mouth like a dead rodent, the whites of her once sparkling green eyes now engorged in busted capillaries. Her hair resembled filthy matted wool. Mascara dripped down her bruised face like wet tar. Her neck was encroached with purple black splotches.

"I don't suppose just sitting there is going to be much help." Mrs. Gaskins cut into a piece of turkey on her plate that had a cockroach crawling on it.

A fourth bang at the door sent dishes crashing to the floor while the chandelier swung even more violent. The teardrop pendants snapped off their chains and rained down onto the table in a hailstorm. Wine exploded from shattered glasses like bursts of blood from gunshot wounds.

"Who are you?" Brandon screamed, grabbing hold of Hank's wrist.

"Why are you doing this to us?"

Hank jerked his arm away from his son's grasp and stared at the boy's shaggy hair in horror.

The teenager's scalp had been torn open like a stuffed animal. The boy held up a broken finger and pointed to his exposed brain, steam rising from the viscid tissue. "Why?" Brandon screamed.

The thunderous crack of a fifth knock shook the wooden foundation of the house. In that instant, the gold and red wallpaper began to peal from the walls and curl inward like silk ribbon on fire.

"I think we better get going now, Roman." Sheila's head tilted towards the half empty glass of merlot in her hand. Dried green vomit encrusted her chin and neck. But the real terror was the look in her eyes— or rather, the lack thereof. Where her brown eyes once rested were now empty black sockets in a gaunt face.

"Roman?" Hank's voice quivered as he witnessed with revulsion of what was left of his brother-in-law's jaw. Flaps of loose skin dangled off the broken bone and hung pathetically from strings of bloody sinew.

"We want to go home," the twins cried hysterically, removing their hands from their mutilated faces. "We want our mommy."

"But..." Hank struggled to find the words. "This is your home now."

In one final knock, the front door exploded, and a swarm of men with helmets and guns stormed inside. Beams from their flashlights sliced through the cold darkness until, finally, they bathed Hank in light.

**

"Police! Nobody fucking move!" Commander Dempsey charged

into the dark cabin, the search warrant secured to the barrel of his gun like a battle flag. The rest of the SWAT officers followed; their guns poised for combat.

Moretti staggered in, his .38 Special trained in front of his chest. Immediately his nose stung from a cloying stench of decay that cut through the frigid air like toxic fog. Dempsey and the officers stopped abruptly, their mouths snapping open in silent terror.

"Holy Mother, Mary of God, what is it, Moretti?" Dempsey's voice trembled as he struggled to keep his beam of light on his target. "What the fuck is it?"

Moretti's heart pounded in his chest like a death drum. His eyes wide and unblinking, he stared at the dismal scene.

The corpses were seated around a decrepit makeshift wooden table covered in frost. Their decaying faces frozen in profound agony. Rotted carrion and moldy cheese on grimy rusted dishes adorned the table.   "We got a baby..." Detective Ross stumbled over to a dilapidated bassinet in the corner of the cramped cabin. He looked inside of it before immediately pulling off his snow goggles. Then he vomited.

"Everyone stay calm!" Moretti ordered.

"I give the orders," Dempsey fired back, but his voice lacked any real authority as he noticed the old, withered newspaper clippings tacked to the walls.

"HIKER AND INFANT VANISH FROM DEVIL'S KITCHEN"; "STILL NO TRACE Of TEENAGED BOY WHO DISAPPEARED IN THE KITCHEN BACK IN 87' "; "POLICE EXPECT FOUL PLAY IN TWINS' MYSTERIOUS DISAPPEARANCE IN SAUGERTIES."

Back at the wooden table, a female corpse was wearing a 1950s cocktail dress, her straggly hair spreading over her putrid skeletal face like old cotton. A second lanky corpse—presumably male in its tattered sweater—was propped crookedly across from it, its dusty grey skull split open like a broken clock.

Two other rotting corpses sat at the table, their boney fingers twisted around wine glasses brimming with a murky crimson liquid that was swirling with sediment. A wooden smoking pipe dangled from the protruding jaw of one of the corpses.

Bile boiled in Moretti's stomach. There were two smaller corpses— most likely children—wearing matching ragged pink dresses covered in cobwebs. From the look of the grey taut skin over their tiny arms, they'd been dead for at least several years.

A seventh and final corpse had its back to the officers. It appeared to be the most ancient and was secured to a wooden chair with nails and screws. A threadbare cashmere sweater draped the dust-covered skeleton like a witch's cloak.

Just to the right of the rotting skeleton, a broken chair spattered with dried blood lay on its side.

Moretti knew whom that chair was intended for. And for the briefest of moments, he felt a meager sense of comfort knowing the girl from the hospital had managed to escape this abysmal dinner party from hell.

Moretti's eyes flashed to the far end of the table where the only living person sat—presumably the host of this morbid affair.

The frail emotionless man rested his bloodstained hands in front of him. He wore a withered wool suit two sizes too small and his greasy unkempt hair shaped his narrow face. A power drill coated in sinew lay next to a plate of rotting meat.

"Alright, get your hands up in the air. Slowly." Moretti shook his revolver in the man's direction.

The man squinted from the flashlights' beams before eventually drifting back to his blank gaze.

"He said get your fucking hands in the air!" Dempsey screamed.

The man slowly began to raise his hands above his head. As he did, the corpses themselves extended their own rickety arms into the air in vile synchronicity.

A loud gasp flooded the room in a swell of shared panic as the SWAT officers cowered back, clumsily tripping over their own boots.

"They're alive!"

Dempsey cried out, his trigger finger trembling.

"No, they're not." The burning bile in Moretti's stomach swam up to his throat as he stared at the lunatic in front of him.

The man's fingers had been wrapped in thin metal wire, like a puppeteer. It extended above him and over crisscrossed wooden rafters in the dilapidated ceiling. From these rafters, the wires continued downward like spider's silk, attaching to hook and eye bolts drilled into the corpses' appendages. Above the bloody chair that had been knocked over, the wires had been severed. They dangled above it like steel tendrils encrusted in bits of flesh.

"He kept saying he was so proud to be my father," The hospital girl's voice echoed in Moretti's head as he stared at the metal wires.

"I kept screaming that that I didn't even know who he was. Then I ripped myself off those fucking wires."

Suddenly the corpse in the 1950s dress began to twitch, its arm slowly descending until its boney fingers began to grope the table in front of it.

Moretti's eyes flashed wide, the puppeteer's hand mimicking the same gesture as his filthy hands reached for the power drill.

In the next instant a deafening barrage of gunfire tore through the puppeteer's body. He thrashed violently, the corpses flailing in deathly unison.

Then as quickly as it had happened, the room returned to an eerie muteness.

"Jesus fucking Christ!" Dempsey stared in horror at the acrid smoke pouring from the barrel of Moretti's gun.

The puppeteer slumped lifelessly in his chair, his arms hanging limply at his sides. His corpse family imitated the lifeless gesture, their skeleton arms dangling from their rotted joints.

Snow was beginning to fall gently from the cracks in the caved-in ceiling as Moretti's daughter's smiling face flashed in his mind.

Bundled in her winter coat and hat with the pink pom poms, he and his daughter were putting the finishing touches on the four-foot snowman in their backyard.

"Do you think snowmen come alive when no one is looking?" his little girl asked as Moretti guided his daughter's hand to place the frozen carrot in the snowman's face. Moretti turned to Sarah who smiled back from the patio, sipping hot cocoa from a Santa Clause mug.

"What did you just do?" Dempsey stared in revulsion at the dead puppeteer slouched in his chair.

A perfect calmness warmed Moretti like a heated blanket as he thought about the promise, he had made to his grandfather all those years ago.

"I killed the Devil," he said.

The Cheap Rooms

Robert Essig

The carpets were severely stained and coming apart at the seams, patched intermittently with mismatched pieces of equal neglect. The walls complemented the carpets with scuffs and mysterious splatter: perhaps a spilled drink (it was Vegas after all), or . . . something else. But Haloran and Stephanie Watts were celebrating their fourth anniversary and didn't have the kind of money that could afford them a stay at a place like Caesar's or even the Flamingo, and they had promised themselves that they would get a room in a hotel at the center of the Strip.

With their budget they purchased the most inexpensive room they could get, which turned out to be in the old Imperial Hotel. Located at the rear of the lot behind the parking structure and a less than charming alleyway. Back in the old days it was called the Sand Dune Inn. Several lots were purchased, and the Imperial Hotel was erected, towering over the diminutive Sand Dune Inn, which was owned by the Imperial, but never held to the same laughable standards.

"Man, I knew the Imperial was run down, but this is too much," Haloran said.

Stephanie smirked. "Let's just hope there aren't any bedbugs and weird stains on the sheets."

They rounded a corner, scanning the room numbers for 519.

"Of course, we might make some stains of our own on the sheets," Haloran said.

Stephanie gave him a playful grin. "We'll just have to see about that."

As they took to the hall, they were both startled not only that there was a housekeeper standing there with her cart of linens, soaps, and cleaning materials who may have heard the soiled sheets comment, but by the fact that she was staring at them with one eye. It wouldn't have been quite as strange had she been wearing an eye patch. But she chose to brazenly walk the halls displaying a rather gruesome cavity of scarred flesh. The scars traveled down the left side of her face onto her neck, disappearing beneath the collar of her uniform.

Haloran nudged Stephanie to keep walking. They had both slowed like lookie-loos passing a wreck on the highway. The housekeeper turned after grabbing several towels and walked into the room she was cleaning.

"Jesus," Stephanie whispered.

"I guess working as a housekeeper is a good thing for someone with those kinds of scars. Don't have to deal with the public. Much. Here it is." Haloran stopped so abruptly that Stephanie bumped into him. She had her head turned, looking down the hall where the woman had been.

"Jesus, Hal!"

"Don't want to pass it up, do we? This place is like a freaking maze."

With a swipe of the key card, they were in. The interior surprised them in that it was much cleaner than the hallway. Only mild stains here and there on the linens and a sprinkling of black mold on the bathroom ceiling. Could be worse.

Haloran plopped his suitcase on the bed furthest from the door (they didn't sleep in the same bedroom at home due to Haloran's snoring, and having two beds was as close to her not being kept awake all night as they could get). He pulled out a bottle of good whiskey (a gift from his father) and they toasted their anniversary.

After a few drinks, Stephanie touched up her makeup and they headed for the odd smelling yet compelling Las Vegas Boulevard.

Slot machines had a way of draining wallets, but Hal and Stephanie knew their limit. They preferred to drop their money on drinks and good food and had already purchased tickets to a burlesque magic show for the following night. It wasn't really what they wanted to see, but there was a great buy-one-get-one-free deal that they couldn't resist. After making their way back through the maze of mismatched carpet and threadbare rugs, they laughed at the conspicuous stains in the halls before slipping into their room where they sipped more whiskey and made love, after which they went to sleep on opposite sides of each bed—Hal's snoring and all. But they'd had enough drink to fall victim to the sandman, easy enough to prevent Stephanie the tortures of his log sawing.

They had a lot planned for the next two nights. The magic show, a fantastic dinner buffet at the MGM they'd heard good things about gambling, people watching.

But none of that happened.

Stephanie's eyes were still gluey from a knockout combo of alcohol and dreams when a disturbance roused her from a deep sleep. Could have been anything in a city that never slept. There were drunks out from dusk till dawn and then till dusk again, and they had the propensity to stumble down hallways and into walls, searching for their rooms and even trying their keycards in the wrong doors.

But this sound was something different.

It was in the room.

Stephanie turned to face Haloran when the sound again issued through the darkness. It was like ruffling sheets, but not the kind of ruffling that resulted from a shifty sleeper.

A whimper?

She had been listening more than looking, trying to keep her eyes closed so she could slip back into sleep effortlessly. But it became clear that she'd better get her bearings, so she opened her eyes. It took a moment to adjust to the dark of the room, and when she did, she had to squint to make heads or tails of what she was seeing in the bed next to hers.

Stephanie bolted upright, yet something caused her to refrain from planting her feet on the floor. Maybe it was childhood fears of the boogey man, or maybe something else.

She stared at Haloran wide-eyed. Something was shoved into his mouth, gagging him. He trembled, sweat beading on his forehead and glistening with the faint light coming in where the blinds were parted. He was restrained with some kind of rope or leather straps.

Stephanie yelped as she jumped out of bed to her husband's aid. He had wild, terror-stricken eyes. The whimpering sounds grew more frantic as the breaths from his nostrils accelerated with rising adrenalin. Then the whimpers hit agonizing and muffled crescendos. His eyes closed tightly, becoming filled with tears that spilled down his face mixing with his sweat.

Mouth agape, lower jaw trembling, Stephanie assessed the situation, doing her best to remain in control. She grabbed the sweaty piece of tape that held the ball gag in Hal's mouth and yanked. He yelped and grimaced. "Jesus it hurts!" he said through clenched teeth. "My back! It hurts!"

"What happened? How did this...?"

Haloran shook his head. "I don't know."

He clenched his eyes again, sucking air through his teeth as pain assaulted him.

"What's wrong, Hal? Can you move?"

"Feels like something's biting me. Cut the straps. Get me out of here."

There wasn't much in their hotel room in the way of cutting utensils. Stephanie frantically checked the stationary desk and her purse for not only a cutting utensil, but her phone as well. Haloran sobbed and cringed from some kind of assault that she couldn't see. She feared that when she cut the straps, he wouldn't be able to move. That somehow, he'd become paralyzed.

"My pants pocket," Hal said.

"My pocketknife."

In a flash of movement, Stephanie retrieved the pocketknife and began cutting the straps that were fixed on something beneath the bed. They wrapped around her husband's frame and reattached on the opposite side. After all the straps were severed and the pressure was relieved, Haloran sat up, which should have been a relief considering Stephanie's fear of his potential paralysis. But something far worse was at play, something that dropped her heart into her bowel and seemed to draw out all the air in her lungs.

Hal's sudden scream was agonizing. It was pain vocalized; fear realized. Stephanie had never heard her man in such a desperate fit. She'd never heard him scream like a frightened child, and that alone chilled her to the core. But what she saw next drove the proverbial ice-pick chill through her heart.

Haloran's face was a shellac of sweat, his eyes and jaw clenched so tightly he looked like a weightlifter attempting to break his max. Then she saw his back. The bed was a mess of torn sheets, blood and gore. His back looked much the same, glistening and red, with stringy muscle and tendons on display. The worst part of the mad spectacle was the implements that held him to the bed. What appeared to be arms protruding from within the mattress. They grabbed onto the shredded ribbons of flesh, little fingers grasping for the solid column of his red, wet spine.

Stephanie took a few steps back until she bumped into the other bed.

"Get them off me!" Haloran screamed.

He struggled to remain upright, the arms attempting to pull him onto the bed again. Stephanie grabbed the old wooden chair from the stationary desk and used it like a lion tamer from the old days. Holding it from the back with both hands she started swinging. She hit one of the strange arms. It dinged metallically as the wooden legs of the chair made contact. The arms began to shake Haloran's body, eliciting further screams and pleas of agony.

Then something emerged from the pool of blood on the mattress. It was a face, smooth and flawless yet hideous and bestial, red with Haloran's blood. The eyes looked straight ahead at Haloran's back, then shifted toward Stephanie. She recoiled, and then the face emerged from the bloody bed, dug its massive maw onto Haloran's destroyed back, latching onto his spine, and yanked him down.

Blood splattered from the puddle as Hal's body hit the tattered sheets, decorating Stephanie with red spatter. She trembled, forced to watch as her husband's body was pulled into the cavity of the bed where the arms and vile sculpted face had protruded.

Snapping out of the terror-daze she'd been submerged in, she grabbed Haloran's arms trying to pull him free. But the horrors beneath pulled him from her grasp and into the bloody pit.

The room was silent with the exception of Stephanie's cries and the bubbling blood pool in the bed. She dared not reach into the muck for fear that one of the arms would reach out and pull her in.

He's gone. I can't believe he's gone.

But beyond the sudden and inexplicable death of her husband, there was something mad and unexplainable in the hotel. Something Stephanie's mind could not register or even attempt to comprehend. And it was in their room. Seething within the gory pool at the center of the bed Haloran had been sleeping on.

She had to get out of there. The image of the marble-smooth demon awash in crimson flashed in her mind. The blood on the bed remained still, as if there wasn't a void hidden beneath. Stephanie wanted to believe that Hal was alive in there somewhere, but her better judgment dictated her retreat from the room. It was better that she get help, not that anyone would believe her story. The bloody pit in the mattress roiled and bubbled and taunted her. Realizing that both of their phones were on the nightstand beside the bed, she inched closer to retrieve one of them. Things in the nasty mattress pit surfaced the closer she got. Sick things. Human-like hands on serpentine coils, dripping blood and gore that hung like strips of muscle, tendons, and clotted blood.

Deciding she couldn't risk getting close enough to snatch one of their phones, Stephanie fled the room.

The hallway was quiet, sullen and distorted, at least in Stephanie's perspective. It could have been paved with gold bars and studded with diamonds and she still would have seen a perfect vision of Hell.   In that moment, as a light in the ceiling flickered like a nervous twitch, Stephanie was overcome by a tide of anxiety-fueled panic. She couldn't decide which way to go. She would have to take the elevator down to the lobby to report Hal's murder. She would have used the phone in their room, but she had to get out of there. The odor and sight of Hal's blood had been getting to her, and there was a general sense of dread and unease. A return to childhood fears, as if at any moment the thing in the bed would get her.

She saw a housekeeper down the hall, her bony fingers latched onto a pushcart topped with toilet paper rolls and off-white linens and towels that were frayed at the corners.

It's too late for maids, isn't it?

"Call the police," Stephanie said. "My husband's been murdered!"

It wasn't the same housekeeper they'd seen with the scar on her face, however there was something peculiar in her expression. Was it fear? Pity? She looked down suddenly and proceeded to turn around and push the cart away, as if purposely ignoring Stephanie.

Stephanie's face twisted into questioning shock. "Wait! Where are you going?"

The housekeeper picked up speed, which came off as more insulting than anything. How was it this woman could so easily disregard Stephanie's plea?

The only sound in the hall was the wheels of the pushcart fighting their way over lumpy patched together carpet.

"Aren't you going to help me? Don't you have a phone?"

The housekeeper glanced back at her awkward speed-walking escape, but Stephanie was gaining on her. At this point she was becoming angry with the woman for her deliberate negligence.

"Where are you going? I need help!"

Close enough to grab her, Stephanie reached out a hand and latched onto her arm. It was an aggressive move, but after what she'd had been through, who could blame her?

The housekeeper grunted as she was pulled to a stop. Her spindly fingers let go of the pushcart that had enough momentum on the old carpet to continue its forward roll until it came to a sudden jerking stop.

That's when Stephanie noticed the length of the chain from the housekeeper's arm to the cart.

Stephanie's mouth dropped open. The housekeeper grabbed her wrist, rubbing the soreness from her shackle, as she stared into Stephanie's shocked eyes.

"You must get out of here before they find you," the housekeeper said.

"They?"

"The ones that killed your husband. They will get you, but they won't kill you. Not yet at least."

"Call the police! Call security!"

In a hushed voice the housekeeper said, "There is no security. Not here. There are no phones." There was a pregnant pause as the women locked eyes as if trying to read one another's thoughts. "You don't know where you are."

Growing impatient and angry with the strange housekeeper, Stephanie said, "I'm at the Imperial Hotel, and if you're not going to help me, I'm going to have to get down to the casino. Something happened in my room, something I can't explain. I . . . I saw something come out of the bed and . . . kill my husband."

The housekeeper nodded rapidly. "Yes, yes! One of *Them*."

"This is crazy."

Stephanie turned from the housekeeper and fled in the direction she thought she could find the elevator. She expected the housekeeper to say something. But the woman remained silent. When Stephanie turned to see if she was still there, the woman had left.

She found the elevator door. A cold slab of metal with ominous scratches and dents pounded into it like urban hieroglyphs. Her finger couldn't press the big C button quick enough, however nothing happened. There was no telltale sound of the hydraulics or a bell dinging that indicated the initiation of the elevator's gears.

She pressed the Casino button again. It didn't light up the way it should have, so she pressed the button for the first floor. It had the same result.

Cursing, Stephanie looked up and down the hallway, afraid of the thing that pulled Haloran into the bed. She looked again at the battered elevator door and screamed. The smooth demonic face she'd seen in the bloody pool on the bed was staring at her. It glared with slanted eyes as smooth as spun sugar. Sugar that would have been beautiful under any other circumstance.

Stephanie stood as still as petrified wood. At any moment the arms could reach out and pull her into the abysmal unknown. Hal was in there, somewhere. She wondered if he was suffering, if he was dead, if there was more pain where he went. Those last moments with him were terrible. His suffering burned in her mind like the black tracings of a branding iron.

She backed slowly from the elevator door as if she would quietly sneak off without the demonic face realizing she'd gone. It stared her down with peculiar eyes that now looked like polished coins. Although Stephanie didn't recognize the president facing the coins. They looked familiar, but something was amiss. They almost looked like George Washington with Abraham Lincoln's beard.

"You won't get out of here," the face said. The voice had a bizarre metallic tone. "There's no way out but through our consumption. And we need you. We've already consumed your husband, but you can serve us in another way."

Stephanie shook her head. "No. I'm getting out of here."

She ran in search of the stairwell; however, she went in the opposite direction, treading over lumpy carpet, stained with black gum spots and splashes of anything from beer to . . . blood? She passed many doors, all of them bearing similar glyphs as that of the elevator door. There was no sign of life whatsoever. No drunken laughter, no dinging elevator bells, no noisy televisions, nothing. When Stephanie wrapped around the entire floor, she grabbed the handle to the first door she saw that didn't have a room number on it.

What seemed like a dozen hands grabbed and pulled her in. She screamed but was stifled by a palm shoved into her mouth.

She was surrounded by tired, desperate housekeepers, gasping and drawing deep breaths of awe. Their faces had a collective look of tragedy and horror. Solemn eyes, dragging faces, scars, broken capillaries—it was terrible. Stephanie was in some kind of hell.

"They're looking for you," one of them whispered after a pause that seemed to defy time.

"Can't you help me?" Stephanie asked. "I need help. Something…

happened. I can't even believe it. My husband is . . ."

"Dead," another housekeeper said, her voice low and emotionless, half-crazed eyes set deep in folds of tired flesh. Eyes that had witnessed atrocities.

The housekeepers began looking upward, scanning the ceiling, and then eyeing the walls for something Stephanie couldn't see.

"We have to hide you," the housekeeper Stephanie had talked to in hall said.

The others erupted into a half-angry murmur, soft and delicate like the fluttering of so many butterflies.

The housekeeper from the hall went into action, lifting the pile of bath towels and linens from the lower rack of her pushcart. "Get down there," she said to Stephanie.

"I won't fit."

"You have to. They're coming. If they find you, they will . . . make you like us."

The woman lifted her arm, the cuff visible around her wrist, a length of chain connected to it that disappeared beneath the linens, connected to her pushcart.

Some of the others displayed their shackled wrists. The pushcarts were all lined up in the storage room, so tight there wasn't much space.

"We were like you," another woman said, her voice heavy with exhaustion. "We came here because the rooms were so cheap, then they came. Killed my husband. Pulled him right into the bed as I watched, and then one of them took me away. We all share the same story, but you still have a chance. You need to get out of here, but for now you must hide, because they're coming. I can feel their presence like static electricity. They are everywhere, fueled by the greed and debauchery of Vegas, but their appetite has changed. The money that once fueled them isn't enough.

They want blood, and they need us to clean the messes."

"Quick," a woman said, her voice only a tone above a hush.

"They're almost here. Climb onto the cart and we'll crowd around you."

Stephanie's mind was a frantic scattering of neurons firing in random succession. She dropped to the ground and crawled onto the lower shelf of the cart, only a foot off the ground. The housekeepers covered her with what seemed like an endless supply of white sheets and towels. She was engulfed in darkness, shivering in fear, sweat beginning to mat her hair to her forehead.

She listened.

There was a gurgling sound, then a guttural chuckle before a voice spoke. She recognized it as the voice of the smooth-faced demon she'd seen in the battered elevator door.

"Where is she?" the voice asked.

Stephanie remained as still as possible, pretending that she was a statue. She clamped her teeth on a towel to stifle the scream she feared she couldn't prevent.

"One of you knows where she is," the voice said. "Tell me and I will have mercy on you."

"We haven't seen anyone," a delicate, frightened voice said.

A loud snap, the sound of bones crunching, liquid dripping, and then a body hit the floor. Stephanie yelped, but her saving grace was that they all yelped at the sudden murder of the housekeeper who dared deny that they'd seen her. What Stephanie didn't see was the demon in the wall, stretching

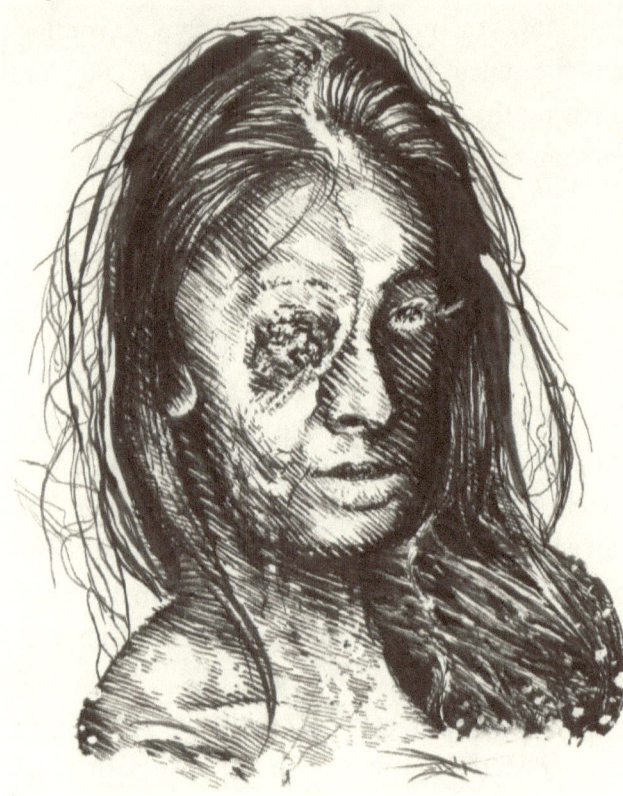

through the plaster, opening its mouth lined with teeth fashioned of sharpened silver coins that orally decapitated the woman. The crunching of her skull could be heard through the cries of the other housekeepers, and then the demon was gone.

They were tense moments as Stephanie lay there on the pushcart wondering if it was safe to remove herself from the tight constraint.

"He's gone," a shivering voice said.

With help from several housekeepers, Stephanie was pulled from the cart. The women were stricken with terror, sadness, and anger. Their decapitated sister's body lay on the ground, the cuffed arm suspended in the air, connected to a pushcart with much less chain than the others, as if perhaps she'd been kept on a short leash. The pool of blood from the raw wound of her neck grew larger, threatening to reach Stephanie's feet like a slowly rising tide that never ebbed.

"Get out of here," one of the women said. Stephanie had misjudged her anger, thinking she'd directed it toward the demon. "You caused this. You're on your own." After a pause and a glance at the body on the floor, the woman finished with, "May God's blessing be with you. And if you get out, you have to tell the authorities. But remember that greedy demons are everywhere. They are the Gods of Las Vegas, and they will do everything to prevent you from ruining what they have here. This place . . . it's the root of all evil."

Another housekeeper opened the door to the hallway. They shuffled toward Stephanie, ushering her out of the room.

She thought to plea for their forgiveness but knew better. They'd helped her enough to lose one of their own. They could have given her up and saved the poor woman.

The door shut. The hall was silent.

A door across from the elevator beckoned to her. It was the stairwell, what most people avoided due to heavy luggage and laziness.

For Stephanie it was salvation.

She took the stairs in doubles, careful not to trip or catch her foot. Nothing to stop her momentum. Hands gliding on the worn and paint chipped iron railings, something beneath her fingers didn't feel quite right. The ridges created by the chipped paint began to feel bumpier. She soon realized that the iron was turning into quarters and silver dollars, pennies, dimes and nickels.

For a moment, Stephanie thought it was by design, but she realized soon enough that it was a distraction, and it worked. She slowed as she pondered the strange currency-lined railing. The steps transformed into wads of cash, and by the time she made it to ground level, the iron-rail turn-coin-rail had become pure gold speckled with blood. The steps became solid gold bricks, the walls covered in a wallpaper of perfect one hundred-dollar bills.

The door was dented and scratched. Ugly in contrast to the wealthy surroundings. There were ominous spatters of blood here and there, but Stephanie made her best effort to ignore the bizarre changes and depressed the large bar that opened the heavy steel door.

A breath of warm air that smelled of sewer and exhaust hit her in the face. It was real. It was Vegas.

Stephanie all but leapt out of the stairwell, turned, and what she saw wasn't gold brick stairs and one-hundred-dollar bill wallpaper, but a filthy, cold stairwell of concrete and iron.

The door startled her by slamming shut.

She had a lot to be thankful for, however there was a hole in her heart for Haloran that would always be there. Here she managed to escape, and he was in there somewhere, suffering or dead.

In the distance were the sounds of people, cars, anger, fun, greed— the spoils of Sin City.

Stephanie closed her eyes, took a deep breath, and then opened them again.

Her scream was so sudden she startled herself. The demon lurched from the door as it had from the elevator, only this time it was accompanied by several reaching hands with claws of molten silver. Before they could grab her, she stumbled backwards and directly into the path of an oncoming car.

###

The last thing Stephanie heard before walking into the hospital was the screeching breaks and the horn as the car hit her. She'd broken several ribs, lost a few teeth, and broken her arm. She had no idea how long she'd been out, but she had a cast on her arm and a lot of bandages on her face and chest.

Where's Hal? Is he all right?

Just as soon as she thought of Hal, she remembered what had happened at the Imperial Hotel. She closed her eyes, prayed for Haloran and thanked God that she was in a hospital.

They're the Gods of Las Vegas, one of the housekeepers had said.

They're everywhere. A nurse entered the room holding a hypodermic. "Just a little something to help with the pain," she said.

Stephanie tried to speak, but all that came out were incomprehensible grunts and malformed words. She desperately wanted to tell the nurse to get the police, but she was unable to properly articulate herself.

"Hush, hush," the nurse said. "Don't try to speak. Just relax."

She jabbed the needle into Stephanie's arm. Stephanie cringed. It burned, which didn't seem right. The nurse smiled, and Stephanie's eyes widened at the sight of veneer-like teeth of silver and gold, displaying the faces of dead presidents.

As the world faded away Stephanie tried to scream, to arouse attention, but she was powerless to the Gods of Las Vegas, and the secret of the Imperial Hotel was safe once again.

The End

Authors

Ryan C. Thomas is an award-winning journalist and editor in San Diego, California. He is the author of 14 novels (including the cult classic, *The Summer I Died*), numerous novellas and short stories and can often be found in the bars around Southern California playing guitar. When he is not writing or rocking out, he is at home with his wife, son, daughter and pets watching really bad B-movies. Visit him online at **RyanCThomas.Com**

Tim Curran is the author of *Skin Medicine, Hive, Dead Sea, The Devil Next Door, Blooding Night, Clownflesh,* and *Bad Girl in the Box,* among others. His short stories have been collected in *Alien Horrors, The Horrors of War,* and *The Brain Leeches.* His novellas include *The Underdwelling, The Corpse King, Puppet Graveyard, Worm,* and *The Sunken City.* His

fiction has been translated into German, Japanese, Spanish, and Italian. Find him on Facebook at:
https://www.facebook.com/tim.curran.77

Bridgett Nelson is a registered nurse turned horror author. Her first collection, *A Bouquet of Viscera,* is a two-time Splatterpunk Award finalist, recognized both for the collection itself and its standout story,*"Jinx."* Her work has appeared in *Counting Bodies Like Sheep, Dead & Bloated, American Cannibal, A Woman Unbecoming,* and several volumes of the *If I Die Before I Wake* series of anthologies. Bridgett has been contracted by Encyclopocalypse Publications to write a novelization of the cult classic film *Deadgirl.* She is an active member of the Horror Writers Association and the co-chair of HWA: West Virginia. She was a 2022 Michael Knost "Wings" award nominee and won second place in the '22 Gross-Out contest at KillerCon in Austin, Texas. Bridgett thoroughly enjoys writing, mainly because wearing a bra is not required. She also likes tarantulas. A lot. To learn more, visit her website at **bridgettnelson.com**

Marc Schoenbach's As a child in the 1980s, he was already enjoying horror movies and playing games that could be seen as morbid by today's  standards. Marc's passion for all things horror would eventually lead him to a career in psychology, and later to writing short stories and screenplays. Marc began creating his own faux-vintage movie posters based on his stories. In 2011 he founded **Sadist Art Designs**. Marc has freelanced for companies such as Fright Rags, Waxwork Records, and Arrow Video, created covers for Fangoria magazine, and even quit his psychology job to pursue his passion full-time. Marc currently resides in Long Island, NY, with his wife, two children, and two black cats, Salem and Spooky.

Nathan Robinson has had over 40 short stories published in numerous anthologies. He is the author of *Starers, Midway, Ketchup on Everything,* and the short story collection *Devil Let Me Go*. He is currently a School Librarian, hoping to inspire the next generation of readers and writers. You can find him at facebook.com/NathanRobinsonWrites or on Instagram @natthewriter

The Never Dead

Dan Henk was born on a small army base in the deep south. He's been homeless, made it through brain cancer, gotten stabbed by a crackhead, totaled three cars, three bikes, and plunged backwards through a windshield. After four hours in a coma, he sprung back and resumed his normal life. There is a running theory that he is a cyborg. He has three novels and two chapbooks out, has done a slew of artwork for books and magazines, and owns a tattoo shop in NYC. Over one hundred books and magazines have featured his art, writing, and tattooing. You can see his latest travails and triumphs on his website, **danhenk.com**

Christine Morgan is the author of several novels and over a hundred short stories, spanning genres from superheroes to smut, with a focus on horror and dark fantasy. She's particularly fond of historical, extreme, cosmic, and blending various sub-genres. She also takes on freelance edit. gigs, does book reviews, is into weird crafts and baking, and spends her free time sleeping or getting bossed around by cats. She can be found online at:ChristineMarieMorgan.wordpress.com, on various social media platforms, or by email at ChristineMarieMorgan@gmail.com

Patrick C. Harrison III (**PC3**, if you prefer) is an author of horror, splatterpunk, and all forms of speculative fiction. Several of PC3's works have been nominated for awards, and he is the Splatterpunk Award-winning editor (with Jarod Barbee) of, *And Hell Followed*. He is also the mind behind the *Splatter Western* series (Death's Head Press.

PC3 has authored ten books as of this writing—including the Amazon best-seller *100% Match* and the award-nominated novella *Grandpappy*. For PC3 news and frequent horror and exploitation movie ~reviews, subscribe to this FREE substack **pc3horror.substack.com**

Jeff Strand is the Bram Stoker Award-winning author of over 50 books, including *CLOWNS VS. SPIDERS, AUTUMN BLEEDS INTO WINTER*, and *TWENTIETH ANNIVERSARY SCREENING*. You can visit his gleefully Macabre website at JeffStrand.com.

Robert Essig is the author of fifteen books including *Baby Fights, Secret Basements* and *Broth House*. He has published over 150 short stories and edited three small press anthologies such as *Chew on This!*, which was nominated for a Splatterpunk Award. Robert lived with his family in east Tennessee. For updates, subscribe to his free newsletter at **robertessig.substack.com**. You can grab signed copies of his books at **essighorror.bigcartel.com**.

Patrick Lacey was born and raised in a haunted house. He spends his time writing about things that make the general public shiver. He lives in a hopefully un-haunted house in Massachusetts with two hyperactive cats, his daughter, and his wife. Follow him on Twitter @PatLacey.

Jack Bantry is the editor of **Splatterpunk Zine**. He resides in a small town at the edge of the North York Moors. His works include *AIN'T WORTH A SHIT*, and the collection *SHALLOW GRAVES*, both co-written with Robert Essig.

Bobby Lisse is a Writer and Filmmaker from New York. He has a daily column for **Morbidly Beautiful Horror** called **The Daily Dig** for which he unearths little-known horror films from the nineteen forties to two thousand  and gives them a spotlight, for better or worse. He has also written for Rue Morgue Magazine You can contact him for film editing at

BobbyLisse@Gmail.com

Bracken MacLeod is the Splatterpunk, Bram Stoker, and Shirley Jackson Award nominated author of the novels, *Mountain Home, Come to Dust, Stranded,* and *Closing Costs.* He's also published two collections of short fiction, *13 Views of the Suicide Woods* and *White Knight and Other Pawns.* Before devoting himself to full time writing, he survived car crashes, a near drowning, being shot at, a parachute malfunction, and the bar exam. So far, the only incident that has resulted in persistent nightmares is the bar exam. He lives outside of Boston, where he is at work on his next novel about the fallout of Satanic Panic of the 1980s. You can learn more about his work at BrackenMacLeod.com.

"But Everyone Disappears, no matter who loves them."
-Dave Eggers

www.ingramcontent.com/pod-product-compliance
Lightning Source LLC
Chambersburg PA
CBHW022018240626
47154CB00007B/2152

Praise for Heather Blanton

"Heather Blanton infuses her stories with immense grace and dignity."

—LINDA BRODAY, *NEW YORK TIMES* BESTSELLING AUTHOR

"Heather Blanton is blessed with a natural storytelling ability, an 'old soul' wisdom, and wide expansive heart."

—MARK RICHARD, EXECUTIVE PRODUCER OF AMC'S *HELL ON WHEELS*

"Fans of Louis L'Amour and Francine Rivers will find Blanton's stories even more enthralling. With wit, a clear author's voice, and storytelling chops that rival the best—you'll have found your new favorite storyteller!"

—CARRIE FANCETT PAGELS, AWARD-WINNING AUTHOR

"Masterful at gritty fiction that points to the ultimate Creator, Heather will become one of your favorite Christian fiction authors."

—KARI TRUMBO, *USA TODAY* BESTSELLING AUTHOR

A Reckoning in Defiance

ROMANCE IN THE ROCKIES
BOOK SEVEN

HEATHER BLANTON

A Reckoning in Defiance

Prologue

MICHAEL PATRICK FLYNN strode across the squeaky wooden floor of the Crow's Pub and laid his hand on the bar. Sean, the barkeep, looked past Flynn at the sparse, smoky crowd. With a shrug, he gestured over his shoulder. "He's in the back."

Flynn slipped around the counter and into the backroom. Dave Bishop, a slender man of tightly wound muscle, eyed a shelf of liquor, hands on his hips, his back to the entrance. Flynn felt for the knife on his hip. "I hear ye've a problem with me."

Bishop spun, scowled, and glanced toward the bar. He shook his head, his thick mustache twitching. "I knew it were a mistake to 'ire a Mick to run the counter. You Cork County mongrels all 'ang together."

The man's rough, Cockney accent grated on Flynn. He hated the British, rich or poor, refined or rough, he hated them all. They all thought they were so much better than the Irish. "If we don't, we'll hang separately."

Bishop reached behind him and pulled out his knife, a six-inch pig sticker, and flashed it with a ready grin. It didn't matter to Flynn. His knife was shorter, but he was faster than the Englishman.

"Let's get this straight then, Flynn. I'm not going to 'ave an Irish gang in Defiance. Leave, or we'll run you and your boys out."

Flynn could launch his knife like a lightning bolt in the flick of an eye. Stick it straight in the Limey's heart. He wanted to, but not till he was ready. A few more bricks needed to be laid in place. "If ye're waiting for us to leave, ye'll be waiting till the Second Coming."

Bishop smiled. "That's 'ow it is then? A bloody war?"

Eventually. But first, a few select deaths at prime intervals. Even the odds a bit more, but he'd keep Bishop guessing on timing. "Think what ye like."

Bishop returned his knife to his sheath and half-turned to the shelf. "Take your Mick friend with ya. I'll 'ave no more Irish in my saloon." He plucked a bottle of whiskey from the shelf and pivoted back to Flynn. "I'll add it to the sign today. Right *below* No Negroes. No Indians."

Hate writhed in Flynn's heart like a rattlesnake ready to kill something. He clenched his teeth and reminded himself to bide his time. "Same goes for my place. No English...except with my permission."

"I don't think you'll 'ave that problem. No English will be busting down your door. At least not to drink."

It was Flynn's turn to smile at the verbal combat. "If any English come by, we'll be sure to make them feel welcome then."

The men stared at each other, the unspoken threats clear. Death would reign soon in Defiance.

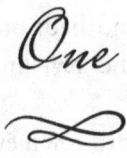

One

CAN HORSES HAVE NIGHTMARES?

A strange thing to wonder, Victoria admitted, but Delilah had been so badly abused. Hard to believe now, of course. The white-socked sorrel was cavorting across the snowy pasture, kicking up her heels, mane flying behind her like fingers of fire. The mare was full of joy.

Victoria laid a hand on the top fence rail and shook her head.

This morning in the stall, though, when she had come to feed her and the others, the click of the stall door had startled the horse. She had squealed wildly, as if emerging from a horrible nightmare, and kicked the wall. She'd spun and looked at Victoria for a full second without the slightest hint of recognition, fear swimming in her eyes, ears plastered to her head. Then, her gaze had changed, warmed, and the animal had come to her senses.

Assessing her now, she appeared in her right mind. This morning, though, that panicked, mindless, *powerful* kick had spooked Victoria. She was still learning to handle the horses for Toby.

Speaking of...

The soft thud of hooves in the snow pulled her gaze to the road. Toby was galloping toward her and her heart did a funny little flutter. She was pleased to see him. Tall and solid in the saddle, strands of blonde hair fluttering beneath his hat, he was a striking man.

He was home early and had, on the way, joined up with Momma. Bringing up the rear in her wagon, she waved. Victoria waved back.

These two got to go into town every day. Victoria was relegated to hiding on their tiny, rented farm, tending a few horses, and staying out of sight of the public.

She hated it.

But she'd brought it all on herself.

Toby slowed his horse to a jog and ambled up to the corral fence. "Evenin'."

"Evening." Toby's gaze always unsettled her. Burning sapphire eyes said everything he couldn't—and she wouldn't let him say until she'd settled things in Defiance. He dismounted and wrapped the reins around the fence. "Everything go okay today?"

"Yes." She hadn't meant to betray any doubts, but he heard them just the same.

He straightened up, pierced her with an intense, questioning gaze, and pulled off his hat. "Uh, huh." He scratched his scalp with a gloved hand and replaced the worn Stetson. "Something happen?"

"No." And nothing had. Victoria regrouped, gathered her confidence. "Delilah startled in the stall this morning and kicked at the gate, but I wasn't in the way."

His eyes cut to the horse, still leaping and running about like a colt. One other horse, an old bay mare, was half-heartedly chasing her like a tired mother attempting to play with her child. "Looks all right now."

"I'm sure it was nothing. But it made me wonder if horses have nightmares. Like people do."

He came back to her abruptly, but his gaze softened as he searched her face. "My guess is yeah. On the surface, she knows we're all right. We won't hurt her. But dreams..."

"They can seem so real," Victoria said, fading off, seeing the faces of men who haunted her nightmares. Most of them dead men now. One or two still breathing and were probably eager for vengeance.

Toby laid a hand on her shoulder and she looked up. "But they're not. Real, that is. Learn the difference between what's in your head and what's real."

She chose not to reply as the jangling wagon announced Momma's approach. Plump, growing a little wider and grayer every day, she set the break and grinned down at them. "You two look like you're solving the world's problems."

"No, Toby here is just speaking the wisdom of God over me."

"Well, that can't be a bad thing."

"I was about to tell her that Rod French has a team of mules he wants to board with us for the winter. One more animal and we'll have a full barn."

Momma nodded, a smile of obvious satisfaction twitching on her lips. "Word's getting around." She surveyed the farm with its sway-backed, two-bedroom cabin, drooping barn in need of paint, the aged but stout rail around the corral. "It's not a pretty place, but it's warm, dry, and secure."

"And it just needs to keep us till spring." Victoria's comment tossed a heaviness on them she hadn't intended and the tension annoyed her. *It's not like they don't know why I'm here, Lord.* Victoria stepped over and started unwinding Toby's reins from the fence. "I've got soup on the stove. You two go on in. I'll get the animals."

Toby tapped his brim in appreciation. "You don't have to tell me twice." The joke fell flat as he nodded at the ladies and headed toward the house.

Slowly, as if her bones were stiff and aching, Momma

climbed down from the wagon. "I wish you wouldn't keep reminding us. We all know what you plan to do in the spring."

Victoria sighed. "I'm sorry, Momma. It haunts me. Until I can make things right—"

"Don't see how you getting lynched is gonna square anything."

"I don't believe they'll lynch me."

"And *you're* not hearing the talk I pick up in the saloon. Your name is Mud in Defiance, baby girl. You need to give those folks time. A lot more time. Years, maybe."

The same argument. Again. For the hundredth time. Victoria understood Momma's concerns. Her pain. Her fears. She hadn't slept well in almost a year. Twelve men dead at the bottom of a mine, your daughter complicit in the deaths, was more than enough to keep anyone awake. "Go in and get some soup. I'll be there shortly."

Momma huffed softly, picked up her skirt, and followed Toby's footsteps in the snow.

Toby shuffled around the little cabin, filling bowls with soup and setting them on the table. He took a moment and surveyed their winter digs. It wasn't much to look at, but somehow Eleanor and Victoria had made it...homey. A large fieldstone fireplace sat at the center of the back wall, and Victoria had done a fine job keeping the fire going all day. The whole house, including the two bedrooms off to the sides, was warm and comfortable.

They'd brought their meager furnishings with them from Dodge. A small settee, a Lincoln rocker, a kitchen table with four chairs, and a cot were the extent of the furniture in the main room. The bright and colorful rag rug set it all off nicely and sort of determined the imaginary line between the sitting area and kitchen.

When they initially arrived in Ruby City, shortly after Thanksgiving, they had tirelessly tried to convince Victoria not to head directly to Defiance. They'd urged her to get the lay of the land. A stubborn woman, it had been all they could do to talk sense into her. Even telling her men in Defiance had tried to lynch Charles McIntyre for his supposed involvement in the mine explosion didn't impress upon her the danger of her idea. She'd finally agreed to wait till spring for no other reason than to shut him and Eleanor up.

He filled his bowl at the stove and set it on the table but stared at the steaming broth for a moment. He couldn't lose Victoria. He prayed she'd see the gift she'd been given by the marshal in Defiance. He'd let her go, expecting her to quietly fade away. He hadn't counted on a guilty conscience driving her to penance.

The door opened and Eleanor slipped in. For an instant, they stared at each other, and he knew what she was thinking. "What are we going to do with her, El?"

She peeled out of her coat, left it on the wall hook, and joined him at the table. "She's bound and determined. But she don't know what I'm hearing at the saloon." When Eleanor had learned pretty quick after their arrival that the Lonely Dog Saloon was looking for a barkeep, she knew it would be a good place to get information. She'd been right.

Toby pulled her chair out for her, then sat down as well. "Still bad?" he asked, reaching for a napkin.

"Town's in turmoil. Some fella that owned the Crystal Chandelier come to town after the mine explosion. Made a big production out of rebuilding and opening up the town, but he wound up running afoul of the law. He's on his way to prison."

Toby was hungry and wanted to dive into the soup, but they needed to wait on Victoria and say grace. "Maybe that's a good thing for her. She told me about him. He was as much a cancer in the town as she was."

Eleanor grunted. "They're angrier than ever. And there's a

couple of pretty vocal groups still want to run their mouths about her and this McIntyre fella being in cahoots."

"They weren't. At least not according to what Victoria told me."

"Mobs don't let a little thing like the truth get in the way of their lynchings."

"I guess not." He picked up his spoon and stirred his soup restlessly.

"How do you like wearing a badge?"

He glanced at the tin star on his chest. With the decision to wait for spring, they'd all had to find work. Eleanor in the saloon, Toby marshaling part-time, boarding horses the rest of the time. That had worked out well. Victoria could handle the animals when he was gone, and the job kept her away from town. This little ranch was the first place they'd looked at and it had felt right. To all of them. Turned out, it was perfect for boarding.

"That bad?"

He'd lost track of the question. "Sorry. It started me thinking how things were working out here. We could have a nice life in Ruby City if—" He stopped the thought and rose to grab the coffee pot off the stove.

"If she'd let go of this fool notion and marry you?"

Eleanor's bluntness made him pause, but he shook it off and brought the coffee back to the table. "That's a crazy idea. I just meant between boarding the horses and marshaling, we stand to make some money. She's handling them well. She's a good partner."

"She could be."

Toby and Eleanor locked gazes and he understood what she was implying. Before they could say anything else, Victoria stomped in, shaking off as much snow at the threshold as possible. "It's getting sloppy out there." She peeled out of her coat and joined them at the table. As she pulled her soup bowl a little closer, her gaze ricocheted between the two. "And just what are you two cooking up?"

"Nothing," Toby said a little too loudly. "Waiting on you so we can eat." He nodded at Eleanor. "Your turn to say grace."

Often after dinner, Toby went to the barn to spend some time with the horses. Usually, Victoria left him alone, but tonight she was restless. The snap in Delilah's personality haunted her and she wanted to talk to Toby about it. She wrapped a wool cloak around her, ignored Eleanor's amused expression, and worked her way through the snow, which was now up to her knees.

The barn was warmed from the animals' heat, and an inviting amber glow spilled through the slats of the last stall on the right. She found Toby brushing down Delilah, the beautiful sorrel with four white socks—beautiful and, at one point in her life, deadly.

Just as Victoria had been when she'd gone by the same name. "You think she's all right?"

The question wasn't all that clear, but she knew he knew what she meant. He continued to brush her without answering right away. This was Toby's way. He often tended to think carefully before responding. More men should be like that.

"Yeah, I do. Any animal coming awake could be confused for a minute. She has a lot of bad memories rattling around in her brain. Don't you, girl?" he said sweetly as he reached over and scratched a spot on her chest. "Trick is not to hang on to them." He cut his eyes at Victoria.

She took a deep breath and leaned back on the wall. "Easier said than done."

Tossing the grooming brush into a bucket, Toby grabbed the blanket draped over the stall door. He spoke as he unfolded it. "That's the thing. It's a choice. It's a conscious effort to keep your mind right." With great care, he spread the blanket over

Delilah and buckled it. "She forgot for a second who she was, but it all came back to her. She didn't run with the panic. She slipped a little, but in the end, kept her head."

"Yes, I suppose she did."

Finished, he turned to Victoria. He was a handsome man, muscular but not overly so, tall, and he moved like a panther. His blond hair showed the distinct imprint of his hat, but it didn't hurt his looks any. Penetrating blue eyes, a dimple in his chin— No, Toby was not hard on the eyes.

"Delilah needs to fill up her head with good thoughts. Eventually, they'll crowd out the bad."

There were so many times when Toby spoke of the horse, yet hinted he was speaking to her instead. Smiling, she tried it for him. "Victoria needs to fill her head up with good thoughts. Eventually, they'll crowd out the bad."

A little smile tugged at the corner of his mouth. "I ain't patronizing you. I know it's not that simple. You're more complicated than Delilah here."

Toby knew everything about her and yet still treated her with such respect. Sometimes he made Victoria want to cry, and sometimes she wanted to jump into his arms. Like now, but she had promised herself to make peace with Defiance first. The air between them seemed to hum, though, fogging her resolve. He took a step toward her. His eyes, deep blue, hypnotic, calming, promised peace and passion. He looked at her the way Logan had. Toby could make her forget, make her want to leave Defiance in the dust...could she leave the memories of Logan behind, too?

She blinked and turned away. "I have to make amends first. Before I try to have a life, Toby."

"Amends. Amends is one thing. Getting lynched is another."

She whirled on him. "Stop trying to frighten me. They're not going to lynch a woman, but they could have a trial. And I'm guilty. If I were to be sentenced to prison—well, I couldn't...I-I wouldn't want to leave a relationship unfinished. Left hanging."

Toby lowered his head and sighed. "Guess there's nothing I could say that might change your mind?"

Victoria felt the weight of the question. A turning point. A fork in the road. But guilt and shame propelled her on her original path. "Not yet," she whispered, surprised her voice had failed her. "I have to make things right."

He was still and silent for so long, she thought he might never speak again. Then he reached for the lamp overhead and took it off the hook. "Let's get back inside."

Two

"GEE, THIS SEEMS FAMILIAR."

Eleanor whirled around from the box of whiskey she was unloading behind the bar and gasped at the young man grinning at her. "Billy Page."

His grin widened and he snatched his bowler off, revealing trimmed but mussed, ash blond hair. Blue eyes glowed with a warmth that kindled great affection in Eleanor's heart. She rushed from behind the bar and gave the boy a big hug around his thick, soft fur coat. "My, oh, my, what a surprise."

"Yes, ma'am." They hugged again and he patted her on the shoulder as she stepped back. "It's good to see you, Eleanor."

"And vice versa." She'd missed that Sweet Southern accent of his, dripping with friendliness. "What are you doing in Ruby City? Can I get ya a drink?"

"No, thank you, but..." He glanced around the gloomy, little saloon, empty except for the two of them. "You have a few minutes?"

"For you I do."

They settled at a table near the buck stove, Billy laying his coat on the table beside them. Eleanor was tickled to see the boy she'd helped back in Dodge. And things had turned out well for him in Defiance. He'd married the little girl he'd gone to fetch. Claimed her and their baby. He'd come by Dodge once more to offer her a job, but she'd still been waiting on Victoria to come home and couldn't leave.

What if she'd taken the job? She might have missed her daughter and who knew where they'd all be now.

"So how is life in Defiance?" she asked, reaching over and adjusting the front grate on the stove to tone down the heat a little. "This thing gets pretty hot when you're sitting this close."

His expression changed and he regarded her more somberly. "That's apt."

"What do you mean?"

He scratched an eyebrow. "I'll cut to it, Eleanor. Toby came to my store just before Christmas. Told me you and she were here."

"I'm the one who told him to find you."

Billy let out a long, weary sigh. "I could use your help, but I am worried half-out of my mind about Delilah being this close to Defiance."

"You better speak a little more plain. And her name's Victoria."

He nodded, accepting the correction. "My wife Hannah has a calling to be a nurse. It's a good, noble calling, and I want to help her. But we have to move back East for a spell."

Eleanor followed the statement but not the point. "And?"

He leaned forward and tapped on the rickety table. "I think you could run my hotel just fine. Maybe even my mercantile. But if word got out you're Delilah's—*Victoria's*—mother, I'm afraid what the town might do. I guess what I'm really here to say is, you should all go back to Dodge."

"She won't go, son. Dynamite won't get her out of Colorado."

"Has she lost her mind? Doesn't she understand—?"

"She wants to go back to Defiance. She refuses to believe the town will lynch her. All she can see is, well, I reckon her own pain. She says it's for them, but I think she just doesn't know how to handle the guilt. We've tried to tell her Jesus cleaned the slate." Eleanor stopped, wrestled down the knot in her throat. "I don't know what to do with her. We've managed to delay her till spring...but then..."

Billy leaned back and fluttered his lips. "I don't know what to make of that."

"Maybe something will happen between now and then and the town will settle down."

"It's possible, but we just suffered through the one-year anniversary."

"Which'll light everybody up again."

"Pretty much."

They sat in a strained silence for a spell, lost in their thoughts. Eleanor racked her brain, looking for a way to stop this wildly naive plan of Victoria's. Then an odd idea bobbed to the surface. *Lord, is this your idea?*

She touched Billy's hand. "What if—what if I did come to work for you? And what if I carefully, gently started telling folks how sorry Victoria was? That she was torn up. The guilt was almost too much for her to bear."

"I'd say that's a dangerous game. A good idea, in theory, but if anybody got wise..." He winced and shook his head. "It's awfully dangerous."

"Nobody in Ruby City has seen me with her, other than when we first rolled in, and it was snowing to beat the band that day. I haven't told anybody who she is. Have you?"

Billy's face froze. His stricken look answered Eleanor's question. He rushed to explain. "I didn't know what to think. About why she was here. I told my brother-in-law, Charles McIntyre. He was nearly lynched—I mean *very* nearly lynched because of Deli—*Victoria*. And he told his foreman Lane, who is our new sheriff now. But no one else." Billy sighed and started fidgeting with his hat. "Has she really changed, Eleanor? Before, when she was running the Crystal Chandelier, she was...she was..."

Eleanor couldn't stand the look of pity in the boy's kind eyes. She rose and wandered over to the end of the bar. "I know. I heard all kinds of horrible things before she came back to Dodge, but then she confessed everything to me. I won't lie. Even I have a hard time believing Jesus could forgive some of the things she did."

Another awkward silence fell, but Billy broke it a moment later with a slap on the table. "Come back with me. Tell Charles and Lane about her change of heart. If they believe you, then at some point"—he shrugged—"maybe they'll let her come in and stand trial."

Eleanor traced a knothole in the bar with a calloused finger, thinking, weighing the risks. "I'd do it. Work for you. But how do Charles and Lane feel about her? Enough to keep me out of Defiance?"

"If I thought they would, I wouldn't be here." He inclined his head toward her. "But you need to meet them."

She chewed on the idea and possible outcomes as the wall clock ticked off the seconds. "Toby and me, we'll ride over tomorrow. I don't want Victoria knowing anything about this. She finds out I might be going to Defiance...well, I need to make sure she'll stay put and wait for things to settle."

The door burst open and a man wrapped in a buffalo robe and wearing a coon skin cap stomped in, shaking off the snow. Eleanor had never seen him before. He was a big man—and it wasn't the robe. He sported a dark, bushy beard—streaked with gray—that hid most of his face. Considering the amount of fur on him, she suspected he might be a trapper.

"Back to work." She slapped the bar. "You want anything—sandwich or anything before you head back over the mountain?"

Billy hesitated, as if considering the offer, but stood, too, and shoved his chair underneath the table. "I guess not. Thank you, though. I'll see you tomorrow. Come to my mercantile. It's the one on Main Street. Toby knows."

"First thing."

He snatched his coat up from the table and slid into it, passing the trapper at the door with a polite nod. When the door closed behind him, Eleanor acknowledged the gent. "Get ya a drink, friend, or maybe some lunch?"

Stripping off his outer robe didn't diminish the stranger's size much. "Roast beef'd be nice if you got it." He hung his coat and strode to the bar. "And some coffee."

Eleanor obliged and poured him a steaming cup, noting the crow's feet at the corners of his amber eyes. He was around her age. "I ain't seen you before. 'Course, I'm still kinda new to Ruby City."

"I come in and out as the mood strikes." He pulled the cup toward him and wrapped his hands around it, warming his fingers. "I seen that boy before. He's a shopkeeper in Defiance. Maybe I've seen him at the hotel, too."

Eleanor set the coffee pot back on the small stove behind the bar. "Owns both of them. I'll be right back with your sandwich. Only it ain't roast beef. It's elk."

The man smiled. At least she thought he did. The hair on his face moved. "Meat's meat."

He was a bedraggled mess. Frizzy, dark brown hair streaked with gray poured out from beneath the coon skin, even though he'd made an attempt to tie some of it back. And while she couldn't see his face, his brown eyes were alert and struck her as friendly. "All righty. Give me just a minute."

As she prepared the man's sandwich, his words came back to her. He knew Billy. He came in and out as the mood struck him. He wandered the valley. Probably had a good feel for the mood in Defiance. When she returned with his sandwich, she'd made up her mind to test the idea.

She slid the plate over to him and refreshed his coffee. "So, you a trapper?"

"I do many things."

"You spend much time in Defiance?"

"A little here and there."

"I heard they had a bad time over the summer."

Nodding with a full mouth, he finished his bite before answering. "Yep. A mine collapsed. 'Bout a year ago. Killed twelve men."

"Really?" She commenced wiping down the bar to feign disinterest. "Seems like I recall something about that. Like... maybe it was done on purpose?"

"Yep."

"Surely not."

"There was a woman in town. Mean as a rattlesnake. Ran the big bordello and saloon. She paid a fella to blow it up."

"Why in the world would she do that?"

"Aw," he licked his fingers one at a time, "she had her nose out of joint 'bout something, wanted to get back at the fella that owned the mine." Fingers clean, he reached for his coffee.

"That's terrible. And people died, you say? How does the town feel about it? What happened to the man who blew it? Did the woman go to jail?"

Finishing off his coffee, he returned to the last few bites of his sandwich. "The man died in the explosion. The woman disappeared."

"Disappeared?" Eleanor leaned toward him, pretending to be eager for gossip. "What in the world?"

The trapper, finished with his meal, cast about for something and Eleanor handed him her dish towel. He wiped his fingers and mouth as he talked. "The sheriff knew if she stayed they'd lynch her. He said it was better that she live with what she'd done."

"Feelings still running pretty high after something like that, I bet. I bet the whole town would like to hang her from the highest tree, huh?"

"And then cut her down and set her on fire." Eleanor

flinched, but he wasn't done. "Drag her burned body down the street and then throw her in the river."

Repulsed, Eleanor took a step back. The image of all this violence done to her daughter cascaded through her mind. "They sound furious."

"Yeah, lot of hard feelings still bubbling up in Defiance." He turned away to belch, long and loud, and then came back to her. "Take a long time for forgiveness to settle in, but I'm trying."

"Trying?"

"I'm a preacher, too." He offered his hand, the size of a bear paw. "Buckley Barr."

"Eleanor..." She trailed off with the handshake, not sure it was wise to give her last name. "Preacher, huh?"

"Yes, ma'am. But I don't go to the church house to share the gospel. I go to the whorehouses, saloons, and mining camps. Even spend some time with the Utes in their camp."

"The Indians?"

"Right now, they are proving to be more interested in the gospel than most of Defiance."

Eleanor's spirits sank, but at the same time, she wondered at the fortuitousness of meeting a preacher. "Mean town, is it?"

"Hurtin'. It's a hurtin' town is the way I would put it. Lots of grief bubbling up as anger. But give the Lord some time. He has told me there is a healing coming." Buckly's gaze at Eleanor changed, intensified. His dark eyes glimmered like he knew secrets. "This spring, as a matter of fact. You know the Lord, don't you, ma'am?"

"As a matter of fact, yes."

He nodded. "Good." He laid down the napkin. "I'll be back. Sandwich was mighty tasty." He laid some coins on the counter.

"You preachin' anywhere around here?"

"Could be." He turned and strode toward his coat at the door. "I never know where the Lord is going to send me."

"Well, if you preach in Ruby City—or maybe even in Defiance, I'll come listen."

He paused before slipping out the door. "I'll hold you to it."

~

The crunch of snow and ice outside his door brought Toby's head up from the arrest report. Eleanor slipped in quickly, shaking off a cold shudder. "My, a chilly day."

"Yes, it is." Toby leaned back. "What brings you by?"

She pulled a sandwich wrapped in butcher paper from her apron and laid it on his desk. "Thought you could use lunch..."

He could. What was that in her tone, though? A skeptical brow raised, he pulled the sandwich across his desk and nodded at the empty chair. "Thank you, but what else?"

"Billy came by today."

"The boy from over in Defiance?"

"Yes. He wants me to come run his hotel for him while he and his wife head East for a spell."

An interesting offer that made Toby's stomach do a sick roll. "You're not thinking of taking it, are you?" It would make it that much easier for Victoria to head that way.

"Well, I was thinking it might be good to have someone there, a set of eyes that could determine the mood of the town, the risks, the people to watch."

A spy. Maybe that *wasn't* such a bad idea. Maybe if she came back with a bad enough report.

"And, honestly, Toby, I was thinking if you had some time alone with her. Maybe you could...you could..."

"I could...get her to see things differently?" Him differently? "Talk her out of this hair-brained scheme?"

"I'd be going just like a spy, get the lay of the land, and report back. Maybe I can scare some sense into her."

He liked this notion. "That's what we should tell her.

You're just a spy. You're not staying. You're going in to scout things."

"And she'll just have to sit and wait on my reports."

He winced at the potential—probable—explosion. "That's gonna make her madder than a wet hen."

"I'll leave it up to you to...soothe her. But I don't want her to know anything yet. I need to meet this Charles McIntyre. See what he thinks of Victoria. Billy seems to think if we can convince him she's changed, he'll offer her some protection, make sure she stands trial. If it goes that far."

"I think this whole thing is a bad idea, but I can't talk her out of it."

"We may just have to watch it play out, much as it grieves me to say that. I'm praying, though, *hard*, for a change of heart in the girl."

"You and me both."

"So, tomorrow, you'll ride with me over to Defiance?"

"Sure."

Eleanor was about half-frozen by the time she and Toby pulled up to the hitching post in front of Billy's mercantile. Stiff, aching, and numb, she eased out of the saddle, snow crunching beneath her boots as she landed. She climbed the steps ahead of Toby and smiled inwardly at the neat, well-stocked store showing in the window. The boy had done good.

The bell over the door announced their entrance and Eleanor made a beeline for the stove. The embrace of warm air wafting from the mercantile's entrance was a welcome sensation. A pretty young girl with a toddler at her side looked up from her desk in the corner. She smiled and laid down her pencil. "Morning, folks. Can I help you?"

Warmth first. Eleanor soaked in the heat from the stove and wiggled her aching toes. Then she glanced again at the girl. A teenager with a warm smile and a golden braid hanging down one shoulder. "I bet you're Hannah." The toddler beside her rubbed his eyes wearily and climbed into his mother's lap. The light-colored hair and penetrating blue eyes betrayed his heritage. "And that must be Little Billy."

Hannah wrapped the child in a warm embrace and joined them at the stove. "We are. And you are?"

"I'm Eleanor and this is Toby."

Hannah's face lit with joy as Little Billy buried his face shyly in her shoulder. "Oh, Eleanor. I've heard so much about you." The girl had the same Southern ring to her voice as Billy. "It's wonderful to finally meet you." The two of them shook awkwardly around the weight in her arms. "And he told me about you. Nice to meet you, Toby."

"Ma'am." He tipped his hat.

Eleanor caressed the pink cheek peeking out from behind his mother's braid. "And you, little one. It's nice to meet you." Memories flooded back of Victoria at that age, wide-eyed and innocent. If life had only stayed that simple.

"Billy knows you were coming. He's across the street right now with Charles. They're meeting with our interim mayor, but they should be done any time now."

As if on cue, the bell over the door rang again and two men entered. Billy's face exploded with a grin and he rushed up to hug Eleanor. "You're here." He shook Toby's hand. "Good to see you, Toby. And this..." He turned and motioned to a hand-some, well-dressed man with dark eyes and an immaculately trimmed beard. "This is Charles McIntyre."

With an affable but distant expression, he nodded at Eleanor and shook Toby's hand. "Nice to meet you. Billy says he wants to hire you, Eleanor. In which case, I'm not sure why I'm here, but if I can help..."

He was also a Southerner, but his accent had the refined ring of cotillions and plantations in it.

Billy and Eleanor exchanged a cautious look and he cleared

his throat. "Well, Charles, it's like this. Remember when I was in jail in Dodge City and I mentioned a woman who helped me get my horse back and set me up with a little jingle in my pocket." As he talked, Mr. McIntyre's expression tightened, ending in a frown as Billy brought the information to a close. "You might recall, she has a connection to someone we both know."

McIntyre's head raised slightly and his gaze slid over to Eleanor. "Dear God, you are her mother?"

She almost backed up an inch, there was so much vile in his tone. "Yes."

"What do you want?"

Billy inched forward. "I'd like Eleanor here to run the hotel for me while Hannah and I are back East."

Mr. McIntyre's jaw went slack. Eleanor suspected that didn't happen very often to this man, but he was in shock now.

"Have you lost your mind? The moment anyone finds out who she is— Good Lord, if they tried to lynch me, they'll have no compunctions about lynching Delilah's mother. She's not safe here."

"She could be. If you and Lane were willing to stand up for her, so to speak, if it comes to it."

"You mean put our necks on the line, and for what?" He whipped his head around to Eleanor. "What do you want?"

She fought off the urge to shrink under his hot gaze. She was here trying to save Victoria. That was all that mattered. "My daughter has this foolish idea of coming back to Defiance and turning herself in."

"That's suicide."

"That's what I keep telling her."

McIntyre turned and stormed away several feet. "I'd like to string her up myself." He paused, took a deep breath, and pivoted back to them. "I'm sorry. She's your daughter. You don't want to hear that, but I'm struggling with my own demons when it comes to Delilah."

"She's changed. She's following Jesus now."

Mr. McIntyre looked at Eleanor as if she'd said Victoria was a virgin. Some things simply could not be believed. It hurt her heart that this man held so much antagonism toward her daughter. "Mr. McIntyre, if you only knew her. If you'd only seen the agony she's gone through bearing the guilt and grief of all these deaths. Especially Logan's."

"I don't doubt she's guilt-ridden. But changed? *That* I doubt."

Hannah tilted her head and regarded Mr. McIntyre with one brow raised in accusation. "May I remind you, my brother-in-law, some of the worst sinners in the world are capable of change if Jesus is really the source of the change."

The gentle rebuke seemed to deflate him. He huffed quietly and straightened his shoulders to address Eleanor. "I can't tell her not to come here. I can't tell you that. But I won't protect her."

Billy frowned and pressed his hand lightly to Mr. McIntyre's chest. "Will you keep Eleanor safe if she comes to work for me? If it comes to it?"

Mr. McIntyre pressed two fingers to his forehead as if a headache was forming. "Tell me again, Miss Eleanor. What is it you hope to achieve by being here?"

"On the one hand, I hope I can learn something that will dissuade Victoria of this idea and send her back to Dodge. Failing that, maybe I can somehow sew the seeds of mercy in this town."

"And you." He looked at Toby. "What do you have to do with all this?"

"I felt it was wrong to let Victoria and Eleanor do this without help. Without protection."

A simple explanation, yet Eleanor would have sworn everyone in the room understood Toby was saying so much more.

"This is a foolish, foolish idea, Billy." McIntyre scratched his beard. "Foolish."

"I'm not going to tell anyone who Eleanor is. Will you? Will Lane?"

"Her secret would be safe with us," he acknowledged grudgingly. "But I urge you..." He passed his gaze over all of them. "Keep Delilah in Ruby City at all costs. And pray she stays there or goes back to Dodge."

~

If Charles allowed himself to curse, on his ride back to the ranch, he would have let loose with a blue streak. However, he didn't want to startle his horse, Traveler.

Delilah had no business coming back to Defiance. Was the woman out of her mind?

Or did she have an alternative motive? As in, building another saloon?

Perhaps she had changed...but not enough to suit Charles. Ever. Nothing would make up for all those deaths.

His mood was grim as he pulled up to the hitching post in front of his home, until Two Spears raced from the house, leaped from the porch, and scurried up to show him a new arrowhead he'd made. Charles climbed down from the saddle and took the object from his son. Smooth, sharp edges. It showed real skill. The ten-year-old was gifted.

He squeezed Two Spears's shoulder and grinned into the boy's dark face alight with expectation and hope. "I'm impressed. Your grandfather taught you well."

"And I have not forgotten."

"Clearly."

"I also made this." He pulled a small piece of wood from his pocket, whittled down with a ball inside it. He shook it and it rattled loudly. "For Adam."

His half brother, the infant born to Charles only a few

months earlier. Charles's heart swelled, knowing his son from an inappropriate arrangement was embracing the family. "I have no doubt he will love it." Charles turned the toy over and over in his hands. Truly skillful work.

"Let's see it."

Charles and Two Spears looked up at Naomi. His beautiful wife bounced their baby on her hip. The boy had a firm grip on her long, golden braid with one hand, and his other thumb was stuck firmly in his mouth. Two Spears rattled the toy in front of his brother, who was intrigued enough to reach for it, letting go of his mother's hair.

"Look, it rattles." Two Spears didn't hand it over fast enough. Adam grunted in displeasure and wiggled his fingers at the toy. Laughing, Two Spears passed it off. Adam shook it wildly and giggled with pleasure.

Charles leaned over and kissed Naomi on the forehead and poked his son in the ribs. Adam barely noticed, enthralled as he was with the rattle. Naomi tugged on a jet-black strand of Two Spears's hair. "What a wonderful gift. That's what you've been whittling on. I am very impressed."

Charles folded himself into his family's routine, enjoying dinner with them, holding Adam, and reading some history with Two Spears for homework. By eight, both children were asleep, and he had a moment to smoke a cigar in front of the fireplace. This was the time when Naomi would typically read her Bible or knit. Instead, she sat on the hearth and gazed up at Charles, an expectant lift in her brow.

"What?"

"You were distracted through dinner this evening. Something on your mind?"

She'd noticed. Her sharp observation surprised him. "I had visitors today. I was not pleased."

"Oh. That sounds foreboding."

He never held anything back from her. He wouldn't now. "Delilah is over in Ruby City. She wants to return to Defiance."

"Dear Lord, what for?"

"According to her mother, she wants to make amends with the town."

Naomi blinked in astonishment. "Wha—amends? Is she serious? And, wait, you said her mother?"

"Eleanor. She wants a job in Defiance so she can ascertain how dangerous it would be for her daughter to return here. She's wholeheartedly against the idea."

"I should say so." Naomi rose, hugged herself, and paced back and forth. "Is this for real, or does Delilah just want to return and cause trouble? More trouble?"

"That is my belief."

"But the town. She won't be safe here. They'll lynch her in a matter of minutes."

"That is also my belief." He puffed on the cigar and lost himself for a moment in the swirling smoke. If Delilah would only dissipate as easily.

Sighing, Naomi reclaimed her seat. "I see no good coming from any of this. Unless...if Eleanor is telling the truth, maybe that would be best. Let her experience the town's feelings."

"If it is discovered who she is, she'll likely be lynched as well."

Charles had no love for the woman he'd just met. If anything, he did have some pity for her. How awful to be the mother of a creature like Delilah.

The thought tweaked his conscience. If he could change, couldn't Delilah?

Not likely. The woman was too far gone. Not just in sexual debauchery with which he was well acquainted, but to cause the death of twelve men, buried now deep beneath their feet. And the sad loss of his friend, Logan. No, if anyone was a reprobate, it was Delilah Goodnight.

He could never forgive her. Or trust her.

Naomi reached out and touched his leg. "I don't like that expression on your face. I've seen it before. It wasn't good then. It isn't good now."

No. Delilah had that effect on people. On him. The mere mention of her name stirred up such loathing. On top of the mine explosion, she'd insulted Two Spears. Almost cost Emilio his hearing in the incident. No, she could not come back into his town. "Delilah is a threat to my family. To this town. If I can, I will stop her from returning. If I can't...the consequences will be on her."

"What about her mother?"

"I advised against the plan, but Billy wants her to run his store and hotel while he and Hannah are back East. As I said, neither Lane, Billy, nor I will expose her identity. There is no guarantee, however, someone can't connect her to Delilah." He studied Naomi's expression. She held a tight, worried pinch in her brow. "What? What is your concern?"

"You. And how this is affecting you."

"I'm fine." He squeezed her hand. "I'm fine."

"I won't pretend that there is any love lost between Delilah and me, but...if she's changed. If she's sorry—"

"She's lying. Trust me on this. The woman is lying."

Three

VICTORIA POKED AT THE FIRE, giving new life to the coals. She was bored. Anxious. Going stir crazy. *I need to get this done, Lord. I'll never have any peace. Just being sorry and trying to get on with my life feels all wrong.*

She flicked a glance at the clock on the wall. 6:30. Where were Toby and Momma? A knot of unease tightened in her stomach. Then—hoofbeats. Low, steady, rolling closer. Strange they hadn't taken the wagon into town today.

A moment later, Momma entered and breathed in the warmth. "Oh, it feels good in here. Long ride."

Victoria rose and scurried to the oven. "Here, I've got fried chicken I've been keeping warm." She began setting the table with plates and food as Momma peeled out of her coat. "Why was it a long ride?"

"Hmm?"

"You acted like the ride from town was longer than usual? Something happen?"

"No. No. I was just...belly-aching. It's cold and snowing again." She approached the stove. "Can I help?"

"You can take the coffee pot to the table and pour some for you and Toby."

"All right."

They were ready to start when Toby came in, shaking snow out of his scarf. "Gonna get another foot tonight at this rate." He took a deep breath and smiled. "Fried chicken. That'll hit the spot."

A few minutes later, they were all seated and eating, the blessing having been said. Yet, Victoria picked up on the quiet. Why wasn't there much conversation? And why wouldn't Toby and Momma look at her?

"Is something...wrong? You're both awfully quiet."

Momma laid her chicken leg back down and laced her fingers. "No sense pussy-footin' around about this. I've got something to tell you. I'm leaving."

The words were clear but Victoria couldn't pull the meaning out of them. "What? What do you mean you're leaving? Are you going back to Dodge?"

"I'm going to Defiance. I've got a job running the hotel there."

More words. Words she was competent to understand, yet Victoria was making no sense of them. "I don't know what you're saying."

"You let me go and be your eyes and ears. See if I can gauge just how mad the town still is."

"That's a foolish idea."

"Why? Because they might lynch me?"

Yes! But she didn't want to say that out loud. She didn't *really* think that was a danger...did she?

"Maybe then you'd abandon this *foolish idea*."

"Stop it, Momma. This is my problem, not yours. You can't get involved like this."

"You are my daughter. Every challenge or problem you face is my problem, to one degree or another."

Yes, there was no getting around that. A mother never stopped aching for her children when they hurt, or rejoicing when they triumphed. Victoria's daughter was blessed and safe

and would never know—

"I will not let you walk blind into that town. I can find out if the threat is real. If we're really talking about a lynch mob or people willing to accept justice. Or offer mercy. Victoria, if you stand trial—"

"I'll most likely go to prison. I can't run from this for the rest of my life. Knowing Jesus, I've got the strength and faith to do what needs doing."

Momma and Toby's expressions fell, but he fought to mask his immediately. Men and their stoicism. It piled on to Victoria's guilt.

I'm hurting them. Tearing them apart.

Perhaps she could offer them a little comfort. She took both their hands. "I'm sorry. I know you don't understand and I know it terrifies you for me...go to Defiance, Momma. Be my spy. I'll listen to whatever you find out." *Probably.* She nodded, coaxing a response from her.

Momma sighed. "Then so be it."

Victoria looked at Toby. The suspicion was plain in his eyes, but he half smiled and nodded as well.

Flynn cringed at the sound of lumber tumbling off a scaffold. Irishmen were good at a lot of things, carpentry maybe wasn't one of them. With a sigh, he looked up from his desk. The shadows on the other side of the tent's wall told the story. Two men shoved each other, and raised voices escalated into a shouting match. Violence wasn't hard to find in Tent Town.

"You stupid Mick," a man yelled, his voice laced with the faint color of the English countryside. "You did that on purpose."

"Ye're calling me stupid? I've brains enough to know if I'm gettin' paid by the hour I need more hours."

"That's crooked."

"I call it good business."

"You're a crook."

"I don't kowtow to anybody, especially to the English, especially Bishop."

"Then you're fired."

"Then this is free." A shadowy fist reared back and clobbered the Englishman. The thuds and grunts continued as Flynn rose and went outside. He was not one to miss a good fight. And if an Irishman was about to lick an Englishman, all the better. And, indeed, a slightly bloody and bedraggled Michael O'Keefe was sitting atop one Whiley Wilmshire and wailing on him good. Whiley worked for Bishop on all his building projects. What a pity O'Keefe here was throwing a log into the cogs, slowing things down.

A crowd formed fast, as men were always ready to watch a good fight. Cheers and jeers erupted as Wilmshire battled back to his feet. Flynn sneered at the small victory. Wilmshire was sucking wind like an old plow horse. O'Keefe would take him. The two men traded blows for a few more seconds, energized by the crowd of men bellowing, laughing, and shaking their fists at the brawlers.

O'Keefe landed a whale of a wallop on Wilmshire's jaw and the man fell backward like a toppled tree. O'Keefe straddled the man's chest and grabbed his collar. "Now who's stupid, ye worthless Limey." Breathing hard, blood dribbling from his nose, O'Keefe looked up and searched the crowd. When his eyes met Flynn's, Flynn nodded and strode forward. Taking a knee, he pulled his knife from his back pocket and began to clean his nails, meditating on this fight.

"Yer call, Mr. Flynn."

Wilmshire struggled for breath. "Please...please. I'm my mother's only son. Would you do that to a good woman? Take her only child?"

The image of the plaque at the Sunnyside Mine rose in Flynn's mind. Joseph J. Flynn was the last name listed. Only a boy of seventeen. "You know, Wilmshire, there's only one person on this planet I hate more than every Englishman on it. Since she's not here, however—"

"Please, Mr. Flynn. I'll leave. I'll leave tonight."

O'Keefe shook the man violently. "Be quiet. Ye'll do what he tells ye. If he says die, ye die."

"Charles McIntyre. Delilah. Our friend Bishop. Rich folks who don't care about the working lads who climb in and out of the mine. My predecessor, Matthew Miller, he cared." Flynn stood up and addressed the crowd. "And I carry on the mantle of giving the hardworking men in this town a place to drink, to come and place some friendly bets, and pass the time with friends. And I charge a penny less than Bishop."

Most of the men in the crowd nodded or smiled in agreement. Flynn might not win over the English, but the Americans were opportunistic. They didn't give a whit about blood feuds. They wanted cheap whiskey.

Flynn cleaned his thumbnail then slid the knife back into place. Sniffing with disdain, he wagged his finger at Wilmshire. "Ye tell Bishop ye're alive because I decided it that way. Let him up."

O'Keefe staggered to his feet. Wilmshire followed, flinching under the cold stares of the crowd, some English, some Irish. Wiping blood from his nose, he swiped his hat out of the dust and lurched off to his hole.

Yep, Flynn said to himself. Ye just as easily could be dead.

"Is it time yet?" O'Keefe asked, dabbing at his lip with a neckerchief.

Was it? "Start it slow," he said quietly. "Here and there. Pick them off one at a time. I'll let ye know when it's time for a full-scale donnybrook."

"All right then."

O'Keefe started to leave as the crowd was dispersing, but Flynn grabbed his arm. "They won't take this lying down."

"I know." He patted the knife on his hip. "We'll be ready."

Naomi liked Eleanor. Her demeanor was humble, affable, and warm. No wonder Billy was drawn to her. Her smile reached her faded, hazel eyes. Even Little Billy had taken a shine to her. Though in Hannah's arms, he kept reaching for the pudgy woman.

They were getting Eleanor settled in the manager's room behind the front desk. A room Emilio had occupied at first. For a man, it had seemed fine. Looking around the cramped quarters now, with its one small window looking out on the alley, Naomi didn't think it would do at all.

Eleanor dropped her two valises on the bed and her arms on her ample hips. "Nice room. Better than what I had back in Dodge. Almost as nice..." She didn't finish the sentence and neither of the girls pried.

Hannah reached over and pushed the red-checked curtains back, letting in more light. "We'd be happy to give you a bigger room upstairs. You'll be managing in our absence. It seems appropriate you have a nicer room."

"Oh, honey, this will be fine. I won't be in here much. Mostly just to sleep. I'll be going back and forth between here and the mercantile. This'll do."

This was news to Naomi. "You'll be managing the mercantile, too?"

Eleanor flipped open a suitcase. "After talking it over some with Mollie yesterday, Billy wants her to be the assistant manager here and that'll free me up to watch over the mercantile too."

"That way we only have to hire one clerk for the store, not two," Hannah explained.

"And I'm happy with that." Eleanor rummaged around her clothes as she talked. "I bet I'll get to meet everybody in town working at the mercantile."

The comment brought Naomi's head up. Was that the

reason she wanted to work there? What had Charles said? She wanted to find out the feelings in the town. The store was a good way to do that. Eleanor would meet everyone face-to-face eventually. And hear all their opinions.

Hannah chuckled. "The mining company opened a smaller mercantile over in Tent Town, but it's not as well-stocked. Everyone *will* filter through our store at one point or other."

"There you are." Eleanor retrieved a pipe from her suitcase.

Naomi folded her arms and leaned back on the wall. "You're going to be a busy woman, Eleanor, but you *will* meet everybody in town. The good and the bad. I hope you get time to rest and to think." To evaluate correctly the hard feelings toward Delilah.

"I'll find time if I need it. I can knit by the fireplace in the dining room. Smoke some." She waved her pipe. Little Billy reached out for it, close to toppling into her arms. "Oh, hey, there, Little Man. And there you go." She let the toddler have it. "We can sit in the dining room and stack blocks, too. What about that?"

Little Billy grinned. "Box. Stack box."

"That's right, we'll stack box." She hugged the boy and smiled broadly at Hannah. "I sure hoped he'd find you. He was set on it, like a dog with a bone."

"Thanks to you, he did find me."

"Aw, I only had a little something to do with it."

"If he'd been much later..." Naomi winked at Hannah. "Little Billy might be calling Emilio pa instead. It was almost a nail-biter there for a spell."

Eleanor gazed lovingly at Little Billy and tweaked his nose. "God had a plan, and it worked out for everybody. No matter the mistakes that were made. Gives me hope."

"Amen." Naomi slapped her hands together in goodbye. "And speaking of children, I need to get Adam from Rebecca. Eleanor, it has been nice to meet—"

The desk bell clanged wildly, startling the girls. Eleanor

handed Little Billy back to Hannah and rolled up her sleeves. "Sounds like we got a rowdy-do out there. I'll handle this."

They followed the woman to the desk, where a giant man with dark, wild hair, a frizzy beard, and a buffalo coat was waiting. His grin stretched clear to Texas. "I thought that was you back there."

Eleanor grinned and extended her hand over the desk. "Buckley, the preacher man." The two shook. "Nice to see you again. You, uh, coming to dine or take a room?"

He leaned down, resting an elbow on the counter, and nodded at her. "I'd like a room, a bath, and a big steak."

Eleanor picked up the ink pen, dabbed it in the well, and spun the guest book around to the man. "We can oblige you."

"I've been up with the Ute these last few weeks. Tonight, I'll be preaching in Tent Town. If you're of a mind to come." He scribbled his name and handed back the pen.

"Might be, at that. Where?"

"You're the preacher I've heard about." Naomi was convinced the man was more a grizzly bear than a human. But she'd bet he had no problems controlling his congregation.

"I reckon." He returned his attention to Eleanor. "Intersection of Water and Bonanza streets. Smack-dab in the middle of everything."

His location puzzled Naomi. "You haven't moved into a building?" Logan's church was still sitting empty. They'd had a pastor for a spell, but the town hadn't been to his liking. The empty sanctuary broke her heart, but she sensed the town and Charles still needed time to deal with all the deaths. "Or even a tent?"

"No, ma'am. I have not been called to preach inside four walls. Yet. The Lord may change his mind, but for now, I talk. I preach. Passers-by either listen or walk on. The Holy Spirit draws the right ones to the Shepherd's voice."

She supposed so, but in the winter, out on the street, on a blustery day like today, he might keep folks' attention a little longer if they were warm and dry. She would pray about it. Determined to do so, she offered her hand. "I'm Naomi McIntyre, by the way. This is my sister Hannah. Her son Little Billy."

"I know you." Hannah shook his hand with enthusiasm. "You've come in the store a time or two."

"Yes, indeed, I have. Well-stocked it is."

"Thank you." She hiked Little Billy a little higher on her hip. "Eleanor, if you've got this, I'll walk with Naomi. If you have any questions, yell for Mollie."

"I certainly will."

"And we'll show you the mercantile's books tomorrow if that's all right."

"Of course."

Buckley was watching Eleanor intently and Naomi sensed she and Hannah were in the way. Was the preacher looking for a wife? Maybe after a shave and a bath, he might have better luck getting Eleanor's attention. Chuckling to herself, she and Hannah bid them good day, grabbed their coats, and left. But Naomi glanced back quickly.

Would this big bear of a man be their next preacher? He sure looked like he could handle a rowdy congregation. Smiling at the image of him tossing a drunk miner to his rear end in the street, she let the door close on the thought.

Naomi and Hannah parted ways just before the newspaper. Hannah rearranged the blanket over Little Billy's head and hurried down off the boardwalk, waving goodbye. "Tell Rebecca I'll see her at dinner."

"You tell Billy I said hello." As Hannah navigated the traffic, Naomi tossed a return wave and let herself into the *Defiance Dispatch*. Rebecca pulled the front page of the newspaper off the press and laid it on the counter. The odor of India ink mingled with the scent of fresh coffee. Adam was sleeping peacefully in the bassinet on Rebecca's desk.

The surge of joy that constricted her throat didn't surprise her. She still couldn't believe the cherubic bundle of joy was hers and Charles's. How blessed they were. Grudgingly, she pulled her attention away to acknowledge Rebecca. "How goes the news today, sister?"

"Either a little slow. Or awful. Depends on how you look at things."

Naomi didn't like the sound of that. She shot Rebecca a puzzled look as she skirted the counter and peeked in on her angel. Sleeping like a log. Snoring softly. Her heart melted. "He even snores like a little angel."

"Yes. Yes he does. And he never cried once while you were gone, but I bet he's going to wake up any second now and he's going to wake up hungry."

Naomi's breasts were full and she needed to nurse soon, but she'd wait a few more minutes. Maybe he would wake up on his own. Resigned, she turned back to Rebecca, who was leaning over the paper, proofing it, and absently brushing her chin with the end of her thick, dark braid. Naomi was glad her sister had returned to this vocation. She'd worked for the town newspaper back in North Carolina but had quit after the fire that killed her husband and daughter.

So, this was the good side of Defiance. People pursued their dreams here. In her forties now, Rebecca wasn't slowing down, and Naomi was pleased the town had given her a second chance at life and love.

But was there something going bad with the town? The thought brought her back to Rebecca's puzzling observation. "Why did you say slow or awful? I don't understand what you mean?"

"The mine hasn't made any announcements. Buckley hasn't given me enough notice to announce his preaching and he's come through twice now. There are no new business owners in town. Mrs. Lee is going to be expanding her laundry, but that's not much to draw readers. So, it's slow."

"If it's slow, why do I hear so much construction going on over in Tent Town."

"Bishop and that other saloon owner, Flynn, are building homes and more saloons, I believe. That's not news."

"Then what's awful?"

"What I *have* had to write up."

She slid the paper over for Naomi to see. *Four Murders in Defiance.* The headline was large, black, unsettling across the top of the page. The first paragraph denoted the noticeable surge in violence in Tent Town and Hell's Half-Acre.

"Four. In two weeks. Lane is worried about the violence getting worse. These murders have been tit for tat between the Irish gang and the English, but I can't print that part because I have no proof."

"Is he planning on doing anything about the gangs?"

"He's talked to Ian about hiring two more deputies. In his words, 'hard men'. He's eager to push some of the worst elements out of town. The gangs won't tattle on each other, so he has no grounds for arrests. Therefore, he argues that some of the worst of the citizens over there need to be made to move on to other locales."

"Make them someone else's problem?"

"Maybe, but at least they won't be ours."

"I suppose." Speaking of problems, maybe she shouldn't discuss this with Rebecca, but Ian had probably already told her. Charles had told Ian. Billy had told Hannah. The circle around Eleanor's secret was already spreading in size. "Do you know who Eleanor is?"

Rebecca pulled the newspaper back from Naomi and splayed her fingers out over the surface of it. "Yes, but it's supposed to be kept very, very quiet. It troubles me." She slid her gaze up to Naomi, brown eyes full of worry. "The town is still seething over what Delilah did. I wish she and her mother were far, far away from here."

"Charles is convinced this is all some sort of a ruse. That Delilah wants to come back and open another saloon. Curse the town with more of her debauchery. If that's true..." She faded off, unwilling to speak aloud her fear, but the thought was there. The town will burn to the ground under the heat of the hate and growing lawlessness.

"Do you think it is?"

No. The opinion struck Naomi firmly and squarely in her heart. Though she had no reason to have an opinion yet, one way or the other. "For some reason, I don't think that's her purpose. I don't know what her purpose *is*, but I'm more worried about Charles."

"Why about him?"

"He hates her, Rebecca. It writhes in his brain, this burning stubbornness to refuse to believe she could have changed. He will not accept the possibility."

"Do you blame him?"

Did she? "I don't think he should be so certain a person can't change, who has met the Savior. If she really has, then she is different."

"Regardless. She's complicit in several murders. She should face justice."

"Can she get it in Defiance? I don't think she can. And Charles's intractability could too easily become a stronghold for the enemy. He's got to at least accept *he* should forgive her, whether she asks for it or not. Otherwise, the hate in him will grow. He gets this look in his eyes sometimes...it frightens me."

"The old Charles McIntyre?"

"If he came back from the dead, we'd lose everything."

"That won't happen." Rebecca tugged on Naomi's braid, trying to lighten the mood. "He'll follow the right path. You and Two Spears and Adam mean too much to him."

Naomi forced out a smile. "I'm sure you're right." But Charles's hate for Delilah meant a lot to him, too.

Four

NO, there wasn't much difference between running a saloon, a hotel, or a mercantile. Eleanor leaned in a little closer to study the mercantile's ledger Billy had slipped in front of her. Thankfully, she'd always been good with numbers.

"Now, you can see here, here, and here..." Billy dragged his fingers across the three months of orders, "the sales on blankets, tents, and cotton mattresses stay pretty steady. Miners like to stay warm. These are some of our most stable products, but the sales will spike again in the spring and summer."

"Men coming in to work."

"That's right. And then canned goods..." He flipped over a few pages. "Stewed tomatoes, canned beans—those are steady all year long."

"Don't they spike when the new miners come in?"

"It's strange. Only a little. I figure the men are spending more on living expenses to get started panning and, so, eating less. Then it sort of evens out."

She flipped through several other pages, spotted some trends easily, and mentioned them. Billy grinned and moved back to lean his hip on the counter. "You're a natural." He crossed his arms and puffed up as if quite pleased with himself.

"I knew you'd be a lot of help. Sometimes it takes a clerk weeks, even months, to spot the trends. You'll be ordering items with great confidence in no time."

"I'll try."

"I have no doubt we'll come back from Chicago and this place will be swept and dusted, and none of our supplies will be gathering moths."

His confidence unnerved her a little. She sighed and splayed her hands over the ledger. A thought bubbled up and she had to ask it. "Do you forgive her, Billy? Or am I here because you needed help?"

He took several seconds to form his answer, running his hand through his cropped, ash hair. "You did me a good turn, Eleanor. I've always wanted to repay that, sure. But I knew you'd do a good job. You're honest, hardworking, and committed. As far as Victoria..." He straightened up and trudged over to the stove. Warming his hands, his stare drifted. "I saw her that night. Logan died in her arms and it tore her up. I've never heard weeping like that in my life." He shivered as if the sound haunted him. "I hurt *for* her. But I believe his death brought back her humanity." He turned to look at Eleanor. "That's why I can believe she's changed."

"It seems it's going to be a lot harder to convince Mr. McIntyre of that."

"Yeah, well, he's not the most trusting soul. He's seen and done a lot of things in his life that make him jaded, even now."

"Even now?"

"He's a Believer. Gave his heart and soul to Jesus...and I think he wrestles every day with how to square that with running a town full of miscreants." He frowned, a deep *v* forming in his brow. "Maybe that's part of his problem. He's not running as much of it as he used to. Ian's our mayor. Lane is our sheriff. Charles used to do all of that, in a sordid, unsavory kind of way. He can't handle things the way he used to. The way he's inclined to."

Eleanor knew all about Mr. McIntyre, but not about his faith. If it was real, he'd have to believe Victoria had changed. Surely, he'd be able to see it.

But what good would that do her?

At least Billy believed. That was something. "Thank you. Thank you for believing me when I say she's changed."

"I saw it in Charles. If Jesus can change him, he can change anybody."

Eleanor smacked the ledger in frustration. "Why can't *he* see that?"

"Look, when Delilah came here, the town had almost tipped toward being law-abiding. She not only swept in with that craziness at the Crystal Chandelier, but she bought and sold women, and paid a man to blow up the mine over a petty squabble with McIntyre." Billy scrubbed his hands over his face as if trying to erase the memories. "It was bad. That's all that he sees right now. And he's not likely to look past any of it."

"Is he...is he the maddest? At her, I mean."

"Not by a long shot."

These observations both gave Eleanor hope and dragged her toward despair. Defiance was no place for Victoria. Would she be able to make her daughter listen?

Darkness settled over Charles, cold, suffocating. His throat tightened up on him. He struggled for breath. From the inky shadows, voices whispered. Familiar, they chilled him to the bone.

"Mighty bold talk from a man about to die."

"You ain't so much, McIntyre. I'll hang this rope on ya, but first I'll have a little fun."

Something scratchy cinched tight around his neck.

Then he remembered with a jolt. The lynching. Naomi—

Charles sat bolt upright in the rocking chair, a choked howl only an instant from escaping. He looked around the bedroom in confusion—his gaze settled on his baby boy, sleeping in his crib, safe, peaceful as an angel. Exhaling his fear, he sat back in the rocker. "Just a dream," he whispered, dragging his hand over his mouth. But he would never forget the feel of the rope dropping over his head, the stark terror in Naomi's eyes. How priceless his family was to him, even more so than before. A rope tended to make a man appreciate—

"Charles?" Naomi called from out in the hallway. A moment later, she appeared in the doorway. She started to speak, but a glance told her Adam was asleep. "Oh," she whispered, walking over to the crib. "Lane's downstairs." She touched a little golden curl at the nape of the infant's neck and gazed dreamily at the baby.

Charles let his anxiety drain away. Naomi could do that to him under any circumstance, but the glow of love on her face when she looked at their baby left him speechless.

God, I am blessed... "Did he say what he wants?"

She shook her head. Charles rose, and stretched the stiffness from his back. "I didn't realize I was so tired." He gave her a saucy kiss to get his blood pumping. "In the library?"

Grinning, she smacked his chest and pushed him away. "That's where I left him."

He kissed her again and then made his way to his favorite room in the house. Lane was standing beside his desk, spinning a globe. "Afternoon, Lane. What brings you by?"

"I had to break up a fight last night over in Tent Town. Picked up a few things. Thought you should know."

McIntyre slipped his hand into his pockets and strode to the window. The glare off the noonday snow was dazzling. Miles and miles of white hills dotted here and there with cows and horses, their short shadows stark against the ivory landscape. The dots were too few, however. He was looking forward to the new herd that would be here by April. "What things," he asked.

Lane didn't answer right away. McIntyre rounded on him and raised a questioning brow. His friend sighed. "We got us a rabble-rouser. A fella that came to town right before Matthew was arrested. He got the Number Two, and now he spends a lot of time talking about you and Delilah."

"Does he now? I gather from your visit he's not being very complimentary."

"His name is Flynn. An Irishman. He talks about you two taking advantage of the town. That Matthew was the only one who cared about folks."

"Is anyone listening to him?"

"That's the scary thing. He's spouting flat-out lies, but a few people are falling in line. Plus, he's got a gang."

McIntyre nodded, resigned to human nature. "There's always someone who wants what you have. If they can't take it from you, they make sure you can't have it, either."

"Yeah, I understand. Flynn is jealous of you and bitter over his brother's death in the mine."

"That damnable mine." Charles had days when he wished he'd never made the discovery of gold.

Lane scratched his chin. "There's more, though."

"More?"

"Some bad blood has developed between Flynn and an English group led by a fella named Bishop. Him and Flynn are bucking for control of Tent Town and Hell's Half-Acre, but they both agree on one thing."

McIntyre waited for the answer.

"They don't like you. They blame you and Delilah for the deaths in the mine."

A good portion of the men in town had a friend or a relative buried in that black hole. The knife drove deep. "It's going to take a while for this grief to run its course. Nothing I can do about it."

"I just think you should watch your back. I may not be around the next time you get invited to a necktie party."

McIntyre understood. Trouble was still on a low boil in Defiance over the mine explosion, and all the new miners coming into town added to the volatility. Who knew what might set off a mob? Certainly if Delilah came back, there would be no stopping the bedlam.

The thought of her return made him want to strangle the woman. Her presence would endanger his family even more so. He kept his thoughts to himself, however, and said simply, "I watch my back. I make sure my family is watched over. I'm praying Eleanor gets enough of an earful to convey the town's sentiments to Delilah. Clearly and without doubt."

"Yeah." Lane bit down on his bottom lip and swiped his hat off the corner of McIntyre's desk. "Guess that's all we can do. Keep our eyes and ears open."

Five

VICTORIA MOVED THE CURTAIN ASIDE. More snow. More wind. Another gray day. Toby was outside, about to mount up and head into town. Leaving her here alone. Again. When was Momma going to be back with some news?

What was Victoria going to do with herself today? She'd cleaned and polished everything she could think of to get her mind off Defiance. To block thoughts of Logan. To keep her thoughts from drifting to Toby.

She needed to get out of this cabin. If there was some way she could sneak into town. She'd risk it, but Toby and Momma would have apoplectic fits.

A gust of wind hit the house and blew Toby's hat off. It went tumbling.

Victoria grabbed his scarf off the peg by the door and raced outside. The cold air shocked her lungs. Ice crystals stung her face as she offered it to him. "The wind is kicking up." She had to raise her voice to be heard over it. "I thought you might want this. It's a long ride into town."

"My favorite Christmas present." He draped it over his hat.

"Your only Christmas present." She grabbed the sides and

tied them under his chin, pausing under his gaze. Even in the merciless, cold wind, there was an unmistakable heat in his eyes.

"Wouldn't matter. It'd still be my favorite."

She cleared her throat and stepped back. "I've been thinking," she yelled over the wind. "With Eleanor gone, I've got to go into town to buy supplies."

"I can get them."

"You could, but I'm going stir crazy, Toby. I need to see a town. Boardwalks. Store fronts. Even people. I just won't speak to them." A shiver hit her and she rubbed her arms. "I have to risk it or lose my mind."

"It's edgy. This close to Defiance. What if somebody recognizes you?"

"Nobody in these parts has seen me without kohl eyeliner, rouge, and lipstick...but I have an idea."

"What's that?"

"I'll dress like a man."

He laughed but sobered abruptly. "You're serious." He scanned her figure. "It won't work. Not sorry to say, you'd never pass for a man."

A smile flitted on her lips as the compliment warmed her cheeks. "Baggy clothes. A big coat. I'll hide my hair. I can pull it off."

"Well, I don't reckon you're asking my permission. If you were, I'd veto this idea right quick."

She laid a hand on his arm. "It will be all right. I know how to fool people. Bring me some clothes? Or I'll wear yours."

He patted the air as he stepped into the saddle. "Get inside before you freeze to death...I'll bring you something. Something big and baggy."

~

"I have to admit, if I was lookin' for a woman, I *might* look right over you."

Victoria grinned at Toby's comment and curtsied, a laughable gesture in her baggy pants and oversized wool coat. She spun for him in front of the fireplace.

"I told the undertaker you're my cousin."

Victoria's face and spirits fell. She glanced down at the coat. "Undertaker?"

"Couldn't afford a new coat. Ain't no church here with a benevolence closet. Only other thing I could think of was the undertaker, whom I know because he is also the town barber. I figured his customers—dead ones—might have left a few things behind. I was right."

Victoria's skin crawled at the thought of wearing a dead man's coat. She shook off the feeling only by thinking of the trip to town it would afford. Fresh air. New faces. A different horizon.

"Let's get the wagon hitched. I'll ride in with ya, tell Eugene at the mercantile you're my cousin and you can't talk."

"Am I deaf and blind, too?"

He appeared to give the idea serious consideration until she punched him in the shoulder. He raised his hands in surrender. "Fine. Maybe we could just say laryngitis? If you have to talk, whisper."

That met with her approval. "Fine."

Ruby City wasn't much to speak of. When they'd first arrived, back in November, the snow had been coming down pretty hard, veiling much of the town. Now, three months later, Victoria got her first good look at it. While the blanket of snow painted it in a picturesque way, Ruby City was anything but. She counted a grand total of six buildings on the main street and a smattering of cabins in the valley, smoke pouring from their chimneys. Most of the homes followed the shores of the stream. Gold claims.

Of the six buildings on Main Street, only two had any real size to them. The saloon and the mercantile. Toby nudged his horse up to the hitching post. Victoria pulled the wagon to a stop just short of it, so as not to block it. He met her at the mercantile door.

"Well, here goes," she said with a wink. Remembering she was pretending to be a man, she did not wait on him to open the door. Instead, she strode right into the long, dim building with all the bravado of a teenage boy. From behind her, Toby sighed, but he was on her heels pretty quickly.

He strode over to the counter as she perused the aisle of canned goods. "Eugene," he called. A second later, a wrinkled but spry man of about eighty knocked the curtains to an office out of the way and took his place at the counter.

"Mornin', Toby." As he snatched his apron from beneath the counter, he nodded at Victoria. "Son." He took his gaze back to Toby. "Which one of you was here first?"

"Eugene, this is my cousin..." He paused and Victoria realized they'd never settled on a name.

"Vic," she offered in a deep whisper.

Eugene's brow rose a touch. Toby swallowed. "Vic. Yeah, Vic here has a case of laryngitis. Anyway, he's picking up the supplies for us, seeing as how Eleanor has taken a job over in Defiance."

"Yeah, she told me about that. Sounds like a good opportunity."

"Yeah." Toby pulled a list from his coat pocket. "Anyway, if you and Vic here could pull these things together? I'll stop back by at noon and pay."

Eugene took the list. "Sure thing." He *tsked* as he unfolded it. "I'll miss Eleanor. She always had a few good stories about Dodge and Wyatt Earp and Saturday night shootouts." He looked over at Victoria. "When you get your voice back, I bet you've got some good stories, too, huh, young fella?"

Memories of things that would curl the man's thinning,

white hair cascaded through her mind, and she grunted in reserved agreement.

"All right then." Toby slapped a hand on his sidearm, nodded at Eugene, and turned to Victoria. "You need anything from me before I leave?"

She shook her head and just as he turned, winked. He paused, bit down on his lip, she supposed to hide a grin and strode toward the door. As he opened it, two women wrapped in scarves and wool coats entered. He tipped his hat and held the door for them.

Eugene came around the counter and waved Victoria's list at the women. "Elsie, Betty. Be right with ya. Let me get this fella squared away."

"No, hurry," one said, unwrapping her scarf. "We want to look over the cloth. Betty here has a hankering to make new curtains for her cabin." Their curious gazes shot to Victoria. "You new in Ruby City?" Elsie asked.

Eugene slapped Victoria on the shoulder. "This here is Vic. He's got himself a case of laryngitis, but he's Toby's cousin and he'll be doing their shopping from now on."

"Oh," Betty nodded. "Cause Eleanor took that job over in Defiance?"

Small towns. No secrets. Victoria smiled and nodded at the women.

"Good to meet you, Vic." With that, the pair drifted over to the five bolts of cloth in the store. Eugene and Victoria wandered the store, collecting the items on the list. Twenty minutes later, everything was loaded in the wagon and Victoria was on her way home.

And no one in Ruby City was any wiser. All in all, the trip was a success. She wouldn't be able to pull off laryngitis for another two months, but she'd think of something. Glancing around the slow, sleepy town, she realized she hadn't been missing much anyhow.

The last building on her way out was Toby's office and she

was considering a quick stop when he hurried out the door, rifle in hand. Their eyes met and she saw the tension in his expression. "Got some sheriffing to do?"

He waved the rifle. "A little trouble over at the saloon." But then he shrugged sheepishly. "Marlin has an unwanted guest in his storeroom. A bobcat."

Victoria chuckled. "A dangerous hombre."

He scowled at the sarcasm. "I reckon I'd rather deal with a wild animal than a wild drunk. Everything go all right at Eugene's?"

She jerked her chin toward the supplies in the back. "*Vic* got everything on the list."

"Good. You going straight back to the ranch?"

"No, I thought I might detour to New York and have a steak at Delmonico's." He scowled again and she sighed. "Unless you know of some mischief I can get into, seems the ranch is my only destination." She hadn't meant for the saucy remark to sound flirtatious, but once out there, it carried its own weight. Clearing her throat, she slapped the reins and said as the horse pulled away, "I'll see you tonight."

Naomi stared into the face of her cherubic little darling. Adam was not yet five months old, but she was sure he was the most wonderful baby in the world. Every time she looked into his chubby, moon-shaped face, she thanked the Lord for him.

Sighing with contentment, she hugged him a little tighter and slipped into the newspaper office. Rebecca and Ian, her sister's tall, balding, middle-aged, Scottish husband, were sitting side by side at their desk. Rebecca was dictating as Ian pontificated. "Furthermore," he was saying, "it is time the infrastructure of Defiance gets its much-needed upgrade. I propose a second firehouse—"

"Look, Adam, it's Aunt Rebecca and Uncle Ian."

Rebecca gasped. "Adam." She quickly set the paper aside and raced for her nephew arms out. "I've missed him. Let me hold him." Naomi didn't have much choice and gave up her son to prevent Rebecca tackling her. Her sister cooed and sang over the baby, who smiled readily and tugged on her braid. "Oh, Adam, you are so pwecious. Two days is too long to go without seeing you, my wittle man."

Naomi grinned, amused at her sister's silly baby voice. Yet, everyone had one when it came to Adam. Even Ian reached over Rebecca's shoulder and gently took hold of the baby's fingers, who immediately grasped his in return. "Oh, my, what a strong grip ye have there, boy."

Moments like this made Naomi a little sad for her sister. Rebecca had lost her daughter and husband in a fire. The Lord had blessed her with Ian, a new husband who loved and honored her. But Rebecca wouldn't have any more of her own children. Instead, she'd watch her sisters have them.

She rejected the maudlin thoughts abruptly. Not today. Today, they would think on happy things. "Ready for lunch? Mollie has a new special at the restaurant. "

"Oh, yes, yes," she said, tickling Adam's chin. "I am weady for lunch. How about you, Adam?"

"He's eaten. Bundle up. Ian, will you be joining us?"

"Thank ye, lass, but I'm working on a platform. A list of things to bring to the voters in the fall."

"You think someone will run against you?"

"It dusnae matter. The citizens have a right to know of my vision for Defiance. Which entails more law and order, and I'm working on a fire prevention program."

Left up to Ian, Defiance would be civilized overnight. He'd proven to be an efficient temporary mayor. She hoped he'd earn the job in the election. "And then schools and more churches."

"Aye. Which will bring in dress shops and other non-saloon-type businesses. We can make something grand of Defiance. If we all work together."

He instilled hope in her. And, judging by the glow on Rebecca's face, in her, too.

~

Flurries greeted them as they stepped out into the gray day. The traffic on the street and the boardwalk was about half what it would be in another month. Soon, they would be stepping around people. Today, a few men tipped their hats, and there was plenty of room to walk. When the weather broke and folks knew the passes were open, the onslaught of miners would quadruple.

A snowflake landed in Naomi's eyelashes and she blinked it away. Winter was hanging on this year. She longed for warmth and sunshine. A blanket by the creek, a book, and her baby. "I wonder how much longer this weather will go on? A month?"

Rebecca hugged Adam a little tighter, warding off the cold. "Maybe less. Ian said the snowpack is about gone on the roads."

An early spring then? "I'm looking forward to the longer days, the warmer temperatures, but not the crowds. And maybe spring will help with the crime. If men feel less confined, if they get more sunshine, maybe their moods will improve. Is that too simplistic a view?"

Rebecca hiked Adam up a touch higher on her hip and tightened her grip. "No. I think you might be onto something. If I could pipe sunshine into town on these gray, snowy days—"

Raised voices from the doorway beside them interrupted their walk. Instinctively, Naomi thrust out her arm to stop Rebecca. Trouble sizzled in the air.

Two men faced each other, their raised chins and clenched fists signaling a fight. "Stop ye're lying. I saw ye take the dice." The Irish gangs. They were always causing trouble, but not usually on the street in the daylight.

"I took nothin'. Your bloody Irish whiskey is givin' you 'allucinations." This man had a heavy English accent. And that explained everything.

"Are ye calling me a liar then?"

"I'm calling you a drunk. Or I guess I'll just call you an Irishman."

Before Naomi and Rebecca could retreat further, the Irishman whipped out a Bowie knife and took a swipe at the other man's throat. As the blood spurted out, the assailant took off running, slamming into Naomi and nearly knocking her over.

Passers-by stopped in confusion as the victim clutched his neck and tried to speak, but only garbled noises and blood came out of him. Shock freezing her rational brain, Naomi reacted only on instinct. She shoved Rebecca. "Step back. Don't let Adam see." Rebecca spun the baby away. Naomi turned and rushed to the victim as he collapsed on the walk, the crimson blood coloring the snowy boardwalk. Others stood by, watching wide-eyed and shocked. "Someone get Dr. Hope," she yelled, dropping to her knees beside the victim. Oh, Lord, what do I do...?

Glassy eyes stared up at her. A gaping wound glistened with steaming, gushing blood. It poured forth from the man like a river. She raised her hands to touch him, to put pressure on the wound, but the slice in his neck was long, deep, and perfectly deadly.

So much blood.

His artery is cut...

A final breath escaped the man, an eery, haunted sound, and he lay still.

Blood slowed dramatically from his neck, but the spreading stain forced her to her feet to avoid it. Was there something she could have done? She hadn't even had a chance to pray for him.

So fast. It happened so fast...

Rebecca laid a hand on her shoulder. "Dear God." She handed Adam back to Naomi. "Are you all right.?"

She hugged her baby to her, keenly aware of how fast life could end. "Yes." Was she?

"I'll go get Lane. Will you let Ian know what happened?" Naomi nodded, eager to get away from this horrific scene. Rebecca looked at the handful of men who had gathered around this sad, shocking death. "If you saw this, please stay here. I'm sure Lane will want to question you." She hurried off.

Like the spreading stain in the snow, shock crept over Naomi. The violence of the attack, the swiftness of it, unnerved her. She couldn't even describe the attacker, it had all happened so fast. And now, a murderer was on the loose.

"It was one of them Micks," a man said.

A Mick?

"Them and the English have been having run-ins."

Naomi couldn't make sense of what he was saying. She turned to find the speaker. A grizzled, older man with a thick beard stared down at the victim. Cold disinterest glimmered in his gaze.

"I don't understand. Are you saying you know the attacker?"

"Nope. I ain't getting involved. I didn't see nothing."

"If you know anything that can help Lane—"

"Lane's got any sense, he'll let them settle it."

"Them?"

"Was a time the worst thing on the street in Defiance was a couple of whores fighting." He shook his head in disgust. "Now these gangs are bringing their problems here. Not even keeping to their side of town." The man frowned at her. "You better not say anything. You could be borrowing trouble. My advice is to stay out of it." The men behind him grumbled and disbanded.

Reflexively, she tightened her hold on Adam. "Where are you all going? You have to answer questions for Lane."

The witnesses ignored her and drifted away, leaving in their wake a wave of sadness that washed over Naomi. She looked back at the man on the street, staring lifelessly at the sky. Mere moments ago, he'd been walking, talking, breathing. In seconds, all that had ended, and now he was facing eternity. Was he a Believer? Had he ever heard the Gospel?

No one on this side of the Jordan would ever have the answers.

Six

⌘

ELEANOR HAD BEEN GONE CLOSE to a month now. Toby rode Dollar into the barn, glancing at the cabin. The amber light glowing in the windows warmed his heart. He missed her, but he was pleased the quiet evenings with Victoria seemed to carry a little tension. The two of them alone together had spiced the air with danger. Desire. He knew she sensed it, too. Was she really such an oak?

He put his horse up for the night, taking his time, dilly-dallying a bit with the currycomb, and giving Delilah a friendly handful of grain. He didn't want to look too anxious to get indoors. He had to treat Victoria carefully. She knew he cared for her, but he couldn't be the lovesick fool. He had to let her come to him. Hard as it was to wait. It sure had been one long month already.

"Toby," she called, her voice slightly muffled by the dusky snow. "Supper's getting cold."

He grinned. "On my way." Still, he spent another few minutes with Delilah, then made for the cabin.

She was setting a basket of bread on the table when he stepped in and shrugged out of his coat. Firelight flickered over the room, the scent of fried ham and warm biscuits made his stomach growl. "Smells good."

She poured them both some coffee, he pulled her chair out for her, and they sat. He reached for her hand. "I'll say grace." But when she slipped her delicate fingers into his, his thoughts scattered like crows in a cornfield. He cleared his throat, managed something thankful, then sliced a bite of ham.

"How'd the wild bobcat incident go?" she asked, tossing her long, auburn ponytail off her shoulder. One of these days he was going to run his hands through all that silkiness. "Did you arrest the offender?"

Toby shook his head and chuckled. "I believe I misspoke when I said I'd rather deal with a wild animal than a wild drunk. That critter howled and hissed and spat and made noises straight from the pit of hell. I've never heard such sounds from an animal."

"Scared you, did it?"

"It absolutely did." He reached for his coffee, pondering the vision of the cat coming straight at him. "I'm just glad there was a window in the store room. Marlin managed to get it open from the outside. The cat charged me, but she was really running for the exit." He started laughing. "I ducked and she used my back to make the leap. I reckon she was as terrified of us as we were of her."

Their laughter settled, and after a moment, Victoria said, "Those two mules came in today."

"Yeah, I saw them in the stall. Did you go out to meet Leroy or...?"

"I started not to, but I was still in the dead man's clothes, so I shuffled out. Kept it to a whisper. Everything was fine."

Something about this made Toby uneasy. Perhaps the possibility that maybe Victoria was getting too confident. The fewer the people who saw *Vic* the better. But he could bring up this bravado of hers later. "And how are the mules? Easy to handle?"

She nodded.

"Good. So we're full. The keep on 'em will get the bills paid. Come spring, maybe we'll consider putting up another barn. The miners'll be back..." he trailed off. Spring. When she wanted to head on over to Defiance.

An awkward silence blanketed them, making the clink of their forks too loud. "Oh, the pie," she said abruptly, rising. "I made an apple pie." She pulled it from the stove and set it near him. "I don't have much experience baking, but I think it'll be tolerable."

He licked his fork clean and eyed the pie with eagerness. "I figure any pie is better than no pie."

They spent a few minutes in light conversation, veering far and wide from talk of spring. He hated her plan, but he had a few of his own. He just needed time. Together they cleared the dishes and stacked them for washing. As he poured hot water over them, he met her gaze and smiled. "I have a present for you."

"Really?" She grabbed a rag and started to pull a plate from the steaming water but dropped it. "Ouch. It needs to cool a minute."

"Good." He set the kettle back on the stove and hurried over to his coat by the door. "I thought this might be nice at night instead of just the crackling of the fire." He pulled a box from his pocket and motioned for her to join him in front of the fireplace. She hung her rag on the sink and sashayed over to him, her expression alight with curiosity.

In the glow of the fire, she was something. All that pretty, auburn hair loosely gathered in the back, delicate little wisps hanging down at her temples, glimmering in the light. Her unusual olive skin was so silky and touchable. Pouty lips that begged for a kiss. He shook himself mentally and handed the gift to her.

Victoria pulled the top off and gasped. She flicked him a pleased look through long lashes and pulled the music box free, tossing the container aside. Eagerly, she cranked the handle, and the beautiful, soft, tinny, but merry chords of Blue Danube filled their little parlor.

She closed her eyes, smiled dreamily, and swayed with the Viennese tune. Toby had to stare for a moment, lost in the possibilities, the dreams of her. He pinched the brow of his nose and stepped back. Maybe the music box wasn't such a good idea after all.

"How did you know?" she asked.

"Know what?"

She opened her eyes, flames reflecting in their chocolate depths. "Blue Danube. It's my favorite song."

"I wish I could say I did know." He hung his thumbs on his belt loops and shrugged. "It was the only music box Eugene had. I happened to see it when I stopped in to buy some jerky. I thought it would be nice to have some music at night."

She laughed, richly and joyously. "Thank God it's not Buffalo Gals."

He laughed, too, and rubbed his neck. Yeah, he hadn't really thought how differently this could have gone.

Suddenly, Victoria reached out and took his hand. "I have to dance." She set the box on the mantel. "Dance with me, Toby."

He didn't hesitate to grasp her fingers and held her gaze as they waltzed on the rag rug in front of the fireplace. They stepped, turned, and glided. His hand on the cleft of her waist belonged there. Nothing had ever come as natural to him as pulling her into this embrace. He gathered her closer, up against him, took her fingers, and pressed them to his chest. Every breath, every curve, every touch of her set his mind ablaze.

And they danced. With no words. Only what their eyes could say, neither fully knowing what the message was. The only thing Toby was sure of was he had a chance to change her mind about Defiance, to turn her heart toward him.

If he had enough time.

~

Eleanor smiled. Thumps and giggles from upstairs told her Billy and Hannah were playing a game with Little Billy. The child's innocent, joyous laughter lifted her heart and she let it soar. Life wasn't perfect, but she could savor the sound of a child who was loved and safe and warm. Billy and Hannah trusted her enough with the store now to sleep in a little and enjoy some family time in the mornings. This was deeply gratifying to her. At her age, she still had the ability to do some good. To make someone's life a little better.

The bell over the door rang and a woman in a frayed shawl entered. Shadows smudged the skin beneath her tired eyes. Oh, Eleanor knew that look. "Let me know if I can help you find anything."

The woman nodded but didn't reply. Two young girls slipped into the store behind her. Pretty, but also frayed and tired, like their mother. Young teens, it wouldn't be long before they'd be forced out into the world. Eleanor hoped they stayed with their mother for several more years. And maybe a good man like Billy Page would come along and rescue them all.

The woman ventured near the counter, perusing the display of wooden cooking spoons and metal spatulas.

"I haven't seen you in here before," Eleanor said gently, "but I'm new."

"I'm not. I still live in the company housing for the mine and shop in the company store mostly. MP&G hasn't told us to leave, yet. But I expect they will. New miners coming in every day, they'll be needing the housing."

"Is your husband not employed at the mine anymore?"

"He's dead." She spat the words like a curse. "I've been living off the blood money Mr. McIntyre gave us, and taking in wash."

The bitterness in the woman's tone gave Eleanor a chill.

"Oh. I-I'm sorry." She wrapped her fingers up nervously in her apron. "You blame him for the mine explosion?"

"His mine. Ultimately, he's responsible. But mostly, I blame that horrid witch Delilah. I ever see her again, I'll claw her eyes out." She snatched a spoon from the tray with unnecessary violence. The two girls didn't move. Only stared at their mother with wide, frightened eyes.

"Some folks have told me this McIntyre was in cahoots with her."

"Maybe. I don't think so. I think they were fighting over the town." She laid the spoon on the counter. "And I need these things." She handed Eleanor a short list of groceries written on a wrinkled piece of butcher paper.

"Yes, ma'am." Eleanor scurried about gathering the small order of coffee, flour, bacon, and sugar. The woman and her daughters counted out a dozen eggs, placing them in the wire basket on her arm.

Eleanor met them at the counter. "There. I think that's everything... What do you mean fighting over the town?"

"He runs Defiance. Delilah wouldn't play things his way."

"You knew Delilah, did you?"

"Everyone in town knew her or at least knew of her. A spiteful, vengeful witch. They said she paid that man to blow up the mine because Mr. McIntyre spirited away some of her celestial girls."

"What in the world?" Eleanor fought the tension in her face, wrestling to keep a friendly expression on it.

"She used to parade 'em, right down Main Street every day at three. One day, they all disappeared, from right under her nose. Oh, she was spittin' mad. A man had made Delilah look like a fool. I heard she threw things in the saloon. Screamed and hollered. Plain crazy, you ask me."

"I understand how that would be upsetting to a woman like her."

"Oh, she raged and raged...then the mine blew up and

Smith confessed his part before he died. Confessed to the preacher yet." The woman swallowed, her eyes misted over. "My Hank is buried at the bottom of the mine. They couldn't get his body out."

Eleanor could weep with this woman. The shared connection to the pain was so real. "I'm sorry." Perhaps she had let too much grief and shame slip into her voice.

The woman regarded her oddly for a moment. Almost suspiciously. Then she shook it off and opened the reticule on her wrist. "She'll be sorry if I ever see her. She's a murderer. My girls will grow up without a father. I don't get a job, they'll be homeless." She snatched her groceries off the counter, passing her daughters each a box of something. "I doubt anybody hates Delilah Goodnight more than I do."

Eleanor didn't breathe until the door closed behind the family. The vitriol the woman had spat spiked the air with a dangerous poison. Dear God, if everyone in the town feels that way...

She wiped sweat off her upper lip and imagined kidnapping her own daughter and disappearing with her to parts unknown.

～

Flynn tagged his man O'Keefe in the gut and pointed down the snowy, muddy street. The bear of a man they called Preacher Buck was preparing to give the passing crowd another sermon. Digging through the pockets in his coat, he was most likely looking for his Bible.

"What do ye think makes a man want to stand on the corner in the snow and cold and shout about Jesus?"

O'Keefe shrugged. "I got no idea. Can you see our priests doing that?"

"Not likely. My ma's priest wouldn't sit down on the pews without his pillow." And this man withstood the cold and the cold stares of strangers to shout nonsense about the Lord. The last time he'd preached, someone had thrown a snowball with a rock in it. Hit the big man square in the back of the head. He didn't even lose his page in the reading.

Flynn couldn't decide if he admired the man or had pity on him for being touched in the head.

"I want to start today," Buckley began yelling, "with a story of compassion and forgiveness." The few passers-by glanced the man's way but didn't stop. "Christ our Lord told a story of a man with great debts." He flipped open his little, black Bible, found a particular page, and started reading. "Therefore is the kingdom of heaven likened unto a certain king, which would take account of his servants. And when he had begun to reckon, one was brought unto him, which owed him ten thousand talents..."

Flynn's gaze danced around the busy, snowy intersection of the street. Women bundled up with laundry baskets on their hips hurried by. Men tugged their coats tighter and headed for or were coming back from their shifts at the mine. A well-dressed gentleman, one of the suits that managed the Sunnyside Mine, tossed a coin into the snow at Buckley's feet, but didn't stop. No one stopped. All of them were pretending to ignore the big man and his story.

"...But the same servant went out, and found one of his fellow servants, which owed him a hundred pence: and he laid hands on him and took him by the throat, saying, 'Pay me that thou owest...'"

Flynn's attention snapped back to Buckley. A fight? Mayhap this story was better than he'd thought. He settled more comfortably on the hitching post holding him up and gave the preacher his attention. Any story that involved choking an enemy had to be interesting.

It was something about a crooked manager who had his embezzling forgiven, but he didn't return the favor to some lad who owed him a small amount. Mean and vindictive, the manager had the small debtor thrown in jail.

"Must have been an Englishman," Flynn muttered.

Buckley continued, "Then his lord, after that he had called him, said unto him, 'O thou wicked servant, I forgave thee all that debt, because thou desiredst me: Shouldest not thou also have had compassion on thy fellow servant, even as I had pity on thee?' And his lord was wroth, and delivered him to the tormentors, till he should pay all that was due unto him.

"So likewise shall my heavenly Father do also unto you, if ye from your hearts forgive not every one his brother their trespasses."

Flynn grunted and stood up, pointing at Buckley. "Now, that's a Gospel I can agree with, lad. We make our choices. We make our deals with the devil. We honor them. There should be no forgiving. The young servant got what he deserved."

Buckley tilted his head. Something in his gaze, intense and hot, almost made Flynn back up. Almost.

"Flynn, is it?" Buckley stomped over to him, his buffalo coat swinging about his thick, leather-clad legs, adding to his impressive size. "We all have a debt, son, one we'll never, ever be able to repay. It separates us from God. The amount is greater than we can imagine. But Jesus paid it for all mankind. He cleared the slate. For me. For you. For everyone. Even though none of us deserved his mercy."

"Then Jesus is a fool. I'll not ask forgiveness for the things I've done, and I'll not give it. No mercy. No quarter."

"How grand it must be to live with such peace." A small crowd of curious on-lookers had slowed and pooled around them. "No regrets." Buckley waved his arms at the on-lookers. Was he mocking Flynn? "No remorse. To have hurt, maybe killed, and you never look back."

"That's right, lad. I've no regrets." He yelled the last part so everyone could hear him.

"No need of forgiveness."

"Not in my book." Flynn glanced at the faces watching

closely. "It's my enemies who need mercy, and they won't be getting it."

"I'm sorry for you, Flynn, but I will keep praying for you."

"My mother, God rest her soul, prayed to the beloved saints over me every day till she died. Did her no good."

"The difference between your beloved mother and me is I will be going straight to the top."

"Go to the devil, for all I care." Disgusted, Flynn waved off the man and continued his journey to the saloon. All this talk of forgiveness, mercy, sin. That mess was for the faint of heart. He pushed through the doors of the Number Two, a rough place, but all his. Maybe not legally, but Matthew was in jail and wouldn't be getting out anytime soon. Flynn had walked in and taken over, implying he had Miller's permission. Long as the whiskey flowed, no one on this side of Tent Town—what they all called Hell's Half-Acre—had cared one way or the other.

I'm sorry for you, Flynn, but I will keep praying for you.

The preacher's promise irritated him. He didn't need any blasted preacher talking to Jesus on his behalf. But, worse, anyone feeling sorry for him angered him. He'd not have pity. Pity the woman who had sent his little brother Joseph to his death in the Sunnyside Mine. One day, her name would surface. She'd be running a new place down in New Mexico, or maybe Nebraska or Chicago, but she would surface again like a dead fish.

And Flynn would be waiting. Joseph had taken his shift that day. Now, Michael believed he'd been saved to avenge the boy's death. Time. It would take time. Patience. Asking around long enough. Asking the right people.

But eventually, he would find her.

His would be the last face Delilah Goodnight ever saw. No, her death wouldn't bring Joseph back. But he'd send the woman to hell on a rail car. Just like the man from the story who had sent the debtor to prison. No mercy. No grace. Only vengeance would do for Michael Flynn.

～

"I hear your sermons are going over like a temperance speech." Eleanor sat down across from Buckley at a table in the dining room and waved for a waitress. Maria hurried over and nodded at the pair. "Maria, this is my friend Buckley. He'll be ordering breakfast. I'd like a coffee."

"Sí"

Buckley ordered eggs and bacon before he responded to Eleanor's observation. "I preach the Gospel. Sometimes, a lot of times, that don't tickle folks' ears. Don't make it any less true."

"Why don't you have a building? A congregation?"

"Church ain't just in four walls. Besides, Pastor Barton has that nailed down. When he comes through the area, he uses the one over in Cripple Creek. Me, I need to move. Like Jesus, I want to go to where the people are. Chase them, pursue them, find them."

"And every once in a while?"

"I find a lost lamb, throw him over my shoulders and celebrate."

"So, you think people can change?"

"I know it. Jesus can change anybody."

"I sure am a far cry from where I started out in life." So many mistakes behind me, though.

Buckley settled back. "Tell me. I'm always interested to behold tales of God's grace."

She waited till Maria had poured their coffee to answer. Then she pulled the mug closer and sighed. "Familiar story. I made some bad choices, but I had a child to support. When she was old enough that the men started noticing her, I sent her away. God as my witness, I thought I'd sent her to a decent hotel to work. Turned out it was a brothel and she thought I'd sold her."

Buckley scratched his jaw thoughtfully and shook his head, pity in his eyes. "Kind of reminds me of Joseph's story."

"Yeah, I guess so. I never thought of it before."

"Have things worked out? You're a Believer. What of your daughter?"

Eleanor took a long, weary breath and let it out with deliberation. "Buckley, my daughter and I both are Believers. I've managed to mostly forgive myself for what happened to her. I had good intentions."

"But?"

"My daughter, her journey was awful. Darker, more painful. People are dead because of her." Victoria's wake of destruction was more widespread than could be described. Like a pebble in a pond, the ripples would go on forever. Children without fathers. Wives made widows. Hearts hardened. And would Delilah ever love again? Logan's death had killed something in her, despite her faith.

"You ever met anyone who couldn't forgive themselves?" she asked. "Even though they'll tell you all day long Jesus died for their sins?"

"That your daughter?"

"She's got this crazy idea..." There was no way to explain without telling Buckley who her daughter was. "She wants to come back to Defiance and turn herself in."

His brow knit in confusion then rose in shock. He cocked his head to one side, like a curious dog. His voice dropped to a whisper. "You telling me your daughter is Delilah?"

Eleanor wrestled with the knot in her throat, the tears filling her eyes. She blinked them away angrily and looked down into her coffee. Huffing a breath, she nodded.

"My lands," Buckley whispered, pulling back from the table. "And she thinks she owes penance. Is that it?"

"What should I tell her?"

Buckley reached across the table and took Eleanor's hand. She looked up and was taken aback by his penetrating stare. "To stay the heck away from Defiance."

"I've been telling her that."

"The demon of revenge has a terrible hold on too many hearts here. But there is other mischief afoot. Men scuffling for power and position. Fighting and dying over a town that won't even be here in a hundred years. Your daughter'll be like tossing kerosene on a fire."

"I've been hearing things and I agree. If she comes back now, one side or the other will use her to set this town on fire."

"I'm praying. I'm ministering. I'm doing all I know to do to fight the devil, but folks have their own free will. She needs to stay away...till something breaks."

"I wish she'd never come to Colorado, but we couldn't stop her."

"We?"

"A young fella came with us...to protect us, but he's in love with her. He knows it. She knows it. He's a good man, but she won't give it a chance until she does what she's come to do."

"They're close by, are they?"

Eleanor hesitated. She trusted Buckley, but still, it was better the fewer people who knew where Victoria was.

He nodded at her delay. "Ruby City, I reckon." He shook his head, scratched his chin through his deep, frizzy beard. "I'll say it again. Keep her away till something changes."

Eleanor's spirits plummeted. Sudden panic out of nowhere gripped her, worked a tiny, choked sob from her. "I can't lose her again." Embarrassed, she hid her face in her hands. "I can't. I won't let this town have her."

Buckley reached over and patted her shoulder with an awkward affection. "There, there. We must trust the Lord has a plan here."

"I know he does," she wept, "I'm just praying Victoria doesn't foul it up."

Buckley pulled his hand away and went silent. After a moment, Eleanor noticed and looked up, wiping her eyes and swallowing the knot in her throat. The big man was staring down at his plate, his half-eaten steak growing cold. "What?"

"Maybe it's time I use a building. Maybe a few more people will come if they can get out of the cold."

Something sparked in Eleanor's heart. Pure hope. "I think they will."

∼

From the moment Adam was laid in Charles's arms, he knew Defiance must be kept civil at any cost. And now Naomi and her son had been inches away from a murderer with a knife. Fear of what could have happened twisted in his guts for days. He and Lane had made their way through the tents and saloons in Tent Town, trying to find the murderer.

No one was talking. Not the Irish. Not the English. They wouldn't point fingers. Not even at the opposite gang. That didn't bode well for what might be coming.

He drummed his fingers on Ian's desk. His old desk. In the old Iron Horse Saloon. The building now served as the news-paper office and the town hall. The town had almost turned the corner into actual respectability. And here it was, teetering on the edge again.

The drive to do something to pull the town back before it went off the cliff burned in Charles's bones.

He knew what he had to do. They had talked to everyone but the ones who mattered. The ones who called the shots. But Flynn and Bishop would not be bluffed. He would have to mean it.

"So, what we've got," Lane began, crossing one leg over the other, "I think a gang war is about to break out. Some of the Micks who would talk would only say they're waiting on the word. And they're ready to get to it, Johnny Reb."

Ian leaned back in his chair and slapped his balmoral bonnet back and forth. "A donnybrook like that could spill over into our streets. As we've already seen with what Naomi and Rebecca witnessed. I say we hire more deputies. Several more, on a temporary basis until this gang situation is cleared out."

Charles drummed his fingers faster. Yes. More deputies wasn't a bad idea. But between now and then? He would not have another incident like the one the girls had stumbled onto. His infant son in the vicinity. His blood boiled every time he thought of it.

He shot to his feet and paced the room. "How long do you think it would take to get a handful of deputies up here?"

Lane shrugged. "Depends. I could get some boys up from here Texas in a couple of weeks and deputize 'em. You want real lawmen, I'll have to scout around. That might take a little time."

Charles had some of those boys from Texas working on his ranch and more bringing another herd up from the Lone Star state. They weren't choir boys.

And maybe that was exactly what Defiance needed.

"Round them up from Texas. Ian, reach out to the territorial governor and see if he'll send a US Marshal our way."

Ian's hazel eyes narrowed and he regarded Charles with a suspicious tilt to his head. "Uh-huh." He stopped his fidgeting with the hat. "And ye, lad. What will ye be up to?"

Confession was good for the soul. And perhaps it was best to have them know his plan. "I'm going to pay a visit to Flynn and Bishop. Give them fair warning to keep their issues in Tent Town. Period."

Ian and Lane exchanged troubled glances. Ian exhaled heavily. "Ye sure that's a good idea? Ye've a wife and a family—"

"Which is exactly why I will explain things to them in unmistakable terms."

"I hate for ye to go down that road."

Lane uncrossed his legs and leaned forward. "If there is a message to deliver, why don't you let me do it?"

"You know why."

Lane eased back. No one knew Lane's reputation. Charles's

was well established. His penchant for violence had been tamped down, but Lord knew the battle for control of Defiance was one that never seemed to leave him. Every time he tried to pray—he'd see a soulless murderer with a knife too close to his wife and son, and his desire for violence stampeded over him like a bull. Did he want justice? Or was vengeance the overarching motivation?

He wasn't sure. He was sure, however, of one thing. "If I would kill to build a town, they'll believe I'll kill to protect my family. Because I will."

Ian slapped his bonnet back and forth again, expressing his agitation. "Getting ahead of the Lord, aren't ye?"

"You think I'm wrong to want to protect them?" Surely not. Ian simply didn't understand something here.

He huffed and wadded his hat up into a little ball. "Protect them, aye, ye must. But, Charles, at some point, this town mustn't hide in the shadows while we—while ye—do the dirty work."

They'd had this conversation before. The town had slipped over the edge under Matthew Miller's hand. Naomi's brother-in-law, the man had snapped when he'd heard about her pregnancy. He'd sabotaged Charles's ranch and railroad operations. His henchmen had committed murder. He'd threatened Naomi and Two Spears. He'd pushed Charles to the point that murder was the inevitable outcome. Sheriff Beckwith had intervened in the last instant and fired the fateful bullet...saving Charles from himself.

Beckwith wasn't here now. Lane was a good man and deadly with a gun, but he was still somewhat of an unknown commodity in Defiance.

Unless God showed up and shared a different plan, Charles was again the man to wrestle the town under control. "Defiance seems to be my responsibility, Ian. Whether I want it or not. Men have died every time I have backed off. I can't let that keep happening."

Lane slumped, his face tightened. "Then why am *I* wearing this badge?" He moved as if to tear it off his shirt, but Charles stopped him with a wave of his hand.

"The law is the best way to deal with the lawless. But men like Flynn and Bishop. They think they're above the law. Almost gods." He drifted over to the window. Men and mules flowed by. Gold Fever still burned in their brains, but the lawlessness drew them here as well. "There was a time I thought it was better to rule in hell than serve in heaven. While I no longer believe that, a foray back across the River Styx is called for, and I am the man to do it."

He didn't know if they got his meaning, but at the moment, he didn't care.

~

"I have a memory of a soldier getting his head bashed in with a rock."

Naomi gasped and looked over at Two Spears. Charles, who was driving the wagon, blinked but otherwise maintained a stoic expression. Two Spears turned and gazed out at the forest of pines around them. "I heard you talking about some white man on the boardwalk. His throat was cut out."

"I-I'm sorry," Naomi stumbled out. "That's not something you were intended—" Reflexively pulling Adam closer to her, she glanced up at Charles. "We should have been more careful. I'm sorry, Two Spears, if what you heard made you remember something like that."

"We couldn't have hidden it from him. He would have picked it up somewhere."

"You must not always try to protect me," Two Spears said, puffing out his chest and turning back to them. "I am not a child. I have seen death."

What did that do to her son's soul? She loved this child as if he were her own and she would have done anything to protect him from sights like...like senseless, violent murder. She moved to hug him, caught herself, and squeezed his forearm in apology. "You're right. I forget what a warrior you are."

"My grandfather used to say death was as much a part of life as eating and breathing. A warrior must accept it."

Warrior. Would Two Spears ever shed the specter of his hero, the violent warrior One-Who-Cries? Chief Ouray, the boy's grandfather, had been a man of peace, but his surrender to the US government had only earned him contempt from most of the young men. Two Spears was following in the wrong footsteps. She glanced quickly up at Charles again. Was he any better of a role model at the moment? His hard heart toward Delilah concerned her. And now, he'd been forced to give two gang leaders a stern warning. And Charles did not bluff.

She prayed none of this would give Satan a stronghold in Charles's heart.

"Are we going to the stagecoach or to the mercantile to say goodbye," he asked.

Today was the day. Hannah, Billy, and Little Billy were leaving for Chicago. Her little sister was going to become a nurse. For income, Billy had already bought a store and would take over management of it. He'd also hired a nanny to assist while Hannah was in class. They had it all planned out.

Naomi was happy for them, but she was going to miss them dearly. Two years from now felt like an eternity. Little Billy would be a different child by the time they returned. "The mercantile. And, honestly, I don't know if I want to watch them ride out of town. I'm already sad enough." Something about watching their stage head off into the distant horizon was too painful, too final. The uncertainty of the next two years almost frightened her. So much could happen in that time.

Charles draped his arm around her and hugged her. "I understand. I'll miss them too, but what a wonderful nurse we will have when they return."

Yes, there was that.

~

They pulled up in front of the mercantile. Dr. Hope and Lane were already there. Hope had hold of Hannah's shoulders and was smiling. "I have no doubt you are going to be one fine nursing student. Thank you for how you have helped me. Now, study hard and hurry back." She kissed Hannah on the cheek and stepped back. "I am going to miss you sorely."

Lane stepped in for a bear hug. "Me, too, little girl. I expect you to make straight A's now."

"I'll try."

He offered his hand to Billy, who was holding Little Billy, and the two shook. "It's been an honor, pard. Little man..." He tugged on the boy's coat collar. "You be good. You hear?" Little Billy nodded and grinned sheepishly. Lane tagged Billy playfully in the shoulder. "Take care of your family, and don't make me come to Chicago to straighten out any problems."

Billy chuckled. "Don't make me come back here to help you fight thugs and bandits."

"Deal."

Lane and Hope stepped back, offered the young family a last, soulful glance, then walked away. Over his shoulder, Lane tipped his hat at Charles. Charles returned the gesture with a nod.

Naomi sucked in a deep breath and approached Hannah. Her heart hurt so much that it almost strangled the goodbye in her throat. "I am going to miss you so much."

Hannah's eyes glimmered with tears. "I know. Me, too. I still can't believe I'm doing this."

"I'm sorry I ever doubted you."

"It's all right. I understand. And a time or two, I gave you reason."

The mountain lion's scars on Naomi's back twinged. All the blood had caused Hannah to assume Naomi had lost the baby. All the more reason her sister should be doing this. "Go and become the best nurse this state will ever see."

"I will."

They hugged, tightly, desperately. It was the kind of embrace that held a thousand goodbyes and the promise of a future welcome home. Adam squirmed, grouchy at being squished by the two women, and protested with a grunt.

"I still say we should have given you a going away party."

"And I said that would make it sound like we were never coming back. We are. I promise."

Ian and Rebecca walked up and Naomi stepped out of the way. The hugs and tears started all over again. Sisters, they'd been together their whole lives. They'd never ever been apart for more than a day or two. They'd celebrated every birthday, every Christmas, every failure, and every triumph together. And all that was changing now.

Naomi swallowed the lump in her throat, wiped the tears out of her eyes, and focused on the future. "You're all packed up and ready?"

Hannah took Little Billy from his father. "We shipped some items yesterday. The rest is either with us or left upstairs."

Billy snapped his fingers, getting everyone's attention. "That reminds me. We asked Eleanor to move into our apartment. I'd feel better with someone over the store and she needs a nicer place. So, if you notice lights on the second floor, it's her."

Naomi nodded. "That's a good idea." But beside her, Charle's lips tightened. His eyebrow dove slightly. He disapproved.

The clatter and jangle of an approaching wagon drew their attention. Emilio and Mollie drove up and regarded the group with sad expressions. Emilio took a deep breath, as if he was trying to inflate some courage he didn't have. "You ready, amigo?"

Billy turned and grabbed two suitcases off the steps, among several others. "We are." Lane and Charles stepped up and gathered the remaining steamer trunk and valises. In a few short moments, they had the wagon loaded. As the last bag landed, the stage rolled by.

Charles plucked his pocket watch from his vest. "It's on time...for once."

Hannah reached out and took Naomi's hand. "Coming to see us off?"

She took a deep breath and shook her head. "I'd rather not. I already want to bawl like a baby."

Hannah sniffed. "And I know how you hate to cry."

Naomi managed a nod, but she couldn't get words out past that darn pretzel knot in her throat. Hannah bent down and cupped Two Spears's chin. "I'm going to miss you most of all, Two Spears. I don't know anyone brave enough in the whole world who would have tracked down a mountain lion all by himself."

The boy straightened and out came his chest. He puffed up like a strutting rooster. Naomi couldn't stop the smile that danced on her lips.

"I will miss you, Miss Hannah." He tried for stoicism but didn't quite accomplish it. He even leaned in a little when she kissed his cheek in goodbye.

And that was it. With sad glances back at them and the store, Hannah and Billy climbed up into the wagon and placed their son between them. Emilio flicked the reins and guided the horses in a big U-turn, pointing them back toward the stagecoach station. With one last wave, they rolled on down the street.

Naomi turned to Rebecca and the two sisters hugged each other. "A part of us is going with her," Rebecca whispered.

"I feel like all of my heart is."

"You know this is best for her?"

"Yes. And I know she will be such an incredible blessing to people. To this town. But I had no idea it would hurt this much to let her go."

Rebecca leaned her head into Naomi's as the departing wagon was all but engulfed by the street traffic. Before it could disappear, Naomi closed her eyes against the painful goodbye. Charles, Two Spears, and Ian hooked their arms around the girls and stood silently in support of them.

~

Charles jangled the change in his pocket and considered the tightness lodged in his chest as Billy and Hannah rode away to the stagecoach station. He hadn't thought their departure would bother him much.

Or perhaps his somber mood was coming from his mission today.

"Charles, Naomi," Ian raised his arms in invitation, "lunch is on me, aye? Will ye join us?"

Naomi's eyes lit up. "Oh, yes—"

"No, thank you." Naomi cut her eyes up at Charles and he dipped his head in explanation. "You and the boys can go ahead. I've some business to attend."

Suspicion crept into her beguiling jade eyes and he kicked himself for being vague. Naturally, it raised her curiosity. "I'm going to inspect the church." Now that he'd said it, he'd have to do it. It needed to be checked on. "It's been empty too long. I need to assess my plans for it. And make sure vagrants haven't moved in."

The lift in Naomi's eyebrow said she understood he wasn't telling the whole truth, but she'd question him later. "All right. Don't be too long."

"I won't."

~

He kicked at a pebble as he strode down the weedy, rutted path that led to Tent Town. He used to willingly stroll down here, eager to find trouble. After meeting Naomi, however, and handing his life over to the Lord, his trips to this side of debauchery had become decidedly less fun. When he'd wandered through here the other day with Lane, trying to find the man who had committed murder right in front of Naomi, he'd known then he'd be back. Tight-lipped gang members who would not turn on each other would have to have the pecking order in Defiance explained to them.

Will it ever end, Lord?

Prostitutes with empty eyes and small bags of groceries eyed him wearily as he passed them. The men looked him up and down with suspicion and some dread. Would he be knocking on their tent flaps again?

No, today he was going straight to the heads of the snake.

He'd start with Bishop. A pale Englishman with a remarkably black bushy mustache, he was sitting in the corner of his saloon playing solitaire. The Crow's Pub was a dingy place with an out-of-tune piano and a small lunch crowd. The gazes of the patrons followed Charles as he made his way over to Bishop's table and sat. Bishop glanced up, showed only boredom at this intrusion, and flipped a card over.

Charles leaned back, crossed a leg over his knee, and reached into his pocket for a cheroot and a match. "Good day, Mr. Bishop."

"Mr. McIntyre. Back to ask me some questions about that squabble on Main Street?"

Charles lit his smoke and waved the match to extinguish it. He'd expected the men to warn him and Flynn of his investigation. "That squabble involved a man with a knife who wielded it inches from my wife and son."

Bishop's hand slowed, then he laid down the cards and looked up. "That is unfortunate. I was not aware. That explains your interest in the matter."

Charles took a drag off the cheroot and exhaled the smoke in a long, calm breath. Now he was aware, and yet, had not offered an apology. "There is talk that the disagreement between your faction and Flynn's is growing. Tempers are getting shorter and shorter. As the situation becomes more explosive, it is more likely to slip out of your control. And your boundaries."

"Boundaries. That makes it sound as if me and my mates are limited in our comings and goings."

"You are now. That little squabble imperiled my family. If it happens again...I will hold you and only you personally responsible."

Surely his meaning was clear.

Bishop's brow dove. "Careful, your Lordship. You might be biting off more than you can chew."

"Defiance is my town. I built it. I allow you to run your little kingdom in this dingy, miserable tent you call a saloon. When your kingdom threatens mine, this game of thrones ends."

Bishop studied him up and down, then snorted. "You and your bloody Yank arrogance. Think you're the top dog, eh? Well, I say you ain't. And I say I ain't afraid of the likes of you."

No, he wasn't afraid. But the slightest dash of uncertainty had slipped into the man's voice. He wasn't *sure* he could take Charles and he was covering the doubt with bluster.

His doubt would get him killed. "If you have any family that you care about, you should write them." Bishop's expression settled like concrete. Charles rose and rested his hand on the butt of his .44. "I will be delivering this same message to Mr. Flynn. It is imperative that you both understand the precarious position you are in."

Seven

CHARLES STOPPED at the sagging doors of the Crystal Chandelier Number Two and, for a moment, imagined Matthew sitting at the table at the end of the bar. The big man had gone off the track, completely lost it, when he'd heard about Naomi and the baby. He'd been a dangerous foe, without reason, like a rabid dog. Would Bishop and Flynn be smarter?

He was still forming an opinion on Bishop. Flynn emerged from behind the bar and shuffled over to a table, his attention riveted on the ledger he carried. He was a slender, wiry man with chiseled, unfriendly features. They suited his personality.

There was no one else in the saloon. Charles strode across the wooden floor with purpose, his boots thumping firmly on the planks, smoke from the cheroot trailing him.

He approached Flynn. The man looked up, looked down, and whipped his gaze back to Charles. "McIntyre. The grand lord deigns to visit with a humble Irishman?"

The gift of blarney. Flynn didn't quite have it.

Charles pulled out a chair and sat, taking a puff from his cheroot. "I've come to deliver a message. One I have already delivered to Mr. Bishop."

Flynn snapped the ledger shut and dropped his elbows on it. "I'm all ears then."

Charles repeated his warning. Keep the gang trouble on this side of the creek, or Flynn himself would pay for it.

Flynn cracked a small smile, but it grew to a huge grin. "Ye realize we'll cower or fight ye. Those are the only two choices. Now, *I* won't lie down like a dog. Bishop, being English, my bet is"—he shrugged ambivalence—"he'll cower."

"I think you misunderstand me, Mr. Flynn. There will be no fight. If my family, if any members of my family, are endangered in any way once more by your men, I will come for you. And you will die. You see"—Charles shifted in his chair—"my philosophy is you and Bishop are one ugly, inbred, malformed snake. One body. Two heads. Cut the heads off, the body will writhe and twist futilely and then die."

Flynn scratched his pockmarked chin, considering things. "I hear yer fast with a gun. Fast with yer fists. And ye give no quarter."

How much longer that reputation would continue breathing depended on Flynn and Bishop, though neither of them knew it. Forced to kill them, Charles would follow through, and pray for forgiveness afterward. He held his peace now, though, neither confirming nor denying Flynn's statement.

After a moment, Flynn accepted the silence. "Duly noted then, Mr. McIntyre."

Charles could read men. Bishop might run if he heard Charles was coming for him. Flynn? No, Flynn would give in to his curiosity. Try to prove he was the faster gun.

And Flynn would die. Charles grunted with regret at the foolishness of men and their blinding pride. "Good day, Mr. Flynn." Charles rose and left without a glance back.

~

Charles would have stormed right past the church if not for the big man standing on the porch tugging at the locked door. He stopped abruptly. Was he looking at a potential squatter? Someone expecting to find Logan?

He hoped it was the latter and walked toward the man. "I own the building. Can I help you?"

The man spun, his buffalo coat swinging with him. He was a big man. Not fat. Big boned. Even his face was large. "I'm Buckley. I'm a preacher. I reckon I need a building."

Buckley's voice, deep and booming, rang a bell in Charles's head. His baritone voice had traveled intermittently on the wind a few days back and Charles had wondered then if a man of God had come to Defiance.

Apparently so. "This one is available. For a brief spell, we've had two preachers. One died. One simply left. Defiance was not his cup of tea. I meant to check on the building today, so allow me." He pulled a key ring from his pocket, sorted through half a dozen keys, and found the right one. The lock turned easily enough and he entered ahead of Buckley.

Gray light poured through the windows, casting a sad glow on the simple, wooden benches. Memories assaulted him. Sitting on the pew with his family. Logan preaching his heart out. New faces appearing with each passing Sunday. Talking a broken and remorseful Logan into returning to the pulpit after his tryst with Delilah. The devastated congregation suffering through a memorial service for twelve lost miners.

He took a deep breath and exhaled the emotions. No sense wallowing in the past. Life had to move on. But he missed Logan. He'd truly enjoyed his sermons and his company.

He'd changed, a voice whispered. *If Logan could change. If you could change*. Then—

Delilah would not change because she could not change. Evil incarnate was simply that—evil.

He rounded on Buckley. "It's yours if you want it."

"Well, uh, I need to pass the hat a few times to gather up the rent."

"No charge." Charles worked the key from his ring and tossed it to him. "Use it as long as you like."

"I—I, uh, that's mighty kind of you. Thank you."

"Where are you staying?"

"At the hotel."

"There's a small apartment in the back."

Buckley's face scrunched and wiggled a moment. He didn't look as thrilled as Charles thought he should. "Something wrong with the accommodations?"

"Nah. I just ain't spent a lot of time indoors. Closest I've come to owning anything is staying in a tipi up with the Ute. They've been right receptive to the Gospel. Defiance, not quite. So, I figured a building might help." He scratched his jaw through his wildly unkempt beard. "Eleanor sure thinks a building will—"

"Eleanor?" How did he know her? Did he know Delilah? What was going on—

"Yeah, from the hotel. We were talking the other day about how stuck this town is on grudges."

Charles relaxed. That would be a natural concern for Eleanor to bring up. "Grudges. Vengeance. Violence." Retribution. He would be the bringer of retribution if Bishop and Flynn caused one small drop of trouble near Naomi, his boys, or anyone in his family. He glanced up at the wooden cross hanging on the wall behind the pulpit.

He would forgive Delilah. *He* would forgive Flynn and Bishop. If they asked.

Charles's conscience constricted like a rope around his heart. It was wrong what he was doing, planning on murder to keep his family safe. He could run Flynn and Bishop out of Defiance. With their tail between their legs, they wouldn't come back.

But he'd already put the threat out there. *There is no walking it back, Lord.*

Buckley's voice intruded on his thoughts belatedly. "What? I'm sorry."

"I said you've the look of a man wrangling the world on his shoulders. Want to talk about it?"

Charles slowly shook his head and let his gaze return to the cross. "I shouldn't have come here today. It has me...second-guessing things I can't get out of now."

"There's usually a way out of trouble. Most often by doing the right thing."

He'd told two bad men he would kill them if they stepped out of line. He would not ambush them. He would simply be faster and more accurate. As they attempted to clear leather, he would already be squeezing the trigger. It was as clear in his mind as Naomi's face. He was not a murderer. But he was a killer. Did that still make it wrong? "The right thing? I don't know."

"Pray about it, son. The Lord'll make things clear if you're willing to listen."

"Isn't that always the crux of the matter? A man's willingness to listen."

"No. More often than not, it's his pride."

The remark nicked his conscience. "Good day, Buckley. Enjoy the building."

Eight

BOZEY O'SHAY.

Flynn pushed his bowler back a hair and dropped his elbow on the bar as the man skirted through the saloon. What was that grubby rat-of-a-man doing back in Defiance? And was his hair whiter than when he'd left? When the mine had exploded, this bugger had jumped on a horse and taken off. He'd said he wanted nothing more to do with mining.

And now he was back. He spotted Flynn, waved, and hurried up. "Mr. Flynn, good to see you again."

Mr. Flynn. O'Shay's demeanor said he was crawling back to town in need of a favor. Flynn was tempted to toss him out. Instead, out of sheer curiosity, he shoved a shot glass at him. "Mr. O'Shay. What brings ye back to Defiance?" He waved a bottle of whiskey and the man nodded.

"I—I believe I might have stumbled on some information that would mean something to this town. To ye."

Intrigued, he poured the shot. "Let's have it then."

"If it is valuable to you, might I ask for a job? I hear you're running a lot of things in Tent Town now with plans to run it all." He fished a coin out of his pocket and laid it on the counter.

A good-faith gesture. He wasn't asking for favors. "How did ye hear that."

"O'Keefe. He was married to my sister. I suppose he still is. Hasn't seen the girl in three years, but me and him have kept in touch. With each other."

"All right. O'Keefe is a good man. If he recommends you, maybe. But what is this news ye have?"

"I've a cousin who works in the livery in Dodge City. One day, a few months back, two women buy a wagon. One woman he knew well from the saloon. The other he didn't. The one he didn't...well, it struck him later. He thinks she might have been Delilah."

Flynn's pulse spiked at the mere mention of the woman. But this was a pretty vague observation. "He just assumed this woman is Delilah because...?"

"He said it was something in the way she moved. The way she turned her head. After he thought about it, he was almost certain it was her. But she was dressed plain as a Mormon's wife. No rouge. No lipstick. No fancy hair-do."

What to do with this information? Flynn licked his lips as he considered it. Delilah did have certain mannerisms that, Flynn agreed, a man might use to spot her. Maybe...?

No. This was wishful thinking on his part. The whole thing was flimsy as onion paper. "I'm not buying it."

"I know the odds are long, except my cousin was pretty dang certain. He's not a man to make up things. Especially if he's nothing to gain."

All right. Maybe a bit more investigation. "Where were they headed with this new wagon?"

"Them and a man was headed North."

Flynn snorted. "North?" The vague answer curled his hand into a fist as his temper ignited. "Well now, North covers a lot of territory. Do ye think ye could be a wee bit more specific?" Before I knock your block off for wasting my time.

"See, now, that's why I'm here. I delivered some horses over to the stage stop in Cripple Creek a few days ago. On the way back, I stopped in Ruby City to spend the night. They got a new sheriff over there. He came into town with two people. The town drunk said he had two women with him, but ain't nobody seen the second woman."

Flynn dragged a hand over his mouth and chin, evaluating the information. Still weak. Interesting but weak.

"And then one day, this new sheriff comes into town with his cousin. His *male* cousin—who can't speak 'cause he's got laryngitis."

"According to this town drunk."

O'Shay shrugged. "According to the town drunk."

Flynn drummed his fingers on the bar. Irritation warred with curiosity. It was a long shot. A million to one. But, what if...?

No. It was outrageous. "If it was her, do ye think she'd be heading back this way? Not unless the woman has a death wish."

"I thought about that. What if she's coming back to open the saloon? Maybe she thinks bygones will be bygones if she serves up enough whiskey and whores?"

Flynn took a deep breath and turned to the wall behind the bar. He caught his reflection in the mirror. The low light and smoky air painted deep shadows on his face, eery and corpse-like. He was only forty. He looked fifty. Joseph's death had been hard on him. Defiance had been hard on him. It would be hard on Delilah if she came back.

Could the woman be that stupid? Or Vain? What if that was her plan? Flynn fidgeted with a shot glass, rolling it between his hands. "When you were in Ruby City, did ye meet the sheriff?"

"No."

Good. "Go back." Flynn slipped behind the bar, rifled beneath it, and came back with his cash box. "I'll give you twenty dollars." He plucked a bill free of its stack, closed the

box, and replaced it. "Nose around. Ask questions carefully."
He raised his index finger in caution. "Don't let anyone catch
on to why you're there."

"What should I say?"

"Say ye're an undertaker, for all I care. Ye're thinking about
opening up a new place. Just get some solid information."

O'Shay palmed the cash. "I can do that."

"Let me be clear so there's no misunderstanding. Come
back with solid information, one way or the other."

The mumble of voices rolled through the little church like the
faint echo of thunder. Eleanor sat on the very back row, eager to
listen and to observe. Mollie and Emilio were in the front row.
A few gals from Hell's Half-Acre—the compound just outside
Defiance's town limits that traded in skin—were in attendance
as well, and various men Eleanor had seen here and there. All in
all, maybe twenty folks. More than she'd expected. Some she
expected were just here to warm up.

The widow from the store, the one with two pretty teenage
daughters, drifted in, her girls in tow. They sat to themselves
one row in front of Eleanor, squeezed off to the left, hugging
the end of the bench. Putting a buffer between them and the
others?

Someone in the group was drinking or at least was madly
hung over. The stench of whiskey was as strong as the perfume
on the soiled doves. If cleanliness was next to Godliness,
Buckley should ask his congregation to bathe prior to services.

He cleared his throat and stomped out of the back room.
Well, look at that. Eleanor couldn't believe it. Buckley had
combed his wild hair, trimmed his beard a little, and was
wearing a worn suit with a wrinkled string tie. He paused for an
instant, surveying the small crowd, and then strode to the

podium. "I don't sing. We get a few more people in here, maybe we'll try it. But not today."

The man didn't stand on formality. Eleanor was not surprised, therefore, when Buckley laid his open Bible on the podium and began reading. "Hatred stirreth up strifes: but love covereth all sins." He looked up and eyed his little congregation again. "You ever notice where there's a lot of hard feelings between folks, there's always feuding, fighting...worse."

"Welcome to Defiance," one of the miners two rows up from Eleanor shouted. The men in the pew with him laughed. Everyone else glanced around uncomfortably.

Buckley scowled but continued. "Now, love and forgiveness don't mean you're a rug for people to wipe their feet on. But you also ain't got to explode over every little thing. Love, the Good Book says, is patient and kind. But"—he pointed upward —"it speaks the truth."

"Well, Henry here must love everybody," the same manner-less miner hollered, "'cause he's always speaking his mind." He ribbed the fella next to him and the pair dissolved into drunken cackling.

Buckley sucked on his teeth for a few seconds, glaring at the man, and then strode over to within a few feet of him. Hands on his hips, he was as big as a grizzly. "I'll thank you to hold your peace, son. Some people here today want to hear the Word of the Lord, not the ruminations of a fool."

The man glared right back. "Call me a fool again, old man, and I'll wrap you up like a Christmas present in that fancy suit."

Buckley cracked his knuckles, loudly, one at a time. "Blessed be the LORD my Rock, Who trains my hands for war, And my fingers for battle. Don't test me, son. Show God's Word some respect."

"Or what?"

"I had intended to preach a lovely little sermon on the power of forgiveness today. That is still my intention. One more outburst and you'll find yourself sobering up in the snow and mud."

The troublemaker tilted his head and opened his mouth. Before any words could spew forth, Buckley snatched the man by the collar from the pew, then latched on to the seat of his pants. The congregation gasped in shock as he quite literally tossed the shocked, flailing man into the front doors. They burst open at the impact. He flew through them, landed on the porch, and skidded off into the snow and mud. As promised.

Buckley brushed his hands of the whole affair, calmly closed the doors, and strode back to the pulpit.

Eleanor snapped her mouth shut. A giggle tried to bubble up in her and she laid her hand across her mouth to keep it down.

"I reckon there are rules in church. I'm not exactly sure." He retook his position at the podium. "This is the first time I've ever preached inside a building. But it seems to me you should respect the house of God every bit as much as you would respect your momma's house. Now, does anyone else want to leave?"

The congregation was still and silent. The men on the pew with the troublemaker subtly glanced over their shoulders at the doors, then back to Buckley. Their shoulders tensed and dread twisted in Eleanor's stomach.

They're not done.

Indeed, three men rose, inched out to the aisle, and approached Buckley. He towered over them, but the odds didn't look to be in his favor. "We don't need yer kind of preaching in Defiance." An Irishman with a good mad on. Eleanor sighed over the trouble coming.

"We'll not be thrown about like rag dolls," the second man added. The third man simply nodded in agreement.

Emilio laid his Bible aside and rose to his feet. Was he going to help Buckley?

The three men dove for the preacher, fists went to swinging.

Buckley roared and hammered back with blows of his own. The scuffle was violent and ugly, shaking the building. Mollie gasped and jumped back as Emilio joined the fray, trying to control the troublemakers. One of them landed a lucky punch, and blood trickled from his nose.

He swung back. The men grappled, punched, and even clawed as they were forced to the doors, yelling in protest, squirming, and raging. Finally, sweaty, red in the face, and breathing hard, both Buckley and Emilio managed to force the men out the doors. Adding insult to injury, Buckley shoved them off the porch as well. "Come back when you can act like you've got some manners."

Cursing, spitting, and gathering up their hats, the men turned to Buckley and glared. "We'll tell Flynn," one bellowed, shaking his fist at the church. "He won't stand for this."

"Be gone with ya," Buckley bellowed right back. "Be gone. Sober up. Come back if you've a mind to, but with your manners." With that, he and Emilio returned back inside.

For the third time, Buckley took the pulpit. "I apologize for the interruption. Now, as I was saying, hatred stirs up strife. Jesus came to give us peace. A peace that passes all understanding..."

His voice faded. Eleanor folded her hands and prayed. She prayed that peace would overflow in Defiance because, right now, it looked like the town was in a drought. *Lord, what will it take for this town to let all this hate go? Only your love can accomplish it.*

I pray the people who need to see your love the most, will. And strengthen the people who can turn back or stomp down violence. Please...

~

A half hour later, the sermon ended and the small crowd drifted out. Buckley spent a few minutes chatting with Mollie and

Emilio. He slapped the young man on the back, most likely thanking him for his help. They left with smiles and nods and a promise to return.

As the door closed behind them, Buckley joined Eleanor, still in her spot on the back pew. "Well, I reckon that was a start. I figure it went pretty well."

Her eyes bugged over his optimism. "You do?"

"Sure. Oh, I know I had to get a little heavy-handed with the drunks, but I tell you..." He slapped his thighs. "Gotta earn their respect. I'll get challenged a few more times, but that will bring in a few more of the curious."

"You think people will come to watch you throw drunks out into the street?"

"Some will. Some will use that as an excuse to explain the tug they're feeling."

"To hear the Word?"

"And the Lord's word will not return void. It will accomplish his purposes, whether I have five people in this building or fifty."

She could only pray he was right. Impressed with his confidence, she laid her hand on his. "I guess you know what you're doing."

"What—what gave you that idea?" As he spoke, he glanced down at her hand. His eyes widened and a blush crept up out of his beard.

Eleanor pulled her hand away. "It was a good sermon," she hurried to add, trying to move them past this awkward moment. What in the world had triggered it?

Buckley looked into her eyes and scanned her face. A hint of fear or concern creased his crown. He shifted, moving away from her in the pew by several inches.

She reached out to touch his arm but clenched her fingers. "Buckley, what's wrong? You look like I'm about to jump up and slap you sideways."

He shook his head, grunted or groaned—she wasn't sure which—and then stood. "You...you..."

"Me?" What in tarnation was wrong with the man?

He pushed his fingers through his mass of dark hair and exhaled heavily. "I'm sorry, Eleanor. I just ain't myself today. The pressure of a sermon and all. I'm being a foolish, old man... and you came to support me."

"I told you I would."

"Yeah. Well..." He swung his arm back toward the pulpit. "Um, I've got some praying I'd like to do."

At first, she didn't understand. Oh, he's asking me to leave. She lurched to her feet. Maybe it was a preacher thing. Maybe he felt he had some important things to discuss with the Lord while they were fresh in his mind. "Of course. I'll let you get to it. I'll see you...soon."

Buckley cleared his throat and stepped over to get the door for her. "Yes, ma'am. Soon."

Reeling, Eleanor slipped into her coat. She met him at the entrance and almost asked if everything was all right. He tugged open the door, though, and her nerve drained away. Instead, she merely nodded and slipped out.

Nine

ON SATURDAYS, Toby worked with the horses in ways that went beyond the simple tasks of feeding or lunging. Since the initial report that Delilah had spooked, he'd gone back to working on trust exercises with her. Always curious to watch, Victoria brushed snow off the corral's top rail and rested her arms on it.

With the sun shining brightly overhead, she squinted against the light and smiled at his patience. He had a long lead line on Delilah but held it loosely while he tossed a rope at her feet with precision. The first time, she skittered and danced sideways in the muddy corral, but Toby repeated the action several more times, each toss easy and slow. Again and again. By the tenth time, the horse didn't move and actually looked bored.

Toby wound the rope up and glanced over his shoulder. "Come here."

Victoria was startled by the request. Toby barely spoke during training, much less invited anyone into the ring with him. A little wary, she nodded. "All right." She climbed through the fence and joined him, slogging through the mud, caking her boots and the hem of her skirt.

"Here." He moved behind her and handed her the lead line

and the rope but guided her actions. "Hold the lead loose. Toss the rope like I did. Slow and easy, no sudden movements."

Victoria couldn't fathom what this was going to accomplish. Worse, she found it difficult to concentrate with him standing so close behind her. Attempting to focus, she did as she was commanded. Delilah did a little hop, more so than the last few times, but she didn't run.

"Now, walk up and pet her."

Willing to go along, curious as to the end goal, Victoria gave Delilah a friendly rub on the forehead. "Good girl. No reason to be jittery on a sunny day, huh?" Victoria then resumed her position in front of Toby.

This time, he reached around her, pressing into her and guiding her arm for the throw. "A little higher," he said softly. Victoria swallowed, trying to force her mind from how nice it felt to be next to him, her back pressed into his chest, his breath in her ear.

Three more times, Victoria tossed the rope and, between each throw, gave the horse an affectionate pat on the forehead. After the last throw, Toby instructed her to rub Delilah down with the rope. Again, Victoria dutifully did as asked, talking sweetly to the horse and using the same tone to ask Toby, "What am I doing? Tell him, Delilah, tell him to share his secret horse wisdom with me."

The horse grumbled as if asking and Toby gave the pair a wry smile. "We're filling her head with calm, steady thoughts. You may not always love on her and bring her a treat. You might have to toss a rope around her every now and then. She needs to know you're trustworthy. No matter what you're doing."

"That I would never hurt her. I will never hurt you, Delilah."

"Eventually, she'll forget it all, Victoria, because it won't be a part of who she is anymore."

Victoria's hand paused on Delilah's neck. "There you go again."

"Again?"

"Most of the time I can't tell if you're talking about her... or me."

He slipped up beside her and laid his hand on top of hers. "Works for both of you, I reckon."

She glanced up at him, willing to get lost in his nearness, in his peace, in a gaze that gave her chills, wondering if they would dance again this evening. It had become part of their nights, but suddenly, he stepped past her and unhooked the lead line. "Turn her out and I'll get Dollar. Today you get your first lesson in being a farrier."

The third sunny day in a row reminded Toby just how close the real spring was. March was iffy, but by April, Victoria had said, she would be ready to go into Defiance. He sipped his coffee and leaned against a porch post. The sun was just cresting the mountains at the end of their little valley, and the horses, their coats sending off steam, were frolicking in the frosty pasture. The two mules stood off to the side, contemplating the antics.

This could work for him. It could work forever. He took a sip and prayed Eleanor delivered a bad report. Only, that was a double-edged sword. He didn't want people hating Victoria, maybe willing to string her up. But if they weren't, then that meant Defiance would put her on trial. With her own admission of guilt, a prison sentence was the only outcome. The idea made him sick with grief, but he'd wait on her. If she asked him to.

"All right, I'm ready." Victoria stepped out on the porch, simultaneously twisting all that silky, auburn hair up tight to hide inside her hat.

Toby tossed the remnant of his coffee into the yard and looked her over. Same disguise: baggy pants, oversized coat, the high-crowned cowboy hat. A spring-like breeze lifted some stray blond hairs across his face, tickling his cheek. "Less this breeze blows in some cooler weather, you're gonna be a might warm in that coat today."

Her shoulders drooped. "I know this disguise won't work forever. It will work one more time."

One more time? His jaw tightened. He was running out of time to change her mind. They needed a report from Eleanor. "Let me get my hat."

"What are you going to do about your voice?" he asked, riding beside her as she drove the wagon.

"I've still got laryngitis."

"For three weeks?"

"Anybody gets nosy, tell them I'm planning to see a doctor if I'm not better by spring. In the meantime, you don't mind the quiet."

Toby was not a man to brood, but her dedication to her plan took the wind out of his sails and they rode the five miles into town mostly in silence. She attempted conversation intermittently, asking about his sheriffing duties and if they could squeeze in boarding one more horse. He answered her, but not with many words or enthusiasm. The last mile into town, his mood seemed to have caught on and she fell quiet. "You want me to go in, like last time?" he asked as they rode up to the mercantile.

Two men stood by the mercantile entrance, counting cash for some transaction regarding a cow. Victoria shook her head and whispered, "I'm fine."

Toby gave a nod and mosied on. Forced to cut between the two older men at the door, she lowered her head, whispered, "Excuse me," and tried to pass through.

One chuckled, looked Victoria in the eye, and whispered, "Ain't a library, son."

She gave him a half-smile and slipped by them, followed by more low chuckling.

"Morning, there...Vic, ain't it?" Eugene asked from atop his stocking ladder. He placed a final can of shoe polish on the top shelf and clambered down.

Victoria nodded and waved her shopping list at him.

"Still no voice, young fella? Mighty good case of laryngitis you've got there."

"The voice comes and goes," Victoria whispered.

"I see. Well," he took the list from her. "Let's get your shopping done."

The wagon was loaded less than a half hour later and Victoria was about to thank Eugene for his help when she remembered something. She snapped her fingers and followed him back inside. "I'd like to get a half pound of black licorice."

"Right this way."

Eugene had a delectable assortment of sweets, but it turned out that both Victoria and Toby had a weakness for licorice, as did all the horses. As she pushed through the door with her final purchase, she wondered if she'd made a mistake in not considering the horses. Perhaps she should have gotten a whole pound—

A giant of a man carrying several trays of root beer plowed into her in the doorway. The impact threw her off balance, her foot skittered down the small step at the threshold, and her ankle rolled hard to the inside. Victoria cried out and folded to the ground like a wet dress. Her head snapped back and bounced off the wood. She managed to save herself a concussion, but her hat went flying and her hair spilled all around her. The man carrying the bottles of root beer gasped and set them down like they were on fire.

"Holy smoke, ma'am, I am sorry."

As he reached for her, Toby suddenly appeared at her side, grabbing for her hat and trying to tuck her hair. "Here, get your hat on quick."

Trying to ignore the pain in her ankle, she attempted to help, but there were too many hands tangled in her hair.

"Say, what's going on here?" The man with root beer asked, moving back.

Toby shook his head and stood up. The stranger was big, burly, and wore a messy beard measured in acreage. Toby had seen him here and there. His name was Billy or Barley? "Look, mister, I'd appreciate it if you wouldn't say anything..." He trailed off. Say anything about what? What did this look like? Other than he and Victoria were guilty of something because they were *acting* guilty.

The man sized him up and then offered his hand again to Victoria. She accepted his help, rising to exchange a troubled look with Toby, who flinched, apparently at his lack of manners or her appearance. She'd managed to get her hair back in the hat, but unruly sprigs indicated she'd done a poor job. On top of this fiasco, her ankle was screaming at her to the point a wave of nausea threatened to swamp her.

"I don't know what I'd say if I was to say something. Reckon it's none of my business why she's dressed like a boy." Toby started to breathe a sigh of relief when the man added, "But I sure am curious."

"Well, I was...I mean, she's..."

"He was trying to protect my reputation," Victoria said quickly, her glance ricocheting off Toby and back to the man. "We're not married. I'm not his wife."

"Y-Yeah, I'd appreciate you helping us—"

"Do you wanna be?"

"I beg your pardon?"

The man's beard moved, revealing a wide, toothy grin. "I'm a minister of the Gospel. I can marry you."

The pain in Victoria's ankle faded away under the shock of the suggestion. She and Toby spoke at once. "Oh, no, we couldn't—"

"That's not something—"

"Come now, children. Living in sin? If you cared about her, boy, you'd make an honest woman of her. You should be ashamed of yourself parading her through town like this." He waved a hand at her disheveled appearance. "Course, I reckon the truth ain't much better."

"It's not what it looks like, Billy or Bar—"

"Buckley. Name's Buckley. And the Word of the Lord says Marriage is honorable in all, and the bed undefiled, but whore-mongers and adulterers God will judge. Hebrews 13:4."

"That's true, certainly, pastor, but—"

"Aren't you the marshal?" he interrupted.

"Sheriff."

The man shook his head, *tsking* in disgust. "A public servant and all—"

"It's not him," Victoria interrupted. "It's me." She cut her eyes at Toby and relaxed under his ever-calming gaze. "I believe he'd marry me today."

"I would," he said softly.

He would? Her breath caught. He would. Victoria grudgingly shifted to Buckley. "I'm the holdout. There are things in the way. Things I have to—but this was the best we could do for now."

Buckley pinned them with a long, steady gaze, but he finished it with an intense stare for Victoria. "You're the hold-out. Is there somebody else?"

The slight hesitation in her answer cut him. She shook her head, but Toby figured she might as well have said *there used to be*. Had Logan leaped to her mind with that question? Did it matter? The man was dead. But he lived on in her heart.

"I'm around in this valley. Preaching here and there. I'll be checking in with you two. Case you change your minds."

"Sure," Toby said, shrugging. "Things could change." He looked at Victoria. "Maybe."

"Maybe," she agreed.

Buckley openly assessed Toby and Victoria and scowled, a

fearsome expression on his weathered, bearded face. "Looks to me like they better change fast." The big man spun, picked up his load of root beer, grunted at them with disdain, and pushed into the mercantile. "Eugene, here's your root beer order from Defiance. And I'll be needing a few things for my trip out—" The door closed on the rest of his words.

Toby swiped a hand over his face as he turned and started to walk away. When he looked back to check on Victoria, he caught her limping and immediately rushed back to her, slipping a supportive arm around her. "Now, here, what's happened?"

"Just get me to the wagon. I need to get out of town."

"I better look at that ankle first."

"It's just a sprain."

"Limp down to my office and I'll take a look. I don't cotton to the idea of cutting your boot off your foot."

"I don't think it'll swell that mu—"

"I've had to do it, so don't tell me. Can you put any weight on it at all?"

"Of course I can." Victoria thought surely she could if she just tried, but the pain was exquisite, like an ice pick stabbing into her ankle, and she collapsed onto Toby. "Then again, I may be wrong."

"Come on."

"Where are we going?"

"Like I said, my office. I'll lock the door and we'll see what's going on."

"But what about the wagon?"

"Pretty much everyone in town knows it's mine. I doubt anybody is going to rob the sheriff."

Victoria chided herself for noticing everything about Toby as he helped her down the boardwalk. He was slender, but not skinny. Muscles rippled beneath her fingers as she grasped his side for support and, with her other hand, gripped the fingers draped over her shoulder. Unruly sprigs of blond hair poking out beneath his hat amused her. She liked the scent of leather, horses, and hay drifting off him. And there was a hint of licorice on his breath.

"You doing okay?" His intense, sapphire eyes touched her almost like a physical caress.

"Yes," she said simply, reminding herself of her mission. Foolish, heart-twisting emotions could not come into play. She knew better.

Besides, she didn't think she could ever love Toby like she'd loved Logan. The gut-wrenching pain of losing him had affected her. Made her deathly afraid of ever experiencing loss again. It still hurt so much to think about the man. The way he'd bled out on the street, died in her arms, his last words about giving God a chance. Right when they'd been on the verge of a new future together.

No, she never wanted to feel pain that exquisite ever, ever again.

"Victoria?"

She blinked. He'd been in the middle of saying something. "I'm sorry, what?"

"Hurts that much, does it?"

"Yes. Yes, it does."

"I said it's just another few feet." And within moments, Toby was helping her to a seat on a cot. "Let's get that boot off before I have to take a knife to it." He kneeled before her and worked the boot off as carefully as if he were removing the frame from the Mona Lisa. He peeled off her sock and winced at the swelling and the bluish color around the ankle. "I bet that is tender."

The warmth of his touch raised goose bumps on her skin as he gently drifted his fingers over her ankle, around her foot, and then back up her calf. If she could stop seeing Logan, stop remembering his kiss...still, it wouldn't be enough to overcome her fear.

"I'll be right back with a bucket of ice-cold water."

There was a well out back from which several businesses on the street drew. Hurrying, Toby returned with a full bucket and carefully dipped Victoria's foot. She gasped at the frigid temperature and the pain it caused but shock settled in after a few seconds. Then a different kind of ache plagued her. "I think the cold hurts more than the twist."

Toby, kneeling before her, dropped to both knees. "Just a few more minutes, and then we'll get ya out." He looked up at her. "I should lock you up."

"I beg your pardon."

"I was thinking, I have a few rounds to make. After that, I could leave early. Why don't you stay here, lie back, and put your foot up? We'll head out together."

Victoria needed to get back. She didn't feel safe staying in town this long. "I should go on—"

"How? You can drive the wagon, sure, but you can't walk. How are you going to put the supplies away?"

Victoria puttered her lips. "Guess I'm waiting on you."

He stood up. "I'll swing the door shut. Just lay back and get some rest. Anyone comes in, tell them I'll be back by four."

She shrugged. "I figured I'd wind up in a jail cell one day."

Toby's face hardened to stone.

Victoria shook her head. "I'm sorry. I forget you and Momma have no humor when it comes to my plan."

Toby hung his head, as if consciously cutting off his words, and hooked his thumbs in his belt loops. "Just hard to stomach is all."

Victoria lightened her voice, hoping to raise the mood. "The icy water helped." She lifted her foot out of the water and settled back on the cot, resting on one elbow. "I'll be here when you get back."

~

Victoria was dozing and absorbing the ache in her ankle when the office door opened abruptly. She sat up and squinted at the man standing in the doorway. A short, slender fellow with white-blond hair, he bounced his bowler in his hand.

"'Lo there, mate. I need the sheriff. Is he around?"

An Irishman. And to her, he looked like trouble. Victoria lowered her voice to answer. "He's running errands." She rose off the cot and limped to the cell door. "I ain't exactly sure when he's going to be back."

The man grunted with irritation.

"Can I give him a message?"

The man looked her up and down, a tense wrinkle in his brow as if he were assessing her manliness. "The sheriff in this town. Is he any account?"

"What do you mean?"

The man's gaze traveled over the open jail cell. "Is he in the habit of leaving his prisoners with no locked door?"

"I ain't a prisoner. I'm a—I was just waiting for him to give me a ride home."

"Uh-huh." He studied the cell again. "Sounds soft."

She didn't know what this man was after, but she wanted him to leave Toby alone. "He's no firebrand if that's what you mean. He's fair and just."

The man scratched his ear and grinned. "I'm just trying to get the lay of the land, lad. I'm thinking about opening a business in Ruby City, not that it's any of yer business."

"What kind of business?"

The man regarded her with his nose skyward. "Undertaker. Like I said, I just want to get the lay of the land. How big the town is. How often new people come in."

She didn't believe him. He was lying. She knew it like she knew her own name. What was he really doing here? A man had once told her *keep your friends close, and your enemies closer.* She wanted into this man's confidence.

"You might be a lot of things, but you ain't no undertaker. Listen, mister, if you're casing the town for a robbery, ain't nothing going on here. Ruby City doesn't even have a bank. I was thinking about moving on myself." Victoria tugged on the jail cell door. "Stayed one night too long and they found out I was playing with loaded dice." She shrugged. "I can leave, or he'll lock the door. My choice. I'm choosing to leave. Them's the breaks, sometimes."

The man chuckled and rocked on his heels. "Shore, loaded dice in a town this size. That was stupid."

"Yeah. I figured that out." She pushed off the bars and limped back to her cot. "Twisted my ankle, to boot, so here I sit."

"Listen, maybe ye *can* help me then." The man crossed the room and leaned in the doorway to the cell. "I heard tell the sheriff is new. And he came into town with two women. Any truth to that?"

This man had information, vague as it was, that was disturbing. "Well, uh, I never actually saw him come in. Just saw him a few days after he was hired. "

"Yeah, but then what's the gossip?"

"Gossip?" This man was persistent.

"Yeah, every town has some. I heard he came into town with two women, but one ain't been seen in some time. But now the sheriff has a male cousin with him."

"I don't spend my time hanging over back fences so I wouldn't know."

Sweat slicked her armpits. How had he gotten this information? Who in town knew anything about Toby arriving with two women? It had been snowing to beat the band the day they'd arrived. No one but...

But the town drunk who had pointed them toward the ranch. He couldn't have seen anything but vague shapes. "Um, we've got a town drunk that sticks his nose into everything. Can't see past his nose, though, without his glasses. He lost 'em a few months back and hasn't replaced them. If he's your source..."

The Irishman studied the ground and grunted. "Guess I'll ask around some more then."

"Are you looking for the sheriff or the women?"

His head came up and there was a mischievous twinkle in his eyes. "Do ye know if the sheriff and his friends came in from Dodge City?"

"Uh, no. I heard they came up from Salt Lake City."

"Salt Lake? Salt Lake." His countenance fell with disappointment. "That ain't Dodge City."

An idea struck Victoria. "Like I said, I don't hang over the back fence. But..." She returned to the cell door and glanced around. "I will say..." She lowered her voice to a conspiratorial whisper. "There is a rumor the sheriff is Mormon."

"That would make the women—"

"His wives."

The repugnant little Irishman recoiled from her. "Debauchery." How ironic his moral certitude. He scratched the back of his head, dislodging his bowler. He squared it up and looked around. "That is disappointing if it's true. Reckon I'll ask around a little more."

"You'd better be careful," she said in a rush. "The sheriff hears you're asking around, you might wind up in here with me. But with the door locked."

"Hmm." He grunted again. "I'll think about it." He turned and left, leaving Victoria behind with a chill. She was sick to her stomach now, and it had nothing to do with her ankle. The man wasn't going to leave.

~

Five minutes later, Toby returned and laid his hat on his desk. "I'll be ready to go in a minute—"

Victoria sprang from the cot and hurried to the door, flinching at her screaming ankle. "Toby, listen to me. If anybody asks, say you came up from Salt Lake City and then act real nervous."

He tilted his head and looked at her as if he hadn't comprehended a single word. "What are you talking about?" He shook off the consternation and met her at the cell door. "Come on out. You've been in there too long or something."

He swung the door all the way open, and she clutched his shirt immediately. "Listen to me. A man was asking if you came into this town with two women. He said he was looking the town over to open an undertaking business. He was lying."

Toby blinked and gave her that same wide-eyed, befuddled look. "First of all, how do you know he was lying?"

She couldn't explain an intuition that had been honed to a razor-sharp skill in her saloons. "I just know."

"Okay. Okay. We'll go with that. I've already told a few people in polite conversation that Eleanor and me came up from Dodge. No walking that back."

"If an Irishman asks you, say that was a lie and that we really came up from Salt Lake."

He chewed on his cheek for a second and rested his hands on his hips. "Let's light a shuck out of here and get home. He can't ask me anything if he can't find me."

Ten

MCINTYRE SHOPPED in the mercantile with quiet focus, avoiding eye contact with Eleanor. She'd greeted him with a hesitant smile. He'd nodded coolly and they'd both let the greeting die there. Her gaze followed him, though, and irritated him. If she had a question, why didn't she just come out and ask it?

After perusing the store for a few more minutes, he found what he was looking for and took it to the counter. He laid a small pair of gloves and a half-size cowboy hat on the counter and pulled a stack of crisp bills from his pocket. Eleanor picked up the gloves. "A little small for you, aren't they?"

His smile seemed to get stuck. With effort, however, he forced it out. "They're for Two Spears. His birthday is next week."

"Oh, that's nice." The woman turned to the cash register and punched in numbers. "Two Spears?"

"My son." He did not offer additional details. To her credit, she didn't ask.

"The hat is two fifty and the gloves are a dollar."

McIntyre slipped her a five-dollar bill. The silence between them was rife with questions and comments. He gave up and opened the door for conversation. "So, have you arrived at any conclusions about the town?"

Eleanor's hands slowed in the cash drawer, but she finished counting up the change and turned to him. "I'm willing to give it a little more time before I pass judgment."

"You think the town will extend the same courtesy to Delilah?"

"Right now, no, I don't."

"Nor do I. I think she'll set off Defiance like a stick of dynamite."

She dropped his items into a brown paper bag and slid them across the counter. "I'm holding out for a change of heart."

"And what in the world could precipitate such a miracle?"

The woman's countenance saddened, and for a moment, he felt badly for her.

"I have no idea," she said. "Right now, if all I can tell her is the town has promised to lynch her, she won't believe me. I need something to happen that will convince her beyond the shadow of a doubt that she's not safe here. Or..." She shrugged. "Or, people find it in their hearts to forgive her, and, as you said, nothing short of a miracle is going to make that happen."

"Hope springs eternal," he muttered, reaching for the bag. "Perhaps she'll fall in love with Ruby City and give up this foolish idea altogether." Something glimmered in Eleanor's eyes and he thought it brought the life back to her expression.

A little smile played on her lips. "With God, all things are possible."

"Indeed." He touched his hat and strode toward the door when the bell overhead chimed and a young woman entered, trailed by two girls, clearly her daughters. Adelaide Johnson. Yet, another widow of the mine explosion. He removed his hat and nodded in greeting.

The woman's face hardened and she seemed to fight for simple civility. "Mr. McIntyre." The air between them sang with tension. It stung, though he was loathe to admit such a thing.

"Mrs. Johnson. And these must be your girls. My, how they've grown since I last..." He trailed off, realizing he'd last seen the girls at the memorial service for their father.

"Anna-Elise and Gracie. You remember Mr. McIntyre. He used to own the mine where your father worked."

Her tone was cold, and the stare from the girls—thirteen or so—was just as frigid. Though she'd been one of the women to accept money from his benevolence fund, the financial solution had not soothed any souls. Too often, McIntyre felt like a fool for having offered it. Had it done the families any good?

"Ladies." He nodded at the pretty little teenagers, blonde, fresh-faced, rosy-cheeked. Full of hope. And hate. "You're still in town. I thought you might have moved on. Most of the widows have."

"I'm working for the mine, cleaning the offices."

"Oh, then you'll get to keep your house?"

"No, unfortunately. They want us out by the end of next month. The miners need the quarters."

"If there is anything I can d—"

"No. You've done enough. Thank you." Adelaide reached back and tugged on Gracie's sleeve. "Come on, girls."

He took a step back, giving them room to pass, admittedly disheartened by the cold reception. He raised his gaze over their heads to Eleanor, who had heard the tense exchange. Her face was blank, but he could read her mind. Changing hearts in Defiance was one whale of a tall order.

~

The cold conversation at the door between Mr. McIntyre and Adelaide made Eleanor's stomach flutter. So much hate in this town. Maybe, today, she could make a tiny start toward turning things around. Is it possible, Lord? Could a little kindness make any difference in the hate flowing through Defiance?

The woman approached the counter, her countenance cut from marble. Eleanor dipped her head in greeting. "Adelaide. Nice to see you again."

"Do you have any black thread yet? You were out the other day. Billy said he was going to order some."

All right. No small talk. The woman never wasted any. "He did. It's right here." Eleanor slipped out from behind the counter and led the woman over to the sewing section. Shelves filled with bolts of cloth and sewing kits, buttons, and quilting supplies reached the ceiling. Eleanor indicated the shelf with dozens of spools of thread, a third of them in black. "It must be a popular color. Half of the black is already gone."

"The miners wear a lot of dark clothes. Doesn't show dirt." She plucked a spool off the shelf to examine it.

"Your daughters are lovely. I don't think I had a chance last time to tell you that. I remember when my daughter was that age."

The woman paused in her perusal. "It's a dangerous age, especially in this town."

The women exchanged knowing glances and Eleanor nodded. "I can imagine. If you have to give your housing back to the mine, you'll be moving on then?"

"Girls, why don't you go get some canned goods while I give our order to Miss Eleanor. You know what we need."

"Yes, ma'am," they said in unity.

"How'd you know my name?" Eleanor didn't remember giving it.

"I saw you at Buckley's preaching. Heard him say your name." She handed her the grocery list. "The job with the mine is a blessing and a curse. I can afford to move us to the boarding house—barely—but to relocate altogether, well, that'll take a little saving. I don't think I'll be able to get us out of here until the end of summer. If I'm frugal."

The bell over the door jangled again and two miners saun-tered in. Their attention went immediately to Gracie and Anna-Elise and lust ignited in their hot gazes. The girls blushed brightly and giggled into their hands. Eleanor cleared her throat and scowled at the men. "Something I can help you boys with?"

They grinned at the girls, finishing their trek to the counter with a saunter and a bold tip of their hats at Adelaide. "Mrs. Johnson," they said in unison.

"Hub. Jeremy."

The exchange was cool. The men's faces iced over as they replaced their hats. Eleanor looked back at Adelaide, noting the tension in her brow, the tight line of her lips. Did this woman have no friends in this town?

"We need twenty pounds of coffee for the camp. Mr. Griffin said to put it on the company's tab."

Eleanor pulled a ledge from underneath the counter and plucked a pencil from a cup. "You two can grab the coffee. I'll do the entry."

Anna-Elise and Gracie giggled under the men's bold stares and turned their backs to them. The pinch between Eleanor's own brow deepened. "And don't dilly dally," she said firmly.

The men took the hint. Nodded at her, Adelaide, waited for the girls to turn around. When they didn't, they nodded once more at Adelaide and strode to the corner to grab the sack of coffee.

"A dangerous age," Eleanor whispered, memories of a young, sweet, and innocent Victoria skipping through her mind.

"Too bad they can't stay that young and sweet." Mrs. Johnson folded her arms over her chest and heaved a big sigh. "They're a handful and getting worse. This town. I have to get them out of here."

"If there's anything I can do to help, please let me know."

Mrs. Johnson scoffed, then seemed to think better of the reaction. "Thank you. That's very kind of you."

Kind? No, just a lament that if only someone had offered to help Eleanor all those years ago—someone she could have trusted—how different their lives might have been. "I have a daughter, too. I would certainly appreciate it if someone showed her some kindness."

～

"Lane, afternoon. I'm headed to the hotel for lunch. Join me?" McIntyre shut the sheriff's door behind him, holding back the cold.

Lane laid down his pencil and pushed away the arrest report he was writing. "You talked me into it." He rose and snatched his hat off the hook on the wall. "You didn't tell me this job had so much paperwork."

"You didn't ask." McIntyre's attention drifted to the new prisoner, his arms dangling outside the bars, but his face was in shadow. Something about him was familiar. He toyed with the idea of taking a closer look, but Lane was already at the door.

"I've been thinking about Lucy's Fried Chicken since about ten this morning. Tom, bring you back anything?"

Tom? McIntyre took two steps toward the cell and the man inside moved into the light, sheepishly. "Afternoon, Mr. McIntyre."

"Tom, what are you doing in there? You usually stay out of trouble." Their local sign painter was darn near a saint.

"Aw, I got a little tight last night and had some words with one of Flynn's boys. All the witnesses said I threw the first punch."

McIntyre pivoted to Lane. Lane shrugged sheepishly. "I know. I didn't buy it, either, 'cause I know Tom. But fifteen people had the same story."

"Yeah," Tom said glumly. "I walked right into it."

"Cheer up." Lane rose from his desk. "I'll bring you some

fried chicken, and at eight o'clock tonight, your twenty-four hours will be up."

"Yeah, okay. Thanks. I guess."

McIntyre chewed on his lip, considering the injustice of the situation. "You better find a different place to drink."

"I don't reckon Bishop's place is any better. They're pushing folks to join up. Pick one side or another. I ain't never been much of a joiner."

So, Flynn and Bishop weren't just looking toward a gang war. They were building an army for something bigger. The revelation was strategic information. "Thanks for the information, Tom."

Lane and McIntyre stepped out on the boardwalk just as a cold breeze struck, icy tentacles snaking around their necks and kissing any exposed skin. "Brrr," Lane growled as snow crunched beneath their feet.

"Get your coat," McIntyre suggested.

"Aw, I can stand it from here to the hotel."

They were on the verge of crossing the busy street when a woman's screams arrested their steps. Lane and McIntyre spun around to the sound. She was pushing through the men on Water Street, fighting her way toward Main Street. The once muddy, rutted path to Tent Town was now a full-bore road with traffic flowing from the mine, its employees and miners wandering back and forth. Blonde hair flashed between horses and wagons, and momentarily, she was on them, clutching at Lane, pulling him down the street. Scantily dressed, haggard, and disheveled, the woman's vocation was more than obvious.

"Whoa, whoa, whoa," Lane said, stopping her. "What's going—"

"You've got to come with me. Drucinda has a wild one." She began tugging again. "He's gonna hurt her. Hurry."

McIntyre and Lane exchanged glances but knew they had no choice.

McIntyre did not miss these days. The rowdy customers. The drunken rages. The injured and bleeding girls. They hurried through the mix of tents and small cabins to Water Street, the main thoroughfare for Tent Town. The MP&G Mine had taken over the Crystal Chandelier upon Matthew's arrest and converted it to offices and a boardinghouse and this was where the woman was leading them. Memories assailed McIntyre. Namely, the night he'd come here on word that the preacher had killed a man. And, truly, Logan had been a drunken, murderous mess.

Thanks to Delilah.

He pushed thoughts of the past back as they entered the old saloon. He did not recognize the place. The once spacious main room had been closed up to provide more rooms. Only a small sitting area, a long hall, and the grand staircase met them now. The woman hurried down the hall, headed for one of the rooms. A woman was screaming in fear and pain. Her cries mingled with the bellowing of what could have passed for a raging bull. Scuffling, thuds, and smacks finished sketching the picture of what was happening.

With resignation, McIntyre drew his Colt. Lane did as well.

The woman with them pounded on the door violently. "Bradford, get your hands off her! Drucinda, the sheriff is here." With that, she stepped back and the raging argument from the room ceased abruptly.

Lane shot McIntyre a quick, worried glance and approached the door. He stayed off to the side and hammered on the wood. "Bradford, Drucinda, this is Sheriff Chandler. Open up!" Silence met his demand. He pounded on the door again. "Drucinda, you all right?" He shared another worried glance with McIntyre then shifted to the woman. "I take it that ain't her husband in there?" The woman shook her head. "Prostitution's against the law," he told her, but McIntyre heard no conviction in the tone, only weariness. "I'm comin' in."

Lane aimed his .44 at the door and fired. The doorknob disappeared in a roar and a cloud of smoke and fire. And just as Lane moved to step inside the room, a voice in McIntyre's head screamed: *nooo*. Without hesitating, he snatched Lane out of the center of the doorway. A shotgun blast roared past him, tugging at his shoulder. McIntyre ducked around Lane and fired at the smoke-obscured shape of a man. A woman screamed again.

Bradford staggered out of the smoke, the shotgun clattering to the wood. A stain blossomed on his chest and he followed the firearm to the floor, collapsing, falling over dead.

Lane squatted down for a closer look. "He's one of Flynn's men."

Charles had seen him around. A bit of a troublemaker, to be sure. And now, no longer.

The girl with them stepped over him and grabbed Drucinda, who was bleeding profusely from her nose. "You okay, honey?"

"Take her on over to Dr. Hope," Charles ordered. He turned and looked back down the hallway. Several men and women had poked their heads out of the other rooms. "You two." He motioned to the two closest men. "Come help us move this body."

They didn't move fast enough for Lane. "Now," he barked, rising to his full height, "Or I'll arrest you on a vice charge. *And* make sure it gets in the newspaper." The men scrambled to gather up their suspenders and hop into their boots.

Charles grabbed the blanket off the bed and draped it over Bradford. Another dead man in Defiance.

Another life he'd taken without much remorse. He'd have to spend some time talking this over with the Lord. Was he regretful? And he was going to have to explain this to Naomi. She worried about his soul turning dark again.

And so did he.

Eleanor scanned the ledger and quickly noted the rise in the number of breakfasts being served here in the hotel. She spun the book around and slipped it across the table to Mollie. Here in the dining room, with every table full, the clink and chatter of a hungry morning crowd made the point that she was going to say. "These numbers right here"—she dragged her finger across the column—"and right here. They tell us we need to up our orders for flour and eggs. You see that?"

Mollie studied the numbers, her eyes bouncing from column to column. She flipped back a page, studied the numbers, returned to the current page. "You're so good with numbers, Eleanor. I'm not sure I've got the experience for assistant manager."

"Now, now." She patted the girl's hand. "I've been doing this a long time. The trends jump out at me. They will for you, too, in time. You're learning every day."

Mollie's blue eyes flashed with suspicion. "Are you just being nice?"

"Honey, when it comes to managing a business and stewarding somebody else's money, there is no nice. Now, trust me, you'll be fine. A few months from now, we won't even need this meeting."

"All right. I'll take your word for it. I do need some coffee. Can I get you something from the kitchen?"

"Well, speaking of eggs, I sure would like a couple over easy with toast and coffee. Thank you."

Mollie rose, swung her long, golden braid over her shoulder, and smiled warmly at Eleanor. "No, thank you. I am learning a lot under you. I'll get that breakfast order in."

She strode off toward the kitchen and for lack of anything better to do, Eleanor took the ledger back and flipped through it. Her mind was elsewhere, though. She wanted a day off to go see how Victoria and Toby were getting along, though she had nothing good to report. Nothing that would change Victoria's mind.

Oh, Lord, I pray Toby is winning her heart. She needs to fall in love with that boy and forget this whole horrible idea of coming to—

"It's a grand hotel with a fine reputation."

The breath caught in Eleanor's chest. The man's voice brought gooseflesh up on her arms. Surely it couldn't be.

"As chambermaids, your daughters will be watched over and kept in safe, respectable working conditions."

Her pulse skittering like a jackrabbit's, Eleanor forced air into her lungs and pivoted in her chair as if she were about to look down the barrel of a gun. Adelaide Johnson sat facing her two tables away. A man sat with her, but his back was to Eleanor.

It can't be...

"And Stillwater is a lovely town," the man said. "It's growing. There are boundless opportunities. The proprietress of the hotel will even guarantee that your daughters attend school."

Bile backed up in Eleanor's throat. A wave of nausea careened over her. Sam Collins. The man who had taken Victoria to a fine, respectable *hotel* in Stillwater. After all these years, he hadn't even changed his pitch.

She stood on rubbery legs, tremors rocketed through them from the fury surging through her veins. Eleanor approached their table and locked eyes on the man.

"You told me all this last summer, Sam," Adelaide was saying. "My girls will be so far away, though. Oh, Eleanor, this is Sa—"

"Sam Collins."

The man looked up at her, his dark eyes showing polite boredom. Eleanor's glare and twitching sneer quickly transformed his gaze to confusion. "Do I know you, madame?"

"Adelaide, this man gave my daughter a job, too. Sixteen years ago." She scanned his face, satisfied to see wrinkles around his eyes, sagging skin at his jowls, and gray spreading through his hair and mustache. She leaned in a little closer and lowered her voice. "I'm going for the sheriff. I'll see you hang for what you did to her."

"I think you must have me confused with someone else."

"No. Not by a long shot." Eleanor waved a warning finger at Adelaide. "Don't let this man anywhere near your daughters." Without waiting for responses, Eleanor rushed out the door, intent on finding the sheriff. Because if she didn't, she'd kill Sam Collins with her bare hands.

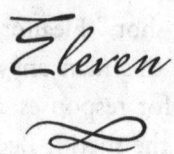

Eleven

CHARLES CURSORILY EXAMINED the shredded shoulder of his new suit as he sat quietly at Lane's desk. Bradford's aim had been alarmingly close. He had told Naomi about his warning to Flynn and Bishop because he did not keep secrets from her, but she was worried now. About his soul.

If she saw his coat, she'd have cause to worry about his health.

He'd had no business going with Lane but, under the circumstances, could not have abandoned his friend, either.

Defiance was quicksand. If he wasn't careful, it was going to suck the soul right out of him. *I need to rethink things, don't I, Lord? I've gotten in a place I don't want to be.*

Lane and the other men had taken Bradford's body to Dr. Clark. As the town MD, she was, by default, deemed the medical examiner as well. Determining the cause of death, however, would not require even slight skill. Charles had drawn first. He'd drawn fast.

He never missed.

Here, in the silence of the sheriff's office, he considered what he'd done. Pulling the trigger. Being there in the first place. He was a husband and a father now. The days of rescuing harlots from violent customers were supposed to be far away in his past. Yet, it appeared Defiance still needed cleaning up. He'd foolishly thought with Matthew's arrest, much of the lascivious behavior would fizzle for lack of a guiding hand. In the absence of a ruler, gangs had formed, and now two were fighting for control.

Instead of letting Lane handle it, he'd leaned into his pride and stuck himself slap in the center of it.

God help the town if Delilah came back now. God help her...

The door jangled and Lane strode in. "Heck of a shot, Johnny Reb." He snatched off his hat, tossed it to his desk, and dropped down in front of McIntyre. "And I owe ya."

"Seems to me the scales have balanced back out." He touched his neck, always amazed there was no scar.

Lane nodded. "Either way, that was some fast shooting."

"I was always fast. You were always accurate."

"With the two of us, it's a wonder the South lost."

McIntyre chuckled grimly. "Best they did."

"I reckon." He put his feet up on the desk. "So it looks like MP&G is turning a blind eye to prostitution in their board-inghouse."

"It would appear so. I'm sure it cuts into someone's business across the creek in Hell's Half-Acre. Possibly one of the points of contention. The girls. Do they work for Bishop or Flynn?"

"They wouldn't say, but they got awfully edgy when I mentioned Flynn."

"I'd love to see an end to trading in flesh." He deeply regretted he'd ever treated women so atrociously.

"Kind of rubs me the wrong way, too." Lane sat back and dropped his boots onto his desk. "MP&G, I mean. I've got no jurisdiction in Hell's Half-Acre, but red light laws are on the books here. I won't let the mining company get away with it. We can't trade one madam for another."

"I imagine the mining officials think they are above your small fines. But you can try."

"I will. And I'll hammer it, arresting everybody over and over if that's what it takes. We can shut it down, at least on this side of the creek."

Charles's mind wandered to Delilah and the debauchery she'd brought to the town. Now, thanks to city limits being established, Lane had jurisdiction over Defiance, including the neighborhood of Tent Town. But Hell's Half-Acre, across the creek, mere feet outside the city limits, was the burr under the town's saddle.

"Flynn is running whores in Hell's Half-Acre, too," Lane continued. "And he's taken over the Number Two. Bishop is running the Crow's Pub and keeps girls in tents out back."

Such industrious men. As Charles used to be. They won't take to more competition lightly. "Delilah will cause a firestorm if she tries to open her own place. I don't think either faction will take it lying down if you'll pardon the pun."

Lane heaved a long sigh. "You really don't buy her change of heart?"

"I think she believes if she can drop enough liquor and flesh in front of the miners, they'll let bygones be bygones."

"Hmmm." His gaze frosted over as if he was pondering something to the contrary, but then he shook his head. "Possibility, I guess. I don't know her well enough to say."

"Most of the new miners won't care about her role in the explosion. She could develop allies quickly. Split the town a third way."

"And start a bigger feud than is already brewing." Lane whistled. "I'll try to nip MP&G in the bud, but what am I supposed to do if Delilah shows up?"

"I will emphasize to Eleanor that if Delilah takes one step into Defiance, it will be one step straight to a jail cell."

Lane frowned and drummed his fingers for a moment.

"What if we're wrong? What if she has changed? What if she really does want forgiveness from the town?"

"Then God help her. Jail might be the safest place for her."

"Sheriff! Sheriff!" a voice called from outside.

Lane's brow dove as he snatched his feet down and surged to his feet. "What? Is there a full moon or something?"

Eleanor ignored the cold, biting wind and moved as fast as her heavy legs would carry her across the street. The second she spotted the sign over the sheriff's office, she started yelling. "Sheriff! Sheriff!" Sheriff Chandler and Mr. McIntyre emerged from the door, leery expressions on their faces.

"Please, come quick." Eleanor hobbled up on the board-walk. "There's a man over in the hotel dining room. You need to arrest him."

"What's he done?"

Eleanor's heart fluttered in her chest. The frigid wind invaded her lungs, stealing her breath rather than giving it. She abruptly collapsed onto a post and the sheriff and Mr. McIntyre rushed to her aid. She waved them off. "Please. Sam Collins. He's at the hotel. You have to arrest him."

Lane drew himself up to his full height. "I'll ask again. What's he done?"

She gulped air. "He created Delilah." His blank look and silence said he didn't comprehend. She grabbed his shirt, frustrated with the delay. "He takes girls. Sells them into prostitution."

Lane reached strong fingers under her arm. "Come on, you can explain this on the way." He looked over her at Mr. McIntyre. "You needn't attend this party."

McIntyre pushed his hat back. "I don't think I would miss this one for the world."

~

They were all disappointed, however, when they found Adelaide alone, dejectedly rolling peas around her plate. Collins was nowhere in sight. Eleanor slapped the table and leaned toward the woman. "Where is he? Where did he go? He doesn't have your girls, does he?"

Adelaide laid down her fork. "No. He tore off out of here after you left. I thought maybe he was following you. I guess not. You just destroyed a wonderful opportunity for my girls, Eleanor. What's this all about?"

Eleanor hung her head and stepped back from the table. Sheriff Chandler touched her shoulder. "Give me a description of him. If he's still here, we'll find him."

"He's tall, in his mid-fifties. Graying brown hair. Mustache..."

What else, Lord? What else?

"He has arthritis in his right hand," Adelaide added. "He's pretty crippled with it." She didn't sound pleased to share the information.

The rush of anger wearing off, sapping her energy, Eleanor slipped into the empty seat at the table.

Mr. McIntyre was moving toward the door. "Let's go, Lane. This man I want to find."

Eleanor waited until the men had left then she gave Adelaide the whole, distasteful story, at least as much as she dared without pointing directly to Victoria. "He sells girls into prostitution. He took my daughter to that hotel in Stillwater. Told her I knew the whole time what he had planned. She believed him, and it took her fifteen years to come back to me."

Adelaide had turned as pale as the napkin in her hand. For a moment, her mouth moved, but words evaded her. Finally, she managed, "Fif...? Dear God. Thank you."

"I'm just glad—" It dawned on Eleanor how easily she could have missed the whole conversation. What if she and

Mollie had had breakfast in the kitchen? What if Eleanor had put off the training till after lunch? But she hadn't. She'd been right where she was supposed to be. A man plans his way, but the Lord directs his steps.

Two little girls were safe. Adelaide wouldn't be chained with guilt. Eleanor wept with gratitude. "Thank the Lord, not me."

~

At first, Charles and Lane considered searching together, but McIntyre was not in the mood to wander about Tent Town *again*, hoping for friendly faces. Instead, he stopped at the boundary between it and Hell's Half-Acre and motioned toward a two-story building. Smoke churned from its four different chimneys. "I've got a few people I want to start with. Like Mrs. Lee here. Maybe one or two others. You work your *friendly* sources. I'll meet you back at the office."

"Friendly sources." Lane rearranged his hat. "This is the second time in a short spell that we've had to come over here knocking on tents. You'll explain this to Hope if it comes up?"

McIntyre tried to work a smile into a disapproving frown but didn't quite make it. "It's official business. I'll swear to that." He touched his brim and turned to the laundry.

Mrs. Lee's place. Eventually, every man in Defiance got his clothes washed here, and the sharp businesswoman picked up all kinds of information from her customers. When McIntyre entered, the young Chinese man behind the counter nodded immediately. "One moment, please."

He spun, his braid whipping about like a rat's tail, and disappeared behind the curtain. Momentarily, Mrs. Lee emerged. A lovely woman, graceful and stoic, she nodded at McIntyre as he belatedly remembered to remove his hat.

"Mr. McIntyre. You honor my establishment with your venerable presence. How may I be of assistance?"

He approached the counter and lowered his voice. "I'm looking for a man named Sam Collins. Older. About fifty, brown hair going gray. Mustache. One hand gnarled with arthritis. He has an unhealthy interest in pretty, young girls."

"I see. You will cure him of this ailment, I trust?"

"Given half a chance."

"I am not aware that he has come here, but if he does, be assured, I will let you know."

"If he does come in, find out what you can about him. Namely, where he's staying."

"It will be my great honor to be of service again."

McIntyre started to go but stopped and added, "Thank you. I appreciate your help, Mrs. Lee. Every time I've had need of you, you and your sons—"

"We thank you, Mr. McIntyre. You have helped us prosper in Defiance when others have tried to hinder us." She bowed her head. "We will keep our eyes and ears open."

She wasn't the most talkative woman, but she was quick to the point. McIntyre returned the bow and left. The mountains had cast long, cold shadows over the street now and the icy breeze bit the skin like fangs. Raising his collar, he stepped into the flow of miners and lumberjacks headed out for an evening's entertainment.

"Thought you didn't frequent this side of town, Mr. McIntyre," one of the passing lumberjacks said. The men with him grinned.

McIntyre toyed with a flippant answer but decided the truth would have the greater impact. "There's a man I'd like to find. Sam Collins. Could be two double eagles in it for you if you get a lead on him."

The men's expressions changed immediately. Serious avarice hardened their features. Another man in the group edged closer as they walked. "What's he done?"

The suspicion in his voice was obvious and annoying. Charles McIntyre didn't gallivant about looking for men for jaywalking. If he was after someone, it was serious. The new men in town still had a few things to learn. He passed his gaze over the group. "He sells very young girls into prostitution. I desire to help him find a new vocation."

The explanation sunk in and the group's suspicion gave way to humbled looks and subtle nods. The first man who'd spoken shrugged his shoulders. "We'll let you know if we hear anything."

"Would it matter," the second man began, "if, say, we found this Collins, and he sort of tripped on his way to the sheriff's office?"

Vigilante justice reared its head so easily in Defiance, even more so when men ran in packs. Worse, McIntyre understood their feelings. Anyone who would hurt a child...but at one point, he'd been on the receiving end of that *justice*, and it made him understandably nervous. "I'd appreciate the chance for the man to face the law. It would be the right way to do this." That was as strong a statement as he cared to make.

The lumberjacks nodded, grunted. "We'll be looking," one said as they ambled on. McIntyre paused, rested his hands on his hips, his fingers brushing the cold steel of the .44. Surely, if they got the word out, no one would protect this man. Which led him to the other person here in Tent Town he wanted to find.

This late in the day, Corky would either be in his tent drinking and planning on where to drink more, or he was already at a saloon. McIntyre opted to try for his tent. He did not hurry through the crowds, which directed curious stares at him and, in some cases, baleful glares. He did walk tall and steady. Hard feelings or not, he was not afraid to walk through Tent Town. What he lamented more was that he'd left his coat in the sheriff's office.

Blowing into his hands for warmth, he turned left at the intersection where the Crystal Chandelier *boardinghouse* was, fell in behind a small group of miners headed toward a section of tent quarters, and kept an eye out for Corky. At a short, lonely pine, he turned again into a small cul-de-sac of five tents. Corky's was the last one on the left. His old home. He rapped on the tent pole. "Corky. You in there. It's McIntyre."

A moment later, the short, dark-eyed, but ever-eager-to-please man emerged. He flashed McIntyre a toothy grin in his round, moon face and the two shook hands. "Mr. McIntyre. It sure is good to see you. Always is. Come on in and get warm."

"Thank you, Corky." He followed him into the small but surprisingly tidy tent. "How's panning?"

The man's face fell as he turned up his lantern. "Aw, I started getting hungry, so I took a job with the mine. Hard work, but it's steady pay. I'll try my luck again later in the spring maybe."

McIntyre was tempted to ask about the fairly large sum of money Corky had left Defiance with last year. As part of his assistance in spiriting away a couple of Delilah's youngest gals, McIntyre had seen to it that Corky had enough to live on for a spell. He should have known the spell would be short. "I have faith you'll make a strike soon," he said generously. "Your persistence is impressive."

"Thank you. What brings you over here? Can I get you a drink?" He motioned over his shoulder. "I've got a little whisk—"

"No, but thank you. I'm looking for someone. I know how you get out and about. If you see him, you'll let me know?"

"Sure. Who is it?"

"His name is Sam Collins. I believe he's only been in Defiance a short time." He gave Corky a description and added the telling part. "He's looking for young girls to sell into prostitution down in Oklahoma. I cannot abide this if it's true. You understand?"

Corky's brow furrowed. "Pretty clearly. I was there when we spirited away those Asian gals."

And burned through several thousand dollars given for the

good deed. "This is worse. It's not women this man likes. He prefers girls. As I said, young girls. "

"Uh, well, yes, sir. I'll—" Corky's gaze jerked to the left behind McIntyre and his round face constricted into a sneer. "Hey!" He shot past Charles and stormed outside, McIntyre on his heels. "Bozey. What do you want?"

A group of six miners had circled the opening to Corky's tent. Each man was holding a pick ax, hammer, or club. One fella, a sloppy gut stressing his dirty, worn shirt and moth holes in his coat, slapped a stick in the palm of his hand. He grinned icily at McIntyre. "How's your neck, McIntyre? Bother you any?"

McIntyre studied the man's fat, pockmarked face for a clue to a memory. In the low light, he couldn't be sure. "Were you there?" A few of the men who had tried to lynch him had escaped. McIntyre had not pursued them, gambling that with Matthew out of the way, men like this would slither back into the dark. Had he been wrong? "Were you?"

The man's brow dove and he curled his fat fingers over and over into tight fists. "Bradford was our friend. We heard you and that sheriff shot him down in cold blood."

"Bradford. The man who was beating Drucinda. He pulled a shotgun on Lane." And none of this interested McIntyre. He inched closer to the man Corky had called Bozey. "I said I want to know if you were at that lynching. *My* lynching."

Apparently understanding McIntyre would not address the issue of Bradford's death, the man shrugged. "Well, now, I believe I was in a card game that afternoon. Lots of witnesses. But I sure heard a lot about it. Heard you begged like a gutless coward for Naomi's life—"

McIntyre launched toward the man, grabbed his filthy collar, and lifted him to his toes. Fury coursed through McIntyre like molten lava. "I don't know who you are, but if my wife's name ever comes out of your mouth again, I will cut out your tongue. Do not test me on this."

The man's bloodshot eyes widened for an instant, chilled with fear, but then heat returned to them. "Miss Naomi is well?"

Before anyone could blink, McIntyre's .44 was pressed into Bozey's fat jowl. "Who are you? How do you know my wife? I will not ask again."

"Bozey O'Shay," Corky said flatly from behind McIntyre, "You should tell me quick-like where your next of kin is." Bozey's wide-eyed gaze shot to Corky as sweat suddenly beaded on the man's forehead. Corky only stared back at him with a dark, bored expression. "You're about to die, if I wasn't clear."

"I—I don't," he said stupidly. Confused, stammering, Bozey seemed to realize he'd poked one big, mean bear. "I wasn't there. At the lynching. I swear. My brother was. He told me. His version anyway."

McIntyre inhaled deeply, trying to calm his stampeding anger and focus clearly on this situation. His gaze, he knew, said everything that lay before this man. His finger itched to pull the trigger. So easy. "And your brother is where exactly?"

Bozey gulped. "Ru-Ruby City. He's over in Ruby City."

"Will he be returning to Defiance then?"

The fear was blatant in the man's eyes now. He'd looked into the face of the Grim Reaper. The scythe was pressed to his neck. Oh, McIntyre could kill Bozey. So easy to shoot first, repent later. Would he always have this battle?

"N—no. He won't. He won't come back. I'll make sure."

McIntyre swallowed, pictured Naomi. And his boys. It wouldn't do to kill over a slight. Still, his trigger finger tensed—

A soft, gushing sound greeted his ears, followed momentarily but the warm smell of urine. Bozey blinked, his eyes wide with fear and humiliation.

That would do.

Charles released the hammer on his Colt and holstered it, inwardly struggling to keep his bravado on display and yet hide his disappointment with himself. The men around Bozey stepped back, grimacing at their friend's humiliation.

Charles smoothed Bozey's wrinkled shirt by way of a sarcastic apology and told him, "Yes, you make sure. Save us both some trouble. You and your brother go far away, where this"—glanced down—"*incident* will never be repeated." Over his shoulder to Corky, he said, "Let me know if you come up with anything on that other matter."

With that, he left the little circle of frightened men, but he was frightened too. In the last few weeks, he'd threatened two men and killed one today. A necessary act. He had some regret, but no guilt. He'd saved Lane's life.

But the Colt had found its way into his hand again...much too easily with Bozey. At least the man's disgrace appeared to be an acceptable alternative to murder.

Twelve

IF VICTORIA DIDN'T KNOW BETTER, she would have sworn Toby liked that she had been laid up for almost three days. He'd set up a chair with a footrest in front of the fireplace and helped settle her there in the mornings. Even tucked a quilt over her lap. She'd limped around the cabin a little, but there was nothing she could do other than a little tidying up and light cooking. Mostly, she'd slept.

Tonight, she'd insisted on sitting at the kitchen table and chopping parsley while he scurried about putting away some supplies and frying up sausage.

"I feel useless, Toby."

He was stirring a pot of something at the stove. The sausage sizzled, scenting the air with a heavenly aroma that made Victoria's stomach growl. "It's just for another day or two," he said. "Won't kill either one of us." He stepped over, grabbed a handful of the parsley, and dropped it in with the sausage.

She sighed. "I suppose." Assuming she was done, she pushed the cutting board and leftover parsley away from her.

"You could read. Knit. Darn clothes. You're not useless."

Oh, she should darn his socks. She never said anything, but

in the evenings, when he walked around without his boots, his big toe and heel peeked at her. "I'll start with your socks."

"That would be appreciated."

"What's for dinner?"

"Well, I did a little trading in town with a fella who came here all the way from Italy."

"Italy. My."

"He gave me a basket full of these little things called raviolis. And he also gave me a recipe for a sauce."

"I've heard of those. I had a lot of Italian cust...omers..." She faded off with a whisper. That life, that Delilah, seemed like another person from a hundred years ago. She didn't like to think about the way she'd lived her life before Jesus...yet it was always there. Like a demon sitting in the corner, watching, accusing.

Toby's stirring slowed, but only for a second. He picked up the tempo again. A few minutes later, he presented her with a plate of steaming ravioli and sausage covered in a savory-smelling tomato sauce. It was even garnished with sprinkles of something white. "Oh, my." She took the plate and inhaled. "I think the wrong person has been cooking for us."

"And I think you hurt your ankle on purpose so you wouldn't have to keep it up."

She picked up the fork and poked at the garnish on top. "Is that parmesan?"

He nodded. "Guiseppe gave me a block with the raviolis."

He glanced at the food, urging her with his eyes to take a bite. She stabbed a ravioli, swirled it in the sauce, and gave it a try. The explosion of flavor made her moan. "That's wonderful. You've truly outdone yourself."

A huge, satisfied grin betrayed his relief and he returned to the stove to make his own plate. They ate in silence for a long, comfortable spell. The kind of quiet that said the meal was worth savoring. Toby licked his fork after the last bite and smiled at her. "Seconds? There's a little left."

"I'd love to, but I can't eat another bite."

He took their dishes back to the kitchen and when he returned, he lay down on the rag rug right in front of the fireplace, exposed toes toward the flames, and breathed a long, satisfied sigh. He crossed his ankles, laid his hands over his stomach, and relaxed. Victoria would have sworn she could see the stress of the day stream out of him. Or was it more like something here, something warm and peaceful, was flowing *into* him?

She reached up and extinguished the lamp over the table. "You like it here, don't you?"

He kept his eyes closed and said, "I do. Ruby City is small but I like the people. The grass is good on this spread, and there's lots of room round about for men and horses. So far, the sheriffing hasn't been too hard, either. No hard cases in town."

She glanced around the small cabin bathed only in the light of the dancing flames. Spartan. Plain. The rag rug and the red paisley calico curtains provided the only splashes of color in the home. Such a far, far cry from her old rooms with red velvet wallpaper, crystal decanters, and shiny brass beds.

And she never wanted to see a room like that again as long as she lived.

Without even thinking about it, she gimped over to him and eased herself to the floor beside him. He raised his head to gaze at her in surprise for a second but then settled back in place. While the floor wasn't all that comfortable, the heat on her feet and the heat coming off him made it more than bearable. Now that she was here, she closed her eyes and wondered about the wisdom of the spontaneous move. What had come over her?

Toby, on the other hand, didn't seem moved one way or the other.

She lay quiet, listening. The pop and hiss of the fire and the tick-tock of the Regulator wall clock seemed too loud. Something had her feeling so antsy. The quiet, *his* easy silence, pressed in on her. Eyes closed, she spoke, just to muffle her angst. "If you were to stay, would you keep the badge or let it go to build the ranch?"

The rustle of clothing said he'd shifted his position, then soft taps, as if he were drumming his fingers on his belt buckle. "I think, soon as I can afford it, I want to put the badge down and turn this place into something."

"You don't want to go back to Dodge?"

"Nah. I might try to get GW up here, though."

That made Victoria smile. GW owned the ranch where she had met Toby. Toby had been the man's head wrangler. "I'd like that. I miss that old coot."

"What about you?" Frustration and resignation shaded his tone.

They were always dancing around this, weren't they? What was her plan? What were her expectations? Would she really go through with this? Was Defiance that dangerous?

"If you can get a fair trial," he said haltingly, "you're gonna do hard time. Have you really thought about that?"

Not in any serious way. If she could apologize to the town, ask their forgiveness, try to make them believe she'd been changed by the overwhelming love of a real savior, the only Savior, then she could go to jail and bear it. Logan had asked her to give the Lord a chance, and she had. Wouldn't he agree that all the pain, the agony, the deaths she'd caused—she should pay for them? Jesus had forgiven her, but she struggled with letting that be enough. So far, it wasn't.

She had to do penance.

Then she had moments like this. Moments that made her think she might be giving up something worth keeping. Lying here beside Toby, in their safe, warm home, dreaming of a future. No, she couldn't let herself—

He rose to one elbow and looked into her face. The light danced in his hair, hid his blue eyes in mysterious shadows. She couldn't ignore how kissable his lips were, how strong his shoulders were. Sometimes his smile made butterflies flutter in her stomach, her heart beat a little quicker.

He reached out and ever-so-lightly caressed her jaw with the back of his fingers. Goose bumps rose up on her body. "You should leave it all in the past and start fresh. Not just a new chapter, a whole new book. You said it yourself, you're not Delilah anymore."

He lowered his mouth to hers, and Victoria gasped with shock, joy, and desire. Before she could think, he gathered her into him, deepened the kiss, commanded her response. She seemed to melt into him, lose herself in the surrender to his mouth, to his will. Her arms went around him and she clung to him, a hurt place in her soul filling up with hope and dreams. For a moment, she drank in the idea of something different, something as mundane as being a wife and a mother...

Dreams she'd had with Logan.

He pulled away, smiled, and tapped her on the nose. "I'm done in. Reckon you can hop to bed on your own, or you need my help?"

His withdrawal, his abrupt change of direction, her own chaotic thoughts, left her floundering. "No, I...uh, no, I'll be fine."

"I should do the dishes..." He clambered to his feet. "But I'm asleep on my feet. I'll do them in the morning. You sure you don't need any help?"

Wasn't he going to say anything about what had just happened? What was he thinking?

And just what was the matter with her? She'd made a living reading men. The old Delilah would have made a game of this. Tempted and teased. She had the feeling now, however, Toby was the one doing the tempting, and it had her off kilter.

He raised his eyebrows at her, interrupting her ruminations. He'd asked her something.

"Oh. No. I want to enjoy the fire a little longer."

"All right. I'll see ya in the morning." He tossed another log on the fire for her and then strode over to his cot.

A few minutes after he laid down, his back to her, she gathered her wits enough to pray. *Lord, I don't understand. Toby confuses me. Help me understand him...what he wants. Sometimes I feel like I'm betraying Logan. Help me understand what I want. No...what I need. What you want for me.*

A memory lighted on her brain. The first time she'd seen Toby work with Delilah. Over and over, he'd touched the horse, talked to her, led her around the corral, then walked away from her. Finally, one afternoon, *she* had walked over to *him*. The moment the horse had expressed her trust in him.

He wants me to come to him.

Victoria's pulse started racing wildly. She wanted his arms around her, his lips on hers again...she wanted whatever was between them to move forward. But it couldn't. It just couldn't. Yet, the compulsion to take a step toward him grew in intensity.

"Toby?"

"Hmmm," he mumbled sleepily.

She licked her lips. "I'm cold."

He didn't move at first—she wondered if he'd fallen asleep —then slowly, he sat up, dragged his pillow and his blanket off the cot, and joined her on the floor. She scootched up close to him as he spread the blanket over them and then pulled her up against him. "Better?"

"Better."

He shifted a touch more to rest his chin on the top of her head, and a moment later, his gentle, rhythmic snoring reverberated in his chest. Smiling, she settled deeper into his arms and drifted off to sleep.

~

Eleanor kept the smile pasted on her face until the last customer of the day left. When the door shut behind the man, she hurried to the front door, locked it, and flipped the closed sign over. With a weary sigh, she leaned against the door, eyes closed, her disappointment warring with her exhaustion.

Coming back to open the mercantile this morning had been the hardest thing she'd ever done in her life. Knowing Sam was out there, skulking around Defiance in the shadows, made her want to tear the town apart.

He can't get away, Lord. Surely you've brought us both here for a reason. I pray it's for justice.

She believed Lane and Mr. McIntyre when they said they wouldn't stop looking for Sam, that Mr. McIntyre had a particular interest in putting a man like Sam away. She also believed they'd find him. They had everybody in town looking for him, and the reward was big.

Should she send a follow-up telegram to Victoria? Something cryptic, of course, but hint at the danger? Other than her usual, 'not a friendly place.' That was all she'd dared thus far. Or tell her in person when she saw her this week. Her first visit home.

She wished Buckley was around. She could use his Godly counsel, but after his last sermon, he'd disappeared. Maybe he'd gone back to rest a spell with the friendly Utes. She sure couldn't blame him. Or maybe he was getting some personal items and would be back Sunday. She hoped so. The big old bear was growing on her.

As she ambled back to the counter, a noise in the backroom brought her head up. An instant later, Sam flipped the curtains out of his way and stepped into the light. Fear and fury jolted through Eleanor, kicking her heart to a gallop. But the fear faded as the fury in her rose to a boiling point. "What are you doing here?"

His suit was wrinkled and there were bags under his eyes. "Thanks to you, barely staying one step ahead of the law."

It didn't hurt her feelings any to hear that. "You ain't changed." She glanced at his swollen, twisted hand pressed to his chest. "Other than you're a crippled old man now."

Sam's mustache twitched. She assumed he was sneering at her. "You know, those things you were saying yesterday. I can't have you spouting nonsense like that. It's not good for business."

"I wonder, do you even remember my daughter?"

"Try me."

"Back in Dodge, sixteen years ago—"

He snorted and spat a curse. "Sixteen years? Why do you think I'd remember a girl from that long ago?"

"Turned out she was special." In so many ways, especially to her mother. "She had a head for the business."

"What was her name?"

Eleanor suddenly realized where her mouth had gotten her. Sam could never learn the truth. He might use it against Victoria. "Doesn't matter. She's out of that world now. Starting over."

He shrugged. "Some of them do. Take a second chance and run with it. Get married, move away. Change their names. Your daughter, is she nearby?"

"I wouldn't tell you that if you put a gun to my head."

"Interesting choice of words." A Derringer appeared in Sam's good hand, cocked, and aimed at her. Instinctively, Eleanor felt beside her for any kind of defensive weapon. Her fingers rested on a canned good. He stepped from behind the counter for, she assumed, a closer shot. He was only a few feet away. Should she wrestle the gun away from him? "I need to know if you've told your daughter. Is she in these parts? I can't have the two of you pointing fingers, busting up my business deals."

"Hell will freeze over before I tell you anything about her."

"Listen, woman, I don't want to shoot you."

"No, you want to shoot us both."

He ran his tongue over his teeth as if considering the observation. Then he grinned. "She's here with you, right? If you don't tell me, I am going to shoot you. Otherwise, I just want you to leave Defiance."

He thought she was a fool. He was going to shoot her no matter what she said.

So be it. But he would never, ever get to Victoria. Never again. Eleanor lobbed the can at him and it bounced off his forehead. Howling in pain, swaying with dizziness, he cocked the little gun. Eleanor dove at him, grabbing his hand. In the same instant, fire shot from the Derringer and a hot streak of pain sliced through her abdomen.

She fell back into a display of stacked cans. Sam cursed and fired again, but Eleanor rolled to the floor with the collapsing heap of metal. Something wet—green beans?—showered down on her.

"I got you," he hissed, holding his swelling head. "I got you. I know I did. That's what matters."

Her side burned so bad the pain threatened to drown her in searing darkness.

Stay awake. Stay awake, Eleanor. Sam's boots thudded back behind the counter, and a moment later, the back door slammed shut.

She waited, listened, pressed a hand to her burning abdomen.

Eleanor fought, clawed at the air, and flailed her way to a sitting position. The pain was excruciating. It set her stomach ablaze and she crumpled to the ground with a cry. Something warm and slick coated her hand. Puzzled, she looked at the red smear glistening on her fingers. Blood. Her blood.

"Oh, Lord, Victoria...please..." The pain burned on and on in her side, but her ability to focus on it dulled. Her vision clouded. "Please keep her safe." Exhaustion like a warm blanket settled on her, robbed her of any strength, and she relaxed on the floor. She was dying but was too tired to care.

Eleanor splayed on her back, looked up at the lamp burning overhead, growing dimmer...dimmer.

The bell over the door rang. Darkness enfolded her. She felt the presence of the Lord, a sweet peace calling her home. "All right..." she whispered, ready.

"Sheriff," a man's voice bellowed.

Buckley? Eleanor's body lifted, and she felt pressure on her stomach.

"Somebody tell the doctor I'm coming."

Thirteen

"FINALLY, SOMETHING DIFFERENT." Victoria dropped the telegram to the table and snatched an apron off the back of the chair. *Not a friendly place. Not a friendly place.* All Momma ever said was 'not a friendly place.' She tied the apron with short, excitable movements. "Now, finally, a telegram that she's coming home. She's got something to tell us." In truth, she wasn't sure how that made her feel.

She joined Toby at the counter, took a knife from the holder, stole a tomato from the group in front of him, and began dicing it.

"What if it ain't good?" he asked somberly.

Her hands slowed, but only for an instant. "I...I need to see this through. If they won't hang me on sight, I have to try."

Toby laid his knife down and turned to her. Victoria didn't want to look at him, but couldn't help herself. His eyes glimmered with a keen intensity that made her insides flutter, but he regarded her with obvious disappointment. His mouth turned down on the corners. His brow creased with concern. "Making amends with someone when you've sinned against them is one thing—but when making amends will only inflame their hate and get you killed"—his voice was rising, a little louder with each word—"that's not helping anybody. Jesus died for your sins, Victoria. *He* forgave you. Throwing your life away makes his sacrifice worthless."

She backed away from him and laid the knife down. "You don't understand. You don't see their faces every night in your dreams. You can't hear the sound of the explosion or feel the rumble in the ground as the rocks fell." She flinched as her throat tightened up. "The eerie quiet in the town as they dug for survivors. The wailing wives—"

Toby grabbed her shoulders. "And nothing you can do will change any of it. You go back to Defiance, you'll just be clawing at wounds that are still raw. You've got to accept what Jesus did for you. You've got to accept you might not ever go back to Defiance."

She snatched herself free and turned her back to him. "What am I supposed to do? Just live like none of it ever happened? Pretend—"

"Forgive. Forgive yourself."

She closed her eyes and took a deep breath. "I don't know how."

Toby sighed and then suddenly he had her in his arms. She pressed her face into his chest and clutched his lapel as he hugged her tighter and tighter. His lips pressed down on the top of her head and he chuckled softly. "The old has passed away, Victoria. Behold, all things are new."

"I don't feel new," she whined into his soft flannel shirt that smelled like hay, sweat, and the fragrance that was unmistakably Toby.

"Would you do it again? Would you send that fella to the mine to blow it up?"

She shook her head. "No. I'd die first." He rubbed her back, and she tried to focus on his gentle hand, the comfort of his arms...and not her raging guilt.

"Then you've been changed," he said in a quiet voice. "Satan is using your guilt to hold you back, to keep you from stepping into everything the Lord has for you. Why can't you see that?"

Grief laced his voice. Surprised by it, she looked up. In his face, she suddenly saw the future she'd dared not dream of. Days filled with hope. Peace. Freedom... Love. A man who knew her past and—like Jesus—forgave it. Toby saw the Victoria she *could* be, wanted to be. He believed in her.

He believed she was a new creation.

She tried to speak, but for a moment, her voice failed her. "Maybe," she croaked, "maybe."

He pulled her back into the hug and chuckled. "Well, that's something."

~

Eager to see Momma, Victoria swept and cleaned the little cabin with an inescapable sense of joy. She paused in her dusting. Joy. Was this joy? Or peace? Or both?

She'd never experienced both of them. She'd only thought she had. She'd felt so happy when it had looked like she and Logan might have gotten a second chance. She'd felt overwhelming relief when Momma hadn't rejected her. But not joy or even peace either time.

What she felt now was new and inexplicable. For the first time in forever, she felt as if she *were* a new person. Unable to stop herself, she sashayed to the window and looked out at Toby. He was in the corral, lunging Delilah. He was so tall and strong. His patience was endless. It seemed he never ran out of it.

"Thank you, Lord, that he didn't. Neither of you gave up on me. You forgave me. He believes in me. I think I can...can I give this a chance? Maybe Defiance can—should—wait, after all."

A rider appeared at the top of the hill, a speck of darkness silhouetted against the early afternoon sun. For an instant, Victoria was sure it was Momma. She was due today.

But her spirits sank and a terrible sense of foreboding crashed down on her. The rider was male. She hurried outside and climbed up on the corral fence. When Toby glanced her way, she motioned toward the road. "Rider coming. It's not Momma."

Toby loosed the rope off Delilah, hurried to the fence, and retrieved his gun belt. He eyed the coming guest warily as he strapped on the Colt. "No, that's not Eleanor."

A minute later, a slender young man with shoulder-length blonde hair and the weathered face of a cowboy brought his horse up to them. "Toby." He nodded, then turned his gaze to Victoria. He studied her briefly. At first, his expression was relaxed with simple recognition, but unmistakable disdain dawned in his eyes. His brow creased with the tension of it. "De —I mean, Victoria."

She knew him as well. "Lane Chandler."

He nodded at her memory but moved past it. "You need to come with me, pronto."

"What's the matter? What's happened?"

"Your ma's been shot. Hope—I mean, Dr. Clark said I should tell you to hurry."

The world fell out from beneath her feet. Instinctively, she grabbed the rail and looked at Toby. Sudden, biting fear rose up in her and froze her mind for an instant.

"You go on, but be careful. Let me get the animals taken care of and I'll be no more than a day behind you."

She tried to respond but found she had no voice. The worst imaginings strangled her ability to speak.

"I'll saddle Delilah while you pack a bag."

Pack. She nodded. "I'll hurry."

～

Shot. Dang, Toby could have gone his whole life without hearing that about Eleanor. When Victoria disappeared inside the cabin, he looked at Lane. "Bad as it sounds?"

"Hope had to do emergency surgery to save her. The bullet bounced around some. Small caliber."

Toby hung his head. "Why would anybody shoot Eleanor?" A horrible thought ignited in his brain. "Does somebody know? Who she is? About Victoria?"

Lane dismounted and trudged over to the fence. "Eleanor came to me and said there was a man in town that sold young girls into prostitution." He cast a glance over his shoulder. "She said it was the man who set Delilah on her path. Sixteen years ago."

The news tried to buckle Toby's knees, but he caught himself. Holy God. "And he shot her?"

"We haven't found him yet, but we think he's the one. She was bound and determined to make him pay for lying to her all those years ago and selling Delilah into that life."

Toby swiped a hand over his face, absently grabbed a bridle off the fence, and started readying Delilah for the ride to Defiance. "So, does...does anyone know?" He was confused as to how or if identities had been exposed.

"That Eleanor is Delilah's mother? I don't think so. Unless she told this Sam or he figured it out."

Toby couldn't clear the clutter and confusion over the impact of this situation. He strode into the tack room, returned with Victoria's favorite saddle, and went through the motions of saddling the horse, but his mind was whirling. "He shot Eleanor hoping to shut her up. Right?"

"That's what we think."

"She may or may not have told him who her daughter is?"

"We don't know what they said to each other, if anything. She's been unconscious since we found her last night."

He cinched the saddle and turned to Lane. "So we don't know what Victoria's walking into. This Sam fella could be telling everybody who Eleanor is. Any woman who comes to check on her could be Delilah."

"Sam's in hiding, if he's even still in Defiance. I doubt he's told anybody anything."

"You don't seem to know much of anything helpful."

Lane's brow pinched at Toby's accusation, but he breathed and nodded. "I get you're worried. I ain't thrilled with the way things are going right now, either. I'll get Delilah to her momma and keep it quiet."

Toby pulled the reins over Delilah's head and walked the horse to the gate. Once out, he locked it behind him and shot Lane a hard look. "Her name is Victoria. Delilah's dead."

Her heart in her throat, her mind whirling with prayers and fears over Momma, Victoria tossed a few things in a bag and burst back outside. "I'm ready."

She raced to Delilah, threw the bag over the saddle, and then paused. She was leaving Toby and didn't want to, but Momma needed her. She laid a hand on his chest and he clutched it with both of his. "It's gonna be all right." He offered her a weak smile. "I'll be along soon as I can."

She wanted a kiss, needed the reassurance of something good between them, but the moment didn't seem to allow it. Instead, she turned, and he helped her into the saddle. From there, she let her gaze linger. "Hurry every chance you get."

He responded with a slow wink. Done, she whipped Delilah around and lunged for Defiance.

They hadn't cleared the first hill when Victoria slowed from the gallop to a jog and Lane pulled up beside her. "Tell me what happened to my mother."

The instant Sam Collins's name came out of Lane's mouth, Victoria had to fight for breath. Her pulse went wild. Memories, so many memories, of lies, deceit, manipulation—the moment she was forced to *entertain* her first customer—it all raced back with the force of a flood. Literally, the fear of falling out of the saddle made her bring Delilah to a standstill.

Lane drew up. "You all right?"

Victoria took a deep, deep breath and let it out with intention...a pitiful attempt to purge the memories. Oh, how she'd hated Momma back then. Thinking she had knowingly sold her into prostitution. And Sam had simply been the buyer in the right place at the right time.

All the plans, the grand schemes of a sleazy huckster, however, had been borne of *his* mouth and dark heart. "I am not supposed to hate anyone...but I believe I could shoot Sam Collins graveyard dead and enjoy it."

Lane tilted his head and studied her hard, his brow creased with suspicion. But momentarily, some other truth flickered in his expression. "'Cause of this badge, I'm supposed to deliver justice...but I understand your struggle. Don't think the world will be missing much when he goes to his grave." He made a *tsking* sound to get the horses moving again.

The road was a muddy mess, forcing them to keep the animals to a jog at best. Still, it was a good half hour before Lane said another word. As they skirted a pine that had fallen across the road, he cleared his throat. "You look a lot different."

"I feel a lot different."

"It's true then? You found Jesus?"

"No." She cut her eyes at him. "He was never lost. I was."

"Lot of people won't believe you. Not sure I do."

"Hang what other people think." But he made her curious. Victoria rolled his comments around for a bit and came back to his observation about her. "Why do you think I'm different? Just because I'm not all rouged up and wearing the latest fashion from Paris?"

"Nah." They rode in silence for a spell, but Victoria knew the cowboy type. Like Toby, Lane tended to consider his words more than other people. "Ain't nothing outward. The whole time I knew you in Defiance, you had your nose in the air and shoulders back, like you were looking for a fight." He slid his gaze to her. "You've been humbled. Some."

Humbled. Oh, yes, she'd certainly been humbled. But more than some. She almost corrected him, but didn't. Instead, she asked carefully, "You think they'll try to hang me?"

She saw, rather than heard, the deep breath he took before answering. "If it wasn't for your momma needing you, I would have told you to stay far away from Defiance."

Her shoulders drooped. "What was Sam Collins doing there? Of all people, in all places."

"Word is, he looks for hard-luck stories. Widows with daughters."

"Like a vulture. And I certainly gave him some widows, didn't I?"

"He never came in any of your places?"

She chuckled bitterly and let the sneer color her voice. "Once. Right after I opened my first saloon. He walked in with a Moral Committee, of all things. A preacher on one side, the mayor on the other. Lectured me about the sins of alcohol and prostitution."

"You didn't tell them who he was?"

"No. But he left town that night. I assume he was a little more careful which new saloon and brothel he campaigned against after that."

"That don't make no sense. What was he trying to do?"

A scripture popped into her head. "Satan comes as an angel of light. Sam pretends to love the light, so he can drag young girls into the darkness."

Lane actually shuddered. "He sounds like one evil rascal. McIntyre has a baby boy now. He takes this fella's treatment of children kind of personal."

Charles McIntyre has a baby. A son. Sadness and jealousy coiled around her heart. She had to fight to keep the emotions from crossing her face. She thought of her own daughter back in Stillwater. A beautiful young lady raised in a Christian home. The daughter Victoria could never know. *Maybe parenting will work out better for you than it did me, McIntyre. Maybe...*

She kicked Delilah up to a lope and pulled away from Lane.

Victoria paused on the doctor's porch. The last time she'd been here, Logan had just died. They'd put him in a room and examined him, but these had been empty motions. He'd died in the dirt just outside her saloon. The memory hurt like a knife in her heart.

She squeezed her eyes shut, wishing she could forget it all. Lane's boots thumped on the step behind her, nudging her out of the pity party. She forced herself to move, to put her head down and muscle her way through the awful memories, as if they were a bitterly cold wind. She pushed open the door. A woman stepped up to her as she entered the office. A young girl, pretty, with auburn hair pulled up into a bun.

"I'm Dr. Clark. Are you Victoria?"

"Yes."

The doctor's gaze flicked to Lane, then she escorted her to the sick room door. "Your mother is in grave condition. I've done all I can do. Now it's up to God."

"Lane said she was gut shot. I didn't expect her to last this long."

"That's not quite accurate. The bullet hit a rib, deflected. It nicked a few organs, including her stomach, but it didn't appear to cause massive damage there."

"That's good then."

"Yes. The concern now is I hope I didn't miss any internal

bleeding." She shrugged. "I don't think I did, but...she was a mess."

"All right." Moving like a ghost, Victoria drifted past the doctor and let herself into the room.

She was not prepared for the breathing corpse lying in the bed. Momma was as white as a January snow. Victoria concentrated on making her legs carry her to her bedside. Shaking, feeling as fragile as glass, she sat down and took Momma's limp hand.

"You said you'd never leave me again, Momma." She couldn't die. Not now. Victoria couldn't lose her yet. "Please don't die." The dam burst inside her and there was no holding back the sobs. So much pain and misery had culminated in this town as if it were some bottleneck designed to gather all of Victoria's sins in one place and press them down on her. "Oh, God, please no more," she prayed. "I can't lose her."

"Baby girl..."

Eleanor's voice was weak, barely above a whisper, but it whipped Victoria's head up. "Momma. Momma, I'm here." Like a crazed nurse, she started tucking the blanket in better and touching her mother. "It's all right. All right."

Momma smiled and managed a feeble nod. "I know."

Something in the response calmed Victoria, and she sat down again. "I'll stay right here. I won't leave you."

With the strength of a dying butterfly, Momma squeezed Victoria's hand. "Won't leave...leave you. Ever."

Charles stared out at the snowy pasture and shifted, uncomfortable in the saddle. Not because of the cold wind or the stiffness in his leg. It was Lane's stare burning into him.

"You really want my opinion?" his Texas friend drawled. "I'd say she's done whoring."

"You think I'm being intransigent."

"If I knew what that meant, maybe. I'm more inclined to say you're being bull-headed."

Charles shook his head. "I simply do not understand how anyone can overlook the conduct of a woman who sold girls into sexual slavery, paid a man to blow up a mine, and was complicit in the murder of twelve innocent men. Thirteen, if you count Logan. Not to mention, she nearly got Emilio killed."

"Yeah, she was no angel, that's for sure. But people can change. Look at you."

Anger spiked in Charles. He was tired of hearing that. "Yes, I changed. It did not happen overnight."

"I ain't saying she changed overnight, either. I'm not even saying she should get away with anything she's done. I'm just saying...she's different."

"And I'm supposed to take her word for it?"

"Johnny Reb, I ain't your conscience and I ain't your momma. Just telling you what I observed. Do with it what you will."

For the first time in a long time, Charles wanted to throw a punch at a good friend.

Quiet down, McIntyre. Otherwise, you're going to say something to Lane you don't mean.

He needed to chew on this a while. Give thought to why Delilah and her story of redemption grated on his nerves. She'd been such a supreme liar and master manipulator.

Could she have changed? The most notorious madam in the West...a Believer? A disciple of Jesus Christ?

It didn't seem possible or likely.

Yet, *he* was living proof the Lord changed people.

"You're gonna go see her, aren't you." It was not a question.

Charles let out a weary sigh. "As you pass by the house, if you would, let Naomi know I'll be late for supper."

"Sure thing."

Without another word, Charles signaled Traveler with a

nudge of his knee and the white gelding lunged forward, eager to move, to fly across the snowy ground. Charles gave the horse his head, even as his fingers went numb and, soon enough, his toes. By the time he pulled up in front of the doctor's office, his thighs felt like huge chunks of ice.

~

Victoria had nodded off, but the scent of fresh coffee roused her, and the hand on her shoulder brought her all the way to wakefulness. She sat up in the chair, saw Momma's pale form, and remembered where she was, though her brain was slow in processing the information.

"I brought you some coffee." Dr. Clark motioned to the steaming cup on the nightstand.

Grateful for the gift, Victoria reached for it, shook off a yawn, and took a sip. Absently, she rotated her ankle, pleased the pain had been replaced with annoying stiffness.

"Miss Patterson," the doctor continued, "it's been twenty-four hours solid. I strongly recommend you get some sleep. I don't want two patients from the same family."

Victoria conceded the point, but she couldn't leave Momma.

"My cabin is a hundred feet through the woods. I left a blanket on the sofa and a cozy fire burning in the stove. I insist you get some sleep."

A warm, quiet cabin. A blanket and a settee to curl up on. A fire to keep her warm. It sounded so inviting, almost dream-like. Truly, if she could just steal a few hours—

"I insist." Dr. Clark clutched Victoria's shoulders and gently pulled her to her feet. "Go get some rest. If anything happens with your mother, you're close enough I can yell for you. Now, please, go."

The woman hung a coat on her shoulders, walked her to the door, and pointed the way.

"You'll wake me in a few hours...or sooner?"

"Only sooner if there's a problem. Now, shoo."

~

Stiffly, Charles dismounted, lugging his cold body through the knee-deep snow. He made his way to the doctor's door and almost knocked but, instead, quietly let himself in. Hope had her back to the door and didn't hear him. No Delilah in sight. He dragged his hat off and cleared his throat.

She spun away from the counter, surgical utensils in her hand. "Mr. McIntyre. I didn't hear you come in." Her sparkling brown eyes widened with concern. "Is everything all right? Is Lane—?"

"Fine. He's fine."

She smoothed a hand over her dark hair. "Oh, good. What can I help you with?"

McIntyre glanced at the closed door. Was Delilah behind it? He tried not to think about the way she'd destroyed his friend Logan with alcohol and lust. Or the astonishing, guilt-free way she'd auctioned off virgins. Tempted and teased the town into violence and debauchery. Hired the men who'd destroyed his sister-in-law's newspaper office. Called his son a half-breed.

"Mr. McIntyre? Charles?"

He blinked himself back to the doctor. "Is Eleanor's daughter in there?"

"No, I sent her to my cabin for some rest. She's exhausted."

This pity people readily offered up for the poor, exhausted Delilah made him want to grind his teeth. The woman was no victim. She was a menace to society.

Hope set the surgical implements down and strode over to him, lacing her fingers at her waist. McIntyre sensed caution in her approach. "She asked me to wake her after a few hours. It's been close to three. Perhaps I could—"

"Why don't I?"

"Well, I don't know. I wouldn't want you to startle her."

"That may be unavoidable."

Before the woman could argue, he made his exit, tromped the short distance through the snow, and marched up to the door. Where, once more, he paused.

He fidgeted with his hat. What was he afraid of? To learn she, perhaps, had changed? Or hadn't? He chided himself for this uncharacteristic waffling. The woman was back in the town where she'd wreaked hell on earth, threatened his friends, indirectly threatened his family.

If she had changed, then that meant she was over the disaster. She'd moved past her guilt. A possibility he was loathe to entertain.

Charles wanted justice. He did not want to entertain the notion the Lord Almighty would do what he often did: show a sinner grand mercy.

He pounded on the door. When he received no response, he hammered again, violently, louder, shaking the frame. The lock clicked and he stepped back. The woman who greeted him took his breath away...and not because of her beauty. He didn't recognize her. Yet, he knew her.

He searched her weary, green eyes rimmed with red for something familiar. Her auburn tresses, always immaculately styled and twisted up with gem-studded combs, hung in a torrent of tangles over her shoulders—shoulders that were bent in defeat more than he'd ever seen. Her face—a lovely one with classical angles and high cheekbones—showed the wear of time and life at the corner of her eyes in her dull, olive skin. Then her chin came up defiantly. A move he'd seen Delilah make a hundred times. "It is you."

She pivoted away from the door and trudged to the stove. "What are you doing here?" she asked absently, looking around the neat, little room, owl-eyed and befuddled. He wondered if she could recall where she was. After a moment, she spotted something, crossed the room, and plucked her coat from a chair.

"That's what I came to ask you."

She huffed a breath and sagged. "You're here. So you must know about Eleanor."

"I've heard for months you were planning on coming back to Defiance."

"Yes. Eleanor's...accident pushed my schedule up."

"You can't be here. The town is in turmoil. I won't allow your presence—"

"Won't allow?"

Some of the fire that he'd expected to see—was used to seeing—kindled in her eyes. "I have as much right to be here as anyone. More, if you think about it."

Clearly, she was delusional. "If you think anyone in this town has forgotten what you did and will visit your saloon or broth—"

"I'm not opening up a business," she snapped. Flinching, she took a deep, calming breath and patted the air with her hands. "I'm going to tend to my mother. Are you going to tell the town I'm here?"

"Spreading that news would only exacerbate the tension. Besides, I gave Eleanor my word I'd keep quiet."

"Why? Why would you do that? I know you hate me."

The accusation stung...because it was true. Scriptures echoed in his head. Thoughts on mercy. Forgiveness. Holding grudges. If he could believe she'd changed...but he wasn't convinced. Had no idea what would convince him. He waved a hand dismissively. "Billy. Eleanor. They believe you've *changed*." He spat out the word. Cheap whiskey left less of an aftertaste.

Delilah's lip thinned into a tight line. She scanned Charles top to bottom, her distaste for him obvious as well. Then an amazing thing happened. Her still pretty features contorted into a pained expression. "But no one else will believe it. Look at you. So certain. So high-and-mighty. Jesus can forgive you, but not me."

"I never took innocent life, Delilah. Not once."

Her eyes downcast, she shrugged into her coat. "I did. And I regret it with every breath." She blinked and sniffed, as if dismissing rebellious tears. "I need to get back to Momma."

Charles let her go. The meeting hadn't been what he'd expected. But then, he wasn't sure what he had expected her to say or do. He hadn't expected...the humility.

Fourteen

VICTORIA WANTED to throw the ticking clock on the wall out in the snow. When Dr. Clark was gone, her office was quiet as a tomb except for the maddening tick-tick-tick, and Momma's soft but labored breathing.

She squeezed her hand. Cool, but not cold. She lifted the blanket. Blood was seeping through the bandage again, but not as much as yesterday. She'd wait for Dr. Clark to change the dressing. Sighing, bored, antsy, she rose and shuffled over to the window. Listlessly, she moved the curtain aside. It was snowing again.

A group of miners strode by and she pulled back, even though they couldn't see her because of the scrub pine that partially obscured the window. Two of them horsed around like kids, throwing snowballs and laughing. Eventually, their chatter and guffawing were swallowed up in the snow.

How long before Momma was out of the woods? Dr. Clark said every day she made it, her chances went up substantially, but it had only been two days. She slept nearly round the clock.

A familiar figure on horseback whipped her attention back to the street. A lone cowboy, his sheepskin collar pulled up, hid his face, but she almost bounced with excitement. "Toby," she whispered excitedly. "Momma, Toby's here."

She hurried out to the other room, opened the door a crack, and waved him in. She wasn't about to step out there in the daylight, though she wanted to jump into his arms. "Come on, come on, hurry."

He wrapped his reins around the hitching post and hurried up the steps. "Hey."

She snatched him inside, shut the door, and hugged him so hard inside his coat that his back cracked. He returned the embrace, then tilted her chin up. "This is a nice welcome. Can I go back out and do it again?"

She grinned and smacked his cheek lightly. "Come on. I want Momma to know you're here."

They slipped into the examination room. Toby exhaled a troubled breath and leaned over to her ear. "Eleanor, it's me, Toby. It's good to see you."

He waited, but nothing happened. As he started to pull away, though, her faded, weary eyes fluttered open. It took a second, but recognition dawned in them. "Toby." Her voice was frighteningly weak. "Good to see you."

"You'll be upright in no time, so you just take it easy, and..." He faded off. Victoria understood. What could they say?

"Fight." Eleanor swallowed. "I will fight." Her gaze moved to Victoria. "I won't lose you again."

Victoria couldn't ask for more. She took Momma's hand again. "You won't. I promise."

～

Later, she and Toby sat in the front room, drinking coffee and sitting at the stove. "How bad?" he asked, raising the cup to his lips.

"It's severe. Momma lost a lot of blood, and Dr. Clark had

to do surgery to get the bullet, which nicked her stomach and her spleen. But she's made it this far, and that's good."

A smile lifted the corner of his mouth. "She ain't going nowhere. She ain't leaving you again."

"Toby..." Victoria leaned forward. "I'm glad you're here. I talked to McIntyre yesterday. He...wasn't exactly cordial. He doesn't believe I've changed."

"You're surprised?"

"No..." She thought about it. "Yes." Shouldn't he be the only one? "Yes, I was surprised. Change is all right for him, but it doesn't happen for anyone else?"

Toby drummed his fingers on his cup. "Billy said McIntyre took the mining collapse real hard. Blamed himself. Said the working conditions should have been safer."

"Not much you can do against a case of dynamite. It's a wonder the whole town didn't disappear."

"Did you...did you think no one would get hurt?"

"I didn't think. I-I..." She searched the ceiling for answers. "I only wanted to hurt him. The miners...I never even thought about them."

"And you wonder why the town is so angry?"

"I don't wonder. I understand it. And it pains me...how I've hurt so many people. I just want to make it right, Toby."

"There's only one way they're gonna think is right." His gaze bored into her. "As soon as you can, you need to leave this place. Bring her with you, and never look back." He reached over and took her hand. "For us. All three of us. Maybe four if you want me to gather up GW."

She laughed. She missed that fat old man with his saucy ways. They would be happy, all of them together. Maybe GW would court Momma. "I...let's make sure Momma's out of the woods and then we'll talk about it."

His face fell. Oh, how she must frustrate him, but she was only trying to be honest. Do the right thing. What she thought was the right thing. "Maybe you can convince me that out of Defiance will be better than in." He was closer than he knew.

"Sooo, I thought I'd come and stay for a few days. Try to understand what's going on. If it looks like you need me, I'll turn in my badge and—"

"No. You keep everything running in Ruby City. If I need you, I'll wire you."

"I don't—"

"Whatever happens here, you've got to have something to go back to. Say you will. Please."

"This makes me feel doggone useless." He wagged his head back and forth in disgust.

"You're anything but. Momma will go back to Ruby City at some point. She can help you keep up your place."

"And you? Us? I thought we were maybe..."

"I don't want to promise you anything yet. Please give me some time." Would she ever quit hurting people? The pain in his eyes broke her heart. He thought she was being wildly foolish. Maybe she was. But she had to let this all play out a little bit longer. She was here now for a reason. She believed that strongly. Maybe it was only to get Momma through this wound and then spirit her out of town.

And never look back. Toby's love could keep her looking forward. She was almost sure of it.

He smacked his hat on his knee and huffed a sigh. "How about I go over to the hotel and bring us back something good for dinner?"

"That'd be nice."

~

Desperation had Toby breaking out in a sweat as he rode through the fresh snowfall. Victoria was running straight off a cliff. Everybody knew what this town was capable of. They tried to Lynch McIntyre on suspicion of being involved with the mine accident. They wouldn't show Victoria any mercy just because she was a woman. This town had no rules.

Settling his horse at the livery, he wandered on down to the hotel, his saddlebag slung over his shoulder. The scent of onions and fried chicken wafted to him from the entrance and set his stomach to growling. He reckoned he'd best get a room while he was here. He didn't figure he should take up a bed in the doctor's office, in case she needed it.

A pretty little blonde met him at the desk. "Hello. I'm Mollie. May I help you?"

"Yeah, I'd like a room for a couple of nights, and I want to get some food to take to my friend."

"Certainly. Here's the menu if you'd like to go ahead and look at it." She handed him the paper with the specials on it and plucked a key from the pigeonhole. "If you wouldn't mind signing the guest book." She spun it around and handed him the pen.

"You wouldn't happen to know where I could find Dr. Clark, would you?"

"As a matter of fact, I do. She's upstairs with a guest."

"Oh, all right. Well, maybe I can talk to her later then."

"You're in number twelve. It's ready now if you'd like to take your bag up."

"Okay. Thank you."

He was trudging up the steps, lost in thought, when he all but walked into Lane. "Oh, sorry."

"Hey, Toby, this is Dr. Clark. Hope, this is...um..."

"A friend of Eleanor's," he said quietly.

"Oh, I see." A pretty girl with wide, dark eyes. She glanced around the room and lowered her voice. "I was just on my way back to check on her. Have you stopped there yet?"

"Yeah, I did. Eleanor was awake. A little. She was encouraged to see...you know, that someone special was there. That she was gonna fight to get better."

"That's good. Very good."

"You think she's going to make it?"

"Every day, her chances get better and better. I'd like to see her make it another twenty-four hours. That would encourage me greatly. Having all the right people around her will be tremendously helpful."

Toby grunted. Doctors. They never committed to much, in his experience. Always cagey. "I'm going to take some food over for...us...I could get enough for everybody."

"Oh, that would be wonderful. I have a lot of work to do and wasn't looking forward to cooking for a guest tonight."

He waved his hat. "My pleasure. Lane, you be joining us?"

He looked at Dr. Clark. "I'd like to." His brow rose in hopeful expectation.

"Please do."

"All right then." Toby lightly slapped the rail. "It's settled. I'll put my bag in the room and get us loaded up with some fried chicken and whatever else smells so good back in that kitchen."

They all nodded and continued on their separate paths. A few steps up, Toby had the certain feeling someone was watching him and turned back, expecting to see Lane about to hail him. The lobby was empty. The door was closing behind Lane and Dr. Clark. The clatter of silverware and laughter drifted to him from the dining room's open doors. He leaned over the stair rail and peered down the hallway to the kitchen. The back door was just closing.

He shook his head, a little embarrassed. Defiance was making him paranoid, was all. Pushing the strange feeling away, he continued toward his room.

~

America. Aye, the land of opportunity.

Flynn chuckled a little maniacally as he counted money

from a good lunch rush in the Number Two. He'd waltzed into this establishment several months back with his best men. They'd taken the saloon without a single shot fired or even a fist thrown. There was no one to fight for it. Matthew Miller wasn't getting out of jail. McIntyre and the old sheriff had made sure of that. The saloon had been there for the taking.

While he did not appreciate McIntyre and the sheriff taking out Bradford, Bradford should have been more careful about roughing up a soiled dove. He stroked the stack of money with feverish glee. No, there was no good reason there to risk a run-in with the law.

The front door opened and Patrick O'Connell danced in. The grimy, stubby Irishman with mischievous eyes was where the legend of leprechauns came from. Flynn was sure of it.

"Mornin', boss."

"Patrick. Ye're spry this afternoon."

Grinning, he sat down across from Flynn. "I met a new gal last night. Ye could say she lifted my spirits."

Flynn frowned. "I'd rather say not at all."

Patrick grunted softly as if the rebuff had hurt his feelings. "Well, anyway, I've something to tell ye I think ye'll find more interesting than a pot o' gold."

"Do tell." Flynn shuffled the bills into a neat stack and gave Patrick his attention.

"A fella paid me twenty dollars to hide him in my tent. He had some sort of an issue with the sheriff and McIntyre. For twenty dollars, I would have hid the devil himself."

Chandler *and* McIntyre were after this man. Flynn's interest rose. "And?"

"This man left this morning to see if Sheriff Chandler was still watching the stagecoach. He was. Then this man decided to try to pinch a meal from the hotel. Daring, but he was hungry."

"And?" Flynn's patience with this drawn-out story was growing thin.

"He overheard something as he was hiding in the closet beneath the stairs." Flynn reached for his pocketknife, planning on sticking it right between Patrick's eyes if the leprechaun didn't hurry. Patrick rushed on. "I'm telling ye, ye want to hear this. The man's outside."

Flynn relaxed and put his hand back on the table.

Patrick turned to the door. "Come on in, Sam."

A middle-aged man in a rumpled suit, with mussed, graying hair and an arthritic hand approached them. His wrinkled, puffy face said he was either mightily hung over or he'd slept in a garbage bin for a few nights. "Mr. Flynn."

"Mr....?"

"Collins. Sam Collins." He sat and leaned forward. "I was trying to get out of town without Sheriff Chandler and this McIntyre fella spotting me. It's been a little dicey. They turn up everywhere. They've asked some miners to be on the lookout for me. Now, though, I've got some information that may be so valuable to you. I hope you'll offer me protection until I can skedaddle."

Flynn sniffed and leaned back in his chair, lifting the front legs off the ground. "If they were to come asking after ye, we could make ye invisible. But the information ye have better be good."

"The woman who was managing the inn and the mercantile for that Billy Page. I know her. I, uh, introduced her daughter to, well, the flesh trade...let's be blunt. I sell women."

Flynn's expression did not change. He didn't care what this man did for a living. He cared that he was getting bored.

Collins seemed to sense it and hurried on. "I shot Eleanor because she recognized me and was attempting to ruin my... recruiting in Defiance. She's in Dr. Hope's care, and I learned by overhearing a conversation that someone special is with her. Some fella was going to get food to take back to the doctor's office. Now, if Eleanor is near death, who's sitting with her?"

"Mr. Collins, I'm a businessman, and ye're seriously starting to put a drag on my day. Anyone might be sitting with a patient."

"The woman with Eleanor is Delilah."

Every hair on Flynn's body stood up. All the sound in the room fell away to graveyard silence.

Collins smiled. "I see that matters to you. Eleanor is Delilah's mother. She sold me the girl fifteen, sixteen years ago. Unknowingly, but still. The long and the short of it is, Delilah has returned to Defiance."

Flynn's brain stopped for a moment. She was back? He couldn't gather the meaning of the words at first. They scattered like feathers. Then, little by little, they all formed into a pretty, vain red-headed peacock. She'd come back to check on her dying mother. Most likely had snuck into town under cover of darkness. Who had brought her here? Apparently, the sheriff? Or this man getting them food?

But now what? Was Delilah under arrest? Was Chandler planning on it? Was Delilah even here? Collins could be bluffing. "Swear to it."

"I-I can't swear to it. It's my suspicion, but I'm fairly confident in it."

"Indeed, I do find this information interesting, but it is only conjecture. I'll offer ye shelter, but ye must confirm Delilah is here." And maybe O'Shay, over in Ruby City, could help him pull all this information together.

"I will. I can do that. If I'm caught trying...?"

"Run. Run like the wind to Mr. O'Connell's tent. Then we'll see ye're not found. If yer information is good, we'll keep ye safe. If ye've misled me, I'll disappear ye myself. Are these terms acceptable?"

Collins swallowed nervously and tugged on his collar. "Well, um...yes, I believe they are. Unless I've been grievously misled, I can't imagine anyone but Delilah coming to sit with Eleanor. It was the way she talked." The man's stare drifted off for a moment. "I'm certain her daughter, Delilah, is near."

"I wouldn't know. I'll give ye a chance to find out, though. Two days."

Mix this information with whatever O'Shay might find out and maybe they could put this rumor to rest...or have a lynching.

Fifteen

NAOMI LAID A SLEEPING Adam down in his crib and padded downstairs, keeping her moccasins quiet. The crackle of the fire laced with the scent of applewood tobacco was all the information she needed to find her distracted husband.

She moved her embroidery out of the way and sat in the rocker across from him. How handsome he was in the firelight, the flames flickering in his jet-black hair. And his beard, slender, perfectly trimmed, had fascinated her from the moment they'd met. She'd also loathed him from the moment they'd met. A man who ran a saloon and a brothel. He'd valued women as much as a shady trader valued a horse.

And look what the Lord had done. Oh, sanding still to be done, certainly. Charles had his rough edges yet. He was a beautiful work in progress. A chuckle escaped her.

But he didn't even look up. She tilted her head, frustrated. "Charles, what is going on with you? You've been so withdrawn or distracted the last few days. Or, no, weeks, really."

"I know. I'm sorry." He heaved a great sigh and leaned back in his rocker. "Where do I start?" He waved his cigar. "I've spoken with Delilah."

Oh. That explained everything. "She's here to be with

Eleanor, isn't she." Naomi liked Eleanor and was deeply grieved to hear about the shooting. Worse, this man Sam Collins was still on the loose. And now Delilah was here. "Why does her presence make me so uneasy?" If the town found out—

"Perhaps because she is the devil incarnate."

His hard opinion of the woman inexplicably irritated Naomi. "I don't know why exactly, but it bothers me that you are so cock-sure she's evil." His brow rose as if the statement astonished him. Naomi raised her hand and waved off his confusion. "I know. I know. She was a horrid person. But so were you." And therein lay the clue she needed. "I think that's what it is. You think you're so special. That the Lord would change you, redeem you, but not her."

"I am not a schoolboy, Naomi. Don't patronize me. It's not that I think I'm *so special.*"

He mocked her with his own patronizing tone and it put a match to her temper. "You certainly think you're better than Delilah."

"That is not it."

"Then what makes her so unredeemable?" They rarely argued, but Naomi was up to it, wisely or not, and now she let her voice rise. "Why is she beyond God's reach when you weren't."

"I don't know," he yelled back, surging to his feet. "The woman is a murderer."

She rose with him. "So were you."

"I never killed the innocent."

"Are you so sure of that?"

"Stop it, Naomi."

"No, you stop it. Jesus died so that anyone could accept his grace. Anyone. You. Me. Her. Who are you to deny—"

"If she can be redeemed," he thundered, "then everyone I ever hurt can be!" The moment froze, seemed to last for seconds as his hot stare burned into her. His jaw tightened and flexed as a sneer tugged at his lip. Finally, he eased back and exhaled. "*Could* have been."

The simple truth of his explanation stopped further arguments from her, like a slamming door. Now she understood. She wilted and sat back down in the rocking chair. "You ended their chance to meet the Savior."

He turned his back on her and rested an arm on the hearth. His hands clenched and unclenched before he shoved them into his pockets. "Before, death was merely a simple consequence. I killed oftentimes when wounding would have been enough, but murder was simpler. It closed the book."

And now he saw his actions in the light of eternity.

"It wasn't merely murder," he whispered. "I damned them to hell."

Just as Delilah had done to most of the miners no doubt. What a wrenching realization for someone who knew the Savior, who understood the eternal consequences of taking a life. Her heart hurting for him, Naomi rose and went to him. "Maybe not all of them." She wrapped her arms around him and laid her cheek on his back. "Maybe some of them were... backslidden. Maybe somewhere in their past..." She stopped talking. There was no way to know. This was theology she wasn't qualified to judge.

He swallowed and released a long, slow breath. "I don't regret them all. Maybe I should, I don't know. I have...so many doubts now, though, Naomi. I don't know how to filter through them."

"In prayer." He had so much to work out, to reconcile with the Lord. He'd been forgiven, of course, but now, he had deep, deep regrets that needed healing. Was he all that different from Delilah? Assuming her regrets were real, as well. "Talk to him. He'll help you find the peace you're looking for."

He rounded on her and pulled her into his arms, resting his chin on her head. "I understand one thing with jarring clarity now. Why a man should never take another man's life if it can be avoided. It is not our place. Still..."

He didn't finish and she looked up. "Still?"

"I fear I have made promises I may be forced to keep."

Promises to Flynn and Bishop? She didn't know the specifics, but she could figure the overall problem and hugged him again. "I'm with you, Charles. Never doubt that. I love you and I trust you'll do the right thing. You know the Truth."

He sighed softly. "Do I?"

A sick feeling rose up in Victoria when Toby announced he was heading back to Ruby City that morning. It took her a few minutes to recognize the unexpected emotion as disappointment. He'd only just arrived. Try as she might, she hadn't been able to keep her heart from falling for him. And now look where she was. Miserable without him. She'd thought no one would ever have her heart again after losing Logan.

Toby had proven her wrong.

Seated at their haunt by the office stove, she looked out the window and sighed. "I thought you'd stay longer, but I understand."

"There's nothing for me to do here."

"I know. Just sitting around waiting for Momma to..." Die? Improve? Whichever way it went, it was for her to deal with, not him. "Go on. Tend to things in Ruby City. Come back when you can...if you want."

He removed his hand from his coffee and clutched hers. The affection in his gaze almost made her weep. "I want. I'm only a few hours away. You need me, send a wire or dispatch somebody. Okay?"

"Okay."

"And you keep a low profile. Don't do anything to draw

attention to yourself. They come in here and drag you away... your momma—"

"I know. It would kill her. I promise I'll stay out of trouble. And if it comes down to it, I'll fall back on my costume and pretend to have laryngitis."

He laughed over the real possibility. "Let's hope that's a last resort."

"In a big emergency."

"Okay."

"Okay." She rose and brought him with her. "Toby, I'm so sorry this is all going sideways."

"It ain't sideways yet." Suddenly, he clutched her shoulders. "I don't like to think like this, but if Eleanor doesn't make it... let's just get out of here. Head to California maybe and start over."

His soft, pleading expression begged her to say yes. And it was so tempting. There were moments she wanted to promise him anything he asked. Instead of saying so, she closed her eyes and kissed him. The softness of his lips brought her peace. Clothed her in a sense of security. *He's a good man, Lord. I pray I don't hurt him any more than I already have.*

Toby pulled Victoria into a desperate embrace and kissed her deeply, passionately. Her thoughts melted into sublime breathlessness. She ran her fingers through his hair, delighting in its softness, then let them drift to his jaw. The stubble poked her. She loved it. She loved everything about him. Toby didn't, in her mind, have one single imperfection.

Except that he loved her.

With a Herculean effort, she pulled back and laid her hand on his chest. "Keep praying. This is all going to work out." One way or the other.

He nodded, grabbed his hat off the table, and slipped out, pausing in the doorway. "I'll be back in four or five days...unless you need me sooner."

"All right. Be careful going home." Home?

He'd caught her use of the word, too. A smile twitched on his lips. "I will."

The door closed behind him and the finality of it added to her sadness. Defiance. She wished she'd never come within a hundred miles of the town, for all the pain it was causing her... and the families of the men she'd killed. And it was sucking Momma and Toby down this whirlpool of pain, too. She'd give anything to stop it.

~

Flynn did not enjoy riding a horse for endless hours through the snow on a cold day. He didn't enjoy riding a horse at any time. One day, he'd be a man of means and go everywhere in a coach. A shiny black one. Not skirting through the woods, taking shortcuts, and avoiding other riders. He'd barely managed to cross in front of the man coming down the road a few minutes ago.

Now, dusk was falling, but lights in the distance led him into town.

O'Shay had asked him to join him. The telegraph was cryptic but clear enough. He'd found out something but needed Flynn to come to Ruby City.

This had better be good, was all he could say, flexing his cold fingers. Otherwise, O'Shay would find himself floating down the river tied to a log.

~

On a clear summer day, Toby figured a man could make the jaunt over to Ruby City from Defiance in a couple of hours. But on a cold day with snow up to the horse's breast collar, it was a longer haul. Hours longer, and it gave him a lot of time to think.

Bottom line: Victoria was going to do what she thought she

had to do and nothing was going to change her mind. He'd come close. He was certain of it. But now everything was up in the air again. Eleanor being flat on her back would keep Victoria out of trouble maybe for another few weeks.

After that?

Decision time.

He prayed she'd choose him over some death wish in Defiance. Good Lord, slap her with some sense. That town will hang her high when they find out who she is.

At the detour in the road, he almost headed to the ranch first, but his conscience got the better of him. If he was going to sheriff, then he should put the town first.

He tugged the reins and pointed the sorrel toward it. Several yards up from the T-intersection, he spotted tracks in the snow and pulled his horse up.

A horse had come out of the woods, crossed the road, and headed back into the woods. That was downright odd. Almost like someone was trying to sneak into town.

Who would want to sneak into Ruby City? The place was a dot on a dot on a map.

So small, in fact, there would be no way for a ne'er do well to avoid detection. Toby just hoped any troublemaker might move on, losing any interest in upsetting the tiny hamlet.

~

Ruby City was small and the saloon was prominent. Flynn stopped in the rough-looking place, not surprised at all to find O'Shay in the corner, almost hidden in the shadows. They'd set no specific time to meet, but Flynn had the sense of an Irishman. It was never hard to find good whiskey and bad company.

He dropped down quietly beside O'Shay so they both could watch the door. "I'm here. It was a long, cold ride. Best be worth it or ye'll not see the sun come up."

O'Shay shoved a bottle of whiskey and his glass toward

Flynn. "I think ye'll be pleased. The sheriff went out of town. I met the man who was going to feed his stock for him. So, I went along yesterday. Bribed the man to be quiet while I went in the house to rummage for liquor."

A flame of excitement sparked in Flynn. The man had found something.

O'Shay turned to the chair beside him over which he'd slung his saddle bag. He fished inside it and came back with two small picture frames. "I nosed around good. And found these. Now, look close."

He slid one picture to Flynn. He studied it. A large, barrel-chested man had his arms over two women. A younger man stood beside them. The one portly, older woman Flynn had seen in Defiance. She managed the mercantile. Or was it the hotel? This was the woman Collins had shot. So the woman next to her...

He peered closer. Pretty. High cheekbones. Full lips. Dark hair. Was this—

O'Shay slipped him the second picture. Another woman. This one Flynn knew well. Delilah, in all her low-cut silk glory, hair piled high and held in place with diamond-studded combs. Rouged cheeks. Painted lips. Kohl-rimmed eyes smoking with challenge.

He set the pictures side by side. The evidence was clear. The same young woman was in both pictures.

Delilah.

"Ye could have brought me this. Why the blue blazes did I ride all the way up here for it?"

"McIntyre threatened my brother. Bozey came through last night headed to Denver. He won't be going back to Defiance. Neither will I. I won't be needing that job, Mr. Flynn. Thank you, though."

"Why did he threaten yer brother?"

"Bozey told him I was at the lynching. To get away from him alive. Some of those boys who tried to hang McIntyre didn't walk away. If he gets to the truth about my brother and me, it won't matter. He'll kill us both."

Flynn grunted but didn't call the men cowards. He was better off without O'Shay if he would rat his brother out. Besides, if both of them were afraid of McIntyre, they were as reliable as rabid badgers.

"Mr. Flynn, I know you're tough and all...but McIntyre...I don't know. There's something otherworldly about the way he takes men down. You might want to respect that."

Respect?

Respect?

Fury sizzled in Flynn's brain like a fuse racing toward a stick of dynamite. He could draw his gun and blow O'Shay's head off in the blink of a gnat's eye. McIntyre was nothing. And O'Shay was a coward of the lowest sort. That he would *dare* suggest Flynn be afraid of a fancypants like that man... "You should leave, O'Shay." Death rattled in his warning.

O'Shay rose, snatched up his saddle bag, and strode smartly from the dark, little saloon without looking back.

But he'd left Flynn with a great gift and he mulled it over to douse his anger. He knew what Delilah looked like without all her paint. Curious, he glanced at the photo of the four of them and flipped it over. Something was written there in pencil. He shifted it around till he could read it in the weak light.

Will miss you all. Come back soon. GW.

Flynn grunted and flipped back to the faces. Who were the men in this photo? Did it matter? Was maybe one of them the sheriff?

As if by magic, the answer walked into the saloon.

"Bob, hey, evening."

Flynn looked up at the man approaching the bar. Then at the young man in the photo. Then back at this man. Light glinted off the badge on his chest as he peeled out of his coat. Flynn sunk deeper into the shadows.

"Sheriff, where ya been? Pour ya a drink?"

"Just a shot to warm me up. Cold ride back."

"Out chasing bandits?" the bartender asked with a chuckle in his voice.

"Something like that. Gonna check on things in town before I head out to the ranch." He tossed back the shot and shivered as it went down. "Woo. That'll do it. Everything all right here? Any trouble while I was gone?"

"Nah. Usually the winter's pretty dead. Oh, except for some Irishman who was curious about the town. Said he might be opening a business here."

"Oh?"

Flynn cursed silently. O'Shay hadn't been subtle and suspicion dripped from the sheriff's tone. He stacked the two pictures and dropped them into his breast pocket beneath his coat. A tight fit, but it wouldn't do to have them sitting out in the open.

"Friendly fella," the bartender continued. "Offered to help Drury feed your stock."

Flynn clenched his jaw, and the sheriff tensed. O'Shay, you're a dead man.

"Big spender, too. I hope he stays around."

"Is this Irishman still in town? I'd like to thank him for helping out."

The bartender shrugged. "I don't know. You'd come in five minutes earlier, you would have seen him sitting over there."

Flynn snatched his gaze away from the men. The deck of cards in front of him called to him and he grabbed it. Just the feel of the familiar in his hands calmed him as he casually shuffled them.

"That him?" the sheriff asked.

"Uh-uh. I don't know him. He was sitting with the other fella though. Just for a minute."

The sheriff shoved his shot glass away and strode over to Flynn. "'Scuse me."

Flynn looked up while still skillfully shuffling the cards. "Aye, ye fancy a game?"

"No. The man you were sitting with. You know where he went?"

"I'm sorry, I've no idea. I sat down to see if he'd play, but he was just leaving."

Suspicion percolated in the sheriff's eyes. "What's your name?" Flynn hesitated to answer, but the lawman tapped his badge. "I'm curious. Hazard of the job."

Flynn smiled. "Sean Martin. I'm on my way to Defiance to get a job in the mine."

"You've never been there?"

"No, but I hear it's lovely."

The sheriff studied Flynn with keen intensity but, after a moment, shrugged. "Thanks." He pivoted to the bartender as he slipped back into his coat. "Bob, put that on my tab. I'm heading on out to the ranch if anybody needs me."

"Sure thing, Toby."

Flynn drummed his fingers, his agitation and excitement growing. He knew what she looked like. He could show this picture to Sam Collins.

He poured himself one more for the ride home. It was late, but he was heading back to Defiance tonight.

Toby checked every shelf, drawer, cabinet, and basket in the cabin, but nothing leaped out at him as different. Nothing seemed to be missing. Near as he could tell, everything was in its place.

He'd have to find Drury tomorrow and ask him about this helper of his. Maybe Toby was just being paranoid, but with Victoria's admonishment not to talk to an Irishman asking questions, and then one volunteers to come out to the ranch... no. Something was wrong here.

He knelt down in front of the fireplace, struck a match on the stones, and lit the kindling. He had to give it a couple of puffs, but it caught. The cabin would be warm in a minute. In the meantime, he needed to rustle up some grub.

He stood and stretched the stiffness out of his back, glancing at the mantle. Victoria had taken to putting a few dried flowers up here in a whiskey bott—

He stepped back. The picture of them with GW was missing. It sat right next to the flowers. He spun and scanned the floor in case it had fallen off the mantle, even looked under the little sofa.

It was gone.

He headed straight for Victoria's steamer trunk in the bedroom. One thing he knew about her. She'd left her saloon days behind, but she kept her dresses and frilly things folded neater than a packrat in a church. He flung open the lid.

Everything was in disarray. Her clothes were bunched up, wadded up, and smashed together. There was no doubt someone had riffled through her things.

Knowing what he'd find, praying he was wrong, he hurried to his own trunk, out in the living room.

Everything in it was chaos as well. His clothes had been shoved aside, jumbled, tossed, and crammed back in. His pulse galloping like a panicked Mustang, he felt around the bottom of the trunk. No, no, no. He tried again. Nothing. Desperate, he dumped his trunk over.

The newspaper clipping of Delilah that he'd framed years ago.

It was gone, too.

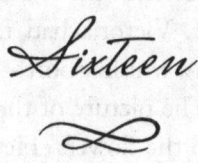

Sixteen

A CRASH from the examination room startled Victoria and she raced in to check on Momma. She was lying on the floor, the water basin shattered around her. Fear exploded in Victoria's heart. "Momma!"

Be alive, be alive, she prayed desperately.

She rolled Momma over and gasped at the heat radiating from her...and the blood seeping through her gown. "Oh, you've opened your stitches again. Here..." Grunting and groaning with the effort, Victoria wrestled Momma back into the bed, but the blood soaking her gown alarmed her even more than the apparent infection. Dr. Clark. She needed her. Where was she?

No, stop. Think. The bleeding. Stop the bleeding first. Victoria rushed to the cupboard out in the examination area, grabbed a handful of gauze pads, and darted back to Eleanor. "Now lay still, Momma." She began pressing the pads to the wound, one at a time, gauging the blood flow with each application. "What were you thinking?"

"Wanted to see...to see my little girl playing in the front yard." Eleanor's eyes were wide and wild, her brow was slicked with sweat. Fear clawed at Victoria's heart. "She has a new doll."

"Oh, Momma, please don't...please don't..." She wouldn't say it. Momma was not going to die. By the fifth pad, the blood was slowing, but not stopping. And her feverish brow wasn't warm, it was boiling as if she'd been sitting on the stove. This was not good. *Oh, Lord, please, she's got to be all right.*

Get Dr. Clark.

The direction was firm and clear.

Where was she? She had said something about a stabbing victim over in Tent Town. Shouldn't be long. Sounded like it would only require a few stitches.

But Victoria couldn't wait. Momma needed Hope now. Panic squeezed her heart, tried to strangle her breathing, but she fought back, taking several deep, calming breaths. She must keep her wits about her. Tent Town wasn't that big. Surely she could find the good doctor without too many people seeing her. And she'd hide her face. "Momma..." Eleanor's eyes fluttered but didn't open. "Momma, I'm going for Dr. Clark. Please stay still." Please...

Only a soft, pained grunt escaped her lips. Whirling away from her, Victoria grabbed her cloak hanging from the front door, pulled the hood over her face, and raced off into the snow.

Even with heavy snow falling, Defiance was busy. Men, mules, horses, and freight wagons traversed the street. Horses were tied up at every hitching post, grumbling about the weather, people were coming and going from the hotel and bakery, and there was a steady stream headed to Tent Town. Avoiding eye contact with anyone, Victoria crossed the avenue to Water Street, the thoroughfare leading to Tent Town. She hurried over the creek and approached a woman carrying a bag of groceries. "Excuse me, have you seen Dr. Clark?"

"Yeah, she's at the Number Two." The woman didn't bother to stop. "She's sewing up Marty Sullivan."

As if Victoria should know who Marty Sullivan was. She didn't, but she could find a saloon. Instinct led her right to the Crystal Chandelier Number Two. It was the last place she wanted to go. And she certainly wasn't going in the front door. Glancing around to make sure no one was watching her, she subtly drifted around to the back door.

If a doctor was called to a shoddy, semi-permanent, half-wood, half-tent saloon, he most likely would be tending to the patient in the back somewhere. There were no windows. Her heartbeat galloping with trepidation, Victoria pressed her ear up against the door. Muffled voices, some excited, some gruff, were audible. She couldn't tell how many people were there, though. Two? More?

There. A softer, high-pitched voice. The cadence was familiar. That had to be Dr. Clark. Taking a breath, she pushed open the door and stepped inside. And wanted to scream at what she saw.

A man, blood dripping down his shirt from a wound in his chest, was holding a knife to another man's throat. Dr. Clark had her hands up, patting the air, obviously trying to calm the situation. All eyes turned to Victoria for an instant, and then the man with the knife pressed it more firmly into his victim's neck.

"No," Dr. Clark screamed. "Stop, Mr. Sullivan."

"Who are ye?" the man with the knife, apparently Sullivan, yelled at Victoria. "What are ye doing here?"

"I-I need the doctor." She looked at Dr. Clark, intent on communicating the desperation of her situation. "Your patient is bleeding from her stitches and she's running a high fever. I didn't know what to do."

Dr. Clark slowly patted the air again, forcing calm into the situation. "Mr. Sullivan, you need to put down the knife and let me finish these last few stitches."

"I'll not have this man stick me again."

"I ain't—" the man started to protest, but Dr. Clark jumped in.

"Mr. Sullivan, you have the wrong man." She spoke in a calm, even tone. "You're going into shock and you're confused. This is Mr. Haggerty. He's a bartender. He is not the man who stabbed you."

Sullivan blinked, owl-eyed. Victoria wanted to shoot him. She did not have time for this. Momma did not have time for this. She inched forward. "I need the doctor. You need the doctor. Either let her sew you up, or she's leaving with me."

Sullivan's face contorted and turned purple with fury. He tossed Mr. Haggerty aside and lunged for Victoria. Instinctively, she reached for a weapon. A frying pan was on the stove to her immediate right. A raging instinct to fight rose up in her and she swung the heavy, cast iron pan like a bat, putting all her fear and all her fury into the motion. Gritting her teeth and growling like an animal, she hit Sullivan with so much momentum that he spun on his heels in a complete circle and dropped to the floor. The hum of the iron pan vibrated up Victoria's arm and rang in the air like a bell.

Dr. Clark rushed to the man, the suture in her hand. "Mr. Haggerty, help me roll him over." The man obeyed and she moved Sullivan's shirt out of the way.

"Victoria, tell me what's going on with Eleanor."

Rotating her shoulder, she set the pan back on the stove. "I was in the front room when I heard a crash and ran in to check on Momma. She was on the floor, bleeding from her wound, and she was hot."

Dr. Clark's hand slowed. She pressed her fingers to Sullivan's neck.

"And I mean hot," Victoria emphasized. "I know a high fever when I touch one. And she was talking crazy like she didn't know where she was. I kept putting gauze on the wound and did slow the bleeding some..."

Dr. Clark pressed a hand to her mouth. She shook her head

and rose to her feet as if she had a weight on her back. Victoria tilted her head. What was she doing? Why wasn't she finishing the stitches? Mr. Haggerty's eyes rounded like full moons.

"Oh, my," Dr. Clark said somberly. "Mr. Haggerty, please go get the sheriff. Um..." She looked back at Victoria. "I suppose I'll go with you now." She reached out and took Mr. Haggerty's arm. "Tell the sheriff to come to my office. He can take our statements there, but I need to tend to my other patient. All right?"

Mr. Haggerty was staring at Mr. Sullivan in a stupor. Hope tugged firmly on his arm. He blinked and came around. "I'll go get him."

What was happening? Hope gathered up her instruments and her bag and pushed Victoria toward the door, but she resisted out of confusion. "I don't understand. What about Sullivan?"

"I can't do anything more for him."

～

I can't do anything more for him.

Victoria didn't remember the rushed walk back in the falling twilight to Momma. She didn't remember any conversation with Dr. Clark. Her mind froze over her words. They repeated incessantly in her head. She'd killed Marty Sullivan. How had that happened? No. She couldn't have done something so ridiculously catastrophic.

She came back to the moment as they pounded up the steps and hurried into Momma. *Thank you, Jesus.* She was still in the bed at least, but she was drenched with sweat. Dr. Clark rushed to her and picked up her hand to check the pulse at her wrist. "Victoria, prepare a bath, but make sure the water is lukewarm."

Bath? Bath. Fever. "All right."

"Start putting some water on the stove while I redo these

stitches. Remember, Lukewarm or even a little cool, but not hot."

Victoria's brain felt like it had been split in two. One-half of her thoughts were twisted up in dread and nausea, worried as she was for Momma. And the other half—dear Lord, she'd killed a man.

Again.

Stop it, Victoria. Momma needs you now. Don't let her down.

Mentally slapping herself out of the shock, she dragged the tub out from beneath the examination table and began running back and forth, scooping up snow from the backyard and dumping it in the large pan on the stove. As it melted down, she poured it into the tub and got more. Half an hour later, the tub filled with room-temperature water, she checked on Dr. Clark. "The tub is ready."

"I'm finished." She laid the suture and needle on the nightstand. "Help me get her in the water."

They left Momma in her shift and carefully laid her in the water. The dip into the cool water worked a raspy gasp from her, but she didn't react further. "I thought for a high fever, a person needed an ice bath."

Dr. Clark shook her head as she positioned Momma to keep the stitches barely above the water. "Common myth, but it can cause hypothermia. This is a gentle embrace of the body, not a shock."

"Should I add more water?"

"No, I don't want her stitches submerged. Besides, we won't leave her in here long. Just a few more minutes." Hope tapped Momma's cheek gently, but she looked comfortable in her dozy state. "Eleanor...Eleanor, how do you feel?"

She grunted softly but managed, "So...hot...but better."

"Good. That's what I wanted to hear. A few more minutes, then we'll take you out, put you in some fresh, dry bedding."

A sudden swell of nausea rose in Victoria. She put a hand over her mouth and sat down. Both sides of her brain warred again with the horrific situation in which she was in the middle. It muddled her thinking. Nothing was clear.

Dr. Clark dipped a cloth in the water and used it to drip cold water on Momma's head. *I should be doing that.*

She reached out to take the rag, but boots stomping across the porch drew her attention to the door. Dr. Clark didn't look up from the patient. "That must be Lane."

The sheriff.

Oh, dear God, what have I done?

He knocked and let himself in, dragging his hat off as he entered. He surveyed the room and then dropped the Stetson on the chair near the stove. He regarded the women with a tense expression. "Maybe this ain't the time, but I've got to know what happened to Sullivan. Haggerty told me his version." He focused on Victoria. "What's yours?"

"Lane." Dr. Clark wrung out the rag and hung it on the side of the tub. "Let us get Eleanor to the bed first, please."

He started peeling out of his coat. "Sure thing."

He aided them in getting Momma out of the tub, wrapped in a large towel, and moved to the bed. The girls took it from there. Several minutes later, sweaty from moving a limp body around, they stepped outside, ready to give the sheriff their statement.

"She going to be all right?"

"Her fever has broken. That's all I can say for now."

With Momma out of earshot, Lane apparently felt free to speak and turned abruptly on Victoria. "Do you have any idea of what you've done?"

"He came at me with a knife. I grabbed the first thing my hands fell on."

He shook his head in total disgust, a slight sneer curling his lip. "If you ain't a magnet for trouble. That man you killed works for Michael Flynn."

"Am I supposed to know the name?"

"Maybe. I don't know. He and his gang and his brother

came to town about a month before the explosion. His brother's buried at the bottom of the shaft."

Victoria's knees almost buckled, and she reached for the rocking chair, barely making it. Her breath came in short gasps as she collapsed into it. "I killed his brother?"

"Yeah. And I don't reckon there's anybody who hates you more."

After Charlie tried to kill her in Dodge City for this same sin, she thought the worst of the haters had come for her. Possibly, she was wrong. "Lovely," she muttered miserably.

"Worse, he's got a gang that's itching to knock out a man named Bishop and his gang. There's a lot of hard feelings trying to boil over in this town. I ain't quite figured out how I can keep your name out of this mess."

"Just don't tell Lane your name," Dr. Clark interjected, earning puzzled looks from him and Victoria.

"I don't get you."

"He already knows my name."

Wiping her hands, Dr. Clark joined them. "It was self-defense. I'm sure that's what Haggerty told you, and it is my testimony as well. There are no charges to be drawn up. You've asked her name, and she opted not to give it to you officially. That's not against the law, is it?"

Lane scrunched up his face and tugged on his ear. "Well, uh, I ain't clear on the law one hundred percent. I reckon not, not unless I was pressing charges or something."

"So, then, if anyone asks, you simply say it was a clear case of self-defense. No charges." Dr. Clark raised her chin imperiously. "You didn't get the woman's name."

"I don't knoooow..." He dragged out the last word. "Sounds kind of fishy."

"The alternative is you reveal her name and someone may put two and two together."

"It doesn't matter." Hopelessness swamping her, Victoria waved away the suggestion. "It's not my name—my real name

—that will get me in trouble. It's if someone recognizes me. My face." She shrugged. "My voice. Either could give me away."

"Yeah." Lane rubbed his chin. "Yeah. We just can't have you out and about over this. Over anything. Just stay here."

She wasn't about to go gallivanting while Momma was fighting for her life in the other room. "Don't worry. I have no plans."

Lane sucked on his teeth a moment, considering things. He eyed Dr. Clark expectantly. "Your version."

"Sullivan had an altercation with someone. By the time I got there, Haggerty had corralled him in the back room, but he was bleeding heavily, going into shock. He got confused and put a knife to Haggerty. Victoria walked in, he got angry with her for no clear reason and lunged at her with the knife. Thank God a frying pan happened to be in the right place."

"Okay. Yeah, that's what Haggerty said, so I'll call it self-defense and be done with it. I have no doubt, though, Flynn ain't gonna like this at all. He was gone somewhere today. When he gets back...I'll expect a visit."

Should Victoria be worried? Would Lane let her secret out? She doubted it, but she wasn't a hundred percent sure of the man, either, though. She followed him out to the porch and was jarred by the brilliance of the full moon reflecting off the snow. It was nigh on to full daylight out here. She stepped out from beneath the porch roof to the top step and sighed at the stars. What a stunning tapestry of diamonds.

"Pretty, huh?"

"Yes. I appreciate it so much more now than I ever have." Since she didn't know what the future held in a more precarious level of uncertainty than ever in her whole life.

"Yeah, I know what you mean."

"Lane, I have to ask."

He paused, unwrapping the reins from the hitching post. "Ask?"

"Will you...if this Flynn comes to you, are you going to tell him about me?"

"Nah, I don't think so. There's no purpose in that." He didn't wait for a reply and jumped into his saddle. He was a few yards off before she turned and—

Snow was missing off the rail at the end of the porch. Probably a bird or some critter had climbed over it, scattering it.

But her feet carried her toward it without much conscious thought.

The moonlight was bright indeed. She looked over the rail. Clearly visible, footprints came from the woods, straight across the yard, and jumped up on the exposed end of the porch... looking in the window into Eleanor's room.

Someone had stood here—someone with sizable feet—had stood here and looked through the lacy curtains at Momma. But the blind was drawn.

She leaned over the rail and peered in the window. The shade was pulled down but an inch gap at the bottom was enough for someone to see in. And there Momma was in full view as Hope fluffed her pillow and pulled the blanket up to her chin.

Victoria's hand went to her stomach as her nerves jangled with fear. Someone had been watching them?

Flynn wasn't one to complain but by the time he was back to Tent Town and had put his horse up, his toes ached fiercely from the cold. Just after two-thirty in the morning, he entered his saloon from the back, eager for a drink by the stove. He might shove his feet right into the coals. "Haggerty." He nodded at the man and grabbed a bottle and glass from the end of the bar. Only a few minutes till closing at three, but the place was still full. He scanned the smoking, murmuring, cursing crowd as he strode to the stove, aware some of the men were giving him a cautious glance. Something had happened.

He wasn't settled good when Haggerty approached. A big man, quiet, confident, he eased into the rickety chair across from Flynn. "We had a little trouble in here earlier this evening."

Couldn't Flynn get five minutes in this damnable town without *a little trouble?* He sighed and pulled the cork from the whiskey bottle. "Aye. What now."

"Sullivan's dead."

Flynn stopped pouring his shot. Sullivan was hot-tempered. It was probably his fault, but the man was loyal and obedient. A loss to the army Flynn was building. "What happened?"

"He got in a fight with a fella, one of them Brits, and was stabbed. He stumbled into the kitchen and I asked one of the boys to go get Dr. Hope. By the time she got here, well, Sullivan wasn't in his right mind. She said it was shock. He put the knife on me."

Flynn scanned him. He looked all right.

"We, me and the doc, was trying to calm him down when some gal came in. Said one of Dr. Hope's patients needed her. It sounded pretty desperate. She tried pleading with Sullivan. All of a sudden, he let go of me and went for this girl. Long story short, she brained him with a frying pan."

"And that killed him?"

"Yes, sir. Just thought you should know."

"The girl. Do ye know her?"

"Nah. She left with Dr. Hope, though. I reckon Lane went to the doctor's office to get their side of the story, but it was clear and simple self-defense."

"So, do ye think this trouble has anything to do with Bishop?"

"I don't know. The fight was out back. Sullivan just staggered in here."

Flynn pulled the picture of Delilah from his coat pocket, the plain one. "This her?"

Haggerty nodded immediately. "Yeah. She's the one who was here."

Flynn had to bite his tongue to keep from jumping up and doing a jig. "All right." He nodded dismissively and Haggerty returned to the bar.

Delilah was here. Somewhere in Defiance. Most likely at the doctor's office. He went over Haggerty's story again. A woman had come seeking the doctor. Haggerty identified her.

Flynn grinned, a dark, smug thing that seeped from a heart cold and black. Finally. His revenge and the takeover of Tent Town were inches from his fingers. How lovely of Delilah to make it so easy. Sullivan was an expensive loss, but Flynn got her whereabouts out of the bargain. It was probably worth it.

"Mr. Flynn."

Collins. The dark, evil thing Flynn called a smile grew. "Mr. Collins. Just the man I need to see." He motioned for him to take an empty chair. Collins grabbed it and pulled up to the stove. "Thought I'd get one last drink before I go back to O'Connell's. He's made room for me, but the man smells of cabbage."

Flynn ignored him. "Take a look at those two pictures."

Collins complied and it only took a second for him to realize what he was looking at. "That's her. That's Eleanor."

"She's at the doctor's office then."

"Yeah. There is a woman there. I spied on 'em. But I didn't get a good enough look before I had to high-tail it out. This is helpful."

Flynn pulled the pictures away from him. "Before noon today, ye must confirm it's her."

"How do I do that?"

"Go down the blasted chimney, for all I care. Just get a good look at her. And do it before noon today. Do ye understand?"

"Something happening today?"

"Do ye understand?" Flynn's jaw clenched with the question. His patience was waning.

Collins read the danger signal. "I do. I'll be back." He left sulking, but Flynn trusted he'd do what he'd been ordered to do.

He had her. Just the ammunition he needed to finish his plans. But Flynn had lost several men in the last few weeks. And who had Bishop lost?

He wiggled his toes for a moment then rose and turned to the smoky room. He had the dynamite he needed to blast Bishop and McIntyre out of Defiance. And he had yet another murder to lay at Delilah's feet. He had to do all this carefully, wisely, and with more men than Bishop could muster.

"Lads, we'll be closing in a few minutes." He rose and turned to the room. "The last round of beer is on me. I appreciate your patronage."

Cheers and whoops filled the smoky tent as the men rushed the bar to take advantage of the offer. Haggerty bellowed at them to calm down and wait their turn. He'd pour as fast as he could. Flynn noted which men tipped their hats at him and thanked him.

He saluted them with his whiskey glass. "Thank ye for yer business, lads. I know ye could be at Bishop's. Beer will be free tomorrow at lunch as well. Pass the word."

Victoria had never been one to chew her nails, but she'd bitten four down to the quick sitting here with Momma. She glanced repeatedly at the window. She'd pulled the shade all the way down but couldn't help wondering if someone was out there watching.

She'd killed a man.

Someone was spying on them.

Did someone in town know who she was?

Was it Sam Collins?

Lane was worried about this man Flynn. Should she be worried?

Did Marty Sullivan have a family?

The jumbled thoughts tumbled over themselves in her brain and she dropped her head into her hands.

The last two nights, she'd left Momma and slept on Dr. Clark's settee, but not tonight. With her Bible on her lap, she'd stayed by Momma's side. As the hours waned, she'd perched in this chair and hadn't moved. She'd tried to read the Word, but her attention drifted to the window.

She scrubbed her hands over her face as another wave of unease cascaded over her. *Oh, dear God, what have I done coming here? Another man is dead. Momma could have been killed.*

She glanced at the window.

And someone is hunting us. I know it. I feel it.

The front door opened. Victoria jumped to her feet and flung open Momma's door, every muscle in her body ready for a fight to protect her. Dr. Clark stepped back with a gasp, startled by the abrupt action. "Is everything all right?"

"Yes, yes. I'm sorry. I didn't mean to scare you."

"No. It's all right." She unwound her scarf and hung it on the hook. "It's four o'clock. You've been here all night. Let me take over now. You go get some rest."

Victoria couldn't sleep. "I can't. I can't stop thinking about what a mess I've made here. And..." She hadn't told Dr. Clark about the footprints in the snow.

"And?" Dr. Clark eased out of her coat.

Victoria looked back over her shoulder at Momma, stepped outside, and closed the door. "I wasn't going to tell you something, but maybe you should know." She motioned to the front porch. "I saw footprints in the snow. Someone was looking in on Momma."

Dr. Clark frowned. "What?" She glanced in the direction of

the porch, the examination room, and then came back to Victoria. "Are you sure?"

"The footprints are plain."

"Well, I'm...I'm sure it's nothing. Lane will be by in a little while. I'll make sure he looks around."

"Sam Collins shot Momma. I killed one of Flynn's men. I should have known...some secrets just can't be kept in the grave."

Dr. Clark clutched her hand. "Don't be so fatalistic. You don't know what God's up to."

"Someone knows I'm here. I can feel it. But I can't—I won't—leave Momma."

Dr. Clark exhaled heavily, squeezed Victoria's hand, perhaps in acceptance, and went in to check on the patient.

Victoria managed a few hours of fitful rest on the settee. But a cup of coffee with the doctor would go a long way in reviving her. She trudged her way through the fresh snow, up to her knees now and filling in her boots. She'd kick them off and let them dry by—

She stopped and stared into the forest of pines and short scrubby cedars. Had she seen movement? No one should be on this path to Dr. Clark's. The muffled laughter of miners headed to work colored the air. Was she merely jumpy, seeing things that weren't there? Maybe it was a bear.

No, stupid, they're hibernating.

Then what?

Was it the previous visitor? How foolish to be out here without at least another frying pan.

She strained to make out the detail in the shadows, now stark in contrast with a bright, sunny morning. But nothing moved. Nothing seemed out of the ordinary.

Yet, the sense she was being watched intently wouldn't leave her. She pulled her hood over her face and rushed on to the doctor's office, bursting inside.

Breathing hard, she leaned back on the door. *I feel it, Lord. The danger is rising, isn't it? I could go. I could just leave right now and maybe that would keep Momma safe.*

The idea consumed her for a moment, and when Dr. Clark called out, she nearly jumped out of her skin. "Victoria, is that you?"

"Y-Yes. How's Momma?"

"I'm hopeful. She was awake—"

Someone pounded on the door and Victoria pushed away from it, her heart in her throat. She had to get hold of herself. "There's someone at the door." She turned and swallowed the fear rising in her throat. "I'll get it." Breathless, her pulse skittering, she cracked the door.

And blinked in disbelief. "Toby." His sheepish grin and the way he was hugging his hat made her want to faint with joy. She grabbed him, pulled him inside, and covered him in kisses and hugs. "What are you doing back? Oh, I don't care." She clutched his face and kissed him again. "You're back and I'm so glad to see you." Maybe it was just a case of nerves, but he was back and she felt safer.

Wait. Why was he back already?

They eased apart and he lowered her hands. His somber expression extinguished her joy. "I've got some bad news." Dr. Clark emerged from the other examination room, rolls of bandages in her arms. She stopped to listen. "Somebody went through our things back in Ruby City. Most likely that Irishman you warned me about. They got..." He exhaled wearily. "They got the picture of us off the mantle."

The one of them all together in front of GW's place? She wasn't necessarily recognizable in it. She had no makeup on. Why was Toby so concern—?

"And they took the one I had of you in my trunk. From your time over in Salt Lake."

She had to unwrap what he was saying. She didn't remember getting her portrait done in Utah. "There isn't any picture of me from there."

"You were photographed for the newspaper. I cut it out and kept it."

What? Why would he do that? A realization dawned on her like honey seeping from a beehive. She wasn't sure if it made her happy or broke her heart for him. "You kept my picture?"

"I've always kind of...loved you, Victoria. Even before I met you. I know that sounds crazy, but there was something about you in that picture that I couldn't get past." He shrugged like a kid caught staring at the cookie jar. "Guess that makes me sound like a fool."

"For love," Dr. Clark said quietly, a sweet smile on her face. Blushing, she cleared her throat. "I'll just go check on Eleanor." She set the bandages on the counter and hurried from the room.

He loved me. Even before he met me. The bittersweet understanding filled Victoria's mind and overflowed to her heart. "I'm sorry." She clutched his hand, then let go and caressed his face lightly. "It can't be easy to love me. I've done nothing but make you miserable, haven't I?"

"Whatever you've done, I have to get you out of here. Dr. Clark will tend to Eleanor. Leave with me right now."

As badly as she wanted to say yes, she couldn't. A tug in her spirit wouldn't let her. At least not yet. "Toby, I—"

Boots on the front porch stopped her. A second later, Lane poked his head in the door and then slipped inside. "Morning." He glanced around and finished on Toby. "Thought you were leaving."

"I did, but I came back. Somebody broke into my home and took two photographs of Victoria."

Lane rested his hand on the butt of his .44 and shook his head. "Let me guess. Somebody can identify her now."

Toby nodded. Lane dragged a hand over his face, sighing in

disgust or weariness. "I heard that Flynn is having some kind of meeting today. Free beer."

Victoria tensed. She had seen that scenario over the years, again and again. "Either he's running for office and wants votes, or he's recruiting men for something."

Lane sucked on his teeth and shook his head. "Yeah. And I don't think he has designs on the mayor's seat."

"He's coming for me, isn't he?"

"I don't know. You could be a piece of it maybe, if he knows you're here. But I don't know that he does."

"Someone's been spying on us."

"How do you know that?"

"I saw the footprints clear as day outside Momma's window." She glanced at the window. "And this morning...I feel like someone was still there, watching."

Lane fell silent. She knew what he was thinking. The footsteps could have been random. Kids maybe. Or maybe somebody looking to steal some laudanum. But it made more sense that somebody was looking for her.

Toby took a step forward. "I think I should take her away from here. Right now."

"You should." Lane cut his eyes at Victoria. "But you ain't gonna go, are you."

"I can't. Not until Momma's out of the woods. Lane..." She took two bold steps toward him. "Arrest me. I'm turning myself in. I want to be tried—"

Lane patted the air. "Whoa, whoa there. I'm not sure that wouldn't be the same thing as handing you over to a mob. I don't know what people are going to do they find out you're here."

"I'm telling you I think someone does know I'm here."

Lane passed his gaze over all of them, ending on the door to Momma's room. "Everybody just sit tight and let me figure things out. I'm gonna look around some more for this Collins fella. And go see what Flynn's up to."

Nothing good. Victoria would have bet on it.

～

Naomi stood off to the side of the crowd, shielded by a little scotch pine. Emilio and Two Spears were with her. They'd come to town for supplies, but the excited crowd of men flowing to Tent Town had drawn them, too. Emilio had urged against this, but Naomi had a feeling something was about to happen and they needed to let Charles know. Adam was safe with Rebecca for a few minutes. She had time.

Flynn flung open the doors to the Number Two at High Noon and a mob flooded in. A man, Naomi recalled his name as Haggerty, recruited Corky to help pour beer. Soon, the lunchtime crowd had grown to over a hundred, and they spilled out into the area in front of the saloon.

The men closer to Naomi muttered over and over something about free beer. Why was this Flynn giving away beer? Naomi didn't understand what he was after. "Emilio, why don't you drift in? Find Corky. See if this is anything we should be concerned about."

"I'll go," Two Spears immediately volunteered.

Naomi smiled at him. "Not for a few years yet. Go on, Emilio."

He did as she asked, and a few minutes later, returned with a grave expression. "Flynn's going to make a speech. Corky said it has something to do with Mr. McIntyre and Mr. Bishop working together."

"What?" As far as Naomi knew, Charles had only spoken to Bishop to warn him, not do business with him. He'd also met with Flynn, but she'd bet he wasn't going to mention that little fact today.

Suddenly, Flynn jumped up on a barrel and fired his revolver. The crowd's murmur faded into silence. "Lads, welcome," he shouted. "Thank ye for joining me. Now, no doubt, most of ye are figuring there's some catch for the free beer."

A chuckle moved through the crowd. "We figured," someone yelled.

"Well, ye're wrong. There's no catch. Other than, I wanted to gather as many of ye together to hear something. How many of ye lads lost a friend or a brother in the harlot's attack on the Sunnyside Mine?"

Dozens of hands shot up.

"All right then, listen up. We all know that McIntyre was in cahoots with Delilah and that's why he was nearly lynched."

"It's not true," a man in the crowd called. "It makes no sense that McIntyre would blow up his own mine."

"He sold it, didn't he? And made a pretty penny. Did any of ye get some of that money, other than a handful of widows?"

The men grumbled, and the sound was decidedly less friendly. Naomi did not like where this was going.

"Exactly. Now, I know for a fact that McIntyre had a meeting with Bishop about business in town." Flynn stopped, he seemed to be looking at someone in the crowd.

Bodies moved as if someone were pushing through them. Then a man approached Flynn. He squatted down to listen, and Naomi lost sight of him. A moment later, he rose again, and there was something decidedly different in his stance. One moment he was cocky. The next, he was standing like the King of Siam. A sinking feeling hit her. What had he just learned? Instinctively, she reached out and clutched Emilio's wrist.

"Not only has Mr. Charles McIntyre had a meeting with Mr. Bishop, but he's also met with Delilah. The woman is back in town."

The crowd roared with hate-filled curses that echoed deafeningly off the sky.

"Go," Naomi whispered, her heart filling up with dread. "Go tell Charles what's happening here."

"He will not want me to leave you, señora."

"Go. Now. Take Two Spears with you. I'll find Lane and then I'll go to the newspaper office." He hesitated and Naomi wanted to scream. "Go," she whispered harshly.

Emilio grabbed Two Spears and dragged the boy with him. Naomi stepped a little further back into the shadows of the pines.

"Now, now..." Flynn yelled, patting the air, calming the unruly group. "Ye must calm down and let me tell ye what I know. McIntyre and Bishop have entered into a dark agreement to run things and keep the Irishmen and the hardworking men of this town under their thumbs."

Lies. He's telling lies. How can he stand there and just say anything he likes? Naomi looked over the faces of the men. Purple with anger, scowling, glaring up at Flynn, nodding as he spewed this nonsense.

"The MP&G lords are all in agreement with McIntyre and Bishop. They want to bring Delilah back for the money she can make them all, off yer backs, and the backs of men who will come here from all over the country. They'll keep us happy and drunk when we're not working in the dark bowels of the earth!

"They don't want us owning businesses or running the town. Just like the English back in Ireland, these rich men want us to be downtrodden slaves!"

Again, the crowd roared with fury. Fists gyrated in the air. The scent of bloodlust filled Naomi's nostrils. Flynn was whipping them up to do something terrible.

"Now, this is what I think we should do. We should ride Bishop out of town on a rail, for starters." The crowd roared its approval. "And second, we get our justice. We hang Delilah Goodnight." The beast of hate roared even louder at that. Men's eyes glowed bright with rancor and their desire for death.

This is demonic. Naomi didn't need to hear any more. She spun and ran from the yelling, salivating crowd. Where was Lane? She had to find him. He was the sheriff. He and Wade. The first line of defense. They could stop this.

She crossed the bridge at a full run as more men flowed toward the murderous rally. Lane appeared at the top of the hill, at the corner of Bonanza Street and she screamed his name. "Lane!" He spun his horse, looking for the caller. "Lane," she yelled again and ran up to him. "Flynn is whipping up a lynch mob. He said they're going to start with Bishop, but he's pointing fingers at Charles and Delilah. He told the crowd she's in town. He wasn't done talking, but I left to find you."

"Where's Charles?"

"I sent Emilio and Two Spears out to get him."

"Holy..." He faded off, scanned the crowd, perked up at a roar and a shout that echoed across the buildings in Tent Town. Naomi turned. The sound of the crowd moving. Were they going for Bishop?

"Get someplace safe, Miss Naomi. Right now." He spurred his horse and headed for the mob. "No, wait." He wheeled back around. "First, find Wade and tell him to get to Hope's office. And expect trouble. Then you get someplace safe." With that, he was gone and Naomi was running again.

Seventeen

NAOMI TRIED the sheriff's office first, but it was empty except for someone sleeping off a hangover. Next, she tried the hotel. Mollie was at the desk. She looked up as Naomi burst in, and her eyes bugged. "Naomi, what is it?"

"Is Wade here? Have you seen him?"

"Um, he was having lunch but left a few minutes ago. What's going on? Is Emilio all right?"

"Flynn is whipping up a lynch mob and Lane rode right into the middle of it. But he wanted Wade to go to Hope's. I think they're going to try to take Delilah."

Mollie slammed her guest book closed. "I'll take one end of town, you take the other."

"Fine. Meet me at the newspaper office. I have to get Adam."

Naomi ran everywhere and asked everyone, from the bakery to the saddle shop, if they'd seen Wade. She stopped in at the livery. Nothing. Her nerves crawling from the tension, she gave up, praying Mollie was having better luck. Time to get Adam, to assure herself he was fine.

She double-timed it down the boardwalk but couldn't avoid the snatches of conversations peppering her. "...Free beer..." "He wants trouble..." "Talking about lynching..." "Says she's back..."

Yes, she was back. Someone had discovered Delilah was here, or Flynn was lying, but that didn't make sense. She skidded to a stop on the boardwalk.

She couldn't believe she hadn't realized this. If someone had told Flynn Delilah was in town...they already knew where she was. Everyone at Hope's was in danger if a mob came calling.

Lost in these thoughts, she side-stepped two brawny miners, and then suddenly someone grabbed hold of her arm and spun her around. She was met by a sneering, pockmarked face she didn't know. The barrel of a gun pressed into her stomach. "Mrs. McIntyre, if ye'll come with me, please."

She glanced down. The man, short, unkempt, with dirty hands, had his finger on the trigger. Oh, Lord...she swallowed and fought to keep a tremble from her voice. "Please take your finger off the trigger so you don't shoot me by accident."

He grinned, revealing tobacco-stained teeth. "Right." He did as she requested, but kept the gun on her, pressing into her ribs now as he shifted to walk beside her.

"Where are you taking me?"

"To Dr. Hope's office."

Where Delilah was. To get there, they had to pass in front of the newspaper office. *Oh, God, please get Rebecca to look out the window.*

They started walking. She risked stumbling right in front of the office. Her captor snatched her up, gave her a good cursing, and tugged her forward. Naomi stole a glance back.

Rebecca was holding Adam and scowling with fear and anger in her eyes. Good. She knows something's wrong. *Get Charles, Rebecca. Get Charles.*

~

Flynn chuckled. Bishop's feet kicked and twitched for several minutes, but the movements grew slower and further between. Finally, the death throes stilled. The crowd, looking up at the man's dangling body, cheered and roared louder at his passing. One man removed his hat and yelled, "Goodbye, old Bishop, our old friend. Nothing but Irish whiskey stands in the end."

Laughter rumbled through the crowd. Time to take control again. Flynn had truly not intended to lynch his rival. If he'd left town peacefully, things would have turned out differently. The sheriff should have kept out of it as well. Hat-tip to his courage, though. He'd taken a good beating and fought hard till he fainted.

But time to move on.

Flynn waved his arms and yelled to get the mob's attention. "Boys!" The crowd still grumbled. "Boys!" This time, they quieted down. "Let's drag the sheriff back to his jail cell. He'll wake up behind bars. We can decide what to do with him later."

Cheers went up and several men spun about searching, but no one came up with Chandler. Flynn stepped into the crowd. "Where is he?" He couldn't get away. He was beat to a pulp, but if he got a gun and made it back to the jail or the doctor's office...

"Find him," he bellowed.

Several men shook their heads and pushed other men aside looking for him. "He ain't here."

"Find him!" He looked at the crowd of drunken, angry men. "The rest of ye, come with me. Now it's time for the big show."

~

Charles peered intently through the eyepiece on the theodolite, his surveyor's site, then glanced at the attached compass. Yes, that was a perfect piece of land to break off and give to Two Spears. He'd survey a second parcel later for Adam, but his boys would start out with their own land to manage or sell back to Charles if they decided to do something other than ranching.

He pulled a small notebook from his breast pocket and scribbled notes in it. He wanted to remember that ridge specifically. It would make a wonderful homesite.

"Mr. McIntyre!"

He spun, not sure if he'd heard his name or if that had been the wind. No. Emilio and Two Speers were galloping toward him, waving their arms wildly. Before they even reached him, he knew their urgency had something to do with Delilah. Forgetting the theodolite, he grabbed Traveler's reins, swung up into the saddle, and cut the distance to the boys. They reined in, dirt flying. "What's the matter?"

"Flynn is whipping up a mob. He told them Delilah is in town. I think he wants them to go after her, but you, too, and Bishop."

"Where's Naomi?"

Emilio and Two Spears exchanged tense glances. "She made us leave her."

"What?"

Two Spears leaned forward. "She was going to go find Sheriff Chandler. Then she said she would be at the newspaper office to get Adam."

His palms sweating over concern for her and Adam, McIntyre swiped a hand over his mouth. She should have come home with these two. But he'd kill her later. Right now, he had to keep Two Spears safe and help Lane. "Two Spears, I want you to ride to the railroad camp and tell Mr. Gunderson to gather up the men. Make sure they're armed and for them to wait for me at the stagecoach office in town. Do you understand?"

He nodded and bolted away to discharge his mission. That should keep him out of trouble.

McIntyre looked at Emilio. "I want you to make sure

Naomi and Adam are safe. Find them and stay with them. I won't be far behind you."

Emilio's brow creased in question, but he shook it off instantly. "Sí, yes, sir." He spun his horse and headed back to town at a full gallop.

Charles headed up the hill toward home.

∼

"Someone's coming."

Victoria looked up from the Bible verse she'd read a million times in the last hour and couldn't recall a word of it. "Do you know who?" Reflexively, she patted Momma's hand, though she wasn't sure if she was assuring her or herself. She stirred slightly at the touch. That had to be a good sign.

Toby dropped the curtain back in place at the window and stared through the lace.

Dr. Clark was at the stove beside him, boiling instruments, and glanced at the door. "A patient?"

Hugging her Bible, Victoria rose and approached the threshold of Momma's room, waiting for Toby's answer.

"I'm not sure. It's McIntyre's wife, but she's with another man."

Dr. Clark carried the pot of hot water over to the counter. "Most likely one of their ranch hands then. They get hurt all the time." She poured alcohol on her hands in anticipation of treating a patient.

The door creaked open, and a sudden, chilling wave of fear crashed over Victoria. She parted her lips to warn Toby—too late. The pair stepped inside. A man in filthy, grimy miner's clothes had a strange grip on Naomi's arm. Suddenly, he shoved her into Toby and brandished a revolver. Victoria's heart stopped. They'd found her.

"Everybody be calm now." The man pointed his gun at

Toby. "Take yers out real slow, lad, so that we don't have a misunderstanding."

Irish. One of Flynn's men?

Dr. Clark rushed to Naomi and pulled her out of the line of fire. "Are you all right?"

"Just fine." Her glare at the man could have melted metal.

Toby cursed under his breath.

Victoria wanted to scream. This was a nightmare. Whoever this man was, he had hostages now. They had to figure a way out.

"Now," the man ordered. "Yer gun."

Scowling, Toby obliged, setting the Smith on the floor. "Who are you?"

"O'Keefe. I work for Mr. Flynn. He'll be along in a bit. He's taking care of *business* down in Tent Town with Mr. Bishop." He shifted his gaze to Victoria. "I understand ye're his next appointment."

Victoria didn't want to know, but she couldn't stop herself from asking. "What is he doing to Bishop?"

"They're giving that toad a good, old-fashioned necktie party." He chuckled, but it was a dark, slimy sound. "Flynn asked him politely to leave. We gave the man a choice."

Dr. Clark made a choking sound and took a quick step forward. "Where's Lane? The sheriff." Panic crept into her voice. "Where's the sheriff?"

"Eh-eh." O'Keefe waved her back with his barrel. "Last I seen him, he was getting his nose bent for sticking it where it didn't belong."

She slapped a fist over her mouth and tears sprang to her eyes. "Please tell me he's not dead."

The man leaned back against the door. "I wouldn't want to talk about things I'm not sure of."

Dr. Clark's expression convulsed into a barely controlled sob. Naomi squeezed her hand for reassurance. "He's all right, Hope. He's tough."

Whatever hope Victoria had that things might go all right for her here in Defiance died a sudden, painful death. Now, all that mattered was saving everyone else. She eased over to Hope and took her other hand. Under the circumstances, *Dr. Clark* didn't feel right anymore. "I'm sorry I brought you into this, Hope. But she's right. He's tough. Pray for him." She turned a glare on O'Keefe. "Enough of this. Take me to Flynn. Let me talk—"

"No." Toby sliced the air with his hand and stepped between her and O'Keefe.

O'Keefe waved him back. "Easy now, boy."

Toby ignored him and kept his eyes riveted on Victoria. "They want you, they'll have to come here and take you."

"Mister, I've worked for Michael Flynn for some years now. And I must tell ye, I've never seen him so determined about a thing. He's lived this last year with the unrelenting drive to avenge Joseph." He shifted to Victoria. "He said ye'd turn up somewhere, sometime. It appears he was right. And ye've gone and made it easy for him."

"Joseph?" Did she want to know who he was and how he was tied to Flynn?

"Aye. His little brother. He said he'd hang ye, as justice for his death. And he'd take Defiance because it's pitiful compensation." He pointed his gun at Naomi. "And *she's* the bait for McIntyre."

"He'll kill you," Naomi said softly, flatly. As if she were saying her own name or that the sun was yellow. "And Flynn." A mere fact.

"He's a dangerous man, yer husband." O'Keefe bobbed his head, agreeing. "But he's not God. He can't take a mob on by himself and live."

Naomi's grim expression hardened like steel. "He won't be alone."

A thud on the porch distracted O'Keefe, but only for an instant. He stepped away from the door just as a bloody, bedraggled Lane stumbled in and collapsed on the floor. Hope squeaked in alarm and ran to him, gathering him up in her arms.

Victoria flinched at the sheriff's condition. His face was black and blue. Both his eyes were swelling shut. Blood smears streamed from his puffy, purple lips and stained his gray shirt. He was holding his ribs. Lane had taken a walloping.

He pointed a bloody finger at Victoria. "They're coming for her."

Her.

Me.

Victoria pressed a hand to her stomach to quell the sick butterflies. Lane's bloody finger declared her guilt...and foolishness.

Hope maneuvered around the sheriff, reaching under him. "Toby, here, help me get him on the examination table."

Toby started to move, O'Keefe stopped him, then relented with a shrug. "Eh, go ahead. It makes no difference."

But Lane resisted as he clumsily attempted to gain his feet. "No...I gotta help—"

"You ain't in shape to help nobody." Toby slipped his arms underneath the man and, with Hope, lifted him up and half-carried, half-dragged him over to the examination table. "Here, I'll get him up there. You get the things you need."

Hope pivoted instantly to get her medical supplies as Toby helped Lane up onto the table. "Lay down before you fall down." He stepped back when Hope wheeled a table of bandages, instruments, and alcohol up beside Lane.

"Lane." She leaned in close to his ear. "I'm here, and I'm going to help you. You're going to be all right. Where's the worst pain?"

His swollen lips moved in a vague attempt at motion. "Everywhere," he whispered. "The things a man will do to see his doctor." Hope chuckled softly and caressed his cheek.

As she tended to her bitterly abused patient, Victoria

drifted over to the window, away from Momma, a vain attempt to protect her. *Dear God, I've handed them hostages.*

Oh, if she'd only leaned into Toby. Followed her heart, not her guilt.

I've lost or endangered everyone I've ever loved. Please break this curse.

She sniffled and quickly wiped her tears away. Toby reached over and took her hand. "It's going to be all right. I promise."

If only he had the power to keep it.

Naomi approached them, her hands reaching toward the stove for warmth, deep sadness etching her pretty face. Another wave of guilt hit Victoria. "I'm sorry."

Naomi tilted her head and studied her for a moment, without any malice in her expression, only pity. "I believe you are. Sadly."

Too little too late. "I've got quite the mess to clean up now, don't I?"

"From what I gather, that's the crux of the problem. You think you can clean this up. You need to quit trying to hang yourself on his cross." She glanced at O'Keefe. "If it's not too late." She let the suggestion sink in, then returned to help Hope with Lane.

His saddlebags full of everything he thought he'd need to quell the mobs in town, Charles and Traveler lunged through the forest, taking shortcuts, racing the devil to beat him to the finish line. *Dear Lord, give me time. Help me stop this. Make them listen.*

He raced into town, going first to the newspaper office. Rebecca's long face told him she wasn't there. "I sent Ian to find you. Two men have Naomi. I don't know where they took her."

The news chilled him to the bone. It made sense, though, that she was with Delilah. At Hope's?

Little Adam reached for Charles and his heart tripped over itself with joy and deep-seated fear. Hugging his son, breathing in the sweet scent of his innocence, he hugged him tightly and begged Rebecca with his eyes.

She understood. "Go find her." She reached out to take Adam back.

Loathe to leave his son but given no choice, he handed him to his aunt. "I won't be long, son. I'll be back soon with Momma." He caressed his pink cheek and tugged at his tiny, fragile fingers. "Rebecca, you may hear some loud noises. Don't be alarmed."

Her brow rose. "If you say so. Just bring everyone home safe."

The door burst open and Emilio skidded in, almost tripping in the entrance. Face flushed and sweaty, he was sucking wind and was beginning to exhibit a black eye. "Mr. McIntyre. It is bad. They beat Lane, but I helped him sneak away. He is at the doctor's office. But so is Señora Naomi, and the mob is on the way there."

The news galvanized Charles, and he lunged for the door. "Come with me." He grabbed Emilio and they raced outside. As he went for his horse tied up at the rail, he spun on Emilio. "Do you trust me?"

"S-Sí, señor." Then he added more firmly, "Yes."

Good enough.

~

Minutes ticked by as Hope and Naomi tended to Lane. Toby continually glanced around the room, looking for a way of escape. Victoria hugged herself and prayed.

Quit trying to hang yourself on his cross.

Naomi's words echoed over and over in her head. *Jesus, I didn't realize. That's exactly what I've done, though, isn't it? It wasn't just penance. I thought by sacrificing myself I would settle all the scores. But they've already been settled. By you. You forgave me. I'm supposed to be a new creation.*

Head down, she turned and went back to the window. *You've changed everything about me, Father. If only I'd let that be enough. And now look at the danger I've brought down.* She choked back a sob, but Toby must have heard it. He eased over and pulled her into an embrace.

O'Keefe snorted. "Enjoy it while ye can, lad."

Victoria cut her eyes at the grotesque little man. There had been one good thing about Delilah. She'd never let a man cow her. She'd had a strength about her, only she'd used it for the wrong results.

Still, you are no simpering, little flower, Victoria. Chin up. Shoulders squared. A brave face. She squeezed Toby's arm and turned to face the room.

No more hiding. I haven't been given a spirit of fear...I haven't been given a spirit of fear...

A low, distant rumble of voices drifted to them. One by one, each of them in the room reacted to the growing crescendo of angry men yelling and shouting curses. Shoulders tensed. Brows furrowed. In unison, their eyes went to the front window. O'Keefe snorted. "Sounds like the next party is about to get started."

Toby pursed his lips and squeezed Victoria's hand, reassuring her they would fight the mob together.

Lane clumsily pushed Hope away as she dabbed at his swollen lips and sat up. "I have to help stop this." He slid to his feet and his knees buckled.

"Lane, you're in no shape," Hope protested, grabbing him and pushing him back against the table for support.

O'Keefe scratched his nose, hiding an ugly grin. "Ye'd best listen to her, boy. Try to take me and someone other than ye might get hurt." He skipped his gaze over the women.

Lane ground his teeth and eased back. He raised a shaky

hand and pointed at O'Keefe. "It's coming, mister. It's coming."

"Please, Lane..." Hope tried to ease him back up on the table, but he refused, keeping his feet on the ground.

Naomi crossed her arms and glared at their captor. "He's right. Trouble is coming for you."

Victoria worried her bottom lip wondering about Naomi. Who had her sons? Were they safe? Were they with McIntyre?

Did she hate Victoria for sweeping her up in this web of disaster?

Seconds later, the mob reached Hope's yard. Victoria looked out the window, as did Toby, and Naomi peered over their shoulders. The tall, slender man in front had to be Flynn. He had mean, chiseled features. Victoria studied the dozens of ugly faces with him, hardened by hate and the lust for murder. A pride of lions ready to rip her to shreds. For a moment, fear threatened to overwhelm her. Her body burned icy hot. They were going to hang her. In minutes, most likely, she would be dead.

She wasn't afraid of death. She was afraid of dying. Terrified of swinging and choking on a rope.

Flynn marched with the most purpose...and glee. He bounded up on the porch. "O'Keefe," he called through the door, "what is the situation?"

"Come on in. They're waiting."

The door flew open. Flynn scanned the room, his gaze stopping on Victoria. Toby released her hand and positioned himself in front of her. "Over my dead body."

Flynn shrugged a shoulder. "If that's the way ye want it."

At least a dozen men swarmed the room, and they flooded over Toby and Lane. Fists flew in the melee like striking rattlesnakes. Furniture flipped and glass shattered. A treaty of medical instruments hit the floor in a cacophony of noise. Three men hammered Toby with vicious blows. Victoria screamed at the top of her lungs. Two men grabbed her, but she fought, kicking, clawing, raging to get to Toby, to no avail. Hope and Naomi leaped in front of Lane to keep the rest of the mob from getting to Lane, but several men grabbed them as others punched and kicked the sheriff. Sucking wind, bleeding from his nose, and teetering on the edge of consciousness, Lane melted to the floor. Hope screamed. Naomi raged and writhed like a wild woman.

Two big, beefy men had Victoria. Gouging their fingers into her arms, they dragged her toward the door. Toby scuffled frantically, taking more punches and kicks. Victoria felt every blow as if they were hitting her. "No," she bellowed. "No! Stop! Don't hurt him!" They ignored her and kicked him again. He fought desperately for her till a final punch to the head sent him to the floor.

Suddenly, Victoria was outside on the porch, staring down into the grim faces of at least fifty cheering, jeering men. The two gang members tightened their vise-like grips on her. O'Keefe kept his revolver trained on her. Their prize wasn't going anywhere.

Flynn straddled the top two steps, leering at her like a gargoyle. Fury and fear arced through her in a lightning bolt and she screamed a curse at him, then sagged with exhaustion. Her fault. All of this was on her. "Take me, but please let everyone else go. Please."

Flynn laughed and slapped her so hard that her eyes watered and stars danced in her brain. For the moment, she quieted, trying to shake off the sting and clear her vision, but murder blossomed in her heart. Flynn, though, glared back at her with murder in his eyes.

Grinding his teeth, he took a breath and pivoted back to the men. "Well, there she is, gents. Delilah in all her faded glory." The men filling Hope's yard settled down, hate and lust glowing in their eyes. "The woman who murdered my little brother. The woman responsible for yer loved ones lying at the bottom of that vile, black mine."

"String her up!" An arm shot above the crowd, waving a rope. "Hang her high!"

As the crowd lunged forward, a deafening roll of thunder boomed over them. All eyes pivoted to the sound. At first, Victoria couldn't comprehend what had just happened. Then she saw him.

Charles McIntyre was standing at the back of the mob, pointing his .44 at the sky. Smoke drifted from the barrel. Curiosity or fear silenced the men. He assessed the scene with a cold, unsettling gaze.

Victoria prayed he wasn't there to help them hang her.

Eighteen

FLYNN CLAPPED his hands together in slow, mocking applause for McIntyre. "Look there, lads. McIntyre himself has come to us. Thank ye, Mr. McIntyre, for making all this so much easier."

McIntyre glared at Flynn. His dark eyes burned with an unholy vengeance. The look chilled Victoria. The angel of death had arrived. But who would the Reaper harvest?

Then McIntyre slowly passed his gaze over the crowd as he lowered his gun, but only to shoulder height. His finger still rested on the trigger. Instinctively, every man in the yard moved back a foot, opening a path straight to Flynn. The air of expectation was almost suffocating.

"Mr. Flynn, you have abducted my wife. Taken and beaten a friend, our sheriff. And lynched a man." He cocked the revolver. The sound was clear and crisp, a terrifying warning. Much like the sound of a rattlesnake shaking its tail. "If I fire my gun once more, the Crystal Chandelier Number Two will cease to exist. It will, in fact, become a pile of toothpicks."

Flynn's hands clenched into fists and his jaw tensed so tight Victoria was sure he'd chip a tooth. "Ye wouldn't dare."

Foolish man. Delilah wanted to scream at him. He didn't know who he was dealing with.

"If I fire it a *third* time, Tent Town will go up in flames." He glanced around again, sneering at the weak-willed, traitorous men watching. "I will burn it to the ground."

Flynn snorted. "Ye're bluffing."

A majority of the men in the crowd reacted. Their eyes widened, some sucked in a breath, and others inched back more. They knew how foolish Flynn's comment was.

"I never bluff, Mr. Flynn. You don't know me well enough to understand that...but many of the men here do." He passed his disdainful, accusing stare over them once more. "Choose now, gentlemen, if you want a drink or hang a woman. You will not do both."

The crowd grumbled, shifted, casting uncertain glances at each other. Men on the fringes surreptitiously drifted away, heads down, hands in their pockets. At first, the departures were hesitant, but soon, the abandonment picked up speed.

Flynn stepped up on the porch, perhaps wanting all the advantage he could get over McIntyre. Veins throbbed in his forehead. Hate ruled his heart and his head. He was as explosive and unpredictable as a sweating stick of dynamite. Another of Delilah's creations.

"Blow up my saloon, I'll kill yer wife. Bring McIntyre's wife out here," he yelled over his shoulder. Scuffles, grunts, and then a smacking sound preceded Naomi appearing on the porch, held in an iron grip by a tall, gaunt fellow. The pink of a handprint bloomed on her cheek. She still had the fight of a mountain lion in her and she jerked and twisted but to no avail.

McIntyre's face was deadly still. His arm lowered a fraction more as his jaw tightened and flexed.

Another man had Hope by the neck and shoved her out on the porch. Toby and Lane, bloodied and beaten, nudged on by another man, followed, barely able to walk, swaying on their feet. They were lucky to still be breathing, but Toby's bloodied condition tore out Victoria's heart.

"No, no, no," she whispered. She couldn't stand it anymore. She wanted to die. She'd caused so much pain, especially to the people most important to her. The weight of it had become unbearable. She had to stop this somehow.

At least the men holding their hostages had lost some of their steam. Their shoulders were hunched and they pointedly avoided looking at McIntyre. They knew to be afraid of him.

Flynn took a breath, looked down his nose at Victoria, then turned his gaze back to McIntyre. "Make no mistake, saloon or no saloon, I will still hang Delilah Goodnight."

McIntyre shook his head ever so slightly. "No, you will not."

"ENOUGH," Victoria screamed. The dam in her burst. "ENOUGH!" Her brain went white hot with self-loathing and anger. The rage numbed her fear. Everything wrong she'd ever done had become a weapon in the enemy's hands. And he was using it to destroy everything and everyone that had mattered to her. *Jesus...Jesus...Help me stop this.* "Hang me!" She fought against her captors, writhing like a wolf caught in a trap. "If that's all that matters to you, HANG ME! Enough innocent people have died because of me."

The man with the rope tossed it at Flynn's feet. It landed like a dead snake on the steps. "I reckon I don't want any part of this. McIntyre's wife shouldn't be involved." The man thrashed his way back through the crowd, offering an apologetic nod to McIntyre...who did not return it.

Victoria tried to calm her racing heart. Would this be the start? Would they let her go? Would Flynn?

Would McIntyre?

A sneer curling his lip, Flynn watched a handful of men skulk away from the murderous group. "Cowards! I call ye all cowards!" His support had thinned by more than half.

"You're losing your grip, Flynn," McIntyre taunted.

Growling like a bear, Flynn pulled Naomi into his arms and snatched his gun from its holster. In the blink of an eye, he had it pressed to her temple. She went stock still and kept her eyes glued to McIntyre.

McIntyre's expression hardened. "That was foolish." He extended his arm skyward again and fired. The .44 roared like a demon, the thunder of it rolling over the scene and echoing ominously off the mountains. Men flinched at the boom and hunkered down a little lower.

Then silence. Perfect, pregnant silence.

Several seconds passed and nothing happened. The men started to relax. Flynn puffed out his chest. "Sounds like someone didn't hear ye. What a pity about yer wife." A chuckle escaped Flynn, but then it grew into full-blown laughter. The remaining mob of men turned their eyes expectantly to McIntyre.

And as Flynn's muscles flexed to pull the trigger, thunder erupted from the other side of town. Like a case of dynamite had gone off in Tent Town. Flynn's laughter died as if someone had slammed a door in his face. Muffled, the wave of sound rolled to them, followed by actual quaking in the ground. A moment later, a man pointed back across town and yelled, "Smoke, Flynn! There goes the Number Two!"

McIntyre casually fired again. Uncertainty and confusion paralyzed the men. No one moved. "And that would be your homes going up in flames," he said as if speaking to daft children.

Suddenly, the shock broke. In unison, the men bolted, yelling, cursing, jostling each other out of the way. In seconds, all but a stunned handful were leaving at a run, knowing their homes, their tents, their belongings were burning to ash. Even the man holding Hope shoved her toward Lane and lunged down the steps.

"I can't lose my tent," one yelled.

"My belongings. I didn't sign up for this, Flynn."

The two thugs holding Victoria exchanged unsure glances, then shook their heads. "I can't do this, Flynn," one said, releasing her. He scrambled down the steps. Before he'd reached the bottom, the other man released Victoria as well and bolted after him. Flynn shouted curses at them that would have made Satan blush. Only a dozen or so men were still standing in the yard, but they wore bewildered expressions.

On the porch, only O'Keefe remained, still holding Victoria in his sights, but fear and confusion warred in his face.

"You should let my wife go."

Delilah marveled at McIntyre's tone. Soft. Gentle. Yet, he sounded like she imagined actual death would, whispering from the mouth of hell.

Flynn snapped. He screamed like a madman, like a banshee, and snatched his revolver away from Naomi, pointing it at McIntyre, as McIntyre was aiming at him. "Dam—" Flynn inexplicably froze, swayed. The gun toppled from his hand, and he collapsed, cascading down the stairs in a violent fall. At the bottom, his face slammed into the first tread and he went still.

Victoria blinked, trying to make sense...then her eyes found Momma.

She stood where Flynn had been, a wrought iron poker in her hands. In nothing but her shift, she swayed unsteadily, her eyes wide and confused. Blood stained the side of the gown.

Flynn lay sprawled on the ground, blood seeping from the back of his head, staining the snow. O'Keefe snatched the weapon from Eleanor, raised his gun to shoot her, and McIntyre's .44 roared again. O'Keefe clutched his chest and tumbled backward into Hope's office.

Eleanor shuddered and Victoria lunged, catching her just before her legs gave way. "Momma, Momma." She clutched her tight, keeping her from falling. "I've got you." Her throat tangled with a sob. "I've got you."

A man subtly easing away from the scene drew McIntyre's attention and he shot him in the shoulder. Victoria jolted at the boom. The victim screamed and cursed him, clutching his shoulder.

"Move again, and you won't have to worry about that arthritic hand."

She blinked. She knew the man. Sam. Sam Collins. McIntyre had shot Sam Collins. She couldn't comprehend any of this, it was all happening so fast.

Naomi watched it all unfold, then her gaze locked on McIntyre. Her chest rose and fell rapidly but she hadn't said a word. McIntyre holstered his gun and raised an arm to receive her. Melting with relief, she flew down the steps and launched into his arms, rocking him on his heels. They embraced like lovers who hadn't seen each other in a decade.

Sam's glare aimed at Momma cleared the fog in Victoria's brain. Blinking, accepting the death and violence around them, she hugged Momma tighter. "We have to get you back inside." Sam Collins was not important.

"Did I do the right thing, Victoria?"

Victoria could have shouted with relief and happiness. She slipped her arms more securely around her. "Yes, but let's not worry about that now." Cheeks wet with tears, she turned her head to check on Toby. He was leaning on the window ledge to hold himself up, but he met her gaze and offered a feeble nod. Blood smeared his lips. A cut in his cheek bled and trailed down to his jaw, but he was alive. He limped over to join them, entwining himself with her hold on Momma.

Below them, Flynn grumbled, made a choking sound, and tried clawing his way to his feet. He only managed to flip onto his back like a dying fish. Gasping for breath, his ugly features smeared with blood, he turned his head and found McIntyre. His stare was crazed and fearful. "Why didn't ye just let me..." His voice was raspy, faint. "Let me hang her?" He was fading. "Let me hang her." He swallowed and blinked several times as if trying to clear his vision. "Why would ye...defend a whore that killed a dozen men?"

McIntyre and Naomi looked up at Victoria with inscrutable expressions. Reading their eyes, Victoria guessed they were weighing a verdict. She held her breath, waiting. What they had to say was important to her. McIntyre was really the law in this town, but his verdict would mean more than a legal declaration. She wanted him to believe she'd changed.

McIntyre rubbed Naomi's arm and smiled a little sadly. "Because Delilah Goodnight is dead."

Flynn groaned and opened his mouth as if he was about to say something else...instead, his chest hitched, a final breath escaped him, and his eyes glazed over. Michael Flynn had gone to meet his Maker.

Nineteen

NAOMI AND CHARLES walked back to the newspaper, arm in arm, each lost in their own swirling thoughts. The violence of the day repeated in her mind and she hugged him tighter. "Did you really blow up the Chandelier?"

"No. Emilio did."

"And the fires?" Smoke smudged the horizon on the other side of the creek.

"He followed orders."

A hard lesson for the men in Tent Town, but she prayed they'd learned it. Charles never bluffed. "Do you remember once you told me my temper was a strength?"

He thought for a moment. "Vaguely."

"You told me this land requires grit and perseverance. That if I was as sweet as Hannah or as kind as Rebecca, I wouldn't last five minutes out here."

"I do recall that."

"Then you said, 'What you see as your greatest weakness, I see as your greatest strength.'" She stopped them and made him look at her. "I think you've found the balance, Charles, between strength and perseverance. I don't think you can be pushed so far you'll become a killer again. I was wrong in worrying about that. You are a warrior. A soldier who protects us. Who will always protect us."

They started walking again, but his contemplative expression said he had a lot going on behind those dark eyes. She was happy, though. She didn't know what they were going to do with Delilah, but Naomi was willing to bet the chapter had closed on her time in Defiance.

She poked Charles in the ribs to lighten the mood. "Don't misunderstand me. I still think you could learn a thing or two from charm school"—she flashed him a mischievous grin—"but the West needs men like you."

He chuckled, but it turned to warm laughter as he apparently caught the reference, remembering the conversation. It seemed to her that he'd said those words such a long time ago.

"Yes, I suppose the West will benefit from both of us." He hugged her to him, still laughing. "Let's go find our boys."

～

Victoria assisted Hope that night in getting Lane and Toby cleaned up and put to bed to rest. Toby had lesser wounds than Lane, so he was assigned to the spare room at Hope's. Hope then hurried to the jail to tend to Sam Collins, under the watchful eye of Wade, the town deputy, who had shown up at the end of the stand-off. He'd locked the man up under orders from Mr. McIntyre.

He had assured her Collins's days of selling girls into prostitution were over. She'd take McIntyre at his word. She wasn't going to waste any more energy on Collins. That part of her life, the lies, the regrets, the hate, was over for good.

She once more spent the night sleeping in the rocking chair next to Momma. And, amazingly, she did sleep. She hoped and prayed—no, she *believed*—she believed the lynch mob in Defiance was done. Momma would be safe. So would Toby.

That was all that mattered. Now, whatever Lane decided to

do with her, she would accept it. She had the strength to face it, and not because she was trying to clear her conscience. She could face it now because she trusted in the Lord's plans for her. He would bring something good out of this for her, and for Momma and Toby.

"Victoria?"

She looked up at Hope's greeting. "Good morning."

"Good morning. Lane is awake, almost feeling human, and he'd like to talk to you. While you do that, I'll go check on Toby."

"All right." Victoria rose, stretched deeply, and failed at stifling a yawn. "What time is it?"

"Nearly ten. I'll be right back."

Victoria yawned again, rubbed her face, and walked over to the other patient's room. Lane was sitting up, sipping on a cup of coffee. A good sign, considering he looked as if a head of buffalo had run over him—twice. "Good morning, sheriff."

"Mornin'." He raised his cup. "I'd pour you some, but I'm still a little unsteady. Help yourself, though." The pot sat on the nightstand next to him.

She waved off the offer. "No, thank you." She took the seat next to his bed. "You look...not as bad as I thought you might."

He tried to smile but couldn't quite manage it with still-puffy lips. "I'll live. Uh, listen, McIntyre was here this morning. He talked it over with Ian. We all don't think the town has the stomach to hang you. The Number Two is a pile of lumber and Emilio set half of Tent Town on fire. That kind of cooled them on you."

"All right." She laced her fingers together and rested them on her knees. "I can get a fair trial now, yes? And I'll plead guilty."

"Yeah. We figured. An accessory to murder. Twelve lives. You'll do a lot of hard time. Probably decades."

She squeezed her eyes shut in shock. A year. Even five years she could stomach. But *decades? Dear God, I'll lose Toby. And Momma...this will kill her.*

"But we don't get where that helps anybody. Most of the relatives of the victims have moved on. A couple of the widows are still here, and they were fixing to leave."

"They deserve justice, the family members." Would decades in prison provide it?

"Deserve it, yeah." His gaze frosted over. "But will it help anybody? I don't think so."

"Then what are you saying?"

"Healing." McIntyre startled them by strolling in and crossing to the other side of the small room. "We all need healing." He rested a hand on the .44 at his hip. "Your mother. She thought she was saving Naomi's life yesterday. I appreciate that. It was unnecessary, as I would have dispatched Flynn. However, she saved me the trouble and ended that ugly situation. We owe her."

"So, maybe it ain't right according to the law books," Lane continued, "but we want you to ride out. Leave today. Take Toby and settle someplace far away from here. Change your name and start over."

"We could start by changing your last name."

Toby. She looked up and half smiled, half flinched. His left eye was swollen shut and his face was black and blue, but again, not as bad as Lane's.

He limped over and sat on the end of Lane's bed, facing her. "If you're willing."

"What about everything you were building in Ruby City?"

"We can walk away from the ranch. We just rent it. I can turn in my badge. I can be a sheriff in a lot of places."

"What about Momma?"

"I have given that some thought." McIntyre pulled a cheroot from his pocket, seemed to consider his surroundings, then put it back. "She recovers under Hope's care. Soon enough, she returns to work at the mercantile. At some point you let me know where you are and what names you're using. I'm sure Eleanor will be glad to join you."

Toby's gaze was warm and hopeful. They'd be broke, but a fresh start would be one heck of an adventure. The bloodlust had died in this town, just as her desire to do penance had. Maybe it is time to truly walk in forgiveness, Lord. Not just give it, but accept it.

"I believe there is an offer on the table." McIntyre smirked at her and cut his eyes at Toby.

A smile started inside Victoria and broke forth like a sunbeam. She rose and extended her hand to Toby. "Come with me."

He did as ordered and the two crossed the office to Momma's room. Victoria stepped over next to her and leaned down. "Momma, you awake?"

Her eyes flew open. "Yep. And I heard every word. These walls are pretty thin." Chuckling, she tried to sit up but flinched in pain. Victoria and Toby rushed to stack the pillow behind her and ease her back on it. She was smiling at them, but a little sadly.

"What is it, Momma?"

"I killed a fella yesterday. That's weighing on me." Her voice was weak and filled with remorse.

Toby leaned against the wall and crossed his arms, his brow pinched in sympathy. Victoria sighed and retook her seat. "You know you saved us. He was bound and determined to kill me, but he had the gun to Naomi's head. You did what you had to do."

"Yeah. And I'd do it again. Just...ain't a very nice thing to go into mother-in-lawing with."

Toby chuckled. "She hasn't said yes yet."

Momma's gaze drilled into her. "What are you waiting on?"

Victoria drifted her fingers over Momma's cheek and whispered, "I wanted you to hear me say..." She slid her gaze up to

Toby and said loudly, "Yes." Laughing, she turned and jumped into his arms. "Yes."

Victoria had been through so many bad men, been treated badly by so many of them. She'd finally found a good one. And he valued her like a treasure. Her heart overflowed with gratitude. She only wished she'd seen his value sooner. But she saw it now. *Thank you, Jesus. Thank you.*

They kissed and Momma sniffled. "Good girl."

Buckley showed up in town later that day. Eleanor was delighted to see him after she got over the shock of his appearance. He'd trimmed his beard down nice and neat, bathed, and combed his still-damp hair to the back, which showed more of the gray at his temples, but she liked it. He was wearing a new set of clothes, too, and remarkably, a blanket coat instead of his woolly buffalo.

Eleanor didn't recognize him at first. "Lord have mercy, Buckley. You clean up fine." There had been a handsome man under all that hair and fur the whole time. "Why didn't you do it sooner?"

He shrugged, fanned his hat nervously, then sat down. "Guess I didn't have reason enough until something caught me off guard. Imagine my surprise at the hotel when I was asking after you. Mollie told me quite a story."

"Yeah, you sure missed some excitement." She swallowed. Every time she thought about parting that Irishman's skull, she wanted to throw up. Right or wrong, it was a terrible thing to have to discuss with the Lord. "Where have you been?"

"Up with the Utes. They need the Word, too. As I've mentioned." Buckley cleared his throat and sat down beside her bed. "And I needed to do some thinking. So, I heard tell you saved a lot of lives, that this Flynn was intent on killing somebody, preferably your daughter. Instead, you did the killing. By the look on your face, it bothers you."

"Yes." She plucked at the covers. "I keep second-guessing it. Wishing I could have done something else."

"The Bible says thou shalt not murder. Killing and murdering are two different things, Eleanor. You took a life to protect life. Reckon that's one of the best reasons."

She nodded. *I'll talk to you about it every day, Lord, till the sick feeling goes away.* Maybe someday it will. "I reckon. Anyway, I'm glad you're here. We were trying to figure out how to get Toby and Victoria hitched. Thought we were going to have to send over to Cripple Creek for a preacher."

"Wait. Wait. Hitched. Who's getting married?"

"We are." Victoria and Toby sashayed in, all cleaned up and smelling of lilac water, though Toby still looked like he'd been kicked by a mule. Victoria grinned at Eleanor. "We just sent the telegraph off to Cripple Creek."

"You don't need it." Eleanor poked her thumb toward Buckley. "He's a preacher. He can marry you."

Buckley stuck his hand out to shake Victoria's, but then he froze, and then she froze, and then Toby froze. "You're..." He pointed at Victoria.

"And you're..." Victoria's eyes widened like full moons.

He scowled at Toby. "Least you ain't dressing her like a boy anymore."

"What?" Eleanor was lost. "What's going on here?"

Victoria sighed. "Buckley and Toby and me have met. Buckley didn't approve of our arrangement in Ruby City."

"We can get it fixed right quick." Buckley dropped his hat on the bed and began patting himself down. "Where'd I put my Bible?"

Eleanor was still confused. "What arrangement?"

Toby rolled a shoulder and scratched his chin nervously. "He thought Victoria and I were, you know, living in sin."

"Oh, pshaw." Eleanor waved the accusation away. "I don't

know why she was dressed like a boy, Buckley, but there wasn't nothing going on between them."

He cast doubtful glances at them as he produced his Bible from an interior pocket. "Well, uh, if you say so. Like I said"—he waved the book—"I can remedy the situation. Whatever it is. Sounds like you're both willing this time."

Victoria hugged Toby's arm and smiled up at him. The peaceful expression of love and adoration made Eleanor's throat tighten up. Her daughter was going to be more than all right.

She was going to be happy. And marry a good man.

Because she'd met the best Man and he'd changed her life.

Toby and Victoria left Eleanor's room, holding hands. She sighed with pure joy over the bright future finally awaiting her daughter. "I'm so happy for her, Buckley, I could sit down and cry like a baby."

"Tears of joy. Those don't happen too often. You should let 'em fall."

She smiled, dabbed at her eyes, and sniffed. "No. I want the time for tears to be over for a while. Tears of any kind." She folded her arms across her chest and tilted her head at him, flinching as her bullet wound twinged. "I would like things to be quiet for a while. Just normal."

"Well, we'll get them hitched here shortly and they can ride off to find their future. You sit tight here, and I'd say things will be quiet for a spell." He cleared his throat and danced his gaze around the room.

Suspicions rose in her mind. "Except? Everything all right?"

"I have come to the conclusion I would like to tell you something, Eleanor, and I just don't know how you're going to take it."

"There goes quiet." She couldn't wait to hear this new problem.

"Maybe it ain't bad, what I want to say."

"Maybe not, but it doesn't sound quiet."

"No, I guess maybe it could be downright disruptive.

Maybe I should wait." He glanced at her stomach. "Till you're healed up."

"Oh, now that you've said that, you've got to spit it out. I won't have any peace till you do."

He scrunched up his face and peered at her with one eye closed. "Eleanor, how old are you?"

Her mouth fell open. Why in the world would he want—? "Fifty-five."

He grunted approvingly. "Eh, me, too."

She looked him over again, baffled by this behavior. What was his story? How had he wound up in the mountains, living like a trapper, sharing the Gospel on the streets and in Indian camps? And yet, here he was in a suit, looking like a real preacher, down to his string tie.

There is a lot to this man, isn't there, Lord?

"Eleanor, do you like me?"

My, wasn't he full of surprising questions today? "I like you fine, Buckley."

He grunted again and smacked the Bible in his palm. "Then here goes. May I call on you?"

Eleanor's eyes bugged nearly out of her head.

Buckley fluttered his lips, and his brow sank. "Not the reaction I was hoping for."

"Well, you have to admit it's a lot to consider. Especially at this time."

He flinched. "Yeah. I guess I didn't think that through, did I?"

An awkward silence fell on them and Eleanor didn't like it. "Buckley, I..." Her wound twinged again and she pressed her hand on it. "I consider you my friend. And I think you clean up real nice. So...maybe you could ask again later. Maybe when I'm not in the hospital and my head is a little clearer."

Buckley considered things a moment, then rose and took Eleanor's hand. "*Tu es une belle fleur et j'attends ton épanouissement.*"

She gasped. "That sounded awfully pretty. What did you say?"

"You are a beautiful flower, and I await your blooming."

Danged if Buckley might not sweep her off her feet, if she wasn't careful. Maybe she shouldn't worry about being careful. Buckley was downright...intriguing.

But first things first. "Let me get my daughter married...and we'll come back to this."

Buckley's wide, handsome face lit up. "Works for me."

Charles lit a cheroot at the jail cell door before looking up to address Sam Collins. The lickspittle hadn't even bothered to rise from the cot. He merely sat there, holding his bandaged shoulder, glaring.

If anyone should glare, it should be Charles McIntyre. This man was a vile threat to society. A destroyer of innocence. He needed to be in a mental institution.

"You can't keep me locked up like this. It's going on two weeks. I haven't done anything. And *you* shot *me*. Unprovoked. I should sue you."

"Disturbing the peace. Inciting to riot. Accessory to murder. We can come up with more charges. And you're a flight risk. So there is no bond. But I'm not here about those charges."

"Then what?"

Charles took a puff on his smoke and exhaled it thoughtfully. "Eleanor says you sold her daughter into the sex trade."

"And Eleanor does not want me telling everybody who her daughter is."

A moot point. Victoria and Toby were living somewhere else under new names. And Eleanor would be leaving soon enough. Buckley would keep her safe. "I have a friend in Stillwater. She is willing to testify you have supplied her with several young girls to work in her establishment. That is the kind of charge that would get you sent to prison for a long time."

Collins thought this over for a moment then rose and approached the bars. "Why would she do that?"

"She's already in prison for various and sundry charges. However, for a shortening of her sentence, she will tell the attorney general everything she knows about you. The attorney general of Oklahoma is a very good friend of mine, and he is eager to hear what this woman has to say. Furthermore, Adelaide will testify you approached her about her daughters working in this woman's establishment."

The color drained from Collins's face. "So, I do a little time in prison. I've done it before."

"You have an unhealthy attraction to young girls. Very young girls. That can be viewed as a mental disorder."

Collins swallowed. "What are you getting at? What do you want? My silence about Delilah?"

Charles took another puff and exhaled smoke rings. Perfect, round, they drifted away...like Sam Collins was going to. "I am not here to make a deal with you. I am here to tell you your future. You are going to spend the rest of your life in a mental institution. I understand they make prisons look like Sunday school classes."

Collins began to tremble. "You can't do that. Those places are hell holes." He grabbed the bars. "I'll go crazy in there."

Charles harrumphed. He liked the ironic choice of words. "Tell me, Mr. Collins, are you familiar with Luke, chapter seventeen, verse two."

He shook his head.

Charles crushed his cheroot out on the crossbar. "I'll see that Wade gets you a Bible before you leave us for Oklahoma." Done with the man, Charles turned and headed for the door.

"Wait," Collins screeched, panic in his voice. "You can't do this. This ain't justice. I don't deserve this—"

Charles closed the door, satisfied justice would indeed be served to Sam Collins.

On the boardwalk, he stopped and watched the traffic for a moment. The sun had popped out, melting the snow in torrents. Winter had ended in the blink of an eye. And the main road into Defiance had become a quagmire, thick, deep mud bogging down the wagons and horses.

Right then, McIntyre made himself two promises. This time next year, most of the streets in Defiance would be paved, even if he had to pay for it himself. And the deputies Lane had hired, arriving soon, would help Defiance make its final turn toward civility, hell or high water.

He sensed a whole new story was beginning. Matthew was not coming back. The Irish gang was broken. And Delilah was dead.

The slate was cleared for a fresh start.

Ian had repeatedly suggested they form a town council, and give citizens a reason to be civic-minded. Give them a voice in noble projects such as opening a school, hiring a teacher, retaining a permanent pastor, and even building a small hospital.

All of that started with Law and Order.

The town was ready for it now. More than it had ever been. He flicked a glance at heaven. "And may I never need to draw my gun again, Father. I pray for peace in Defiance. I know it's a tall order."

A scripture immediately whispered to him. *With man, this is impossible, but with God, all things are possible.*

Epilogue

Dear Mr. McIntyre,

Have arrived in Hot Springs. Thank you for the loan. The purchase of the horse ranch with a contract to supply mounts for the army has been completed. We expect to pay you back sooner than agreed.

We look forward to having my mother join us as soon as she's ready. Thank you for passing our mailing address along to her. And please extend our appreciation to Hope as well. We're sure her care for Eleanor was vital to her quick recovery.

And thank you again for believing people can change when they truly give their lives to the Savior. You believed it and you acted on it. I will be forever grateful.

Sincerely,
Susan and Robert

~

My darling daughter Susan,

How wonderful to hear you and Robert have found a ranch place to call home. I am eager to see it and South Dakota. I know you will be very happy there.

As for me, I have unexpected news. After a brief courtship, Buckley has asked me to marry him. I would have thought I was too old for such an adventure, but I am happy and excited to say yes to him. I won't be coming to live with you. Instead, I will come alongside Buckley, helping him share the Gospel with the Indians and in the mining towns. We have decided to leave the Defiance area and venture up to Deadwood first. On our way there, we will come by for a visit.

I'll be honest. I thought my final days might be filled with rocking your babies on my lap and watching my hair turn gray. Instead, I feel the Lord has restored something the enemy stole from both of us—a chance to be a helpmeet to a good man.

We expect to visit in June and I can't wait. I hope you are as happy for me as I am for you.

Love,

Momma

~

THE SUN WAS SETTING, washing their brilliant jade valley in warm shades of tangerine, crimson, and rose. The Black Hills in the distance and the towering, mysterious rock formations on the hillsides made their choice to settle here feel solid. Like they belonged and would build prosperous lives here.

The amber lights began to glow in the windows of their cabin, beckoning them in for the night. Her home. *Their* home. So inviting. So warm.

Peace swelled in her heart. Beneath her, Delilah shook from nose to tail, casting off a blanket of dust. From behind her, whistling. It grew louder, and then he was beside her. Together, in silence, they studied the sublime view. He exhaled, the sound of complete contentment, and reached for her. She gave him her hand. His fingers were warm and strong. "I love you, Susan."

"I love you, Robert."

"The old things are passed away..."

"Behold, all things are made new."

And now they could write a new story.

Coming Soon

IN TIME FOR CHRISTMAS

A Romance in the Rockies Novella

AVAILABLE JULY 2025

About the Author

Heather Blanton is a *USA Today* bestselling author of thirty Christian Western romances, including the highly rated and awarded Romance in the Rockies series. She is also an award-winning script writer. Her Romance in the Rockies series has been optioned for a limited TV series, and her script *Unbridled Hearts* is currently optioned as well.

She grew up in the mountains of Western North Carolina on a steady diet of *Bonanza, Gunsmoke,* and John Wayne Westerns. Her daddy taught her to shoot when she was five, and she can hit that at which she aims.

Her novels are all Christian Western romance because she enjoys creating feisty pioneer women who struggle to find love and hold on to their faith. Like all good, old-fashioned Westerns, there is always justice, a moral message, American values, lots of high adventure, unexpected plot twists, and often a touch of suspense.

www.authorheatherblanton.com